THE
LONG RIDE

by

Johnny Carlton

New Year's Day, 2008

Dear Cecil,
May God bless you.
Thank you for your
longstanding friendship

Johnny
Carlton

PUBLISH AMERICA

PublishAmerica
Baltimore

ISBN: 1-4241-8071-6
PUBLISHED BY PUBLISHAMERICA, LLLP
www.publishamerica.com
Baltimore

Printed in the United States of America

To my wonderful and very patient wife,
YVONNE,
who, like some of the characters in this story,
has a great talent for seeing the needs
of people around her and for
going to their rescue.

AUTHOR'S NOTE

Some small segments of this novel, particularly parts involving *John Pinetree*, were inspired by historical events. Pinetree and his activities are loosely based on a Cree Indian outlaw of the 1890s by the name of *Almighty Voice*. The true story of that man's troubled but fascinating life can be found in the annals of the Canadian Northwest Territories.

Chief Beardy, a true-life native leader after whom a Canadian Indian reserve has been named, also makes an appearance.

From the Southwest, four actual Apache leaders are briefly mentioned: *Tudeevia, Victorio, Mangus Colorado*, and *Cochise*.

Then there is *Geronimo*, whose fame/notoriety stands out among the Apaches; but the only part of his doings in this story based on real life—other than the depicting of his warlike nature—is the mention of his stay at *Fort Sill*. No doubt what happened there was highly significant to the real Geronimo, namely that he became a Christian, but in this story the matter is only touched on in passing.

The two featured real-life characters, Almighty Voice in the Northwest, and Geronimo in the Southwest, never met. They were almost 2,000 miles apart as the crow flies, at a time when the world was much larger because horses were the fastest means of transportation. This also applies to their fictitious counterparts. However, in my novel the lives of Geronimo and John Pinetree become connected in a sense. This is because of the far-flung adventures of two other men: One is a law officer in the *North-West Mounted Police* force, who, just before the fulfillment of his plan to marry the beautiful woman of his dreams, finds himself stripped of badge and uniform; the other is a Cree Indian whose circumstances isolate him from both his own people and the white culture that has educated him.

Please note that the hyphenated spelling of *North-West*, as in *North-West Mounted Police*, is the correct spelling for that usage.

Ladies and gentlemen—readers—I invite you into the exciting lives of courageous men and women facing overwhelming challenges that may affect the generations following them. Step into the 1890s and the western frontier of North America.

Contents

PROLOGUE

Two men stood in the shadow cast inward by the stockade. One was an elderly North American Indian, and the other was white. The Indian, wrinkled, tough looking, and fit, wore a loincloth, leggings, moccasins, and a white man's shirt and hat. His hair was in braids ornamented with buckskin thongs and little feathers.

The white man appeared to be a few years younger than the other and apparently was dressed to render a refined impression at a time and in a part of the world where refinement was scarce. He wore a white shirt, dark suit, a totally clean black hat, and polished riding boots. And his collar was that of a clergyman. The expression on his face was gentle.

The Indian spoke, and as he did the hardness in his black eyes seemed, at first, to soften just a little. His words were uttered in reasonably good English.

"For many suns you have tell me that you are a messenger of the Great Spirit, and that the Great Spirit has a new way of life for all to follow…. I have thought much about your words. I want to believe you. I want to follow your words and no longer follow my way of blood and death. I want to believe you, for your words have a good sound of peace…. But I think I cannot believe you."

The clergyman responded gently and sincerely, telling the old Indian that he needed to pray more than he had been and to let the Creator, the Great Spirit, guide him. For a few minutes longer the two men exchanged their differing thoughts; then they parted company, the minister of God's word looking sad. A guard in a cavalry uniform let him out of the stockade prison.

The old Indian, after walking past half a dozen other prisoners, found a man—a coppery skinned one like himself but a lot younger—sitting alone on a rough wooden bench near one of the high walls. Easing himself down beside him, the old man spoke softly so no one else would hear, starting out by referring to the clergyman he had just been talking to. "He is a good man, but he does not know the way of the Apache. There is much blood to be repaid."

The younger Indian grunted his agreement.

The older one continued, "I will escape from this place just as I have planned. Then I will go and gather my warriors, and if they feel as I feel, we will kill many white men. Then still more warriors will join us, and before the sun rides low across the southern skies, the land of the Apache will overflow with the evil blood of the white man."

The place was Fort Sill, Oklahoma. The man who spoke was, perhaps, the most ferocious Indian warrior of them all. He was Geronimo.

PART ONE: BLOOD BROTHERS

1

Sergeant Don Roman of the North-West Mounted Police stepped out of his saddle into a mixture of crisp snow and frozen horse manure in front of the police-station stable. He handed the reins of his black gelding to a young constable who was on chore duty.

Normally Roman fed and groomed his own horses—he had two of them—but he had been told that Commissioner Bancroft was in a bad mood about something and didn't want to make things worse by keeping him waiting any longer than necessary. So, as the constable led the horse into the barn, Roman was already walking briskly toward the log station building.

He had been on a routine patrol only about three miles away when another officer, on his way to his own duties, had intercepted him and delivered the verbal message that Roman was to cut his patrol and ride back to headquarters in the frontier village of Duck Lake to see their disgruntled superior.

Sergeant Roman was tall for men of his day in this winter of 1894; he was just a shade over six feet in his boots, and he entirely looked the part of an officer in the North-West Mounted Police force. Even his shaggy buffalo coat and fur cap could not smother the soldierlike straightness of his athletic body. His poster-boy, clean-shaven face, like the rest of him, also seemed to be grimly standing at attention, for it was not allowed to slouch or become involved in any sort of frivolous or out-of-control expressions.

Yet some who knew Roman wondered if all this rigidity was a façade; for the sergeant had a reputation for being a soft-hearted old grandma who wouldn't step on a spider if he could avoid it, who had been seen to cry tears at the reunion of a mother and child, and who could absorb insults like a floor mop absorbs water, and without ever sloshing any of it back at his abuser.

Had he been in the army instead of in this amazing frontier police force, he might not have fared so well; for his softness and self control in the face of insults might have been mistaken for weakness. But in the force the men were actually trained to not react emotionally to anything; and this had often stood them in good stead in touchy situations with renegade Indians and bootlegging white men. In time, the history of the redcoats would be well sprinkled with cases in which one or two police officers stood outnumbered and refused to react to provocation. And their enemies, in the face of such seeming confidence and fearlessness, would generally hold off their attacks long enough to allow the heat of their anger to be replaced by the common-sense knowledge that these outnumbered poker-faced redcoats, had, after all, the strength and resources of a nation backing them. Sergeant Don Roman was a master of this non-reaction technique.

The nation was Canada, the area was the Northwest Territories (a part of it that would later become the province of Saskatchewan), and the little frontier town of Duck Lake was situated on the well-traveled *Carlton Trail* that led from Fort Garry farther east to Fort Edmonton to the west. Fort Carlton had also been on this route less than a day's ride west of Duck Lake, but only nine years ago, in 1885, this fort had been burned to the ground during the brief Metis rebellion led by Louis Riel.

Don was already unbuttoning his coat before he got to the Commissioner's door. He wasn't about to enter and then stand there beside a red-cheeked stove waiting for "Ornery Oliver" to give him permission to remove his coat. So, after he knocked and heard a disgruntled sounding "Enter!" he didn't even look toward the desk area before taking off his coat and fur cap. He hung them on wall pegs, then turned to face Commissioner Oliver Bancroft, making sure to look very soldierly, erect, and respectful as he did so.

"Sir!" said Don crisply. He was not required to salute, but he made sure there was plenty of "salute" in his voice. "I was told to come in at once to report to you, sir."

Commissioner Bancroft was five-five in his heels, and no one seemed to know how he had made it into the force in spite of his small size and large defects of character. And he had gone on from there to beat and boot his way up through the ranks to become the Commissioner of the Duck Lake detachment.

When he was angry, Bancroft always made Don think of a little firecracker that had gone off but was still standing on end with its top part blackened. This was due not only to his dark hair and large black mustache, but to the thundercloud rage in his weather-beaten face that drew the features together into a murderous focal point somewhere around the opening under his mustache—an opening that appeared ready to spew out no end of fire and verbal cannon balls. On his good days he generally looked a little angry, but today he was definitely a firecracker. Too inflamed to be seated, he stood there behind his desk and just glared at Don for a moment. And for the millionth time, Don wondered at how Bancroft was the exact opposite of everything the force stood for, including its reputation for not reacting emotionally to stressful situations.

"Took you bloody long enough to get here!" said Bancroft.

"I had already ridden to a point well past Frenchie's cabin," said Don calmly. I turned back as soon as I got your—"

"What the hell were you riding?—a cow? All right, you're here, so now listen." Bancroft stepped toward his chair, but his movement from standing behind the rough wooden table-desk to sitting in the winged chair appeared to be some sort of acrobatic stunt that might have cracked a normal man's spine; but Bancroft didn't even seem to take a breath before he ranted on. "The Indian situation around here is going out of control, just as I've been warning for months!"

"I'm sorry to hear it, sir," said Roman, knowing well enough what kind of reaction he'd get to that.

"You're sorry to hear it! *You* should be the one telling *me*! You're out on patrol every day!—and *I* have to tell *you* that there's trouble brewing with those powwowing pemmican pukers?!"

"Any in particular that you're referring to, sir? And do you mind if I sit down?"

"I'm referring to the whole bloody works of them!—and to one in particular…. All right, get your ass on a chair if that'll help you to listen."

Sergeant Roman scraped a chair from one side of the small room to a position nearer the desk—not that he wanted to be closer to Bancroft's spewing hot saliva, but it seemed like the respectful thing to do. Bancroft waited for him to be seated before he continued his verbal attack on red men and redcoats alike. "The one in particular is John Pinetree, and if you and the men under you had only one eye for every three of you, you would have seen long ago that Pinetree is a first class troublemaker!"

"He drinks and gets into the occasional fight—" began Don, but again was cut off by his superior.

"He preaches rebellious redskin propaganda!—that's what he does! And last night he induced his village to have a war dance! If you and the men under you can't see where that's going…your eyes must have gotten mixed up with your balls! So maybe you should flick out your balls, just for a moment, and have a good look around!"

"I'll do whatever's required," said Roman, trying hard to keep from smiling but not being entirely successful.

"Don't get smart-assy with me," said Bancroft, yet his fury seemed to be subsiding a bit. "Now, I want an end to this easy-going Indian-lover shit. You're supposed to be the head sergeant here, so I want you to start acting like one."

"What do you want me to do, sir?"

"For a starter go have a talk with Pinetree. Lay it on heavy. Let him know he can't mess around and make trouble and get away with it. Let him know that you've got a big boot and he's the horse turd that's gonna get kicked around if he doesn't smarten up."

Bancroft was so far out of line that Don knew it was useless to remind him that the work of the North-West Mounted Police was to protect everyone by keeping the peace—through diplomacy rather than confrontation as much as possible. Maybe, thought Don, the time had come to get some of the men together to secretly discuss the matter of Bancroft's near-insanity, and maybe deliver a letter, signed by as many officers as possible, to headquarters at Regina. Still, that was tricky, because there probably wasn't enough solid evidence to make a convincing case to the top brass who always tended to take the side of higher rank over lower. Without a totally sound case against the commissioner, the accusers could end up being court marshaled themselves.

The seeming firecracker smoke around Bancroft's head cleared a little more and he looked almost like a human being as he said, "From now on, Sergeant, I want a personal report from you once a week, every Saturday, telling me everything that John Pinetree has been up to that week…. And when we have enough on him we'll make our move. Now, get out of here, ride to his village and give him a talking to. Then organize some way of keeping track of him. You don't have to do it all yourself. Take turns watching him. When he goes to town, have a man out of uniform, or more than one so he doesn't get suspicious, keeping close to him and seeing who he chums around with and what they talk about. You might have to hire one of the half-breeds who can speak Cree. We have some funds that can be used for that…. All right, Sergeant, are you clear on everything I've said?"

"Yes, sir."

"All right, then, I want you to report to me tonight after you've had your talk with Pinetree. And on Saturday I want a full report on what you've set up to keep track of the blighter's doings…. You're dismissed."

"Yes, sir, thank you." Sergeant Roman got to his feet, stood straight for a moment, then turned and put on his coat and cap. He left the office and walked back toward the barn on the narrow path of hard packed snow.

The overcast day was moderately cold and the low hanging clouds seemed menacing even though they didn't appear to be snow clouds. These bulging forms looked more as though faces might appear in them at any moment and scream out orders for Indians and white men to go to war. A fantasy, yes; nevertheless, Don knew that Duck Lake and a wide surrounding area had a serious and threatening problem. The combination of John Pinetree and Commissioner Bancroft was a wagonload of gunpowder waiting to be ignited.

Roman shivered in his buffalo coat. Snowflakes began to fall.

2

Just a little ways down the street from the police station, Jim Longfeather reined in and climbed out of his saddle in front of the livery stable. His breath and that of his horse were like horizontal geysers in the cold, snowflake filled air. He led the bay stallion toward the large front door which had been opened for him by Thomas LaMoove, the barn owner.

"Hallo, Jim," greeted the short, bearded man as he held the door open and Longfeather, returning the greeting, led his horse into the dim interior. It radiated the warmth of its four-legged clientele along with the cozy smell of horse manure.

"Looks like you have lots of room in here," observed Jim.

"Yeah, lots a' room." Thomas closed the door and now the place was almost completely dark to unaccustomed eyes. "Didn't hardly know you, Jim, with that big collar up around your ears.... Just joshin'—I'd always know you by your size...an' that stallion of yours too, even if you showed up in ladies underwear."

"I'd look cute in a corset, but my horse wouldn't go for it. Besides, neither of us would fit into one."

"Unless it belonged to Sally," said Thomas, "then it'd be too big."

"Yeah, but Sally's got a heart as big as her butt."

"I know it, said Thomas. "I think I'm gonna ask her to marry me."

Jim laughed a short unbelieving laugh and Thomas extended it as he took the bridle reins and led the horse into a stall.

Jim turned down the collar of his handsome buckskin coat, revealing a coordinately handsome face—a high-cheekboned dark face, with features that managed to be strong and sensitive at the same time. They were bold, definite features that seemed just right to top off the ruggedly graceful buckskin-covered physique that held them up to well over six feet above the ground. Jim Longfeather was almost certainly the biggest man in all of the Territories.

After Thomas had removed the bridle from the stallion's head and was replacing it with a halter, Jim asked, "What's all the racket in there? You got some kind of a party going on in there again?"

Thomas headed for the hay bin. "Yeah, I guess you could say that." He grabbed up a fork and made several quick stabs to work up a large forkful of hay. He crowded past Jim with it. "You want some oats for 'im?"

"Yeah," said Jim as he brushed snow from his horse's rump, "make it a double. He's a big boy."

"All right, you go ahead an' git in there, and git warmed up...outside an' inside."

Jim walked a short distance back toward the front of the building, then turned through a little side door that led into the "office." It was in this small room that the merrymaking was going on. Jim was cheerfully greeted by a half-dozen half-loaded old boys who sat around the heater. There was an empty whiskey flask and one about half full on a little homemade wooden table. There was also a coffeepot, smelling good.

Only one person in the room looked entirely unfamiliar to Jim. He was a big man—almost as big as himself—thick chested and broad-shouldered, with a wide face that seemed molded into a look of scorn. A long Adams revolver hung on his right hip over the edge of the wooden chair he slouched on. It seemed he was the only armed man in the room, but when Jim Longfeather removed his coat he uncovered a beautifully tooled gunbelt of mahogany-brown leather that supported a pearl-handled Colt forty-five on his right hip and a stag-handled hunting knife on his left. The disdainful eyes of the broad-shouldered man looked Longfeather over from head to foot, apparently taking note of details like the clean, perfectly shaped brown Stetson, the soft tan shirt, the black and brown narrow-striped pants that anyone present would have been proud to get married in, and the extra-high boots of tooled mahogany leather that were exactly the same shade of color as the gunbelt and the narrower belt that rested in the loops of his pants. It seemed that Jim Longfeather's whole outfit had been made as a matching set. The broad-shouldered man looked increasingly scornful.

"Pretty fancy lookin' redskin, ain't you?" he said, shocking everyone present with the blunt rudeness of his words.

Jim looked at the man, then smiled but said nothing.

A little man called Louis brought Longfeather a cup of coffee. "Here, Jim, it's on de house." He laughed. "Jim, I like you to meet Chuck Scote—he's from de States. Chuck, dis here is Jim Longfedder, de bes' bloody redskin anyones could ever find anywheres, even if he don' care for whiskey." He laughed again.

Jim, still standing, said, "I'm pleased to meet you."

"You're a breed, ain't you?" was Scote's way of returning the greeting.

"He ain't no breed!" said Little Louis, distaste and anger bristling his voice. "*I'm* a breed! He's pure Cree In'ian...an' he's proud of it!...Better remember dat, Scote. He's proud of it!"

Jim put in, "And if I was a breed I'd be proud of that too. There's nothing wrong with being a Metis. If you're any example, Louis, I'd say the mix turned out pretty damn good."

"Tanks," said Louis, and reached up to slap Jim on the shoulder. "You're one 'ell of a good frien'!"

Scote snorted, "Wal, I'm glad I ain't no breed or Injun."

"Hold it right there, Scote," spoke up one of the other men. He was mustached and with a narrow-brimmed dress hat with the brim down all the way around. "You better lay off the whiskey for a bit. An' you better lay off this here redskin. He's got you outweighed all around. He's even bigger'n you are, an' he's edicated up to the gills, he's filthy rich, he can lick his weight in wildcats...an' he's our friend.... So my advice is lay off him."

"Ah, take it easy," returned Scote. "What did I say? I just asked him if he was a breed. There ain't nothin' wrong with that, is there?" He pivoted back comfortably with his chair.

Jim said, "No, there's nothing wrong with that."

"Edicated, eh?" said Scote, once more turning his scornful face toward Jim. "How'd you manage that?"

The Indian moved closer to the stove to warm himself. Louis popped up and put in a stick of wood. Jim stepped back to give him room and said to Scote, "I guess I was just lucky."

"Who paid for your edication?" Scote persisted in his rudeness.

"The government," answered Longfeather calmly, not smiling, not frowning, but looking steadfastly into the bright flames that licked up out of the open stove. Although there was no need for it, little Louis stirred up the fire with a long poker.

"Jim was de smartess kid in school," Louis informed Scote while continuing to stir the fire like a kettle of soup. "De govermin' fine'ly sen' him to Englan' for finish his schools…. Now he's back here to help his own peoples." Louis pulled the poker out of the stove and shut the lid, to everyone's relief, for the sharp smell of wood smoke was beginning to dominate the small room.

Scote laughed so stinkingly it was almost beautiful, then said, "Help his own people? Help them fartin' Injuns? There ain't no way to help 'em 'cause they don't wanna be helped. Now take that critter, John Pinetree…."

Jim had been looking down at the closed lid of the stove, but at the name of Pinetree his until then calm black eyes suddenly flashed an intensity as though the fire in the stove had somehow been transferred into them; and they swung and directed their fiery quality at Scote's face. That stubbled, rugged countenance modified its contemptuous expression a little in recognition of the change that had come over Longfeather, but then the scornful mouth continued, "Pinetree is gonna make trouble, you watch and see. He's gonna make a lot a' trouble. He's one a' the worst."

"You're talking about one of my best friends," said Jim Longfeather in a voice that was just a little quieter than the way he ordinarily spoke.

The man in the slouch hat and a tough looking baldheaded man who made his living by hauling freight had been muttering together and now they both stood up. The muscular freight hauler said to Scote, "C'mon, Chuck, let's go…. We want to see Alice, don't we?"

Scote looked up at them angrily from where he sat. "Nobody tells me when t' go an' when t' stay. I'll leave when I'm damned good an' ready!"

Jim found an empty chair and sat down. He sipped his coffee while Chuck Scote stared at him evilly.

"Injuns like Pinetree ought t' be shot afore they start trouble…that's what I say," Scote carried on.

"I suppose you have a right to your opinion," said Jim, leaning back with his chair, stretching out his long legs relaxedly, "but you're wrong about John. He's a good man.... I owe him my life. He saved my life once." He looked steadily at Scote for a few seconds, then added, "We're blood brothers, John and I, an' that's at least as close as a family relationship."

"I don't give a damn if you're married to him," returned Scote, "I call a spade a spade. John Pinetree shoulda been shot long ago."

It finally got through to Jim that Scote was simply picking for a fight and that there was no use in talking to him. So he turned to Louis and said he wondered how long the snowfall would carry on. Just then Thomas, the barn owner, came in complaining in a good-natured way about why horses had to shit so much. The conversation began to get back to normal, but every now and then Scote would prod at Jim with an insult, and a couple of times the two men who seemed the most familiar with Scote renewed their efforts to get him to leave, but without success.

Finally Thomas had his fill. "Get out of here!" he ordered with an abruptness that startled everyone. "I don't want none a' this kind a' shit in my place! I get enough from the horses! You can come back when you learn to talk like a man! Now go get your horse saddled and git outa here!" He slapped some change on the table. "Here's your money back!"

"Lemme get this straight," said Scote, looking happier than he had up till then, probably because he was almost twice the size of Thomas. "You really gonna try to throw me out?"

"You damn right I will!" returned Thomas, his round eyes fairly glowing above his black beard.

The freight hauler said, "You won't have to do it alone. We'll all throw 'im out together."

"All right, I'll leave...you bunch a' bastards!" said Scote as he got to his feet. He looked huge then, the top of his hat almost touching the ceiling, his shoulders and chest seeming too big for the small room. "I'll leave...but I want the Injun to step outside with me. I'd like t' do a little work on 'im."

"Just git out!" said Thomas.

Jim remained sitting and silent.

"Well, Injun...you comin'?"

Jim looked up and studied the large man for a moment before saying, "You're in no shape to fight. Better go sober up first."

"You chicken-shit bastard!" exploded Scote, and moved quickly toward Jim. Jim remained sitting, but his booted foot came up and found an easy target—the attacker's crotch. The big man came to a sudden stop and bent over to the front, his face pained to the point of ridiculousness. Still bent over, he took a step backward. Without rising from his chair, Jim kicked up his foot again and connected solidly with Scote's chin. He fell sideways to the floor like a shot bull.

Cheers and laughter filled the small room. It quietened down a bit and Louis said, "Hey, look, boys! Jim never even spill a drop of his coffee!" It was true. He still held the half-full cup in his hand and was leaning back comfortably in his chair as though nothing had happened. He couldn't resist increasing the effect by casually taking a sip of coffee. This brought out another round of laughter and compliments.

Scote came to but was so groggy there wasn't a chance of any more violence on his part at the moment. His two acquaintances helped him out through the door, saying they would take him over to Alice's. "He's really not such a bad guy when he's sober," said the man with the slouch hat just before they left.

This was the first meeting of Jim Longfeather and Chuck Scote.

* * *

Jim stayed overnight at a friend's place. The snow had quit falling, the sky was clear now, and the moon was almost full. Longfeather lay in a bed with his head propped up on pillows that smelled faintly of chicken feathers, and looked out through a bedside window at a silvery, calm, silent backyard scene—bare trees and a woodshed beside a leaning rough-lumber yard fence.

He was disturbed by what the drunk Scote had said. He tried to tell himself that the man had just been pushing for a fight; but why had he, of his own accord, picked out John Pinetree for special abuse? What made the matter worse was that Jim had heard earlier remarks—although less insulting ones—about his friend from other quarters. There was talk going around that John Pinetree was planning a rebellion of some kind. Could there be something to the rumors? He hoped not. He hadn't seen his friend for over a month; now he decided that tomorrow he would ride out to the One Arrow Reserve and talk to John. He felt he had to get to the bottom of this thing, for an Indian uprising led by his friend and blood brother was highly undesirable. Jim Longfeather was all for helping his own people untangle themselves from their present difficulties, but to his way of thinking the warpath did not lead in that direction.

I'll go talk to him, thought Jim, *and see what he's up to.*

But he didn't look forward to this, for he was afraid he might find out more than he wanted to know.

3

Cold sunlight streamed out of a clear blue sky and sparkled on the snow covered prairie. Here and there bushes of naked poplar trees protruded from the glistening white banks, pointing their wooden fingers skyward, reaching for the sun.

On the crest of a little knoll and darkly magnificent against the bright background, stood a handsome bay gelding straddled by an Indian—John Pinetree.

The man was tall, rangy, and good looking in a rugged sort of way. His dark skin had the clear, healthy appearance that comes as a result of living out of doors, and his black eyes flashed the fierceness of a plunging hawk. He wore buckskin and had a folded red bandanna around his head, partly covering his ears. An equally vivid red was the color of the Hudson's Bay blanket wrapped around his shoulders. His hair was in braids.

John Pinetree was a warrior at heart. He had been brought up by parents who clung to the beliefs and customs of their ancestors, who, like all the Cree Indians of their time, had lived lives of proud freedom and had called the Northwest prairie wilderness their own land. But that appeared to be something of the past. Other beings from a different world, with different ways and superior weapons, had come and conquered. A new power that rode a horse like the Indians did, and wore a red coat, and was called the North-West Mounted Police, had made known the strength of its authority. And then there were the foot soldiers. Only nine years had passed since General Middleton's troops had beaten down Louis Riel's Metis and Indian forces at Batoche—a small settlement not many miles from where Pinetree now sat his horse. But the Indians were not content with their present lot. They could not adapt themselves overnight to an entirely new way of life. However, they were given no choice. They lived on reserves—the patches of land that had been left to them by the white men—and many were dissatisfied.

John Pinetree had received his white-man's given name in honor of a brave and kind-hearted Metis *coureur do bois*, John Dumont, who had been a close friend of his father. And that was pretty much where Pinetree's willing association with the palefaces ended. Pinetree chafed under the restrictions imposed on him by the law. He mourned the loss of the old way of life.

He was popular among his Indian friends—both male and female. They considered him dashing. They enjoyed his cordial manner and the sound of his self confident low voice. They admired his athletic ability. He was an expert rider, could fight any man, and was more or less famous as a long distance runner.

The air was bitter cold as the Indian sat on his bay gelding and scanned the bright-white scene before him. He found what he was looking for. A lone cow not far distant stood behind a scraggly row of small leafless poplar trees.

Pinetree had no difficulty in roping the cow and leading her behind his mount. She was a tame animal, not given to running away, but the makeshift corral gate had come open and she had strayed away aimlessly.

As Pinetree neared his somewhat isolated teepee he heard the sound of snow-muffled hoofbeats in the distance. He was riding at a walk along a trail through a thickly wooded area when a rider on a pinto horse came into sight from the rear at an easy lope.

As Pinetree looked back over his shoulder at the gaining rider his face showed no change, but he felt brighter and warmer inside than he had a moment ago. A few seconds later the colorful pony came to a sliding stop beside him. The rider was an Indian woman, young and pretty. She was his own woman, but they had not been together for some days because she had been attending to the needs of a sick aunt in another village. It turned out the aunt was much better now.

As Pinetree and Flying Blackbird rode on together at a leisurely horse-walk through the crunching snow, she asked, "Is that your cow?" She spoke in the Cree language and Pinetree answered her in the same.

"No, this cow belongs to the white men. She got away. I went to look for her, found her."

"How is it that you have a cow that belongs to the white men? Did you trade something for her?"

"Do you not know?" said Pinetree. "The palefaces gave us this cow to raise calves. The calves, they say, will be ours. But the cow will still belong to the white men and to the Great White Mother."

This matter having been settled to Blackbird's satisfaction, they talked about other things as they rode side by side. Blackbird said she was on an errand, delivering a message of no great consequence to friends in another camp. She assured him that she would be home in his teepee before the day was over. When they were out of the forested area and about half a mile from Pinetree's camp, the woman said good-bye, and, turning her pinto, galloped off into the bright winter landscape.

Pinetree was glad that she was leaving in spite of the fact that he liked her company. He had things to do. He needed to make a few simple preparations before killing the cow; and then he hoped to find one or two men to help him with the work of cutting up the meat.

As soon as he had put the cow back in the pole and brush corral and repaired the gate, he started out toward the village to find the helpers he needed. He had not ridden more than a quarter of a mile when he heard the unmistakable sound of a stallion whinnying somewhere up ahead. A second later Jim Longfeather came riding around a bush that bordered the trail. The two friends greeted one another and then Jim turned his horse and rode alongside Pinetree.

"You cannot butcher that cow!" said Jim in no uncertain tones when he found what the purpose of Pinetree's trip was.

"You will see if I cannot," returned the other. Both men spoke in their native Cree except for an occasional handy English word.

"That cow belongs to the *government*. They will put you in *jail*."

"Everyone here is starving," said Pinetree. "The white men have driven off the game. They have made captives of us and taken away our right to eat…. But we will eat their cow." When Jim was silent, Pinetree added, "Not all red men are as fortunate as my good brother, the white man's friend."

Jim caught the obvious bitterness. "Pinetree, good brother—" Jim knew that his friend liked to be called by the Indian part of his name. "—I have been working with the agent on Beardy's Reserve, trying to better the lot of our people there. I did not know that things were so bad here. I did not know that anyone was going hungry. But something will be done.... I will try to have food brought in."

"You will try.... That is good of my brother." Pinetree looked neither grateful nor hopeful.

"Then you will not butcher the cow?"

Pinetree did not answer but smiled a slight, mischievous smile that did not help to allay the other Indian's apprehensions.

"There is something else I would like to talk to you about," said Jim. "There are stories flying about in the wind that you, John Pinetree, are dreaming foolish dreams—that you are planning to make trouble...that you are planning a new rebellion against the whites."

Pinetree allowed himself a little laugh. "I have heard the stories too, but it is not true.... Yesterday a redcoat came and talked to me about that—the one called Sergeant Roman. He asked me to live in peace with the white men. I told him I do live in peace with the white men, for they have stolen everything from our people including our freedom and our food. The redcoat looked sad and afraid. But I assured him I was not going to start any rebellion...And so I tell you the same, my brother. Perhaps I have said a few things about the white men, but I have no plans to start a war. It is only talk."

"You should be careful what you say."

"And maybe I should pass the time living with the white men in their great splendid teepees, like my good brother."

Jim let a few seconds pass before he said, "We are brothers forever, are we not?"

"Forever," answered Pinetree, and his face relaxed into something that could almost be called a smile. Jim read sincerity in his eyes.

They had reached the Indian camp now—a couple dozen or so teepees in a clearing. Horses whinnied and dogs barked.

Pinetree began looking for a particular brave and quickly found him. When he asked the man if he would help him butcher a cow, Jim realized that further pleading on his part would be useless. Pinetree had made up his mind and no one would change it.

"I must leave now," said Jim. "I can have no part in this. I wish you would not do it.... I will do my best to bring food as soon as I can."

* * *

Jim Longfeather left then, and rode back across the frozen Saskatchewan River toward the town of Duck Lake from which he had come.

Longfeather wished that he had more control over his own financial resources. Little Louis had told Chuck Scote that Jim was filthy rich. In a way that was true, but in a way it wasn't. The wealthy family that had adopted him continued to support him in his adult life, and he could have just about anything he wanted. Charity was a tradition with this family and they were also progressive enough to consider new and innovative ways of helping the natives. They had even liked the idea of Longfeather keeping his Indian name, and when he showed interest in helping his own people to find a better lot in life, they were all for it. So Jim had taken advantage of the situation, and, instead of worrying about earning a living, had set about doing everything he could for the Cree, using his own education and his adopted family's money to equal advantage.

One problem was, though, that everything he tried to do had to be approved by his father and uncles—the whole raft of them as they sat around a mahogany table and took great enjoyment in discussing things for days…or weeks…or months before they reached a conclusion.

* * *

By nightfall the cow had been butchered and some of its flesh eaten. By noon the next day Pinetree had generously distributed the meat. Hungry stomachs were grateful and his boldness was praised by many Indian lips.

On the following day Pinetree had a visitor in the person of the white agent who managed the reserve affairs. Flying Blackbird was not with Pinetree at this time because, expecting trouble, he had arranged for her to stay in the village, in the teepee of her widowed mother.

"Bad cold wedder, eh?" said Pinetree in English when the agent had squatted Indian fashion on the fur hides which covered the floor of the large teepee.

"Yeah," said the agent. Then, abruptly, he came to the business at hand. "I heard you butchered a cow, John—a government cow. Is that true?"

"Yeah," said Pinetree. He sharpened a sliver of wood with his hunting knife as he spoke. "But I got toe doe it. I got nutting toe eat."

The stern faced agent took off his heavy winter cap and scratched his bald head. "You shouldn't have done it. You'll be jailed for this. I have no choice but to report you."

"Please not report. Yoe not tell, no one know. I say dat cow run off and we not find her." Pinetree smiled hopefully as he picked some beef out from between his perfect straight white teeth. "Only me and yoe know, eh?"

The agent rose to his feet without saying any more. Anger was smoldering in his eyes. He shook his head as though to say he couldn't believe what he had just heard, then turned to the door flap and opened it. He shook his head once more at Pinetree, then stooped through the opening, strode to his horse, mounted, and rode off.

Pinetree knew he was in for trouble.

That evening, after dark, trouble arrived. Two fur-coated, fur-capped members of the North-West Mounted Police showed up. One was the same tall one, Sergeant Roman, who had come to talk to Pinetree two days earlier about being at peace with the white men. He now informed the Indian that he was under arrest and instructed him to saddle his horse and ride with them. Soon the police officers and their prisoner rode out into the night.

The dark overcast sky contrasted with the dim white of the chilled earth. The crunch of snow under the horses' hooves seemed loud in the icy stillness. Cold saddle leather creaked.

John Pinetree looked to the side at one of his captors—the tall one who seemed to be in charge—and at that moment made up his mind firmly that he would not always be a slave to the will of the white man.

4

About two hours later the three riders reached Duck Lake, their destination. They dismounted at a hitching rail in front of the police station and the police officers steered Pinetree through the building and out a side door that connected with a short passageway—only about four feet long—that led toward another closed door. There was a large, double-paned window in one side of this passageway, and Pinetree noted that there were no bars on it. One of the officers opened the next door and this led from the passageway directly into a little log-house jail. The tall policeman motioned for him to step inside. Pinetree did so. The door was closed and locked behind him.

"See you in the morning," said Sergeant Roman through the small barred window set into the heavily planked portal. "I have to leave now, but I'll be replaced by another man, so there'll be at least two officers nearby all night. Please don't make any trouble. I promise to do all I can to get you out of this mess." Then he and the other redcoat walked back into the police station proper.

In the dark, Pinetree inspected his surroundings. There was a heater with fire in it, burning low, and in one corner of the room a pile of firewood. Along one wall stood a narrow cot with blankets and a pillow. Two small, square windows, one on each side of the little log house, had glass panes but from the outside were barred with iron. Not much later Pinetree could hear someone putting the horses in the barn behind the station.

He added a couple of sticks of wood to the fire. Then he removed some of his outer clothing—his blanket and buckskin shirt—and lay down on the bed. Not a bit nervous about this experience of being in jail for the first time in his life, he fell asleep promptly and peacefully.

After a while he awoke because the room had become much too hot. He had left the stove damper wide open. He closed it and was about to lie down once more when he heard a door open and close, then the sound of two sets of feet walking outside, not far from the little jailhouse. When he looked out the window he could see nothing but dim snow, dark sky, and one of the back alleys of Duck Lake. But he could hear the conversation of two men, along with the sound of two streams of urine hitting snow.

"He'll be moved to Prince Albert as soon as possible," said one voice.

"Yeah. It's just as well. With Roman having responsibility for him, we might end up bringing him another government cow so he can butcher it right in the jail." They both laughed about this.

The Indian pressed his face against the window in his effort to see who was talking. They were not in his line of vision, but it was obvious that they were police officers talking about him.

"Wonder what they'll do to him," said the first voice.

"Who knows?" replied the other. "But with any luck they'll hang him."

The two voices blended in another short laugh. Then one of them cautioned. "Better not talk so loud. He might be awake."

"Well, let's get back inside and finish the game."

Once more came the sound of boots crunching through snow, the door opening and closing. Then all was quiet.

Pinetree seated himself on the bed and thought over what he had heard. He found that only one part of the conversation remained with him: *"Who knows? With any luck they'll hang him."*

They were talking about me, thought Pinetree. Having little knowledge of the workings of the white man's law, and having seen his share of violence from both white man and red, it did not once occur to John Pinetree that the police officer might have been joking. The big Indian sat in the same position staring into the darkness for a long time. Then he lay down on the bed once more, but this time hours passed before sleep was finally victorious over his troubled mind.

He slept soundly until breakfast was brought to him in the morning. The day seemed very long. Sergeant Roman did not return, yet Pinetree could hear that there were always two or three men about. Flying Blackbird did not show up, but that was because he had instructed her not to in the event that he was arrested. Jim

Longfeather also did not come to visit. There could be only one reason for that: he did not yet know about the jailing of his blood brother. This was just as well, thought Pinetree, for he didn't wish to be scolded by his fancy white-thinking friend.

There was a noon meal, and, after dark, another meal. Along with the supper, the police officer brought a lighted coal-oil lamp and placed it on the wooden box that served for a table.

Pinetree glanced at the plate of food. "No knife toe cut meat," he complained.

"Can't bring you a knife," said the redcoat, "but I see I didn't bring you a fork either. Sorry, I'll get you one." He closed the door but didn't lock it and walked up the short passageway into the police station.

Pinetree rose to his feet. Here was an opportunity for escape. But could he actually get away even if he got out of this cell? He knew he had to make up his mind before the policeman returned with the fork. He took a step forward. He hesitated.

The door of the police station opened and the lawman returned through the passageway holding a fork in his hand. He came briskly to the prison door and stuck his arm through the barred window, holding the fork out to Pinetree. The Indian took it. The officer turned and walked back into the police station.

Pinetree set down the plate of food. His hawk eyes narrowed and a slight smile came over his face. He began to move toward the door, then turned suddenly and went back to the food. He picked it up in handfuls and wolfed it down.

He threw the empty plate on the bed, pulled on his buckskin coat, and wrapped the Hudson's Bay blanket around his shoulders; then he walked to the door and opened it cautiously. He was still stunned by the fact that the redcoat had forgotten to relock it.

The window in the passageway had no bars; but the challenge was to slide it up without making enough noise to bring one of the guards to investigate. Therefore it had to be done slowly and with great patience, balancing the danger of making too loud a sound with the possibility of one of the officers coming into the passageway for some other reason. There was always the chance that the one who had brought the food and the fork might suddenly remember that he had left the jail door unlocked. Patience, cunning, calmness under stress:

Pinetree had it all. He slowly worked the window up with only a little scraping sound; he climbed through into a dark back alley; he patiently lowered the window, again making very little sound. Then he cautiously circled the jail building and headed toward the barn.

As he had hoped and expected, the barn was dark and occupied by horses only — including his own. He did not take his own however, for the horses of the redcoats were sturdier, larger, and well fed. He chose one without being able to see the animal. It took him half a minute to find the tack and another two or three minutes to get a bridle, saddle blanket, and military style saddle onto the horse. The horse, normally handled by any number of officers and chore boys, remained calm through the whole thing, and soon was being led out of the barn. Pinetree mounted and rode off at a walk, the horse's hooves in the snow sounding to him like gunshots. But in a couple of minutes he was leaving the sleeping town of Duck Lake behind.

* * *

Pinetree reached his camp on the One Arrow reserve. He fed his new horse from his meager supply of hay, then took a short rest.

For the next half hour he worked rapidly, sorting out his belongings and deciding which to take along and which not. Finally he had the most important items in a pile on the floor of the teepee. Among other things there were blankets, food, a repeating rifle, and a considerable amount of ammunition that he had been saving and hoarding for months.

Now all that was left to do was to go to the village and collect one of his horses that he kept there...and...to say good-bye to Blackbird.

* * *

They guided their mounts around a deep snowbank and then took a trail that led north. They rode at a brisk canter. The packhorse loped along willingly behind them without a rope, for he would not leave the other horses.

Blackbird had been determined to go along with Pinetree, and although he had tried to dissuade her, he was glad that she was now riding at his side. It had not taken them long to decide that they would go north into the wilderness. There only could they hope to hide from the white face and the red coat.

They galloped on into the night. Something cold touched Pinetree's forehead. A moment later he saw snowflakes drifting downward. Pinetree smiled in the dark. In another minute the snow was sifting down heavily and filling the night air like a white cloud of fog. There would be no tracks.

Walking their horses now, the man and woman rode on in silence. They rode northeast, into a land of lonely wilderness.

* * *

Jim Longfeather was walking past the Duck Lake general store when he met an excited looking Little Louis.

"Hey, Jim! Have you hear 'bout John?" The little Frenchman's round face, red with cold, peered out from toque and scarf like a pig poking its nose out of a straw pile. Only his eyes were too round to fit the impression.

"No, what?" asked Jim anxiously as the two stopped and stood facing each other.

"Dey took him in here de night before last. Dey had 'im in jail. An' de crazy bugger busted out!"

"Oh, no!" This was worse than Jim had expected. "Did he hurt anyone?"

"Naw...dey don' know how he get out—pick de lock, maybe."

"Let's step into the store," said Jim. "It's cold."

They walked into the warmth of a properly cluttered general store, found a couple of chairs beside the heater and sat down.

"I hear it from George," said Louis as he began to roll a cigarette. "He's a brudder of Stan, you know. I guess John he wen' an' butcher a guvermin' cow a couple day ago, or sometimes dis week."

"Why did he have to do it?" Jim asked the cluster of kettles and coffee pots that hung on a nearby wall. "And why did he make it worse by running away?...I wonder where he went."

Little Louis was unwinding six feet of scarf from around his neck. A large drop of moisture depended precariously from the end of his roughly constructed nose. "Dat's hard to say, Jim, but he proBABly went nort.'"

Longfeather was resting his chin in both hands—a gesture of despair, or maybe of concentration. "I've got to try to find him...talk some sense into him."

"Dat's not easy ting to do."

"He probably went north all right. Could be he followed along the river and..." He let the sentence become a mumble. Then he stood up. "I'm leaving, Louis, right away. I've got to get on his trail. I'll get ready and go to One Arrow's—maybe I can pick up a clue there—and then I'll do my best to get on his track. I'm afraid that if the police find him first he's liable to get himself into real trouble. I've got to find him and try to get him to give himself up."

"I sure wish you de bes' of luck," said Little Louis.

* * *

For John Pinetree and his woman there were days of hard travel. They rode in the daytime and made camp every night.

Early one cloudless winter morning, just as the two runaways were about to break camp, they heard the sharp flutter of a prairie chicken's wings. Pinetree took a quick step and grabbed up his rifle. He saw the fowl rising into the air from behind a willow clump. He raised his carbine while at the same time levering a bullet into the chamber and smoothly squeezed off the trigger. The discharge shattered the crisp winter air. The prairie chicken fell from its flight and hopped around crazily in the bloody snow.

Blackbird went to where it was and picked it up by the legs. Pinetree put another cartridge into his rifle to replace the one that had been fired.

It was then that they heard the sound of horses' hooves galloping in the snow. They exchanged glances, and Pinetree stood waiting with his rifle in a ready position.

Two horsemen rounded a thick growth of bare poplar trees and pulled their mounts to a stop when they saw the Indian camp. One of them was a Metis scout whom Pinetree had seen once or twice before. He was bearded, wore ragged buckskin, and had a bright yellow scarf around his neck. The other man was a fur-clad member of the North-West Mounted Police. They stood out sharply against the snow which was brightly lit by the early morning sun.

Pinetree remained calm. To his way of thinking, there were only two logical courses of action for him to follow. One was to shoot both men immediately; the other was to warn them off and then shoot them if they didn't cooperate. He knew that the first plan would be by far the safest. But Pinetree had more softness in him than he himself cared to admit, so he chose the second alternative. And on that he didn't hesitate. He lifted the rifle to his shoulder and aimed it at the officer's heart. "Turn horse and ride away!" yelled Pinetree, "or me kill yoe!"

Instead of obeying, the officer tried to spur his horse forward, but the Metis scout grabbed the bridle of the policeman's horse and held the animal back. "He means what he says," said the scout. "You ride at him and he'll shoot!"

"Let go," said the policeman. "He won't shoot. It's a bluff."

The scout released the bridle. Once more the officer set his horse moving and rode forward, now at a walk.

"You come closer, I shoot!" warned Pinetree.

The lawman continued to approach. "John Pinetree, you're under arrest. Put down your gun before you get yourself into even worse trouble."

Pinetree squeezed the trigger. The rifle coughed blue smoke and the police officer's frightened horse leaped to one side. The officer tipped out of his saddle and fell heavily in the snow, then rolled onto his back but did not lie still. His arms and legs were thrashing about. A small splotch of red appeared and grew larger on the front of the officer's coat as he continued to convulse.

The scout jerked his horse's mouth savagely and wheeled him around, partly on his hind legs. The shaggy bay sprang into a gallop. Knowing that he would regret it later, yet not wanting to kill a man who was part Indian, Pinetree let him go. In a moment horse and rider were out of sight behind some trees.

For a few seconds more the police officer kicked about in the snow just as the prairie chicken had done, then lay quietly.

John Pinetree stood motionless, as though in a trance. The Indian did not try to fool himself about what had just happened. He knew that in the eyes and laws of the white man he would now be classified as a murderer; and no time, money, nor sweat would be spared in the effort to hunt him down.

Blackbird, standing nearby, still held the dead prairie chicken. Her hand trembled and her face was pale.

Pinetree walked up to his fallen foe and removed the gunbelt. He strapped it around his own waist. He found no difficulty in catching the officer's horse. Pinetree removed the saddle and bridle and turned the animal loose. The only parts of the policeman's gear that he kept for himself were the bedroll which was made up of heavy woolen blankets, rifle and handgun, and all of the ammunition.

Pinetree turned to Blackbird. "We will go far away," he said. "Very far away. We were not safe here before, but to stay now means death. We must hurry."

They broke camp quickly and without another word.

Soon they were once more riding in a northeasterly direction. The sky became gloomy with clouds. Around midday they rode into country that was lightly wooded with evergreens. The change of scenery was refreshing and the fugitives began to feel more confident that they could escape from the law by ensconcing themselves in the seemingly endless maze of timber, brush, and lakes of the unexplored North.

* * *

The sky was so heavily overcast that Jim Longfeather could see no indication of how far the sun had progressed on its daily route; but according to his gold-plated, engraved, monogrammed pocket watch, the afternoon was already half finished. He wondered about the distance-muffled sound he had heard—possibly a shot but more likely a tree cracking from expanding sap—and turned his horse in that direction.

He rode at an easy walk, listening to the crunch of the big brown stallion's hooves in the snow, the sound of the wintry wind, and his own thoughts.

He thought, as he often did, about his strange past: how as an orphaned teen-ager he had been adopted by a wealthy white family; how for some years they had lived in the east, where he had been labeled a child prodigy and no money nor effort had been spared to carry out this experiment to see what would happen if a native genius was given every opportunity to learn. He had even spent some time in England, in what they called "schools of higher learning." He had been on display there, like a trained bear in a circus. He was the intellectual savage.

Still, in fairness, he knew that there had been many who had accepted him simply as a human being whom they liked, and even admired. Certainly he experienced no lack of popularity. When he wrote scientific articles on anthropology and archaeology, the publishers stumbled over one another trying to get to him first; when he lectured, the halls were packed.

His adopted family's economic fortunes did a down-spiral then, and he used his own financial resources—which were considerable by that time—to help out. But things deteriorated still further after that, leaving him personally penniless but having a special interest in the failing family businesses.

There was some shuffling of authority resulting in Jim's parents having less control and a smart but hardhearted uncle having about ninety percent of it. The business empire revived, but now Jim, like his parents, were in the outer circle. There was lots of money available, but it had to cross over that big mahogany table where Uncle Ross, with some advice from the others, sat at the head and decided which way the bucks would be channeled.

Jim's great interest in the welfare of his own blood people, along with his knowledge that many of their present distresses came as a result of the white man's coming along and turning their way of life upside down, directed the further course of his studies along lines of social work and agriculture.

Back in the Northwest Territories, he determined to put his knowledge and training to work for the betterment of his people. But what had he done since he got here? He had been advised to work together with one or more *Indian agents*, the white men that the government stationed one on each reserve to help the natives get along in their new way of life. So that's what he had done. He had been able to give a bit of advice on occasion, to the agent and to the Indians, which sometimes was heeded and sometimes wasn't, and altogether progress hadn't been what he had hoped. There had been real setbacks too, like the one resulting from the incident during which Pinetree saved his life.

A smile came to Jim's lips as he reminisced. What a fight that had been! And the whole thing had started just because some dopey Indian whom he didn't even know and an equally dopey white man had both gotten drunk and were insulting one another out on the main street of Duck Lake. The worst of it was that the white man had called in extra help—two big lunks who seemed to hate the world in general and Indians in particular. The three whites would have made pemmican out of the lone Cree if it hadn't been for Pinetree and Jim who happened to come along just then, one from each end of the street. Now it was three against three.

At first the whites had been getting the best of them, but during the course of the fight—which began at Judson's general store and slowly progressed half a block to Bellanger's blacksmith shop—the picture had changed until finally the three whites, bloody faced and desperate, had been thinking seriously about calling it quits. But a last-ditch blow had knocked Jim down. Then Jim's antagonist, wanting to wrap up the whole thing properly, had grabbed hold of a long-handled hay scythe—there for sharpening—and made straight for Jim with it. The battle-crazed maniac had definitely looked like the Grim Reaper, Longfeather remembered, as he bore down on him and swung that hideous weapon.

Jim rolled to one side but not quite far or fast enough and got his shoulder nicked. He rolled to the other side. The blade missed. He saw the blade raised for the third time; and it hovered in the air for a moment, for this time the man was taking a more careful aim. But the blade never descended, at least not in a thrust. The strong arm of Pinetree had snaked around the maniac's neck from the rear, and the man, after a number of seconds without oxygen, was willing to release his grip on the scythe.

But Pinetree was not at all willing to release his choking hold on the white man's neck. The two other whites, bloody faced and limp looking, now stood by dumbly without making any move to intervene, either because they didn't have the strength left to do so or because the whole thing had gone too far to suit them and they wanted nothing more to do with it. Jim had to do some earnest and eloquent preaching before Pinetree agreed to let his poor victim fall gasping to the floor.

Well, that was the end of it, except that the whole thing had to go to court. Jim took on the lawyering for Pinetree and himself. The maniac got a one-month jail term; the other two whites and the one Indian got away with a warning to refrain from disturbing the peace; Pinetree and Jim were recognized as being innocent. But the trouble was that the incident aroused a lot of bad feeling among a certain segment of Duck Lake's white population. The maniac had a few staunch followers—Indian haters, all of them. They stirred up a bit of trouble and slowed Jim's work, a good part of which was trying to bring about better relations between red and white.

Perhaps the only good thing that came out of the whole mess was the close friendship that sprang up between Pinetree and Jim. At Pinetree's request they became blood brothers. (The blood brotherhood institution was not a regular item in the culture of these particular Indians, but had suddenly arisen among them, likely an import from farther south, and, after a few years, was no longer practiced.) A tiny knife cut was made on one forearm of each man, the arms were pressed together so that the blood mingled; tom-toms beat while vows were made. When it was over the two men were married—not in a sexual love relationship, but in a love relationship nevertheless. For they had vowed to always do their best for each other, to be loyal, and to stand together in any emergency—to stand together to the death.

Jim had agreed to the rite because he had known it would mean a lot to Pinetree; it was Jim's surest way of showing his gratitude for having his life saved. But after going through with it he began to have some qualms. After all, his way of life was entirely different from that of the other Indian. He began to doubt more and more that such a pact could actually be kept, yet he was determined to do so.

Jim's thoughts were interrupted by the sound of hoofbeats ahead of him. He pulled his own horse to a stop. The snow-crunching sound drew rapidly nearer, and in a few seconds the hurrying rider pounded into sight through a narrow opening between two arms of the clearing-riddled pine forest. When he saw Jim he reined his horse away to one side as though he had just sighted a new enemy and must flee him also; but then he pulled to a stop, and, after a moment's hesitation, rode at a walk toward Longfeather.

The approaching rider was a rough looking person—this effect being created mainly by the beat up clothing he wore. Although Longfeather's attire was as neat as this man's was shabby, there were similarities. Both men wore a hat and buckskin coat. Jim, however, had a big fur collar turned up to keep his ears warm, whereas the other man had a ragged, bright yellow scarf tied around his ears, with his lumpy hat fitting over that. His face was protected from the cold by a short, dark beard, replete with many little icicles around the nose and mouth.

"Hello," said Jim.

"Hello," returned the other. The remaining distance between the two he closed in silence, and when he brought his horse to a stop near Jim there was a look of inquiry on his face.

Longfeather said, "Say, you were really moving along there. Any trouble?" It was only then that Jim recognized the man. He was a Metis scout who worked for the police, but the name had skipped.

Instead of introducing himself, the scout asked, "Who are you?"

"Jim Longfeather."

"Oh, I've heard of you," said the scout. "You're a good friend to John Pinetree.... Well, I got bad news for you."

Jim stiffened. "What's happened?"

"You're blood brother killed himself a policeman today." A long barreled forty-five appeared suddenly in his hand; he had brought it out quite smoothly from behind a fold of his buckskin coat. "I'm goin' now to report it."

"How did it happen?" asked Jim, ignoring the gun—in fact, hardly being aware of it, so startled was he by what he had just heard.

The scout looked at him sternly. "Sergeant Walker an' me was on his trail. We found him, an' that woman he's got with him, an' Walker tried to take him...but he wouldn't let himself be took. I warned Walker, but he wouldn't listen. So Pinetree shot him. An' you can bet your best boots I didn't stick around there very long.... I'll tell you one thing, friend—no one's goin' to take that outlaw alive. They'll take him dead or they won't take him at all."

"I hope you're wrong," said Jim. "What's the idea of the gun?"

"You're his blood brother, ain't you? You're gonna stick with him to the death, ain't you?...I suppose you're goin' out to find him now."

"I'm going to find him and try to talk him into giving himself up," said Jim. "That's the best way I can help him."

"By putting a rope around his neck? They're gonna hang him sure—or they would if they could catch him alive, which they won't. And you sure as hell ain't gonna talk him into giving himself up."

In his heart Jim had to agree. "You sure the sergeant was dead?— not just wounded?"

"Oh, he's dead all right...I'm pretty sure. If you know your blood brother, you know he don't miss at fifty feet—not by a hair."

Again Jim had no choice but to agree. "Yeah.... What about Sergeant...who did you say?"

"Walker."

"What about his body? Shouldn't someone go and pick it up?"

"Well, sure," said the scout, "but don't think I'm goin' back there alone."

"If you tell me where he is," said Jim, "I'll put the body up in a tree so the wolves don't get it."

The scout considered this for a moment. "All right," he decided. "You shouldn't have any trouble findin' it. Just follow my tracks. It ain't far."

"Right."

"I appreciate what you're goner do," said the scout. "It don't show proper respect to just leave a man's remains out to the wolves. I'll bring someone to come back for the body just as soon as we can."

"Good," said Jim.

The scout finally put his gun away. He said, "Well, I better git goin'...an' I wish you the best a' luck. I guess the next time we meet it could be over flyin' lead." He laughed in a way that sounded as though he was embarrassed at the melodrama in his own words. "I mean with you bein' his blood brother, standin' by him to the death, an' me workin' for the police, it kinda looks like it could happen.... But if it does, I just want you to know that I got nothin' personal against you...an' I hope you feel the same."

"Well, I sure do," said Jim, and he could think of nothing else to say. There was no way of explaining to this man that he did not intend to become a murderer simply because his blood brother had become one. And yet, wasn't that what the pact implied? As the two riders parted company and rode their opposite ways, Jim Longfeather searched his conscience deeply and wondered what really was the right thing for him to do.

About thirty minutes later he came to the spot where the violence had taken place. He quickly got through the unpleasant job of tying the cold, stiff body up in a tree, sacrificing his own good lariat for that purpose.

Then he started on the trail of his blood brother. The tracks were plain—three horses. He knew, as did the police, that Pinetree's woman, Flying Blackbird, had disappeared at the same time that he did and was assumed to be with him. Now the scout had verified that. So there would be two riding horses and the third would be a packhorse.

About an hour later Jim made camp in the shelter of some high willows close beside the Saskatchewan River as a premature darkness slowly swallowed up the heavily overcast wilderness. He heated a mixture of meat and vegetables over his fire, ate it out of the pan along with bread, then wiped the pan clean with snow and a cloth. He bedded down for the night. He fell asleep feeling fairly confident that he would be able to catch up to his outlaw friend on the following day.

But when morning came, and he awoke to see fresh fallen snow lying six inches deep, it was plain enough that looking for Pinetree was now hopeless.

He saddled his horse, packed up his things, and started back toward Duck Lake.

* * *

From police headquarters in Regina orders were issued that the murderer must be taken at all costs. Scout-guided patrols ranged the area for many miles around, particularly to the north. But they also combed every square inch of the One Arrow Reserve. They could find no trace of the hunted outlaw.

A year and a half passed by. Pinetree and his woman seemed to have magically evaporated, leaving no trace of their former existence.

5

It was a cloudless bright day in late spring. Jim Longfeather was hitching a team of horses to a wagon in preparation for a trip to town. Some of the supplies were running low and they were out of salt for the cattle. He was still working together with the Indian Agent out of the Beardy's Reserve station.

"Don't forget about the salt blocks." It was the agent, sneaking up behind Jim. The man got some kind of satisfaction out of trying to prove that he could move as quietly as an Indian.

"'Course not," said Jim, making sure he didn't sound in the least bit startled.

"If we don't get salt to them cattle on the south side," said the agent, "they're gonna eat themselves clean down to China." He was referring to the way the mineral-hungry cattle were chewing at the soil in an attempt to satisfy their craving.

"Well, let's hope it got here," said Jim. There had been some previous delay in the arrival of the shipment which was supposed to be coming by train from Regina.

Quickly finishing hooking up the horses, Jim gathered the reins in his hands and climbed to the buckboard seat at the front of the wagon.

"Say, Jim," said the agent quickly before Longfeather could tongue-click the horses into motion, "see if you can find out in town if it's true about the reward for Pinetree. 'Course I guess we'll be gettin' a poster in the mail, and the department should be writin' me about it."

"I'll sure ask around and find out what I can," assured Jim. "I'm very concerned about it."

"Ah, go on," said the agent, waving a big hand at Jim in a gesture of disbelief. "I thought you had quit worrying about that silly renegade."

Jim looked down into the habitually grim face of the agent. "How could I quit worrying about him? He's my friend, Bernie, and he's my blood brother. And he's a man in bad trouble."

"I sure gotta 'gree with that last part. So what're you gonna do if you find out they've slapped a big reward on him?—dead or alive. What're you gonna do to keep people from goin' after him to get the money?" He took off his hat and scratched his bald head, as though to show that he was asking tough questions.

"I don't know," Jim answered honestly. "But for their own sakes I hope they don't try it. John won't be easy to take, with or without a reward."

* * *

When Longfeather got to town he headed straight for the general store which also housed the post office, because he knew that people would be gathered there to pick up their mail and to visit. In a few seconds he had the information he wanted, and he hadn't even needed to ask anyone. A large printed poster on the wall, complete with an artist-rendered head-and-shoulders picture, proclaimed that one-thousand dollars would be paid to anyone who brought in John Pinetree. In smaller letters it added the information that you could bring him in dead or alive, as you preferred.

"Hello, Jim, ain't seen you for a time."

"Hello, Edward," returned Jim to the tall, thin, middle-aged man who had separated himself from the rest of the concourse to come up alongside the Indian.

"Too bad about the reward," said Edward, glancing up at the poster. "This is gonna make it a lot tougher for him to stay hid. Some bastard might know where he is and give him away just to get a share of the money."

Jim studied the farmer's face intently for a few seconds. Was the man sincere in the sentiment he had just expressed?—or was he saying that just because he knew Jim was Pinetree's blood brother? *He might mean it*, thought Jim, for it seemed, strangely enough, that there were a lot of folks on the outlaw's side—who hoped that he would continue to cunningly evade the persistent clawing and searching of the law's long arm. Sometimes it seemed to Jim that these whites were more supportive of Pinetree than he himself was; for Jim never had been able to condone his friend's killing of Sergeant Walker. Still, Jim supposed that less than ten percent of the area's population were strongly on Pinetree's side. The others seemed to be of the opinion that Pinetree should be shot down like a dog without the complication of a trial.

Jim and the farmer discussed the situation for a while, Jim holding back some of his feelings about the matter. Then the farmer came up with new information.

"I guess you know that Chuck Scote has gone out after the reward money."

"No," replied Jim. "Who's Chuck Scote?"

"Don't you remember Scote? You had a fight with him one time in the feed barn office."

"Oh, that one," remembered Jim, as the ugliness of what this might mean to Pinetree settled in. But Jim tried to look unaffected. "I think you were there, eh?"

"Yeah. I guess it wasn't hardly a fight." The farmer laughed. "You gave him a good trimming without even getting out of your chair.... Yeah, and he don't figure on bringing in Pinetree alive either."

"How do you know?"

"That's what he told everybody, before he left. He was goin' around town shootin' off his mouth about how he was goin' to be back real soon draggin' the carcass of Pinetree. That's the way he said it—carcass. I hope Pinetree puts a bullet square between his rotten eyes."

"Well, I wouldn't want to be in his boots when he comes face to face with John," said Jim.

"The trouble is," said the farmer, "that he's not going to try to come face to face with him. I'll bet my bottom dollar and every acre of land I've got cleared against a...a horse turd that Scote is gonna try an ambush."

"Yeah, maybe," said Jim, "but how's he figure on finding him?"

"Says he knows where he is. I doubt it though, but he must have some kind of clue."

"Yeah. You have any idea what it might be?"

"I'd say your best bet would be to talk to Little Louis about it," suggested Edward in a lowered voice. "He knows more about the whole thing than I do."

"You mean he's got an idea where Pinetree is?"

"Could be," said the farmer, and he looked distinctly uncomfortable now. "I'd say your best bet would be to see Louis."

"Yeah, I guess I will," said Longfeather.

"Well, I'd better get t' hell going too," said the other. "Got a few things to do."

Jim collected his mail and headed back out into the warm sunlight.

Little Louis was not at home in his bachelor cabin where he slept when he wasn't out hunting, fishing, trapping, or drinking. Jim was afraid the man might be out of town, but after a bit of walking around and asking several people if they had seen the miniature Metis, he found Louis where he then realized he should have logically begun his search—at Alice's place. Alice was a widow and the mother and supporter of nine children. She was a part-time whore; and she drank a lot, probably to try to forget about what she had become.

Alice and Louis were both feeling no pain when Jim arrived and knocked on the screen door.

"Wal, hallo der Jim, you fartin' good ol' bugger! Come in!" greeted the little Metis from where he sat at the kitchen table.

"Yeah, C'mon in," said Alice. She stood beside the table with a half empty glass in her hand. Jim maneuvered his big frame through the somewhat smaller than normal doorway and quickly closed the screen door in the faces of a lot of noisy flies who wanted to join their many buddies already in the house. He removed his hat which had been almost brushing the low ceiling.

Alice was a rather handsome woman—red haired, strongly built, dressed in simple homespuns.

Little Louis said, "Dis ain't my house, but I'm askin' you in anyhow." He laughed then, apparently because the whole world was funny. His dark hair seemed longer than usual, or maybe it only looked that way because it was so mussed up, and his round, rough-nosed face was almost as red as the wine in front of him.

Jim worked his way around half a dozen children, two dogs, and a fat yellow cat, and finally arrived at the table. Alice was already pouring him a drink.

"Easy there," pleaded Jim.

"Hey, Alice, what you doing?" demanded Louis. "Don' you know dis guy he don' guzzle down booze like me and you." He laughed loudly again.

"Ah, shaddup," said Alice good-naturedly. She picked up the glass of wine and handed it to Jim. He took it, studying her strong, good looking features as he did so. The expression on her face was just a little blurred because of too much firewater in the brain behind it, but Jim could see there evidence of gentle qualities. It was not the first time that he had decided there was still considerable goodness left in this fallen woman.

Little Louis said, "Alice, I hopes you knows dat dis here man is one of de bes' fran' I got…. Have a chair, Jim."

Jim pulled a chair close to the table across from Louis and Alice, who was still on her feet, and seated himself. "And you're one of *my* best friends, Louis, you know that." The yellow cat jumped on the table and tried to get at Jim's wine.

"Cat! Git off there!" hollered Alice boomingly. Surprisingly, Cat obeyed immediately as though it was a well rehearsed act. Alice pulled a chair up to the table now too and sat down unsteadily, at the same time pushing away some dirty dishes to make room for her own glass of wine.

Louis said to Longfeather, "Ain't seen hides or hairs of you for a long time. What you been doin'?"

"Oh, keeping pretty busy at the agency."

The children were playing a game that required the whole kitchen area and appeared to be a test of strength during which some of them would run from one side of the room to the other while the remaining ones would holler at them, apparently trying to knock them headlong by the sheer force of lung power.

"Say, Louis, is it true that Chuck Scote has gone after Pinetree?" asked Jim, wanting to dig up whatever information he could as quickly as possible and get out. The last half of his sentence was drowned out so he had to repeat it.

"Yeah," said Louis, "dat's right."

Jim took a sip of wine just in time to rescue it from the cat who had reappeared in front of him. "Well, how does this Scote know where Pinetree is?"

"Cat! Git off there!" hollered Alice. The cat jumped down.

"I wouldn' tell anyone else but you dis," said Little Louis, "but I know you won' tell no one.... So here's how she go." He leaned his unkempt head closer to Jim. "Scote been makin' fran' wit an In'ian on One Arrow's.... Funny ting, de way he hate In'ians. But don' worry, he know what he dooz. He make good fran' wit Sleeping Wolf...an' Sleeping Wolf, he know where Pinetree hide."

"Sleeping Wolf, eh?" mused Jim. He knew the man when he saw him but had never talked to him.

"Yeah, Sleeping Wolf he say he know where Pinetree is at.... I'm tell you dis 'cause you his blood brudder...but don' you tell noBODY, Jim."

"Don't worry, I won't. How does Sleeping Wolf know where Pinetree is?"

"I don' know...but I tink Pinetree been der back in One Arrow's one time, an' I tink he have tell Sleeping Wolf his place where he hide. You can go talk wit' Wolf, but I don' know if he tell you anyTING about—"

"Cat! Git off there!" hollered Alice.

"How long since Scote started out?" asked Jim.

"Sometime yesterday—I dunno what time."

Jim drank half his glass of wine, set the rest down, and got to his feet. "Thanks a lot, Louis. I've got to go now."

"Aw, not yet," Alice smiled up at him. "You ain't finished your drink."

"Sorry, but I just don't have time—got some important business to take care of."

Little Louis said, "Wal, I'm sure wish you luck. But Jim, I guess you knows dat if you goes agains' Scote, you goes agains' de law too."

Jim was silent for a few seconds, then got a secret wink across to Louis when Alice momentarily looked away to the side to yell at her rowdy children: "Shut up you noisy little bastards!"

"I'm not going after Scote," lied Jim. "What do you take me for?"

The children's clamor was reduced by only a few decibels, leaving it at about the level of hail on a tin roof.

"Wal, yeah…I know you ain't," stumbled Louis, his mind still clear enough to catch on to the necessary intrigue.

Jim said, "My pressing business is to pick up some salt at the station, if it got here, and take it to the cattle as soon as I can. So, see you again."

"Yeah, sure ting, Jim," said Louis, "an' good luck…wit dat salt."

"Good-bye," said Alice. "Come again."

As Jim ran the gauntlet to the door, he noticed that one of the two dogs he had to step over had a sore on his nose and the other had a hairless inflamed area under his tail. Jim supposed this indicated that the dogs were victims of the same contagious disease.

Longfeather quickly did his shopping, picked up the salt which finally had arrived, and headed back toward the reserve—driving his horses at a pace he would not usually have required of them, especially under a load.

Once back at the agency, Jim immediately relieved himself of all his ordinary responsibilities.

"I'm going on a trip," he told the agent. "Might be gone for a couple of weeks."

"Goin' to look for Pinetree, eh?"

"No," lied Jim, "this is something else."

"You know I really gotta have your help with that hog breeding program you started," whined Bernie. "You can't just run off. And there's a lot 'a other things." He complained for some time.

Jim loaded his best packhorse with food, oats, and bedding. On the saddle of his mount, the bay stallion, he slung a seven-shot carbine and a good supply of ammunition. He cleaned and oiled his pearl handled Colt forty-five and filled the empty spaces on the back of his gunbelt with cartridges.

* * *

It was late in the evening when he got to the camp of Sleeping Wolf on the One Arrow Reserve. The middle-aged, sober faced bachelor Indian received Jim with hospitality. They squatted on furs in his large teepee and, in the Cree language native to both of them, spoke of many things and made their acquaintance real before Jim broached the subject that was the purpose of his visit.

"I have come to speak to my new friend about my blood brother, John Pinetree. I have heard that a man with death in his eyes has gone to seek for my brother."

"What man is this?" asked Sleeping Wolf.

"His name is Chuck Scote."

Sleeping Wolf was very much awake. "Has Chuck Scote…in truth gone to seek for our friend, Pinetree?"

"Yes," said Jim, "to seek and to kill him. Scote desires to have the reward that is offered."

Sleeping Wolf was silent for a long moment, then said, "I have heard that you are a good man—a man who is doing all he can to help the people of his own blood. You would not lie about this…. Sleeping Wolf has been tricked. I have told Scote where Pinetree has his camp. Now our friend may die with an evil bullet in his heart…. And Sleeping Wolf will be to blame. Ah, I have been well named indeed, for the big white man with his clever words of friendship and his gifts of tobacco and firewater did lull me into the sleep of carelessness."

"How did you know where Pinetree is?"

"He came here last winter. His woman had a child, born in the wilderness. They left the child with the mother of Pinetree, Laughing-Buffalo-Calf. They took ammunition and a few supplies and rode away. But Pinetree told me the place of his camp and told me that if any illness or harm should ever befall the child, or any threat of danger should come to him, then I should come at once and tell him…. Instead, I have betrayed him."

Jim could not help but feel sorry for the sober faced Indian as he squatted there, his tall brown body slouched and with his head hanging forward so that he looked surprisingly small.

Jim said, "Take heart, Sleeping Wolf. Perhaps we can yet help our friend. Tell me where Pinetree is, and I will ride there as though my horse had wings on his feet. I will warn Pinetree of the danger that threatens him."

Sleeping Wolf slowly looked up. "No more will I tell anyone where Pinetree hides. I will go there myself."

"My horse is faster than yours, or any that you could find. Let me go."

"I will not tell."

"Sleeping Wolf, you know I am the blood brother of Pinetree. You must tell me so that I can help. Pinetree would want you to."

The other thought this over, then got to his feet. Back to his full height, with his shoulders squared, he had lost his look of defeat; and when he spoke it was with the full, strong voice of a man who knows what he's about. "We will both go. I trust the blood brother of Pinetree."

Once the matter had been decided there was no time to lose. They left Jim's packhorse in Sleeping Wolf's camp, for speed was more essential than most of the things that were loaded on the packsaddle. Sleeping Wolf threw a beat-up old military saddle on his best horse, a colorful yellow buckskin, and the two Indians, whose lives and purposes had become related through the plight of a mutual friend, took to the trail that very evening.

6

The spring air was still cool at sunrise. After riding all night, morning found Jim Longfeather and his new friend many miles into the northern wilderness. The yellow black-maned horse of Sleeping Wolf almost always stayed half a neck ahead of Jim's big brown stallion, for the less civilized Indian was leading the way. They rode out of bush into a large clearing and there splashed through a shallow creek.

Both men were tired to the point of near-collapse. Jim pulled the stud to a stop. "We should let the horses drink here," he said.

"No," disagreed Sleeping Wolf, "we will cross this creek again, more than once. It winds like a snake. We must hurry."

But Jim turned back to the water. "Our horses will make better time if their thirst is quenched."

Wolf gave in then, and both men let their mounts drink, but stayed in their saddles. The animals needed no coaxing. Jim took off his wide-brimmed hat, rubbed hair and face, then sat quietly hunched over the saddle horn. His sleep-hungry eyes kept trying to pull their lid-blankets over themselves and Jim kept pulling them off. "How much farther is it?" he asked.

"A quarter day's ride," answered Sleeping Wolf, and, after a moment's silence, added, "Maybe we *should* stop here for a short while to rest the horses."

Jim glanced at him in surprise. He noted how bone-weary the man looked, and wondered if he looked that bad himself. Sleeping Wolf let both his bridle reins fall to the water. Then he dismounted, managing to reach the dry bank without getting his moccasins wet. He got down on his knees and splashed the cold water into his face. His long, ebon braids dangled into the creek.

Jim dismounted and gave himself the cold-water treatment too. They tethered their horses on lariats—Jim using a metal ground-stake he always carried with him—and removed their saddles and bridles. The Indians had a quick breakfast from the limited amount of food they had packed in their bedrolls. After that they slept for a few minutes. Altogether, their stop delayed them for less than an hour.

Jim was mounted and Sleeping Wolf was halfway into his saddle when a shot rang out clear and sharp in the morning air. The riveting sound came from the north, dead ahead—and close.

It was followed immediately by a woman's scream.

Longfeather and Wolf exchanged startled glances; then, simultaneously, they dug heels into their horses' sides and the buckskin and bay both uncoiled into a headlong, neck-on-neck race in the direction from which the shot and scream had come. The smaller yellow horse was superior for a quick dash; in a few seconds he gained a widening lead over the big stallion.

They pounded through the clearing, had soon crossed it. Sleeping Wolf galloped his horse into the timber at a point where there seemed to be a vague deer trail. Jim was still fairly close behind.

Another shot cracked the atmosphere—very loud and close now. But the two Indians sped forward without the slightest show of caution, except that Jim unleathered his forty-five. It was the woman's scream that had triggered something automatic and fiercely daring within both men.

Another shot. The yellow horse of Sleeping Wolf dropped down, skidding on its nose—went into a roll. Jim's mount, close behind, could not sidestep this unexpected obstacle of limb-flailing horse and rider. The big stallion stumbled over them and went into a wild somersault. Jim left the saddle, floated smoothly through the air, hit the ground hard, rolled fast, and came to a stop by batting his head against the trunk of a tree. He went blank, but only for a few seconds. Scrambling to his knees, he was at once surprised to see that his companion appeared to be unhurt.

Sleeping Wolf was running toward him in a crouching posture; he scooped up Jim's fallen gun and continued on to Jim's side. But he didn't stop moving there. He grabbed hold of the civilized Indian and more or less bundled him down a slight incline on the side of the trail.

They rolled several yards before they came to a stop among high weeds. Then they lay there quietly, listening.

Jim had had enough time to see that the yellow horse lay kicking, probably fatally hit, but his own horse had been out of sight.

"Here is your little thunder-stick," said Sleeping Wolf quietly as he handed the revolver to Jim. "Are you hurt?"

"No, and you?"

"I have no broken bones," replied Sleeping Wolf.

They lay silently for a few seconds. Jim asked, "Do you know where the man with the thunder-stick might be?"

Sleeping Wolf thought about it. "There is a rise of ground on the other side of the clearing where the shot came from. He is somewhere up on higher ground shooting down on us. There is a creek up there too—the same one we crossed, and a little waterfall—" he pointed, "—where the water drops to this lower level. You can hear it if you listen close."

Jim listened but could hear only chirping birds—until that tranquil sound was disturbed by the deep booming voice of the Indian they had come to warn. Pinetree was calling to them from somewhere a little farther up the deer trail. "Come this way, my friends, there is safety here."

"It is Pinetree," said Sleeping Wolf. "He is not dead." Great relief showed through his words. "Let us go to him."

Longfeather followed Sleeping Wolf as the latter, walking stooped over and sometimes lowering himself to hands and knees, with Jim doing the same, led the way toward the area from which the Indian outlaw's voice had issued.

The place of safety turned out to be a tiny ravine—not much more than a natural ditch with banks of gravelly shale and rock outcropping. Here sat John Pinetree and his wounded mate, Flying Blackbird.

The young woman had been shot in the arm, high up on the outside of her right shoulder. Pinetree had stripped her to the waist, the easiest way to uncover her upper arm. The beaded buckskin shirt lay beside her. She sat leaning against the ridge of rock, looking down at what Pinetree was doing to her arm. Jim thought her to be very beautiful with her dark braids against her dusky, flawless skin—flawless except for the wound. When she looked up at the approaching pair, both of whom she knew, she smiled pleasantly, showing not a sign of the hysterics that could well have been expected after her close call.

"How bad is it?" Jim asked his blood brother.

"It is a cut," returned Pinetree. "The bullet did not stay inside. But someone will die for this." He was wiping away the blood with a rag that looked anything but clean.

"We must use something more clean for the wound," said Jim as he removed his buckskin coat, then his shirt. "Here, this is cleaner," he said, indicating the shirt. "At least it's cleaner than what you have there…. Maybe I should do it. I have learned to tie a good bandage." He began to rip up his shirt into strips. It irked Jim to know that he had real bandages in his saddlebags but couldn't get to them.

Pinetree knew that his blood brother was skilled in such things so he let him take over. As the civilized Indian worked a strip of cloth around the woman's slender arm and over her smooth shoulder, the feel of her skin, warm and satiny under his finger tips, hit him hard. He was a lonely man and as naturally horny as any, and he craved a woman of his own. But circumstances had put him in a bad position in this regard. All the available Indian women he knew were too uneducated and backward to suit him. And the white women? He wasn't sure he'd want one even if he could have one. Those of them who were educated seemed standoffish and probably looked down on him for having been born an Indian.

Jim drew a long strip of the shirt around Blackbird's upper chest to better hold the awkward shoulder bandage in place. He was hardly aware of Pinetree and Sleeping Wolf talking in low voices, making a plan to surprise the ambusher. As Jim worked the supporting bandage around Blackbird and stroked it into place, he knew that he was touching her unnecessarily—actually, though almost unintentionally, caressing her.

She smiled up at him. "You have very gentle hands."

So she was quite aware of what he was doing. Hoping he wasn't blushing like a fool, he said, inanely, "I must try not to hurt you in any way."

Pinetree said, "We will go now to kill the coward." It was a simple statement, and no one, not even Jim, voiced any dissent.

Jim asked, "How is it that Blackbird was shot at instead of you?"

"The coward on the hill is a poor shot," returned Pinetree. "The bullet was surely meant for me. We were riding close together."

Jim had finished the bandaging. "How do you plan to kill him?" he asked, surprising himself with the ruthless sound of that question. Somehow he felt no large-sized qualms about joining forces with these two savages who were bent on extinguishing the life of a law-abiding bounty hunter. Yet he wondered about it. Should he not rather be telling his less civilized blood brother that he ought not to stack crime upon crime—that he should still give himself up and take his chances in court with a good lawyer? Maybe the reason he did not was because he knew how futile such suggestions would be. Maybe. And maybe it was because he himself, civilized Jim Longfeather, was as desirous as his two savage friends to lock horns with the bloodthirsty devil up on the hill. But if the latter was true, there at least was no desire for vengeance in Jim's heart; it was, rather, simply a matter of wanting to put an end to the danger. In any case, Jim had his forty-five ready in his hand as he listened to Pinetree outlining a simple plan.

"Sleeping Wolf will circle around to the right. You, brother, will circle in from the left. I will go straight ahead. We must hurry for he may be fleeing—only to come back later to try again. But the high creek is nearby behind him and the bank is very steep at the place closest to him...where he would most likely try to cross if he fled. And there is much driftwood. This will slow him. Now, let us move quickly and quietly."

Pinetree seemed to be taking it for granted that "the coward" was alone. Jim didn't bother to suggest otherwise, for he felt sure that the ambusher was Chuck Scote, and Scote was not the kind of man to share the reward with anyone.

Jim noticed that Pinetree was wearing a police gun rig, the big forty-five unleathered and already cocked. Sleeping Wolf was now armed with Pinetree's Marlin lever-action rifle.

Pinetree told Blackbird to remain quietly where she was. Then the three Indian braves parted company, and, like silent shadows flitting among the tree trunks, made their way separately up the rise. Longfeather and Sleeping Wolf followed a curved course on either side of the supposed location of their quarry; Pinetree climbed straight up the low hill, keeping his shoulders bent over low and his cocked gun in front of him.

Jim was not used to going through bush without a shirt on. The heavy foliage scratched and tickled him by turns, and now and then a thirsty mosquito would land on his back and suck his lifeblood to proliferate her evil species. He still had his wide-brimmed hat on though, and this helped to keep annoying cobwebs out of his eyes.

Longfeather thought he probably had a considerable ways to go before he came anywhere near the gunman he was looking for, so he got quite a surprise when he suddenly found himself face to face with Chuck Scote, with a distance of only about twenty-five feet separating them.

Scote looked surprised too, and a little scared, but Jim didn't have time to study the man. The bounty hunter's rifle swung up and shattered the air with its thunderous belch; the slug crackled through branches a few inches above the Indian's head. Automatic reflex pulled Jim's trigger as he dropped down to the comparative safety of some underbrush before he could determine if his bullet had connected with Scote.

Jim crawled quickly on hands and knees. Scote's rifle roared twice more and covered up the sound of the pounding lead so that Jim couldn't tell on which side of him the bullets were striking. It was plain that Scote could and would riddle the underbrush so that Jim's chances of not being hit would be slim. The Indian wished now that he had emptied his gun at Scote when he had the chance—when Scote had missed with that first shot. Jim knew he could easily have gunned down the bounty hunter before he had time to lever another cartridge into his rifle's chamber. Why then, wondered Jim, had he fired one careless shot and dropped for cover? At the moment he was not inclined to analyze all this is any great detail, but he knew that his civilized nature balked at the thought of killing a man—in this case a man who was doing what the law allowed and encouraged.

Scote's rifle cracked again. Jim knew that the lead must be coming close. He moved forward a few inches on hands and knees; then, without really trying, he found himself peering through a small, leafy opening in the brush—a peephole that afforded him a perfect view of Scote. And that individual obviously did not see Jim, but looked rather mystified and seemed to be wondering where to place his next shot.

This time Jim didn't hesitate. But he had to bring his gun up slowly to avoid being detected, for Scote was ready with his finger on the trigger. Quite suddenly, before Jim could get his revolver's sights on the man, Scote turned and ran. In two seconds he had disappeared among trees, heading in the direction of the creek. It was plain that he had seen or heard one or both of the other two Indians.

Jim thought that he had glimpsed a smear of red on the side of Scote's shirt as he spun around and fled. It seemed that Jim's shot had not been a complete miss.

Now Pinetree and Sleeping Wolf, having come together, moved into sight from the side, running low, disappearing again in seconds behind foliage as they pressed hard after their prey.

Longfeather got to his feet wondering what he should do now. In a way he felt like staying out of it from here on. After all, Scote was on the run now. But Jim found himself walking in the direction of the pursuit, and as he did he ejected the empty shell from his Colt and replaced it with a fresh cartridge. It didn't seem right to forsake his friends at this point. If they cornered Scote, one or both of them might die. Jim felt that he at least wanted to be near the action, ready to do whatever might need to be done.

It wasn't long before he reached a bend in the creek, but there was no sign of Scote or his pursuers. The bank was very steep here. Stopping beside a long-trunked tree that grew on the very brink of the cliff-like bank, he looked down and saw that the water was black-deep with much windfall driftwood in it, as Pinetree had said. Jim listened carefully but could hear no sound from any direction.

As he stood there, gun in hand, he dreamed a little terrible daydream—as a twelve-year-old boy might—of a further gun duel between himself and Scote. He imagined that the big ugly bounty hunter came running out into the open from the side and toward the creek, and saw him, fired, missed, and then that he himself fired back in return, shooting Scote through the heart. In the eye of his imagination he could see Scote tumbling over the edge of the creek bank. Down went the bounty hunter in a spectacular headfirst fall, and splashed into the black water.

Jim's little involuntary daydream was over, but now he heard the very real sound of someone running, coming closer fast. Jim drew back; however, he was not quick enough to find concealment.

Scote came into sight, but not from the side as in Jim's daydream. After reaching the creek, Scote had no doubt been following along it looking for a better place to cross, still chased by Pinetree and Sleeping Wolf. Because Jim was standing on the edge of the high creek bank, Scote's course of progress was taking him directly toward him. Scote saw him and came to a quick stop, then dropped to one knee and raised his rifle.

Jim had no time to aim. He pointed and fired. Scote rocked back from the impact of the bullet somewhere on his person, but his rifle discharged and Jim's face was sprayed with particles of bark from the tree beside him.

Scote dropped his rifle as he rolled over on the ground; but he got up on his hands and knees and began to crawl away. Jim suddenly felt immensely sorry for the man.

Now came the sound of running moccasins beating through brush and undergrowth as Pinetree and Sleeping Wolf raced into view. They had been trying to head off Scote and were running toward the creek at an angle rather than directly along it as the bounty hunter had been. They emerged from the bush about fifteen yards from the scene of the action.

Scote saw them, made an effort to regain his feet, and, in spite of a bloody wound in his side, did so quickly. No doubt he still considered Jim to be the greatest immediate threat, for he turned in that direction and drew his revolver.

It was a fast draw for a wounded man. Jim saw the shiny blue-black weapon snake out of the holster and level up toward him in a split second.

Jim fired, once, twice. As the Colt bucked in his hand, the target that was Scote lurched backward in two jerking steps and then tipped headlong over the stony cliff that bordered the creek's edge. Jim could not see all of the twenty-five foot fall, but he heard the crash as Scote hit driftwood and water, and it was more horrible by far than the way it had been in Jim's imagination a moment ago.

Pinetree and Sleeping Wolf came running up and, together with Jim, stepped up to the very edge of the steep bank. Scote looked dead, that was sure, half floating there among bloody driftwood; but Jim found a place to climb down. Leaving his boots, hat, and gun rig on dry ground, he waded into the water, swam a distance, and finally worked his way among the deadwood to where he could do a close inspection of the body. It was quite lifeless.

Jim freed the body and floated it to a place where the bank of the creek—the first tier of it—was low and level enough so that he could drag the body up on it out of the water. The other two Indians climbed down and joined him there. Jim dried his feet on his bandanna before putting on his boots.

"Yes, you have done very well, my blood brother," approved Pinetree again, for he had been praising Jim's victory all the time that Jim had been fishing Scote out of the water. "I hoped to kill him myself, but you have done it for me…. But how is this, brother? You do not look happy."

Jim, strapping on his gun rig, replied, "I find little to smile about in the taking of a man's life…. Then too, I will now be called a *murderer—*" he said the word in English, "—according to the white man's law, a hunted killer like yourself."

"That is as is should be," returned Pinetree with good humor that Jim found extremely irritating. "We are blood brothers and we should ride side by side."

"If you had not killed that cow, none of this would have happened!" exploded Jim.

"The people were hungry," answered Pinetree calmly.

Jim slammed his hat back on his head. "You should not have broken free from the white man's *jail*! That was where the trouble started."

"They said they were going to hang me."

"It was not true. They do not hang a man for stealing a cow. It was stupid talk."

"I heard them say they would hang me, so I fled. I do not want to be hanged."

"And then you shot a redcoat and killed him. That was the worst thing of all."

"I had to shoot him. He wanted to take me back to hang me."

Longfeather sat down on a fallen tree a short distance from the body. He began to reload the empty chambers of his gun. "I have important work to do on the reserve. How can I hide in the bush?...I will feel like a useless coyote."

Sleeping Wolf had been listening in humble silence, but now he spoke up. "Perhaps you need not hide in the bush. We could bury the body of the coward, and no one would ever know what happened to him."

Jim was silent, sad. He holstered his gun.

Pinetree looked a little sad now too, for he was disappointed to learn that there was such a simple way for Jim to get out of the mess, but then he admitted, "Yes, it would work. My blood brother would be safe...to go and live as a white man again. Is that what you wish to do?"

Jim thought this over quietly for several seconds, then rose to his feet. "It is the only thing to do," he said. "I must go back to my work."

Once that was settled, there was one other thing to be ironed out. Pinetree wanted to know how Scote had found him. He broached the subject by explaining how the ambush had taken place. "We were riding back to One Arrow's on the only trail that leads toward my hiding place. We were riding back because we wanted to see our child again. We rode into an ambush. Scote was waiting on the deer trail for me. I think he knew where my camp is. Tell me, brothers, how did he know?"

This was the cue for the penitent Sleeping Wolf to tell all—how Scote had soft-talked and boozed him into giving away the secret of Pinetree's whereabouts. The Indian outlaw was angry but in the end forgave Sleeping Wolf, as Jim knew he would. The whole thing took some time, however, and Jim left the two to go look for a suitable spot to bury Scote.

When Pinetree and Sleeping Wolf had settled their matter, the outlaw went to get his mate who by this time was probably half dead with worry, having heard several shots fired and not knowing the outcome.

Then the three men buried Scote in a shallow grave that they dug with their hands and Jim's tethering stake.

Jim was in a hurry to leave the scene of his crime. He wanted to get back to the reserve and pretend that the whole thing had never happened.

Pinetree made one last attempt to keep Jim with him. "We are blood brothers," he began, using his basic argument. "We should be together in our trouble. Are you not afraid that if you break your vow bad things will come upon you?"

"I am not breaking my vow," said Jim. "And how can you say that I should ride where you ride? I can say as well that you should go where I go. Ride with me back to the reserve, and back among the white men at Duck Lake. You are my blood brother—stay at my side."

"You talk useless talk," said Pinetree. "You know I cannot go back, except in secret."

"Why not?"

"They will kill me if I go."

"And they will kill me if I do *not* go back. I am safer doing my work on the reserve than anywhere else, for there no one will suspect me of any crime. But if I do not come back they will start looking for me and asking questions."

Pinetree considered this. "It is true," he admitted. "Then you must ride your way and I will ride mine.... But we will remain blood brothers."

"Always," said Jim. "I have not forgotten the day that Pinetree saved me from the man with the hay blade."

"You have repaid me well this day," returned Pinetree, "by slaying the man who hurt my woman—the man who hoped to trade my life for money."

And so on this note of reciprocity and trust the blood brothers parted.

Although Pinetree and Blackbird had planned to go see their child, they now decided to postpone this trip for a while. There was the possibility that Scote might have told someone else where the outlaw's hideout was. It was a comparatively permanent type of camp, and Pinetree intended to move to a new location now as quickly as possible.

Longfeather found his mount grazing not far from the horses of Pinetree, near the scene of the ambush. An inspection of Sleeping Wolf's lifeless buckskin showed that the animal had been shot through the head.

A hot spring afternoon saw two Indians riding double on a big brown stallion, silently making their way through wild forest and grassy clearings as they moved back toward a peopled part of the country. The one who sat in the front, in the saddle, the most civilized looking one, hung his head forward in a way that suggested he was carrying a burden on his mind. He was, and it was an unfamiliar one for him.

Even though his crime was a secret one, Jim Longfeather knew that according to the law of the land he had suddenly become a murderer at large.

7

Without a doubt, Commissioner Bancroft's house was the most beautiful and expensive one in Duck Lake. It had been built by a successful former merchant. He had used real lumber shipped in from Regina, which made the building stand out distinctly against most of the others in both the town and the surrounding countryside, for almost all of them were made of logs.

Only a year after building the house, the merchant had volunteered for action during Riel's Rebellion, on the side of the government, and had died when his horse, frightened by gunfire, had bucked and pitched him headfirst against a tree trunk. The house had been purchased by the North-West Mounted Police to be used as a headquarters for the area.

When Commissioner Bancroft was assigned to the post, he had pulled some strings which allowed him to use the building mainly as his home, while a smaller log building, on the business street, had become the station proper. However, it was understood that the large house would have to be available at all times for any needs or functions that the brass in Regina might require. Bancroft couldn't complain about that, for he and his wife were allowed to take up residence in a mini-mansion that made them look and feel like the king and queen of the prairies.

It was more than just being made of actual planed lumber that set this house apart from the rest. It was a two-and-a-half story structure with fancy trim and a railed and pillared veranda, and with a huge brick chimney that told everyone on the outside that there must be a whopper of a fireplace on the inside. There was. The interior also boasted a variety of expensive furnishings throughout its assortment of rooms including a number of guest bedrooms. The featured space was an overly large drawing room where at least twenty-five upper-class frontier couples could gather and rub well attired elbows.

On this spring evening, with darkness already having set in, the house looked warm and inviting, for most of its windows were bright with yellow light from any number of oil lamps, and, since some of these windows were open, they also exuded graceful waltz music, and at one large window any observer on the outside could see dancing couples moving by. This cozy, peace-enchanted feeling, however, had a counterpoint.

The large landscaped yard, under the light of lanterns hanging from trees, was fairly vibrating with movements and sounds of a different character. A couple dozen Indians were dancing a powwow around a blazing campfire and a drum. The drumbeat was savage and loud, and the five men beating it were doing a blood-curdling chant. At least for white people it was blood curdling, but it was not intended to be that, for this was not a war dance, but, rather, a prayer requesting peace and healing.

For Commissioner Oliver Bancroft, who stood at an open window looking out, it was neither blood curdling nor healing. It was just damned irritating. But there was nothing he could do about it. Those bloody idiots in Regina didn't know their asses from that many holes in the ground! *Throw a party for Chief Beardy,* they had said. *Invite him into the house and make him feel wanted and respected. At the same time let his people have a powwow on the yard. Let them know that we want peace and to work together with them in their new way of life.*

Bancroft slid down the window hard enough to risk cracking a pane. He turned sharply to a constable who had, up until that moment, been standing there enjoying the cool breeze and trying to look rigid and handsome for any of the single women who might happen to be looking that way. Bancroft, in a low voice, told the constable, "Damned pemmican burpers! Can't they enjoy themselves without sounding like a bloody pack of coyotes?"

"It would seem that way," said the constable, not because he minded the powwow sound, for he rather liked it, but because he didn't want to spend his whole first year as a policeman shoveling manure in the police stable.

* * *

Sergeant Don Roman, with his beautiful blonde fiancée on his arm, arrived late at for party. As they crossed over the yard they navigated a friendly gauntlet of Indians, male and female. The powwow was between rounds just then, and a number of the men greeted Don and he returned all of these with a smile and a friendly word of his own. Other greetings he initiated and these were responded to in the same spirit of goodwill. But some of the well-wishers were just a bit too animated to suit Don.

As they climbed the few steps onto the front veranda, Rita, clinging tightly to Don's arm, said, quietly, "Didn't you say there wasn't going to be any booze allowed?"

"Yeah, it isn't allowed, but that doesn't mean there isn't any."

They entered the building amid more greetings, now from whites, and soon were in the large drawing room where they at once slipped into the circular stream of waltzers. For a few seconds neither Don nor Rita said anything; both were looking about as they danced, letting the color and gaiety soak in. The predominant color was brilliant red, for all the police officers, including Don, were dandied up in their scarlet dress tunics accentuated with gold braid. And the women, not to be outdone, did not let down the color scheme with its emphasis on brilliance. Their floor-length gowns boasted shimmering, silky materials in greens, yellows, blues, and with a smattering of feminine pastels, all accentuated with glinting necklaces, earrings, and broaches of glass and colored glass. There were also a few real diamonds, small and overshadowed by the more showy and prolific fakes.

Rita was as showy tonight as any of the women, although she was light on jewelry. Her dress was a powdery yellow with a white sash that accentuated her slim waist. She was young and had a petite figure except for her no-nonsense mammary glands. Her puffy golden hair and her fine-featured, blue-eyed face brought about pleasant excitement in any man who looked at her—and *that* they always did.

In regard to her face, it wasn't only its great bone structure and perfect complexion that had this effect on men. It was the look on it. She had many looks, but almost always there was an ongoing theme—one that Don sometimes thought she was unaware of, while at other times he was sure she was willingly responsible for it. If this subtle theme of facial expression could have been written out in words, Don thought it might have read, *I'm a sexy, horny woman but I'm unavailable to you, so keep your pants buttoned*; but he kept this interpretation to himself. In composing this theoretical line, Don had chosen the words partly because Rita sometimes talked that way, but only when she was with people who she thought wouldn't mind. Don was one of those, and he had heard her come out with things that would have jarred a whiskey runner. Although her mouth sometimes made her seem like a loose woman, Don knew from personal experience that her sexual morals, along with other morals, were distinctly on the straitlaced side. The result for Don was that she could turn him into a blazing fire with a few shocking words about the fun they'd have as soon as they got married, and then pack him in ice by reminding him that they were good Christian people with sound morals and so not much was going to happen until the vows had been made. And he was sure that the heat-ice treatment tortured her as much as it did him. Yet she would never let it rest for long— as though she thought that to quit talking about the joys of sex would somehow put her in danger of becoming frigid.

That, thought Don, was highly unlikely. She constantly exuded sexuality. It was like a delightful perfume that a man could smell with his mind. She was doing it now, too, for, in between glancing around to take in the whole room, she would throw in quick little looks up at Don, and each one was loaded with that amazing saturation of femininity that could not be explained but only enjoyed and endured.

The room had a low bandstand with about half of it being used by the four-piece orchestra made up of some of the numerous members of the force who had musical ability. On the other half a head-table had been set up, and behind it sat three Indians—as stiff and erect as though they had awakened from a bad dream and in that moment had petrified. In a way they were in total contrast to the rest of the room's occupants, who were smiling, dancing, milling about, and flapping their lips in lighthearted small talk. If there had been a contest that night between white man and red man to decide who looked the silliest and who looked the most noble and concerned about the issues of life, the three Indians at the head-table would definitely have walked off with the prize; but the silly white people, like the Indians on the lawn outside, definitely seemed to be having the most fun.

The middle Indian of the three sitting on the bandstand was Chief Beardy. The other two were his two top lieutenants, and they were also serving as his personal bodyguards for this occasion. Beardy was a reasonably peaceful man whom Don had spoken to on a number of occasions. From what Don had heard earlier in the day, the chief had been pleased with the concept of this party to honor himself and his band and to strengthen good relationships between the two races.

The chief and his lieutenants had donned their best finery, short of war bonnets, and presented an appearance appropriate to the occasion of promoting peace and goodwill between the two peoples; for they wore a fascinating mixture of Indian and white articles of clothing. The chief, with his hair in braids, wore a flat-topped, flat-brimmed white man's dress hat with a great yellow feather stuck in its band. His white-man's shirt was as red as the tunics of the police officers, and over this he wore a buttonless Indian vest of tanned deer hide. Wide bands of colorful beads weighed heavily on his shoulders and chest.

Rita, her attention in a different direction, told Don, "Look, there's that good looking civilized Indian, Jim Longfeather."

"The Indians are all civilized now," said Don. "The old days are over for them."

"Yeah, sure," she responded. "They live in teepees and slick back their hair with beaver fat. They're civilized all right."

"Well, give them a little time."

"Of course, they can have all the time they want. I love 'em...especially Jim Longfeather." She gave Don a mischievous glance. "I'd like to check out his hair close range, to see if he still uses beaver fat. And I wouldn't really care if he did or didn't. I could take him either way." She took another look at Longfeather who was standing in the stag section, a head or more taller than most of the men to either side of him, broad-shouldered and muscular, looking both massive and sharp in his white shirt and brown pants tucked into tooled boots. She carried on: "He is the biggest, handsomest, stud-iest looking Indian I've ever seen."

Don had known Rita for almost a year now, but he still had not been able to determine exactly how the daughter of a respectable, widowed police officer had learned, at least to some extent, to think and talk like a bawdy barroom woman. At the same time, in other ways, she displayed strong evidence of education and refinement. Don had learned not only to accept this ironic mix but to actually enjoy it; and he knew how to handle her.

He said, "If you carry on getting all soupy about that overgrown clotheshorse, I'm gonna go outside and dance a few rounds of powwow with that big-eyed, buckskin beauty that gave me a smile just before we came in the house. You *saw* that smile, I hope."

"Oh, yeah, I saw it. She's cute. I'm sure you and she could warm up a wigwam without hardly putting your minds to it. If there's enough room maybe we could make it a foursome."

"I'd sooner make it a twosome with just you and me in a bedroom."

"Sounds good," she said, "but I'd like us to spend our wedding night in the livery barn hayloft." She put her cheek against his and kept her voice low enough so that the other nearby dancers would not be likely to hear her next words. "There's something very exciting about sex in a hayloft, don't you think?"

"Oh, definitely," said Don, feeling a distinct beginning to the enlargement of his manliness. "What do you say we get married tonight?"

"Well, seriously you know that won't happen…but, also seriously, we should talk about when it *is* going to happen."

"Yeah," agreed Don. "I was hoping we could soon get alone somewhere and carry on our discussions regarding the matter."

"Yeah," she said, "it's like an ongoing play entitled, When Will the Handsome Red Coat and his Beautiful Blonde Fiancée Quit Talking About Hopping into the Marriage Bed and Actually Do It?"

"That's kind of a long title, isn't it? How about, *The Horny Couple*?"

"Shame on you!—using a word like that. You need to cool off."

"Let's leave here and go jump in the lake." He was referring to the nearby lake that the town of Duck Lake was named after, but was not serious about the suggestion.

So she surprised him when she said, "Well, you can't leave now, Sergeant, but after this do is over, I think it'd be great if we snuck out there for a dip in the dark."

"You're serious?"

"Why not? We don't have to be married to swim…. But, for now, a cool breeze is the best we can hope for to get you back under control. Did you know that this palace has a back veranda as well as a front? If the powwow people are sticking to the front yard, which I admit is doubtful, we might be able to have a moderately private conversation on the back porch."

"Yeah, in the swing-seat."

"Oh, you know about that. Let's go see if it's available."

* * *

Jim Longfeather, still standing in the stag line and wishing he hadn't been more or less forced to come to this party, saw Sergeant Don Roman and his beautiful blonde fiancée work their way off the dance floor and move toward an exit at the rear that led directly out onto the back veranda. Roman had his hand on her waist and the sight of that increased Jim's frustration and loneliness which had set in even before he had arrived here.

There were only four single women here tonight, all nice looking enough to be distinctly touchable, but all presenting problems that, rightly or wrongly, were holding Longfeather at bay. Anna was too young. Bessie he knew to be a pain in the ass because of her nonstop chatter and tendency toward cruel gossip. Laura was a tart and was being energetically courted tonight by Melvin Davis who appeared to be getting drunk and would probably want to fight if Jim got in his way. Melvin made Jim think of a little ornery dog who would take on a St. Bernard just for the hell of it. He decided that Melvin and Laura deserved each other so he wouldn't interfere. The remaining single woman, Isabelle, was as pretty as a touched-up photograph and kept her pert nose slanted an inch higher than any nose had a right to slant. Jim would have liked to dance with her, just to see what a China doll with oversized tits would feel like in his arms; but he was sure that when Isabelle would agree to dance with an Indian—even one in expensive white-man's clothing—Commissioner Bancroft would immediately go over to the bandstand and kiss Chief Beardy on the mouth.

* * *

The swing-seat on the rear veranda was not occupied when Don and Rita emerged into the cool evening breeze, so they immediately got into it, and Rita lost no time in leaning her softness thoroughly into Don's side.

"Honey," he said, this…closeness is not exactly cooling me off."

"Oh, I'm sorry," she said, and at once moved into the swing-seat's far corner so they were separated by at least two feet. She said, "From this moment on, for the rest of the evening, we mustn't do anything or say anything that would tend to give either or us a hard-on."

* * *

Without bothering to pick up his hat, Jim made for the front door and got out into a cool evening that would have been tranquil if it hadn't been for the drumbeat, the wailing chant of the men around the drum, and the intermittent whoops of the dancers. The flickering orange light of the large campfire added phantom movement to the actual movement of the hunched-over dancers. A bit of the light reached a far corner of the yard where, under a spreading elm tree, a small group of buckskinned and feathered men were taking turns at a jug. When they were done, one of them hid it behind the tree trunk.

Jim felt uncomfortable—not so much because of the forbidden booze, but because he wasn't sure he belonged here, out on the yard. He was an Indian, but he wasn't dressed like an Indian, and, even if he had been, the other differences would have been obvious. They knew, as well as he did, that he was not really a part of them.

He looked back at the house from which bouncy polka music was now halfheartedly competing with the Indians' drumming and chanting. Should he go back in the house where he would be tormented with subtle isolation and having to look at unavailable white women? Or should he stay out here and feel isolated by his own upbringing which wouldn't allow him to take a swig of bootlegged whisky, join the powwow, let out boisterous whoops, and, if he went the whole route, end up in the bush behind the yard impregnating some primitive hot-blooded young woman whom he would never spend the rest of his life with.

Against a side of the house and facing toward the powwow dancers was a wooden bench that no one was using. Jim walked over and sat down on it. He knew his tiredness was mental and emotional. He needed to be at this party because both whites and Indians considered him to be a reasonably important link between the two entities. He was not a big star with either, but when a white-red problem needed solving or a negotiator was required to help settle some tricky dispute, Jim was the most likely person to be chosen— whether by the police or the Indian elders. He knew they particularly wanted him here tonight in case trouble broke out.

Jim Longfeather fervently looked forward to getting back to the agent station, into his own bunk in his own little room, where hopefully sleep would bring him a new and brighter day.

* * *

Don and Rita, in the swing-seat, still had the two feet of space between them and were heroically keeping it that way.

"I will, of course, wear a *white* wedding dress to symbolize that I'm still a virgin," said Rita's sweet voice. Don could see her only indistinctly by a bit of lamplight coming through a window and by some of the flickering red light from the bonfire around the corner of the house. It reflected off leaves of the backyard grove of poplar trees. She continued, "But, if you don't mind, I won't be wearing anything under the dress—to symbolize that I'll be in a big hurry to rip if off as soon as we're alone."

"I'll help," said Don.

"You'll be busy ripping off your own clothes. So let's get down to business. Exactly when is this big event going to take place?"

"When do you want it to?"

"Tonight...or at least this week."

"One is expected to announce a wedding at least a month before it happens," ventured Don, feeling like an old lady.

She said, "So the sooner we announce it, the better, right? Besides, everyone knows. We've been engaged long enough for a dog to have grandchildren. They're all expecting it."

"The dog's grandchildren?"

"Just tell me—when do you want to get married? I'm tired of being held in the breeding pen with a lick and a promise—mostly minus the lick. Speak up, Sergeant."

"Oh, I've got something pretty definite in mind," said Don. "Bancroft is sending me out on a mission, so we'll be separated a for a couple of weeks or longer. And, I was thinking, how about if we set the wedding for right after I get back?"

"But you said a couple of weeks or longer. How can we set a date for right after you come back if you don't know when you're coming back?"

In spite of this worry, Don could see that Rita was pleased. He said, "Well, let's make it a month from tonight."

"All right!" she said and flung herself on him. He pulled her slight form even closer against himself so they were molded together like two loaves of bread squished into a saddlebag; and for a moment he thought he might be about to have sex with her without her even knowing it. It didn't help that an Indian couple from the powwow fire were trotting by hand in hand toward the bush. They were the third couple to head for relief, and the first hadn't yet come back out. But then Rita pulled back a little and said, "What kind of a mission? Where to?"

"Way up north to the Dunlap area—you know, the Dunlap logging camp."

"That place is in nowhere-land. Dad says there's nothing there but bush, a log-cutting operation, and a kink in the river."

"He's right."

"Why do you have to go there?"

"There's a rumor—well, maybe more than a rumor—that John Pinetree was sighted working at the mill. Bancroft wants me to go check it out and, if it's true, bring him in."

"Not by yourself, I hope."

"Yeah, by myself. Bancroft keeps expecting a full-scale Indian war to break out here in his backyard any moment and can't spare anyone else."

"According to what I've been seeing of his backyard, I'd say the Indians have other things than war on their minds."

Don lowered his voice. "Yeah, if anyone starts a war here it'll be Bancroft himself." Then he got back to their normal level of quiet talking. "One man is enough to pick up Pinetree anyhow. I'm not worried."

"Well, *I* am," said Rita. "Everyone says Pinetree will never let himself be taken alive."

"Everyone is right," said Don grimly, sadly. "I'm sorry, Rita, but I'm a member of the North-West Mounted. Pinetree has killed a police officer. I have no choice but to go bring him in if I can find him—dead or alive."

"Only if he doesn't kill you first." Rita slumped back into the swing-seat. "Shit! I might be a widow before I even get married."

Another buckskin-clad couple, hand in hand, were trotting toward the bush.

* * *

Jim thought he'd walk a circle around the bonfire and dancers, just to kill time, then go back inside and somehow kill time there. But just then another powwow round came to an end, and, since the Indians were becoming more rowdy, Jim decided to head straight back toward the house.

He saw that his friend, Sleeping Wolf, and two other Indians had parked themselves on the veranda steps—maybe because they were too unsteady to be on their feet. Wolf was between the other two and had an arm around each of them so that the three tended to sway back and forth simultaneously, although occasionally one would lean south when the other two would lean north, or some other such combination, thus momentarily destroying the rather pleasing pendulum effect.

As Jim approached them, Sleeping Wolf withdrew his right arm from his buddy's shoulder, pulled a flask out from under his shirt, and took a swig, and all this considerably upset the rhythm of their swaying. Wolf then lifted the flask high and greeted Jim in English but with an accent he had picked up from the French and Metis: "'Allo, Jeem." Then he switched to Cree. "You are my good friend." Next he looked first at one of his two booze buddies and then at the other, as he carried on: "Jim Longfeather is my very good friend.... Oh, yes, we share a secret that only he and I know.... Is that not true, Jim, my good friend?" He smiled a blurry smile and started to upend the flask again, but his buddy on his left took it away from him and had a go at it himself, spilling about as much as he drank.

Jim was alarmed at what Wolf had just said, and wasn't sure what to do about it. He thought of calling him aside and talking to him about the importance of never making any mention of the secret they shared; but Wolf was in no condition to absorb anything, nor to remember anything he did absorb. Jim said, "You shouldn't be drinking out in the open like this."

Wolf's buddy on his right side now had gotten hold of the flask. He looked up over it at Jim and said, smiling broadly, "We have a treaty with Bancroft. He says we must all drink much firewater tonight and make babies in all the white women in the house." The other two laughed at this fascinating vision.

"Try not to get too drunk," said Jim inanely as he stepped around the men and climbed the steps—inanely, for they were obviously already well past the point of respectable social drinking. Not that the latter concept was known to a great many who lived on the reserve, thought Jim, but they had lived for centuries without booze, and suddenly this mind-numbing liquid magic had been unloaded on them. He expected they would need decades of experience, mostly bad, to get a grip on it.

Halfway through the open front door, Jim stopped and looked back at the three Indians sitting on the steps. He was getting more disturbed by the moment with what Wolf had said—that he and Jim shared a secret. Their backs were to him now. Sleeping Wolf was telling the other two: "Jim Longfeather is a good man. A great warrior.... And I, Sleeping Wolf, am a great warrior too. I am a greater warrior than any of you others think. I have fought to help John Pinetree stay free. But I will tell you nothing more."

The other two men at once badgered Wolf to tell them all about it, but Wolf replied, "No, I will tell you nothing more.... It is enough for you to know that Jim Longfeather and Sleeping Wolf are great warriors, and together we have bravely come to the defense of our good brother, Pinetree."

Jim had heard all he cared to hear. He carried on into the house only deep enough to retrieve his hat from where he had left it upon arrival. Then he headed back out and down past the three on the steps. He turned and looked back at Wolf.

"Sleeping Wolf," said Jim in Cree. "We are friends, are we not?"

"We are friends," agreed Wolf at once.

"We have a secret that must be kept between us—is that not true?"

"That is true, my friend," said Wolf with obvious pleasure.

"Then do not speak any more about it, not to these good men, nor to anyone else."

"I will never say anything. It is our secret."

"That is good," said Jim. He turned and walked away, leaving the yard.

* * *

At the livery stable, Jim saddled his horse and retrieved his gun rig from where he had hidden it in the hayloft. Guns were not allowed at the party.

As he rode back toward the Indian agency on the reserve he met no one. The moon had come out and bathed the wilderness trail in a peaceful but contradictory pale-golden wash. It was contradictory to the lack of peacefulness that Jim felt inside.

So this was it. What he had worried about was coming true. Sleeping Wolf was hitting the bottle and letting slip the terrible truth that could put both him and Jim at the end of ropes swinging gently from the gallows in Regina. He had always doubted that the secret was safe with Sleeping Wolf; now he knew it wasn't.

Many times since the killing of Scote, Jim had wondered if he should flee the area, change his name, become a full-fledged fugitive. But he had always decided against it. So long as Wolf could be trusted there was very little chance that anyone would ever find out. But now....

By the time Jim arrived at the Indian-agent station it seemed to him that he had asked himself about a hundred times if he was overreacting; but each time he had heard, in his memory, the booze-blurred voice of Sleeping Wolf saying, "*...we share a secret that only he and I know,*" and "*...together we have bravely come to the defense of our good brother, John Pinetree.*" How long would it be before Sleeping Wolf came out with the whole story? Actually, chances were pretty good that he had already done so.

Jim made up his mind then. Sadly realizing that his life had changed forever, he packed his saddlebags and bedroll. He would not take a packhorse but, rather, travel as lightly as he could.

While his stabled horse rested and ate hay and oats in the barn, Jim lay down on his cot and allowed himself an hour's rest. He was glad the agent would not be back until late the following day, for he had gone to an agency meeting on the One Arrow Reserve.

Just before leaving, Jim wrote a note to the agent:

Dear Bernie,
I'm sorry for running out on you and everyone else like this, but I can't stand staying here any longer when my blood brother is in such serious trouble and needs help and guidance. This time I'm going to find him. Best wishes.
Sincerely, Jim.

He left the note lying on the table. From a hiding place under his cot he brought out a sock containing more money than any fugitive had likely ever before hit the trail with, and headed out to the barn.

The pale-gray of dawn was working its way along the northern horizon toward the east when Jim Longfeather climbed into the saddle on his bay stallion and headed north.

He was careful to ride along the banks of the nearby creek for a bit, to make sure that he left tracks. But after a couple of miles, in a grassy area, he began to circle. By sunup he had changed the direction of his progress entirely, now heading south. He intended to stay clear of all civilization and humanity for a good number of days. No one must learn that he was heading south instead of north. Allowing himself no less than twenty miles per day, Jim expected to reach the U.S. border in a week. He didn't know how deep into Montana he'd go before surfacing and trying to start a new life, or if he might go even farther, into Wyoming.

Would there soon be reward posters out for him in the States? How could he modify his appearance? If only, thought Jim, he wasn't so bloody big; he would stand out like a swollen thumb everywhere he went. And how many drifters rode a stallion?

These were somewhat discouraging facts, but human nature is strange. In spite of all the negatives, in spite of the fact that Jim found himself this morning to be a fugitive fleeing for his life, the pleasant morning sunshine and the birds singing among the breeze-trembled aspen leaves did something to him. Of course, it wasn't only the sun and the birds. *Hope blooms eternal in the heart of man,* and whenever a man turns over a new leaf in his book of life, he can hardly help but feel that maybe, just maybe, he is on the brink of a glorious new adventure and the best years of his life.

Jim was a positive sort of person. He regretted what had happened, but, now that it had happened and the page had been turned, he began looking forward with pleasant anticipation to learning what that page held. And a meadowlark, so close beside the trail and so synced with his passing that it seemed more than coincidence, sang him a brilliant little song of hope and happiness.

PART TWO:
THE TREK

Roman moved his hand away from the holster. He could hear footsteps behind him, and, turning his head part way, caught sight of two more men coming out of the bush, one from either side. One of these was leading a horse.

Don felt his hair peacefully settling down once more, and a feeling of ultra-calmness spread through every part of his body—as it always did once the show had begun. He turned his head back to the men in front. "Good morning, gentlemen."

"Good morning, Sergeant Roman," returned one of the men over his rifle. Don noted that he was exceptionally well dressed, if not appropriately, for this backwoods part of the country. He wore clean, gray-striped riding pants, a spotless white dress shirt, and an equally dressy looking cloth vest. The black hat that shaded a handsome but long face also seemed, like the rest of his outfit, to have been bought in a store this very morning. The long, handsome face added to its greeting by saying, "Please step down from your horse, sir, and make sure that your hand stays away from your gun."

As Don Roman obeyed, he made a quick sweeping inspection of the other three men, mostly out of curiosity as to whether they were as ridiculously well dressed as the spokesman, but also to check on how they were armed and how vicious or kindhearted they seemed. He was relieved to find that as far as their clothes went they looked like ordinary dirty cowpokes, but there was nothing encouraging about the repeating rifles they held in their hands and the man-sized revolvers that dangled from gunbelts around their hips. Don stood on the ground beside his horse now, waiting.

The handsome clean man came a little closer. Like small boys who respected their daddy so that they imitated his actions, the three dirty henchmen also moved in closer. Clean-man said, "This wasn't much fun—too easy—capturing the great Sergeant Don Roman without even a fight." The fact that these men knew Don's name didn't surprise him too much. He had a bit of a reputation in the Territories.

"Better make him take off his gunbelt. Better play it safe," said a taut voice behind Roman.

"Oh, shut up," said Clean-man without sounding too annoyed. "Do you think I'd let him keep his gun? All right, Sergeant, unbuckle it."

For a member of the North-West Mounted Police (at least for those who had the new features of the uniform) to take off his gun rig was no simple thing; it was almost a chore. First there was the shoulder strap which had to be unfastened, then the white lanyard cord that led from the butt of the revolver to a loop around his neck had to be slipped up over his head, which involved removing the wide-and-stiff-brimmed hat, and finally the belt that supported the covered holster and held the scarlet tunic trimly to the policeman's waist could be unbuckled and removed. Don dropped the whole rigging to the ground.

"Kick it over here," ordered Clean-man. Don did so. The man picked it up without taking his eyes or his gun away from the sergeant. "All right, now walk in there." He waved the hand that held Don's gun rig toward the bush on one side of the trail, indicating a bit of an opening in the foliage. "But don't try to make a run for it, 'cause I'm gonna be right behind you."

As Don started walking slowly into the bush he could tell quite plainly by the hard rifle barrel poking at his back that the nicely dressed man was indeed right behind him. In just a few steps Don had entered a small clearing within the grove of trees.

There was a team of horses there hitched to a wagon—an odd looking, closed in, high, box-like conveyance, and Don remembered having seen caravans of Gypsy families traveling about the countryside in the same kind of rig. It also looked somewhat like the ones driven by sellers of medicine and household goods. But then he noticed that the small windows in this one had iron bars. The four owlhoots who had him under gun were obviously not Gypsies, and not likely sellers of medicine either, so Don supposed that they had bought or stolen the wagon and converted it into a portable prison.

At Fancy Clean-man's order everyone came to a halt. Roman stood ringed by the four.

"Well, what do you think of her?" asked Fancy, gesturing loosely toward the wagon.

"Looks fairly secure," returned Don.

"Oh, she's secure all right," assured the other, "as you'll soon find the first time you try to break out of her.... Yeah, I hope you like her, 'cause you're going to be traveling a long, long ways in her. So we'd better get started pronto.... But first, take your clothes off."

"Eh?"

"You heard me. Get out of those fancy duds. You're riding this whole long trip naked. Ha! C'mon, peel! Or is that too much of a dishonor for a proud member of the North-West Mounted? Or maybe you lose your courage when you lose that red coat, is that it? Well, anyways, you'd better take it off if you don't want it decorated with a different shade of red. You get it?"

Don began to unbutton the coat. "All right, but what's the idea?"

"I have my reasons. Just strip—take off everything. And don't worry, we're not gonna screw your hairy ass." The other three men laughed at this, and Fancy continued, "I'd sooner screw a frog," which got another laugh, so he was encouraged to elaborate further. "Anything would be better than copulating with one of you red-backed, yellow-legged law beetles." This brought on still more laughter.

Don, as he carried on undressing, said, "Sounds to me like you gents have had a lot of experience pokin' various forms of wildlife. You might want to try a woman for a change."

"A regular smart ass, ain't he?" said one of the men, and he didn't sound pleased.

Fancy said, "Good. He'll be more entertaining that way." This seemed to put the others at ease and they continued laughing, sometimes uproariously, as though the sight of an uncovered male body was colossally hilarious. One of the men, laughing like the others, picked up each item of clothing that Don cast off and neatly folded it in a little pile, sitting on his haunches to do this. Another man, obeying Fancy's orders, unsaddled and unbridled Don's horse before turning him loose.

Then, still laughing, they marched the stark naked sergeant toward the prison wagon. The one in charge of the clothing brought that bundle along.

One of the men opened the door at the rear of the portable prison; the leader told Don to climb inside. As he put one leg up high into the doorway in preparation to hoist himself up, this brought an extra loud gust of laughter from the men. Don walked stoop-shouldered into the low-ceilinged, dim interior. There was straw under his bare feet. The door closed behind him and he heard the metal bolt slide firmly into place.

"Make yourself comfortable," said the voice of the handsome man. "We got a long, long trip ahead of us." He seemed to enjoy emphasizing this.

There was a small square window in either side of the caboose prison and one equally small one in the door at the rear. All three were barred. There was no opening of any kind in the front. In about the middle of the floor was a four-by-four inch square hole that Don recognized at once as a simply-made indoor toilet.

Partly by seeing through the windows and partly by sound, Roman could make out that two of the men mounted saddle horses and the other two climbed up into the high seat on the front of the prison wagon. He heard the signaling *click-click* of a tongue to which the wagon horses responded at once by jolting the rig into rollicking, bouncing motion. Sergeant Roman landed squarely on his bare behind on the straw covered floor.

Still sitting, he got his back up against a lurching wall and tried to follow his captor's suggestion—tried to make himself comfortable for the long journey that lay ahead. Since he could come to no conclusion as to where it might lead, he amused himself by pretending that the horses could fly and that he was on his way to the moon.

9

As days and nights passed by for the captive Don Roman, the only thing he learned about where he was heading—and this from his own visual observation—was that the wagon was constantly rolling southward. It was exciting and boring at the same time. Exciting because of the mystery of the situation—not knowing where he was being taken; boring because there was not much to do day after day but sit on his bare fanny in a pile of straw and listen to the bumping and creaking of the wagon wheels. He did spend some time standing humpbacked at any one of the three windows, peering out at the slow-passing countryside, trying to pick out new clues as to his changing location; but because of the uncomfortable posture the low ceiling forced upon him, he never stayed at a window for more than a few minutes at a time.

They kept him well fed. They gave him a cowhide to cover up with at night. They took good care of him in every way except that they would not relieve his curiosity about where they were taking him and why. During the first full day on the road he had asked twice. Both times Fancy Clean-man, whose name turned out to be Byron, told him that he would find out soon enough. The other men's names were Harry, Sam, and Bull. This he learned, along with a few other trivial things, partly from overhearing their daily conversation and partly from having them answer at least some of his questions. But in all the talking that Don's captors did, which ranged from telling jokes to bragging about the hot women they had "poked," never a word was let slip about the purpose and meaning of this whole vagabondish enterprise.

They crossed many rivers, most of them shallow enough to ford easily, but on two occasions they crossed by ferry. Both times the ferryman on duty was told that the wagon was delivering a dangerous lunatic to a mental hospital in some town to the south. Don didn't dare make any denials. He was afraid that to do so might endanger not only his own life but also the life of the ferry operator. If there was anything that particularly struck him about his captors it was that they were determined persons.

Don Roman was not as anxious as many individuals, including experienced policemen, might have been in this situation. But, then, Roman was an adventurer by very nature and had been living an exciting life since his early youth.

* * *

His pioneer parents had settled at Fort Garry, in Canada, when he was a boy of four. He could not remember much of his previous childhood in the old country except for the docks and the ships and the embarking. And he could remember the ocean voyage. It had been a great hazardous affair that somehow seemed like the beginning of his life.

At Fort Garry, a Hudson's Bay post, his father carried on with his trade which was blacksmithing. Don was able to go to school and did well in his studies. But a powerful desire to travel wooed him into leaving school and home at the age of sixteen. He came farther west with the settlers. In the Northwest Territories he got a job as a laborer, helping with some enlarging work on Fort Carlton for the Hudson's Bay Company. While working there he met a prospector who later took him along on a mineral and fur hunting trip much farther into the north. They didn't find any gold, silver, or copper, but the lonely winter that followed brought them enough furs to have made the trip financially worthwhile. For young Don, however, the greatest gain was the experience he acquired in rugged living.

After that he went home and back to school. He found that what stuck in his mind the most about his brief wanderings was the memory of the North-West Mounted Policemen he had come in close contact with while working at Fort Carlton. There were members of the force at Fort Garry too, but somehow it wasn't the same. In the wild country around Fort Carlton these riding adventurers had a special glamor of their own; and that glamor, very real to a young, healthy, teen-aged boy, had impressed itself upon Don so that he decided to join the force as soon as he was old enough.

He was trained at Fort Garry, then sent west to Regina, and later he was stationed at various forts and settlements in the far Northwest.

These were tough times that quickly made or broke a man in the force. A recruit required qualities of hardihood and daring, and a sense of diplomacy, and the all-important imagination that can enable one to think of answers to a problem when it seems there are no answers, and plain, raw courage, and the basic quality of having a strong enough motive to be doing this kind of work in the first place. This included, in the minds of many of its members, a sincere desire to help make the Northwest a good place to live. Those recruits who had these qualities were destined, as a group, to make this unique Canadian police force one of the most famous in the world.

It turned out that Don Roman had what it took. It may be that he was not the very greatest of his time, but the five years of accomplishment that turned him from a green constable into an experienced sergeant proved beyond a doubt that he was one of the most capable and fearless men who had ever donned scarlet serge.

* * *

He had no scarlet serge now; he sat naked and dirty like a pig in a pen—a portable pen that was taking him to where he would not at all have wanted to go if he had known the purpose of this journey.

Days followed nights followed days followed nights. Roman lost accurate track of time but judged from the length of his beard that at least a month and a half had passed by. Don knew that they were now deep into the United States of America. Through the little barred windows he had seen a great variety of North American countryside ranging from heavy timber through level, treeless prairies, to hilly country with snow capped mountains in the distance. Occasionally there was an encounter with passersby, but never anything that seemed to worry the kidnappers very much, although twice they hid the rig in bush and were silent as hoof and wagon sounds approached and went by. On one of these occasions Don was warned to be still if he didn't want his "bloomin' head blown off."

Eventually the terrain became arid and sandy with rocky outcroppings. Only a little grass grew here and there and Don's captors were often involved in conversation regarding feed for the horses and which water holes they hoped to get to. Apparently they knew the area. The heat in the caboose increased to the point where Don was allowed to occasionally pour a little water over himself even though he gathered that it was not in abundant supply. But they apparently did have a small barrel fixed somewhere to the front end of the wagon, and they filled it at every opportunity.

So it was obvious that their purpose in kidnapping Don included the need to take good care of him. After a time they even went so far as to open the door of the caboose wide during the hottest times of each day's travels, allowing Don to sit in it with his legs hanging out so the breeze could reach him, and they let him use his hat to shade his head and eyes. His whole body was soon as brown as that of an Indian, for he allowed the light to strike him from every angle, sometimes lying on his stomach on the floor with the sun beating down on him. During these times when the door was open, the two men on horseback would ride behind the wagon and keep a close eye on him. They were not really taking much of a chance in giving Don these benefits, for he was weaponless, naked except for the hat, and somewhere in the middle of a no-man's-land southwestern desert.

And still the days and nights passed by and the wagon continued to bump along as though there would never be an end to the journey. Roman kept himself from going flabby by doing daily pushups and other standard police exercises, always during the cool mornings and evenings. He kept himself from going crazy by making up corny jokes. Once, after hatching out an exceptionally juicy one, he laughed out loud. The men heard this, and the leader, Byron, commented, "Damn it!—hope he doesn't crack up on us." So it was clear that they needed him both mentally and physically sound.

During earlier parts of the trip, Don had spent a lot of time thinking about Rita; but he soon realized that this brought him more inward pain than pleasure. However, he found that if he granted himself just the occasional thought of her—and what powers of mind control that involved!—it became a positive thing. So, with amazing psychic discipline, Don would allow himself to willingly think about Rita two or three times a day and then only for a minute or so, always, among other related thoughts, looking forward to getting married to her. He was so full of faith that this would actually come about, that he sometimes almost expected her to be waiting for him in a wedding gown when he got to the end of this southward trek.

And there were also times when he wondered if the heat and isolation were slowly destroying his mind.

One day the men suddenly got excited. Don could hear them cursing as the horses slowed from a trot to a walk. It was in the cooler morning hours and Don was locked into the caboose. Whenever he was locked in, his hat was taken from him and hidden away with his other clothes, wrapped in a sheet and somehow secured under the wagon, probably in a box they had fixed there.

"It's too late to turn and make a run for it," Don heard the leader complain from the driver's seat. "We'll have to try to bluff our way through...and if that don't work, shoot our way through. Keep cool, but be ready for quick action if necessary."

"You sure it's the law?" asked the other man who was sitting in the wagon seat at this time, namely Bull.

"Of course," returned Byron. "Can't you see the sun shining off their badges?"

"Yeah," said Bull. "We can take 'em easy. It's four against two."

"Just make sure you don't miss," said Byron. "But don't make a move unless I do. You all got that straight?" The other two were riding close on either side of the wagon. They grunted acquiescence. Byron now addressed Don in a somewhat louder, yet low, voice. "Sergeant, we're coming up to some lawmen. If you want to live through this then not a word outa you till we're clear of them. You hear me?"

"I hear you," said Don.

A little later Don heard a new voice ordering the wagon to pull to a stop. It did so.

"Dave Lindner, sheriff of Garner Flats," the same husky and totally masculine voice introduced itself, "and this is Depity Cliff Fullbright."

"Pleased to meet you, Sheriff...Deputy. Name's Ross Gibbens," returned the voice of Byron without any hesitation. "This here is Ed, and that's Judd and Matthew...all Slater by way of last name— brothers."

"I see," said the husky voice. "What you got in the wagon, boys?"

"A mental patient, Sheriff," said Byron. "We're takin' him to the mental institution at Stony Hill."

"Stony Hill's quite a stretch from here," said the sheriff. "Where you from?"

Byron said, "From Duncroft. Sheriff Allison there rounded up this one. Crazier'n a loon, this one. Won't keep a stitch of clothes on his body, and thinks he's a werewolf—y'know, thinks he can turn into a wolf when there's a full moon. Goes around trying to bite and strangle people—real dangerous. You care to take a look at him?"

"Yeah, reckon I will."

Don heard Byron climb down from the seat and caught a glimpse of the gray-shirted sheriff riding past the window on a dapple-gray horse.

"Don't y' all bother t' open the door," said the sheriff. "I'll just look in through the bars."

"All right, sheriff—probably just as well," said Byron.

Don was thinking hard. Was this his big chance? Could he somehow secretly let the sheriff know that he was not really a mental patient?—that there was foul play afoot? Small chance. He could come right out and tell the lawman what was going on, but then even if his own life was spared—for his captors obviously had some use for him—the sheriff and deputy would most likely be gunned down before they had half a chance to defend themselves. But he had been locked up in this damned caboose for probably close to two months. He felt that he couldn't pass up the small chance that had suddenly come his way. Maybe a sly wink that only the sheriff would see. And then what? If the sheriff *did* catch on that the wink meant more than the twitch of a nervous imbecile's eyelid, he would ask more questions and would probably end up dead. The sheriff's saddle creaked as he dismounted at the rear of the caboose.

A normal sized man would have stayed on his horse to look through the window, but not the sheriff. Standing behind the wagon, his deep-tanned face, shaded by a wide-brimmed gray hat, lined up quite nicely with the barred opening.

Don stared back at him more intently than he had planned to, for the face was quite familiar looking.

Although it couldn't be, it seemed to be the face of Jim Longfeather, the educated Canadian Indian who worked with the agent on Beardy's Reserve.

No, it just couldn't be him; besides, this man had a southern, uneducated accent. Yet it was amazing how much they looked alike. Whoever he was, Don finally decided firmly that he did not want to put the man's life at risk.

Don was on his knees in the straw. He let out a loud vicious growl, at the same time cupping his hands into the shape of claws and arcing them through the air as though he would like to tear to shreds anyone who might dare to come within reach. He contorted his bearded face into an expression of maniacal fury. The sheriff, poker faced, studied him for a moment and then drew back. Don reached a grasping, clawing hand through the bars and continued to growl fiercely. He saw the mildly stunned looks on the faces of the Byron and the other owlhoots, for they had all come around to the back of the caboose along with the sheriff and deputy.

Looking out through the window, Don took further note that the sheriff was an exceptionally big man and built like a fort—just like Jim Longfeather. Maybe, thought Don, this was Longfeather's twin brother, although he had never heard that he had one, and the two had somehow been separated at birth with one growing up in Canada and one here in the southwestern United States. Like Longfeather, this man stood well over six feet tall and packed at least two-hundred and fifty pounds of solid muscle, maybe more.

"Say now," said the big sheriff, still looking toward the barred window, "he is kind of a mean fella, ain't he?"

Byron said, "Yeah, an' then some."

Don sank back down onto the straw-covered floor. He heard the sheriff's deputy speak for the first time. "I guess you fellas will be mighty glad to git him to Stony Hill, huh?"

"Oh, no," said Byron, "I wouldn't say that. We're used to him now. After a while you kind of get to like the critter."

"You're kiddin, huh?"

"Oh, no, I mean it."

The sheriff said, "Wal, I guess you kin go on yore way an' we'll go ours…. But I should really ask to see yore papers…like maybe a letter from the sheriff at Duncroft, or whatever you got."

For a couple of seconds Don feared that his world-class performance had been for nothing, but then the voice of Byron surprised him by saying, "Sure thing, Sheriff, here you are." Next came the sound of paper being unfolded and handled.

"Uh huh," grunted the sheriff after a few seconds. "Yeah...okay." Paper crunching again. "Wal, the best a' luck on the rest of yore trip, fellas. C'mon, Cliff, we gotta finish our little scoutin' patrol an' git back to Garner Flats afore our horses die of starvation or old age."

Don wondered about the papers. They had to be some sort of fakery. He was astounded at the foresight and cunning that had gone into this thing. What was the meaning of it all?

The prison wagon covered many more miles before that day drew to a close.

Around sunset Don felt the jolting floor of his room slope to the front and stay that way, at various uncomfortable angles, for so long that he decided they must be going down the banks of another river. He began to rise from the straw, intending to look out through a window, but only managed to get up on one knee. At that moment the floor underneath him did a heave and he heard both men in the driver's seat yell in alarm.

The wagon tipped over with a wood-rending crash.

Don fell from the floor, along with the straw, to the lower side of the caboose which was scraping the ground. He bounced about like a rubber ball as that side hit something and skipped upward a foot or so. Don rolled over, voluntarily now, to get away from the barred window under him which was spewing up a thick jet of sandy dirt. He could hear Byron hollering, "Whoa! Whoa! Whoa!" to the horses from somewhere off to the side; but by the way the upset caboose was hopping along and dirt was shoveling in through the ground-side window, Don didn't get the impression that anyone had a hold of the reins, or that the horses gave a fiddler's fart about their master's commands to them to stop. If anything the pace increased, and as the dragging caboose began to shake and jolt more and more—as a result of either greater speed or rougher ground or both—Don had all he could do to keep his head from hitting the sides of the cubicle and the rest of his bruised self from being injured further. He managed to get into a crouching position with his hands braced against the surface below him. Strangely enough, in all this danger, the manner in which he was bouncing up and down on his haunches put the thought into his mind that he was like an ape hopping along through the jungle. But he wasn't long able to enjoy this humorous concept, for in a few seconds the now loud, wildly galloping hooves of the horses were drowned out by the second grinding, splintering smash-up as the skidding caboose hit a large rock. This time Don was not able to protect his head.

When he opened his eyes it took him a moment to remember anything. One of the first things he figured out was that he had been unconscious, although maybe only for a few seconds. It took at least a few more seconds before his billowing brain leveled off enough for him to realize that he was on his back on the ground with a wide, clear, dusk-blue sky above him. He was conscious enough to realize that he had been smashed free from his prison.

He tried to get up but caved in immediately. Lying on his side now, his head once more swimming, he waited patiently until he regained his concepts of up and down, and then tried again, only this time more slowly. He made it to his knees, stopped to listen as he heard voices from higher up on the riverbank. Byron was cursing while Bull was shouting, "You can see where they went—here, through the bush."

Don looked around to all sides now, sizing up his chances for escape. A few yards downhill from him was the wreck of the caboose. One wall had been completely wrenched out of it and there was a variety of other damage. The horses were no longer attached to it and were not in sight. Looking back, uphill, Don saw an axle with both wheels still attached, the axle broken over a three-foot-high rock.

Roman completed this overall survey by inspecting his own body. That was skinned and bloody down the front, but seemed to be hanging together in one piece.

He made it to his feet, swaying, managed to walk to the wrecked caboose and steadied himself against it. The voices on the brushy hill above him were closer now. Roman took a deep breath, let go of the wagon, and walked as fast as he dared toward a rocky, brush-filled ravine—or *arroyo*, as Don had heard Byron referring to this sort of deep water-eroded but dried out channel—that angled down toward the river. The edge of the ravine was not far from the wreck, and Don half expected to find the team of horses there. He looked over the edge, saw nothing but jagged rocks, high brush, and a few scraggly trees. He lowered himself over the side, at the same time taking a look back at the higher banks. There was much brush up there. He still could not see anything of his captors, but just then Byron's voice came through loud and clear again.

"There's the wagon!"

"Looks beat up pretty bad," said one of the others.

Partly to get away from the renewed outburst of cursing, Don speeded up his descent into the gully. Once at the bottom he stumbled along barefooted over rocks, low brush, and fallen trees as he made his way downward toward the river. It wasn't long before the ravine widened and flattened out in front of Don, and there just ahead of him, looking muddy-dull in the twilight, was a stream about forty feet wide.

Don walked up close to the water, crouched behind a clump of willows as he tried to make up his mind whether or not he should try to cross. Under ordinary circumstances he could have swum it almost without effort, but now.... And he could probably hide just as well on this side as on the other. Yet it seemed sensible to get the river between himself and his pursuers; there was a chance that none of them could swim.

He got up and walked down into the wet sand. The water, particularly after it was up to his knees, seemed colder than reasonable for such a warm evening. He was also surprised by the slowness of the drop under his feet. By the time he was almost halfway across, and still only hip deep in the flow, he began to realize that he would probably not have to swim a stroke.

The riverbank ahead of him sloped much more gradually than the one he had come down. When he looked up at the highest point of the bank—which was the horizon line from his viewpoint and about three hundred feet away—he was quite startled to see, in the dim light of dusk, a lone rider sitting motionless astride his equally motionless horse. There were feathers on the man's head and on the horse's bridle. He was framed by brush and one scraggly tree which partly covered him, so that he was not all that easy to pick out unless one's eyes happened to fall directly on him.

Don, standing rock-still in the water now, didn't know if the Indian had seen him. Nor did he have time to think about whether it made any difference if he had, for at that moment the sergeant was addressed from the rear.

"I think you'd better come back here, Roman," —it was Byron's voice—"unless you want to be feed for the catfish. You'll never get to the other side with a dozen or so forty-five slugs in you."

Don turned slowly to face Byron, Harry, Sam, and Bull who stood there on the bank like a row of wooden soldiers, each holding a revolver. The sound of the stream's current had covered up their sneaking footsteps.

Don waded back to them. As he stepped out of the water he took note that the three henchmen looked madder than picadored bulls, almost as though they were blaming him for the wreck of the wagon. Byron alone, in spite of the fact that the fresh white shirt he had put on in the morning was now quite soiled, had regained his good humor. He was smiling as he said, "You know, Sergeant, you almost had a lucky break, and all because of my careless driving."

"What happened?"

"Hit a hole with the front wheel just when the wagon was already leaning too much," explained Byron. "Looks like you took quite a beatin'. Well, I'm glad you didn't get killed."

"Thank you for your concern. I'm deeply touched."

Byron laughed. "You're valuable to me, almost precious in fact. But don't let that fool you into thinking that I won't kill you in a second if I have to."

"Yeah, sure," agreed Don, "no use gettin' carried away."

Sam spoke up. "What're we gonna do with the bloody wagon?" He was the tallest of the four. One side of his beard-stubbled face was streaked with dirt and blood.

"Fix it—what else?" said Byron.

"Yeah? An' what're we gonna do with this stud horse in the meantime?"

"Tether him to a tree—what else?"

Roman felt fairly sure that the men had not seen the Indian high up on the hill. He ventured a look now and saw that the horse and rider were gone. Partly to supply a reason for having looked away from the men, Don said, "It's a long time since I've been in water. If you don't mind I think I'll finish my bath. Without waiting for permission, he stepped back into the stream.

"Sure, go right ahead," said Byron. "It's a good idea. You were starting to stink clear up to the driver's seat."

So Don had his first bath since leaving Duck Lake—as best he could, without soap. His captors waited patiently during the two minutes it took him. Then they marched him back to the broken wagon, kindly gave him a towel to dry himself with, wrapped him comfortably in a fur hide—for the desert evening was cooling quickly—and tied him up firmly, fur and all, to the nearest tree.

10

They had found the runaway horses, tangled up in brush and their own harnesses, even before they had found the runaway policeman. By noon the next day they had both wagon and harness repaired, although in a pitiful, makeshift way. The rear axle was splinted together with a limb from one of the few trees that grew along the stream's edge, the wall that had come out of the caboose was now held in place mostly by lariat ropes, and the broken harness was knotted up in places with lace leather they had cut from other straps of the harness that could afford losing a bit of their width.

They had untied Don for last night's supper and this morning's breakfast; now they loosed him for dinner. After everyone had a big feed of their staple cured beef and hardtack, the journey got underway again. They drove and rode through the narrow, shallow river without any difficulty.

Once more in the privacy of his portable room, Don immediately began to inspect the repaired side. But there was not much to be seen, for the wall fit into place well. From the inside it looked almost as secure as it ever had been, but Don knew that except for a few wooden wedges and three lasso ropes, there was nothing to keep the thing from falling out. If only he had some sharp object, he thought, he could slip it into the crack between wall and floor and so might be able to cut the ropes—at night when the men, save the one on guard duty, were sleeping. But he had no sharp object.

The afternoon turned hot, although not as hot as some of the past days had been. Don was reasonably comfortable in his shady prison. A slight breeze passed through the barred windows, but the main reason that the caboose was not always an unbearable oven as might have been expected was that the walls, floor, and roof were all of double construction with the inner space insulated with wood shavings. Some of the shavings had been lost now, but the dead-air space was enough to prevent much of the heat from soaking through and building up in the interior of the cell. The bedding and gear packed on top of the roof provided further insulation.

Don was beginning to like his captors. He was one to see the best in everybody, and he saw qualities of manliness, ambition, and boldness in all four of them; and in Byron, the leader, he saw resourcefulness, stubborn courage, and what perhaps appealed to him more — a sense of humor. Then too, thus far none of the men had gone out of their way to torment him, which, of course, they could have done in various ways had they so desired. So, in spite of his daily confinement and the humbleness of his position as captive compared to theirs as his captors, he could not help but feel a weird kind of comradeship with these men.

That feeling changed abruptly on the day they repaired the wagon and continued their journey on the other side of the river. Late in the afternoon Don's slight admiration for these mysterious men was shattered completely and replaced with sickening disgust.

They had stopped to rest the horses. Bull must have just come back from doing a bit of scouting, for Don heard him say, "I found me a redskin family, Byron, just over the hill. They was jest makin' camp so they'll likely be there fer a bit."

"No shit. You mean just one family?"

"Yeah, and there ain't no other redskin fer a hunert miles, by the look of it."

"A slight exaggeration, I'm afraid," said Byron. "What's the family look like?"

"Three bucks an' two squaws."

Lanky Sam spoke up now. "Wal, it ain't no family — it's a huntin' or scoutin' party of some kind...and you kin bet yore bloody spurs there's a band a' the bastards not more'n a few miles away."

"So what?" said Byron. "They're not so dangerous anymore. What's the matter, Sam? You scared of an Indian uprising?" For some reason this remark brought laughter from all four of the men, or perhaps one of them had done something funny which Don, inside the wagon, couldn't see.

Harry put in his opinion now. "It ain't no huntin' or scoutin' party if there's a couple a' squaws with 'em." He added, "I don't know what it could be."

"Wal, anyhow," came in Bull again, "there ain't no other redskins around fer miles. I was right on top of the hill. You kin see fer miles."

Byron said, "Then they were probably up there at some time looking at us too."

"You mean the family?" said Bull. "Wal, maybe so, but it don't matter none. They ain't told no one yet......an' man, we could sure have us some fun!"

"I think I know what you got in mind, Bull," said Byron, "but that *family* you're talking about might not be such easy pickings."

There was a whole lot more discussion on the matter, and as it progressed Don began to get physically sick to the stomach. After they had agreed on the best plan for dispatching the Indian males— in the event that they should actually decide to do so—they began to argue about which two of themselves would have the first go at the squaws and which two would have to wait. Don was still hoping that they were only blowing off hot air, but at the same time couldn't help but realize that they were spending far too much time on the subject to be anything but serious. This matter was settled completely for Don when Byron said, "All right, you horny bastards, if that's what you want to do then let's get started on it."

Roman had been pressing his ear between the window bars. Now he hollered, "Byron!"

The leader came over at once. "Yeah? What do you want, sir?"

Don's bearded mouth opened and moved a few times before his tense voice could begin to express the thoughts and feelings of his outraged mind. "You're not going to...to really...do this, are you?"

Byron, looking up at the barred window with his usual good-natured grin, said, "Yeah, I reckon we will. Got anything against it? Hey, boys, C'mon over here. I think the sergeant has got something to say." The "boys" came at once and stood obediently near Byron.

"Well, sir, we're waiting," said the leader.

"I heard you say," began Don, "that you're going to kill the men and rape the women! You just can't mean it! You mustn't do it!"

"Rape?" said Bull. "What's that mean?" Perhaps he was only pretending not to know.

"It means," explained Sam, seriously or otherwise, "to screw 'em when they don't want you to."

Bull said, "They never want you to unless you pay 'em for it."

Sam carried on, "Raping them's the best way t' handle women. What's the matter, redcoat?—don't you know anything about women? Ha! You probably don't even know they got a soft spot between their legs. There's a difference between men and women, y'know."

"Yeah, I know," said Roman, "and I also know there's a difference between men and snakes! And right now you're not sounding like men. Listen…please don't do this thing. Somehow I haven't got you figured for the kind of men who would do something that rotten and low."

The four stood silently for a moment; then Byron turned to his men. "What do y' say, boys? Are we the kind of men who would do something that rotten and low?"

"You fuckin' right we are!" said Sam. Harry and Bull tried to drown out each other with foul-mouthed agreement.

"Well, there you have it, Sergeant," smiled Byron.

There was desperation in the eyes of Don Roman as he watched the men turn and walk toward the horses. For a few seconds Roman thought that they were going to leave him unguarded, but then, while they were unharnessing the team, they began to discuss the matter of who would go and who would stay. It almost turned into a quarrel. However, Byron settled the matter with his usual confident dispensing of authority. Byron, Sam, and Bull would go. Harry would stay. Byron and Sam would ride the two saddle horses; Bull would ride one of the team horses without a saddle.

The three mounted and left without Roman being able to think of anything to say that might change their minds. He sank down to a sitting position in the straw and tried to encourage himself with the hope that the Indians would kill Byron, Sam, and Bull, instead of the other way around. Somehow that didn't seem likely. These men had revealed their true nature to him today, and from this revelation Don felt safe to conclude that his captors were hardened killers— hardened and experienced. They would make certain that the three braves did not have a hair of a chance to defend themselves. In fact,

Byron had decided on a sneak ambush during their first discussions of the matter.

Then Don began to wonder if he might somehow be able to outsmart them and escape—and get to the Indians in time to warn them. If only there was a way to get out of the caboose and around the obstacle called Harry, the remaining team horse was there ready and waiting. From that point on he would have a chance of getting to the Indians in time. But there was so little time.

He called to Harry.

"Whadaya want?" asked Harry in a tired, resigned sounding voice. He was not over his disappointment at having been left behind.

"I want to talk to you," said Don. He still had no real plan in mind, but felt that if he had any chance at all to escape, it probably lay in getting Harry within reach.

"Talk to yourself," said Harry.

"No, listen—I've got something important to tell you. Come here." Don knew he sounded foolish, and he didn't know what he'd do if Harry *did* decide to come over, but there was no time for making elaborate plans. It was a short distance to the Indian camp that Bull had described.

"Wal, you got somethin' to say, say it," said Harry. "I can hear you good from here." .

"No, I've got something to show you." Don realized unhappily that Harry would have to be stupid beyond words to be unaware that his prisoner was up to something.

"Oh, so you got somethin' to show me. Wal, ain't that nice." There was a hint of improved humor in his voice, as though his spirits were rising with the thought that he might get some action after all. In a few seconds he had come around to the barred window. "Wal, show me whatever you got. I want to see what you got to show me."

Don felt the burden of limited time growing inside of him. The Indian camp was just over the hill. By now the three gunmen, armed with their rifles, would likely already be within firing range or their unsuspecting prey.

"All right," said Don. "It's pretty important what I've got to show you…and tell you," he said lamely, his mind groping desperately. He considered the foolishness, for a second, of asking Harry to come close so that he could whisper into his ear—so that any nearby sand lizards wouldn't hear—and then he would grab Harry around the neck and....

"What you waitin' fer?" asked Harry, his eyes glowing hopefully. "You scared someone will hear? Maybe I should come a little closer to you."

Sergeant Roman considered the man in a new light. Harry was looking for trouble. "Well," said Don, "I don't suppose you'd take the chance of coming any closer to me. After all, I might just be looking for a chance to get at you.... I mean...I'm not, really, but since you don't know that, I guess you'll make sure and stay your distance—I mean a good safe distance."

"That's all right, I trust you," said Harry, warming even more to the game. "See, I'll come real close to yer window." He came within three feet. "Now let's hear what you got to say."

The sergeant was silent for five seconds before he said, "You're not close enough."

This was too much for Harry. His round, red face crinkled up into a laugh as he reluctantly gave up the farce that had been affording him so much pleasure. "You shore are crazy.... Did you really think you could fool me into comin' close enough so's you could grab me?" He relieved himself of a few more pressing laughs, then continued, "No, you can't fool ol' Harry that easy. But now that you know you ain't foolin' me, I tell you what I'll do. I'll step right up close an' give you a chance t' grab me...if you really got a mind to. But first I'll take my hat off so's I kin see you better." This made good sense because the barred window was just a little higher than Harry's eye level, so the brim of his hat would possibly have tended to come between his eyes and Don's right hand which was lying ready on the sill between the bars. Harry was pitting himself against that hand, wanting to prove to himself and to the pathetic naked prisoner, that he was faster and smarter.

Tossing his hat to the ground, Harry immediately stepped forward to the window, at the same time putting his hand on his holstered revolver—but he was not quite prepared for the unhesitating and unerring movement of Don's hand through the bars. Taking advantage of Harry's lack of a hat, Don grabbed a hold of his hair, then yanked his head forward so that his skull came in sharp collision with the side of the caboose just under the window.

But the blow wasn't hard enough. Cursing loudly, Harry jerked back with desperate effort and got free from Don's grasp. He was also freed from part of his hair. Harry staggered and fell, but by now he had his gun in hand. He got up on one knee and aimed at the window. Don had time to glimpse a face gone completely primitive with rage peering over the top of the leveled forty-five; then the policeman flung himself down on the straw. Two slugs ripped into the walls of the caboose as Harry's thundering gun began to express its owner's displeasure.

Then, from a distance, came three more shots, almost like an echo of Harry's fire, but Don knew what it was. So did Harry. He regained control of himself enough to lower his revolver, then hollered, "Did you hear that, Roman? That's the end of the Injuns, 'ceptin' fer the squaws, of course. No use you tryin' t' git out now no more.... Leastwise you don't hafta be in such an all-fired hurry about it." He laughed then and it sounded unhinged.

Still, Don knew that what Harry had just said was true. He lay quietly in the straw, still hearing, in his mind, the three distant shots. Somehow the memory of them seemed louder than the memory of Harry's close gunfire. Those three distant shots had been fired very close together, almost at the same time. And after that there had been no more shooting. Don was near certain that Byron, Sam, and Bull had accomplished their mission with all success.

Harry, after picking up and putting on his hat, came and looked into the rear barred window to see if he had killed Don, and hoped fervently that he hadn't. Having regained his sanity now, he remembered that this prisoner had been brought many weary miles. Harry was aghast at the thought that the man might be dead.

"Hey! You kin git up now," said Harry through the barred window in the door. "I wasn't really tryin' t' kill you—jest give you a scare." He had some hope that the policeman had not been hit, for there had been no moan of pain nor sound of thrashing about as might have been expected; still, the sight of the naked form lying there so quietly in the straw put new alarm into his mind. Maybe he had scored a direct hit through the brain. "Look, don't try any more tricks...'cause you know that don't work with me. Now git up! Blast yore fuckin' hide!"

Don lay very still, even holding his breath for a while, and then breathing as shallowly as he could endure. He waited to hear the scraping of the door bolt sliding open, but it didn't come.

Harry continued to look in through the window for a good thirty seconds, stubbornly hoping to detect some sign that his prisoner was playing possum—so that he would not have to venture into the caboose to make certain. His forehead felt as though all the hide had been taken off it, and his scalp hurt where some of his hair had been yanked out. In his mind he could still see the blur of the unbelievably swift movement of the prisoner's hand snaking out toward him. Although Harry wouldn't go so far as to admit it to himself, he no longer had the slightest desire to ever again tangle with this man in close, physical, fair combat. He turned and walked away from the caboose. "You can't fool me," he said over his shoulder. "You can't fool ol' Harry that easy."

Don remained on the floor, but he relaxed and took a deep breath of air as he heard Harry's retreating voice and knew the game was over. He had failed in his bid for escape; his captors had been successful in their ambush of the Indians. Roman felt so badly about it that he continued to lie motionless, even though there was no longer any practical reason for him to do so.

He got to his feet only when he heard the returning hoofbeats of the killers' horses. Through a barred window he saw what he had expected to see, with a single exception; they had only one woman with them. Bull had reported that there were two in the camp.

The one they had brought sat in the saddle in front of Byron, chained by his arms. For just a moment Don let himself become happier with the thought that perhaps the other one had gotten away—had managed to hide somewhere, but then it seemed to him that this was highly unlikely. This latter thought was confirmed in a few seconds.

"How come you jest got one squaw?" asked Harry with a note of sincere disappointment in his voice.

"The other one wasn't of any use," said Byron. "She had too much fight in her to make a good woman."

Lanky Sam was swinging down from his horse as though he was in a hurry about something. "I had to quieten her down a little with my knife," he said. For the first time Don noticed a long, sheathed hunting knife hanging from the back of Sam's gunbelt. Possibly he had strung it there just before leaving for the Indian camp.

"What was the shooting about?" Byron asked Harry.

Harry had his hat pulled down low in front to cover his bruised forehead. "Ah, I was foolin' around with the monkey." He jabbed a thumb carelessly toward the caboose. "Nothin' serious."

"I don't want any unnecessary shooting," reproved Byron. He continued to sit his horse, behind the saddle, apparently reluctant to take his arms away from being wrapped around the woman.

Don studied the squaw. She was young and beautiful, and her darkness and facial features testified that she was a full blooded Indian, although of what nation or tribe Don did not venture to guess. It seemed to him that her clear, perfect skin had a more bronzed look to it than had the complexions of the Cree, Blackfoot, and other kinds of Indians of Canada that he was used to, which might be accounted for by the hotter climate of the Southwest. The woman was silent; in despair she hung her face down toward partly naked breasts. Her doeskin shirt hung in tatters from her shoulders. The shirt was long enough to cover her hips, but a tear down the side revealed that if she had ever worn anything under it, it was no longer there.

Because of training, experience, and an inborn ability to remain calm under stress, Don Roman seldom lost his habitual grip on himself; but now his face became pale above his dark beard and his lungs sucked in a deep breath in preparation to hurl a tornado of vocal violence at the four devils who called themselves men. Byron had dismounted now and was reaching to pull the woman down after him, and before Don could engage his voice, the woman exploded into action and vocality so that Don was startled into remaining silent. She had seen a chance for escape at the moment when Byron's feet hit the ground and she herself was still in the saddle. She made a grab for the reins, at the same time kicking her moccasined feet against the horse's sides and loudly yelling something in her own language. The surprised animal lunged forward, but Byron still had one hand on the rein and his grip held. The horse was wheeled around before having a chance to get up speed, and came to a stop; Byron staggered, held his footing; the woman kicked at him frantically and yelled in the best enunciated English that Roman had heard since he was kidnapped: "You dirty bastard! You dirty rotten bastard!"

The other three came to Byron's rescue. In a few seconds they had her off the horse and pulled down to a half-sitting position on the ground. With a savage jerk that must have hurt the woman physically, Sam tore the remainder of the doeskin shirt from her body. The feminine beauty of that naked, helpless girl, being insulted and abused when instead she should have—to Don's way of thinking—been tenderly caressed and loved at all times, was almost enough to change the police officer into the insane maniac that he had been pretending to be just the day before.

He saw Harry getting ready to take his turn. He saw the woman continue to struggle, silently, between Byron and Sam. Roman gripped the bars, meaning to tear the whole window frame out of the wall, but even his anger-inspired maniacal strength was not capable of that. For a moment he watched Harry having the woman. Then Don turned to the opposite wall and began to kick at it with all his might with the bottoms of his bare feet. It was the wall which was held in only by the lariat ropes. He found that turning his back to the wall and delivering mule kicks worked the best. At first it resisted Don's furious kicking with calm solidity, but then when he began to concentrate on the rear lower corner there was a definite spring-out every time his foot struck. Seeing the corner of the wall spring away like that gave him more hope, so he stopped kicking and began to consider the situation in the light of returning reason.

"Bull, go see what the son of a bitch is doing. Make him quieten down!" It was Byron's voice, sounding uncommonly ill-humored.

Bull's big jawed face appeared at the window in the door. "Quieten down! What're you tryin' t' do anyways? You can't git out."

Don stood quietly.

Bull said, "I don't want t' hear no more bangin' aroun' in here...or we'll take an' tie you to a tree an' whip the shit outa you!" He turned and walked away.

Byron's voice came in again, once more sounding cheerful. "Now, now, Bull, let's not be disrespectful to mister...to Sergeant Roman. After all, he *is* a sergeant."

"I don't give a shit what he is. An' you called him a sun of a bitch yourself," said Bull. Byron laughed.

Don was sitting on the floor now, knees bent, forcing both feet against the corner of the wall. It gave enough so that by stretching one arm forward at the same time he could get his fingers into the crack. This gave him a big help for now he could hold himself from sliding backward when he applied pressure with his feet. The corner of the wall began to bend outward—three inches, four inches....

"Nah, I've had enough for now," Bull was saying.

"I'll tie her up," offered Sam.

"No need for that," said Byron.

"Whadaya mean?" said Sam. "I ain't figurin' on settin' here holdin' her till somebody's ready to have another go at her."

"Put her in the caboose with the sergeant," said Byron. There were a few seconds of silence, then Byron continued, "Ain't you fellas got a heart? Ol' Sarge ain't had a woman for a long time—just as long as us."

"I don't know," said Sam. "I don't see why we should give him anything."

"You're so selfish," said Byron. "Now listen, boys. We gotta get moving. We gotta be at Shallow Creek before noon tomorrow. We've fooled around here long enough."

Now that the whole thing was over for the time being, Roman had quit trying to get out. He sat silently and listened.

Bull asked, "So we're gonna take the squaw with us?"

Harry answered before Byron could. "Sure, why not?"

Byron said, "We'll take her along a little ways. But tomorrow morning we get rid of her. We can't have her with us when we meet Ruizo. I don't care about him and his men, but you never know who it could get to from there."

"Yeah, that's right," said Bull.

"All right," said Sam, "so we git shed of her just before we get to Shallow Creek."

"We get shed of her a good while before we get to Shallow Creek," modified Byron. "Ruizo could come riding out to meet us.... All right, give her something to eat, and then put her in the caboose. You can do that, Harry—you and Sam. Bull, you come and help me get the horses ready.... Hey, Harry, what happened to your head? A horse kick you?"

"Wal...yeah," said Harry, "ol' Brownie. Never thought I'd see the day when that horse would kick at me. Guess I surprised her some.... Come up behind her without sayin' nothin.'"

Bull let out a loud laugh. "So y' couldn't wait till we got here with the squaw."

The other three picked up the laughter.

Harry said, "You're *all* fulla shit!"

Roman watched through a side window as they offered the still-naked woman a tin plate of cold food. She took it and the fork and began to eat without hesitation. *Smart girl*, thought Roman, but was astounded at how calm she looked sitting there helpless between two ugly brutes who had just defiled her body. Was an Indian woman so different from a white one?—who, in this circumstance, would likely still be screaming and/or crying. Or maybe this Indian woman was simply past the stage of being hysterical or terrified. Or maybe she was exceptionally brave and coolheaded. In any case, Don was glad to see her eating and drinking.

When she had finished, Harry and Sam brought her over to the wagon prison. Seeing them coming, Don quickly sat down at the far front end of the caboose, trying to make himself look small, weak, and helpless, so that the sight of him would perhaps not strike new terror into the poor woman's heart. And yet she would surely expect another episode. The fact that he was completely naked would do nothing to help calm her natural apprehension.

The thought of attacking the men and trying to escape together with the woman when they opened the door came into Don's mind, but he dismissed it at once. The woman would be as afraid of him as she was of her captors. He needed to gain her confidence before he could have the slightest hope of helping her. The idea of escaping without her did not blemish even the fringes of his mind.

The door opened; the naked woman was lifted, pushed up and into the caboose. She came no further than to where she had been forced so that the door could be closed. When the bolt slid into place she turned her back to Don but stood quietly with her arms hanging at her sides. She was almost a foot shorter than Don and could stand without stooping her shoulders. Don took note, not for the first time, that her nudity was complete—they had even taken away her moccasins. He could see pale bruises on her arms and one on her left buttock.

As the police officer watched her in pity and tried to formulate his first comforting words, he could not help but think how healthy and beautiful this young woman looked. She was small and curvaceous but not skinny, yet with a waist that was pleasingly slim. Her hips, her behind, her legs, were well filled out—smooth and womanly soft, yes, but giving an impression to the eye that they could, in a half second, flex into firm feminine muscles with much athletic ability. However, Don realized this latter thought might have come to him more because of what he had already seen her do in trying to escape when she was still on the horse than from the way she actually looked. She also looked pathetic, standing there motionless, seemingly with no one to turn to for help.

Before Don could think of anything to say, Byron's voice sounded through the walls. "Well, Sergeant, we've got the horses ready except for hitchin' up the traces, so we'll be pullin' out now. I want you to enjoy yourself with the squaw. And don't ever say I never did anything for you." When Don remained silent, he continued, "Now we'll see who's rotten and low and who isn't."

Don's three-worded reply was carefully planned psychology. "Aw, shut up!" He was successful in making his voice sound annoyed and defeated. He knew that nothing would please Byron more than if his noble, upright, reputable, redcoat prisoner would break down and give in to temptation. Roman wanted to make sure that Byron did not change his mind about putting the woman in the caboose with him; otherwise he might decide to "get shed of her" sooner, maybe even immediately. Don was quite sure that Byron had no intention of letting her live.

Byron did not miss the note of surrender in Don's voice and laughed happily. He said no more after that. Trace chains rattled, then came the sound of two men climbing up into the high seat.

"Better sit down," said Don to the woman. "The wagon might start with a jolt." He was amazed at how straight and strong she stood after all the abuse her body and soul had been through in the past hour.

She turned partly and looked at him, her lovely dark face showing mixed feelings of fear, hope, doubt, anger. Then she followed Don's advice and sat down in the straw—and not a second too soon, for the wagon did start off with a sudden lurch that likely would have thrown her hard against the door.

"Thanks for warning me," she said in perfect North American English.

In reply he gave her what he intended to be an encouraging, friendly smile, then was afraid it might have looked like a lecherous leer. He thought of commenting on her surprising control of English, but decided not to. "How are you feeling?" he asked instead, then realized it was a pretty dumb question.

He must have been right about that, for she looked at him but did not answer. She sat with her legs pulled up in a tight bunch, swaying slightly to and fro as the horses pulled the creaking, groaning wagon over the rough trail at a fast trot. Roman was grateful for the noise of the wagon; it helped cover the sound of their voices.

"I'm sorry," said Don then. "It was a stupid question. After what you've been through, how could you feel anything but rotten?"

Her eyes dropped but came back to him again, now studying him more carefully than before. After a few seconds she said, "Why have they got you in here?"

"I wish I knew. They've hauled me like this all the way from Canada. Do you know where that is?"

"It's another country," she said, "far to the north."

"That's right. I'm a member of the Royal North-West Mounted Police. Don Roman is my name."

Her eyes had opened wider at the words, *North-West Mounted Police*, as though that was significant to her.

Don continued, "Please excuse the way I look. They've been feeding me well, but I haven't been able to do much about grooming." He smiled and ran a hand through his long, uncombed hair, then down through his beard. "I haven't even got a decent press left to my trousers," he said, glancing down at his naked legs which he had unconsciously pulled up shieldingly, just as the girl had done with hers. "This surely is no way to look in front of a lady, which you obviously are," he finished.

"I don't feel like one," she replied; then, after a moment of mental dispute, she added, "I think you must be a gentleman."

"That's kind of you, ma'am. I'll try to behave like one while I have the pleasure of your company."

One of her long, black braids had come partly undone. She began, for a few seconds, to work at rebraiding it, but then quickly changed her mind, once more sitting quietly and looking down at her bunched up knees.

Don said, "If you'd like, ma'am, why don't you lie down in the straw? You need to rest. There's a cowhide here that you could cover up with if you want to."

"All right," she said, "I will. Thank you."

Don unfolded himself out of his prudish posture and reached for the hide. He moved a few feet toward her so that he could hand it to her. She took it and held it in front of her while Don retreated to his place at the front end of the caboose.

"I'm sorry," she said, "that I didn't tell you my name before when you told me yours. My name is Meadow.... I'm a daughter-in-law of Geronimo and the wife of Cloud-Chaser." Her voice broke on the last two words—the name—and she buried her face in the cowhide and began to shake with crying. It seemed to Don that the name, spoken by her own lips, had shattered a trancelike state of stoical defense that she had gotten into through the personal ordeal she had just come through, and had once more made her aware of a larger tragic reality that had for a time been forced out of her conscious mind.

She began to cry louder and more uncontrollably. The sound cut into Don like a blade. He moved a little closer to her. "Your man, Cloud-Chaser—he was killed by these devils who took you?"

"Yes," she sobbed. "And they killed the others too...even Little Brown-Calf. She's very strong, and she fought hard when they tried to.... They killed her! Maybe it would have been better if they had killed me too!"

"I don't know what to say to comfort you when your sorrow, and your reason for sorrow, is so great," admitted Don. "Yet I'd like to say that...somehow things will change for you again.... And you'll be happy again."

She continued to cry with her face in the dirty cowhide. After half a minute or so Don couldn't stand it any longer without going over to her. She heard him walking through the straw and looked up but showed no fear of him. So he sat down beside her and put a gentle arm around her shoulders. "Go ahead and cry," he said softly. "It's probably the best thing for you right now. But I want you to know that you're not alone.... I mean...I'm gonna do my best to get you out of this mess.... And I...don't want you to be unhappy."

She looked up at him. He was almost startled by the beauty of her dark, tearstained face which was so close to his now. She said in an unsteady voice, "You're a good man. I'm sorry for crying." She tried to stop crying then, but that was impossible, for the delayed nervous reaction to her ordeal was just beginning to set in. She fell against Roman's chest, sobbing loudly and shaking from head to foot.

He put his arms around her, gently, protectively. "Easy, now, it's gonna be all right. I'll help you." He continued to speak to her quietly with whatever soothing words came to his mind, but after a while he simply stroked her hair and her shoulders, which seemed to have more effect that anything he could say. She stopped shaking almost at once, but cried softly for several minutes. Now she was almost limp in his arms.

After a minute or so she straightened up slightly and separated herself from him by a few inches. "Thank you. I'm all right now.... I'm sorry." She pulled farther away from him.

"Sorry for what?" asked Don. "You haven't done anything wrong."

"You're a man," she said, then stumbled around a bit for the right words but couldn't find them. Roman knew what she meant though.

"Don't worry," he said. "You're very beautiful, and, under other circumstances, you'd be driving me out of my head with desire.... But right now I'm so full of...other feelings that you haven't really worked on me in that way." This last part was an outright lie, for though pity and compassion had been his main feelings while she had been in his arms, he had also been thoroughly aroused sexually — and right now was doing his best to keep her from seeing his enlarged state of being.

"I think I'll lie down for a while now, like you said, and cover myself with the fur," Meadow decided.

"It's a good idea for you to lie down and rest and try to get some sleep," approved Don, "but don't steam yourself under that hide just to keep me from losing my head. I only said it before, about covering with the blanket, because I thought it would make you feel better, but I think you trust me now. You'd never be able to rest under that hide—it'd be way too hot.... You *do* trust me now, don't you?"

"Yes, I do," she said. "And you don't know how much it means to me. If you had been like the others.... They'll be stopping the wagon and coming in here to get me again!"

"Don't even think about it," said Roman. "I'll kill anyone who comes in here for you." It almost gave him a start when he realized how sincerely he meant this—that this was precisely what he *would* do: kill the first man of them who attempted to come in and bring her out…and the second, and the third, and the fourth—or die trying. He knew that this latter was what would happen to him, for his enemies were armed, whereas he had only his bare hands and a fierce determination. And when he was dead they would still take her, amuse themselves with her, and then kill her too. But if there was even one less of them left alive at that time, the world would be a slightly better place.

Meadow must have been thinking somewhat as he was, for she said, "But you have no gun."

"I don't need a gun. "I'll kill them with my bare hands."

"You'd risk your life for an Indian?" she asked, then quickly added, "I'm sorry, I shouldn't have said that. You've already shown me the kind of man you are."

He put his hand on her shoulder and smiled at her. "Lie down, little Indian, and try to get some sleep. You need rest." He could not tell what was in her mind as her large, dark eyes looked steadfastly up into his, but there was something soft and gentle there. As for him, a new warm feeling, that was not altogether sexual, began to well up from some wonderful spring within and flooded through every part of him.

Her face was still very close to his, and still with that look of softness on it; but then she pulled the hide toward her and said, "I think I'll try to get some rest now."

"Good," said Don. He moved away from her to give her room to lie down, then decided it would be best to go all the way to his place at the front end of the caboose and did so.

Meadow lay in the straw on her stomach. Don was glad, for her sake more than for his, that she took his advice and didn't cover herself with the heavy cowhide. The low, gentle hills and valleys of her back, buttocks, thighs, and calves made the most scenic horizon line that his eyes had ever beheld. After a time she began to breathe the deep, even breath of sleep; and Don was grateful again, for he knew how much her jangled nervous system needed a bit of respite from the world of reality.

As he sat beholding her, still feeling shaky from the emotions that had been more or less tearing him apart, he began to think more fervently about how to best help her to escape from the four devils called Byron, Sam, Harry, and Bull. He was sure that they fully intended to kill her—after they had insulted her body once more with their lower-than-animal passions. By what they had said it seemed that they did not plan to kill her until sometime tomorrow morning, but there was no telling when they might decide to use her sexually again.

Don hoped they would wait till after dark. He had not at all forgotten about the loose corner of the wall, and he had a picture in his mind of himself using his feet to push the wall outward as far as it would go while Meadow quietly squeezed through—to sneak away, nude, unarmed, completely defenseless, but alive. And he might never see her again. That couldn't be helped, but the thought was surprisingly painful.

He got back to wondering about the woman's ability to speak perfect English. She seemed to be educated; also he was sure that she had spent a good part of her young life in some center of white civilization—some big city, perhaps in the East; for one did not learn the kind of clean-cut, precise English she used in a settler's shack or frontier cow town. But for some reason she had come back to the rugged Indian way of life. Don wished that he could hear her story; it would, no doubt, be interesting. And she had given herself to a man called Cloud-Chaser, and had said that she was a daughter-in-law to Geronimo.

Sergeant Roman had heard about a ferocious old Indian chieftain by the name of Geronimo who had been doing his best to make a menace of himself by slaughtering every white settler that he and his bloodthirsty followers could get to. This had been going on somewhere in the southwestern part of the United States, in the New Mexico and Arizona territories, if he remembered right. That could be right here; this was certainly the Southwest. Geronimo had been captured by a General Miles and imprisoned at some fort in Oklahoma. In any case, thought Don, surely this lovely, gentle young woman would not have married the son of such a savage, cold-blooded killer; so perhaps there was more than one Geronimo.

Don's mind went back to thinking about helping Meadow to escape. It would soon be dark, and the sooner the better.

She moaned in her sleep, began to twist about restlessly. It was not hard to guess what nightmare was haunting her. She was likely seeing her husband and friends murdered, and then herself being knocked about and sexually abused. She became more agitated in her sleep, moving her arms and legs frantically, fighting off the booted, spurred, gun-toting dream devils who tormented her.

Don couldn't stand to watch her without trying to do something about it. He knelt close beside her, not knowing if he should put a hand on her. "Easy now," he said, "it's all right...it's all right.... Wake up."

With a sudden twist, Meadow turned over onto her back and at the same time let loose and ear-shattering scream. She woke herself with it, then sat up with a jerk and began to move away from Don, but the rear wall of the caboose was in her way.

Don said quickly, "You were having a bad dream. I tried to wake you up."

Her face relaxed its hold on the look of nightmarish fear as she came more fully awake. "Oh, I dreamt that...it was happening again!.... It was happening all over again!"

"Don't think about it," said Don. "It was only a dream." But of course they both knew it was not really only a dream; it had happened, and her dream was an echo of that reality.

She put her face down in both hands and released a deep moan. Don reached out and touched her shoulder. "It's all right now. Nobody's going to hurt you."

She came against his chest, letting her head fall on his shoulder and clasping her arms around his back. She was crying now, softly. With his cheek against her hair, Don stroked her shoulders and said encouraging and calming things to her.

Minds are strange things, and, just at this time, Don's mind came up with an image of his own beautiful blonde Rita sitting close to him in the swing-seat on Bancroft's rear veranda—sitting close to him and looking at him lovingly and seductively. Don put this out of his mind as quickly as he could, for it somehow seemed quite inappropriate, and continued to stroke Meadow's hair and shoulders comfortingly.

The interior of the prison wagon was already quite dim, for the sun had sunk into a cloud bank close to the horizon, but now the little room became even slightly darker. One of the side windows was almost completely closed off by the shoulders, face, and hat of Sam. No doubt the woman's scream had attracted his attention, so, in his own good time, he had steered his horse in close to the side of the caboose for a look. He could see that Meadow was in Don's arms.

Between the bars, his wide mouth spread into an evil grin. With his degraded mind completely misinterpreting what he saw, he let out a stinking laugh. "That's it, Sergeant," he said. "Give 'er shit while you got a chance. It'll soon be our turn again."

11

Dusk began to settle more heavily over the badlands. The wagon creaked and rattled onward.

Don wanted to learn all he could about Meadow and about the surrounding area that she apparently was familiar with; but the only way they could talk without being overheard by their captors was to get so close together that the magic of intimacy became not only a pleasure but a problem for both of them. They did nothing sexual; and yet it felt sexual to be in physical contact, cheek to cheek so they could whisper into each other's ears. And when a naked man and a naked woman are that close together, breasts and nipples have a way of making their cushioning presence felt. And thighs are right there too, finding it impossible to be segregated. Don knew that Meadow was a totally recent widow who had just been raped by the dregs of humanity, so he couldn't quite imagine what she was feeling toward him; but he knew what he was feeling toward her. At times his greatest fear was that he would unwillingly ejaculate over her, and thus maybe lose her trust. It was the most pleasant ordeal he had ever experienced.

Nevertheless, he stoically pressed onward with his good intention of learning what he could, for that was important to the escape he was planning for her. He had already told her a little about that.

His lips were almost nibbling her ear as he whispered, "If you manage to get away as I plan, what'll you do? I mean what chance do you think you have of getting somewhere where you'll be all right?"

"A pretty good chance," Meadow whispered back, her breath entering his ear and seeming to seep into his brain. "There's an Indian camp not far from where we were when...they came. That's my band. The whole camp may have moved already, to Yellow Valley for the sun dance, but I know the way that they'll come. My husband,

Cloud-Chaser, he's the…he was the son of Geronimo, as I told you. You must have heard of Geronimo."

"Yeah," said Don, "we got reports on him in Canada. I'm amazed that you're married to his son."

Meadow's whispering continued. "My husband, Cloud-Chaser, called himself *Bill* later. You see, he ran away from his family and band when he was only fourteen. I met him in San Carlos. I was brought up by a white family there after I had been traded to another man for guns and managed to get away from him. The white family adopted me."

"You were traded for guns?!"

"Yes, but that's another story…. Bill hadn't been adopted by anyone, but because he was so young and so bright he got a lot of help from the government. Later the two of us went to school together at San Antonio and we showed everyone that Indians are just as smart as anyone."

"Of course you are," he said. "But why did you and Bill come back here to the Indian way of life?"

"Geronimo had become a terror to every white man in this territory. Bill felt that it was his duty to try to convince his father that it was an ugly thing he was doing. Bill was determined to stop him somehow. But he was sure that he couldn't even talk to the old man about it with any hope of influencing him unless he first proved himself as an Indian. We joined with a more peaceful band, the one under Chief Strong-Hand—the band I was telling you about."

"The one you said you hoped to find?—who are on their way to the sun dance?"

"Yes," answered Meadow's lips close to his ear, "only it's not really a sun dance that they're going to—not in the ordinary sense. It's really a big war council in disguise."

"A war council? How serious *is* this?"

"It's a very big thing," replied Meadow. "There's never been anything like it before. Every Indian nation of the Southwest, and almost every tribe and band is to be represented there. Most of them are there already."

"Shit!…I'm sorry…sorry for the bad language."

Meadow said, "It's okay, I don't blame you—it really is a frightening thing…. Of course not all the tribes want war, as far as we

122

could make out, yet they seemed interested enough to come. Messengers have been busy riding in all directions, but it's all been kept very secret. And Geronimo is going to do his best to convince the others to join him. He hopes for all the tribes to unite and make full scale war against the whites to drive them from the Southwest. He's been working at this ever since he escaped from Fort Sill. This kind of united stand has never been accomplished, but if it *did* happen it would mean a horrible bloodshed, worse than any Indian war ever. Geronimo, in his grandiose way of thinking, sees it as being even bigger than it really would be. He sees it as spreading over the whole continent—even up into your Canada."

"I'm glad I found out about this…. This thing has to be stopped before it gets totally out of hand."

"Bill and I were at a preliminary part of the meeting. Bill tried to convince his father to give up the whole plan. Geronimo ordered us out of the camp—Bill and I and two braves from Strong-Hand's camp who were with us, and my friend, little Brown-Calf. We were almost back to Strong-Hand's camp—had a half day's ride—when these men came…. I can hardly believe what happened—that Bill and the others…that they're all…gone." She rested her face against Don's shoulder. "Oh, I wish we had never come out here, away from civilization! Why was I so willing? Why didn't I try to convince Bill not to come?"

"Probably because you knew it was very important to come and try to stop Geronimo from doing the slaughtering he was doing at that time," suggested Don. "And if your husband was the kind of man I think he was, I don't think your talking would have changed his mind, if you had tried to talk him out of it. You should be real proud to have been married to a man like that, who cared enough about the whole thing to want to do something about it."

"I am," trembled her voice, and she began, once more, to wet his shoulder with tears.

"Please, don't let yourself go now," begged Don. "We have to try to get you out of here before it's too late. You'll have to be strong now."

She lifted her head. "I'm sorry. I'm okay…. I'm ready to try this. But I wish you'd try to get out too."

"No," refused Don. "There's no way for me to get out without making noise. I'll get a chance later on. If I can get you out of here and you manage to get to Strong-Hand's band, and he takes you with him to the war council, will you be safe there? Or will Geronimo want to harm you?"

"I'll be perfectly safe at the council so long as I'm with Strong-Hand."

"Good," said Don. "Just remember to be very, very quiet while you're slowly squeezing through the opening. And then, the second you get out, lie flat and don't move for a time—till the wagon is a good distance away…. And I sure hope you can find your band."

"I will," she said. "Don't worry."

He *was* worried. "The sun will be scorching tomorrow, and you'll have no water…and you haven't even got anything to cover your head."

"I never have anything to cover my head," she said, "but I'll be with Strong-Hand's band before the sun rises anyhow. Don't worry. I know this part of the country." Then she drew her top half close against his and said something about not wanting to leave him; but all he could really absorb just then was the feel of one of her nipples pressing into his abdomen. He exploded all over his own thigh, and somehow she was immediately aware of it. "Don't worry," she said, "it's all right. You'll feel better now."

* * *

When true darkness finally came without the wagon having stopped, Sergeant Roman's hope grew. Yet this hope was increasingly being interfered with by the knowledge that with each passing second the chances became greater that Byron would decide it was time to once more torment the woman.

She was sleeping again. He sat close beside her, listening to her quiet, even, relaxed breathing. The horses were walking; the wagon creaked only slightly. Roman got up and went to the loose wall side of the caboose and looked out the window. His eyes, used to the almost completely dark interior, found the starlit evening nearly as visible as though the moon had not been hiding behind a small pile of cloud. Clouds had been scarce for some time now, and quick desert showers even more scarce, so Don didn't expect any precipitation and hardly gave that matter a thought.

What *did* grab his attention was something else he saw — or, rather, didn't see — and this gave him another shot of relief and hope. He had expected that Harry would be there on his horse, for he usually rode on that side, but there was no one. Don went to the window on the other side. He could make out the tall, hawk-nosed form of Sam astride his tired-walking horse, but there was no sign of the other rider. Maybe he was riding behind the wagon. Don did a quick check through the rear window. He was relieved to see only an empty desert trail. So Harry must be in front of the wagon, maybe scouting some distance up ahead.

Now was the time. There could never be a better.

He knelt beside Meadow and softly said her name. She awoke, this time without hysterics, and immediately sat up and reached for Don in the darkness. It got to him how in such a short while she had learned to trust him, and the thought of sending her out alone and defenseless in the middle of desert badlands was so unpleasant that he almost changed his mind about his simple plan for her escape. But then he thought of Sam riding out there, probably with a grin on his face and evil thoughts building up more and more in his depraved mind, and Byron and Bull riding up on the wagon — bulls, both of them, but without a real bull's natural ability to please his partners — and Don knew that he had to send Meadow out into the dark night. He would gladly have tried to go with her, but he hadn't figured out any way to getting out of the wagon himself.

When he put his lips close to her ear she did not pull away.

"Meadow," he whispered, "the time has come for you to escape. But we're going to have to be very quiet."

"You mean right now?" She also whispered close into his ear, and the warmth of her cheek against his once more sent pleasant prickly feelings up and down his neck.

"Yeah," he said, "now's our best chance. I think I can pry the loose corner far enough out so that you can squeeze through."

"You must also try to squeeze through."

"No, I've told you — it's a stiff bend, and I'll have to push on it with all my strength to get it open wide enough for you to go through. And as soon as I quit pushing it'll spring shut again. If I'd try to force my way through it would make too much noise."

"I'll try to pull it open once I'm outside," she said.

"No!.... No," Don whispered almost too loudly. "Once you get through, I want you to drop flat to the ground and don't move. Let's hope that none of them look back for a little while.... And we'll roll up the cowhide in a bundle and you can pull it out after you as you're going through. You'll need it for warmth to get through the night."

"No," she said, "I'll be running all night, and I won't need it in the daytime. The hide would only get in my way."

He considered that. "I guess you're right.... Okay, as soon as you get outside, fall flat and lie still and hope and pray that they don't look back."

"But I want you to escape too!" pleaded Meadow. "What are they going to do with you?"

"I'll be all right. But as for you, you know they intend to kill you sometime tonight or early tomorrow morning." He hated to put it that bluntly, but she needed to be motivated.

Don got to his feet and made another check at one of the side windows and the rear. Harry had not returned.

Sitting in the straw, Don pushed his feet against the loose corner of the wall. It made only the slightest of creaking sounds—one that could just as well have come from any part of the noisy wagon. He got the fingers of one hand into the crack between wall and floor and applied a more steady foot pressure against the bending wood and the tightening, somewhat stretching ropes that held the wall in place. Fortunately, the ropes were not fixed directly over the corner.

Meadow lowered herself into the opening feet first and face down as silently as the true Indian she was. It was a tight squeeze but once her hips were through, the rest of the passage was comparatively easy—while Don kept up a relentless pressure. Then he could see only the dimness of starlight reflected from sun-whitened sand and desert grass through the opening that he was still forcing with his feet. Slowly he let it come shut. He waited in suspense for about two minutes before he let himself accept the fact that Meadow's escape had been successful.

Don lay in the straw but there was no thought of sleeping. In his mind he could see the naked woman running through the night down the desert trail; but she would quickly find her way to rocky areas where she could not be tracked. Running? Maybe she was too sick with abuse, fear, and sorrow to be able to run. But she had seemed to be basically uninjured; he was so grateful for that. For a few seconds he contemplated how awful her fear must be that she had become pregnant from the monsters who had raped her. He then found himself praying that she was not. He prayed for a few other things after that, the most important of which was that the war council would decide not to wage the large-scale war.

When he had finished talking to God he tried to sleep, but still could not. The walls of the prison wagon, which had penned him in for so long now, were working on his nerves more and more. He longed to smash his way through the weak corner of the wall, if that was somehow possible, then smash his way through Byron, Sam, Harry, and Bull—to be free again, to be his own master again, and to get to the authorities of this territory and let them know what was brewing so that perhaps something could be done about it before it was too late.

But Don knew that he had to be patient just now. Every moment of peace and quiet gave Meadow that much more of a chance of getting away. And anyhow it would be foolish to try to make a noisy escape through the corner; for it *would* be noisy with no one to hold it open for him. It would be much better, he decided firmly, to bide his time and try to find out what these men were up to. They were going to meet someone tomorrow—Byron had said that to his men. Perhaps then, thought Don, he would find out what was going on. He wondered if Byron and his men had anything to do with Geronimo and his council of war.

A couple of hours passed. Don was beginning to think that the men would drive all night. No one had been talking for a long time, but then Harry's rasping voice insulted the peaceful stillness. "Don't shoot. It's me, Harry."

The wagon came to a stop. "What're you worried about?" returned Byron from up on the high seat. "I knew it was you 'cause even in the dark I could see your belly hangin' over your saddle horn from a mile off."

"Aw, shaddup," said Harry. "I ain't got no more guts than.... I mean my belly ain't no bigger'n anybody else's."

There was laughter, then Byron asked, "Well, how was the water hole?"

"It's all right, I reckon," said Harry. "Lots a' water...an' no fresh tracks around. Looks like it ain't been used since the last time we was here. I'll bet most of the Injuns don't even know it's there."

"Oh, they know it's there all right," asserted Byron. "They just don't use it 'cause there's one closer to the trail."

"Yeah," admitted Harry's voice glumly.

"How far did you come back? How long have we got to go before we get there?"

"Wal, you was comin' to meet me at the same time," calculated Harry. "I'd say we'll be there in about an hour."

"Well, then, we'd better keep pushin," said Byron and started the team and wagon into motion again.

* * *

It seemed to Don that a good two hours passed before the wagon finally pulled to a stop at the out-of-the-way water hole. The men unhitched the horses and built a fire before any one of them let their mouths be the overflow to the brew of evil thoughts and emotions that had been boiling continuously higher in the minds of each of them. It was Sam who spoke about it first. "Okay, let's get her outa the wagon. What're we waitin' fer?"

"Why, Sam, you're so excited," said Byron in a voice that was intended to convey jolly good humor, but, because of the situation, came through to Don's ears sounding only like the sick voice of a sick man. Byron continued, "Don't you want to have your supper first, Sammy? Don't you know it's bad for you to poke a woman on an empty stomach?"

Sam disdained to answer; Harry and Bull laughed nervously. Then there was a bit of mumbling talk about campfire and supper and wagon tracks, and some that Don couldn't catch at all; then Byron's voice came loud again. "All right, go get her."

Immediately there came the sound of boot-steps approaching the wagon. Don's heart was busy pumping an extra supply of blood to his muscles in preparation for whatever might be required when the men found that the woman was gone. He knew there would be at least an outburst of anger, but his face held a grim smile and he couldn't hold back a quiet chuckle of sincere pleasure. He sat on his haunches at the front end of the caboose farthest away from the door.

The door opened. Sam and Bull stood there, Sam holding a revolver, Bull a lit lantern which illuminated the interior of the caboose with what seemed, to Don's expanded eye pupils, an uncomfortably bright light.

"Where the hell is she?" asked Sam in a startled voice. The question was not really directed at Don or at anyone else, but then Sam hoisted his long body through the doorway and extended his gun-bearing hand threateningly toward the sergeant. "Where the hell is she?" he repeated, this time louder and definitely requiring an answer.

"I don't know," said Don from where he sat at the front end of the caboose. "She just disappeared in a puff of smoke. Must be some kind of Indian magic."

Byron was coming to the wagon now. Don could not yet see him, but his voice, sounding a little nervous, was drawing closer. "What's goin' on there? Why don't you bring her out?"

"How the hell can I bring her out if she ain't here?" roared Sam.

Byron climbed in now, taking the lantern from Bull as he did so. He straightened up as much as he could under the low roof, looked around sternly. Satisfied that the woman really was not there, he turned at once to the damaged wall and began to kick it hard in various places. He was not long in discovering the springy corner. Still standing slightly behind Sam, he turned to face Roman. "When did you let her out?" he asked quietly.

Don kept to his squatting posture. "I dunno. You took my watch."

Byron's unfailing sense of humor failed. He yelled, "Don't try to get funny, you naked, shitty son of a bitch!"

Now Sam went into action. He kicked at Don's head, but Don fell to one side, avoiding the blow. Sam took one step closer and held the barrel of his gun to Don's face. He put his intention into clear wording. "I'll kill you, you bastard!"

"Don't!—you fool!" hollered Byron. He hauled Sam back savagely just as that furious gunman pulled back the hammer on his forty-five, cocking it. Don, on his knees now, spun himself to one side, trying to get away from the business end of the gun. However, Sam controlled himself enough to keep from pulling the trigger.

Bull, still in the doorway, also had a gun out and was covering Don. Byron cursed Sam thoroughly and ended with, "You flea-brained idiot! Don't you know we gotta keep him alive?!" He turned back to Don. "Look, we'll find her...and kill her! We're not worried. But you're causing a hell of a lot of trouble."

"That's tough," ventured Don.

"We'll get even with you tomorrow," promised Byron. He turned back to Sam. "If you're so all-fired anxious for action, then get on your horse and go find the squaw. She'll be somewhere on the trail behind us—so get goin'!"

"Sure," said Sam, "it'll be a pleasure."

"Find her and kill her. And bring back something to prove that you did."

"Sure," said Sam again.

Bull spoke up now. "Why can't he bring her back before he kills her?"

Harry was looking in through the door. "Yeah, that's what I say."

"Who gives a fucking shit what you say?" barked Byron. "I've had enough of this fooling around. We came out here with a job to do and we're gonna do it!"

Sam was climbing out through the open door past Harry. Harry said, "Wal, maybe me an' Bull should go along...in case he needs help."

"No!" said Byron sharply. "I need the two of you here to help me fix the wagon wall...so that we don't lose this bird too.... And Sam," he called after the evil-faced owlhoot who was already mounting his horse, "take the spade along. You'll have to bury her."

"How's he gonna find her in the dark?" protested Harry sulkingly.

"I don't know," said Byron, "but if he can't find her tonight, he'll find her tomorrow." He raised his voice a little to make sure that Sam would hear. "He damned well better not come back until he does find her."

On this cheering note they left the caboose and bolted the door. There followed banging on, pushing on, and cursing of the damaged wall. Finally Byron's voice said, "Well, that ought to do it. But from now on we'll keep a close watch." He raised his voice a little. "And anything that comes pushing through anywhere will get chopped off!"

After that the men went about preparing a meal and eating. They didn't bring any food to Don. It was the first time, on this trip, that he had missed a meal. Byron and Bull turned in for the night then, leaving Harry to guard the caboose.

Don covered himself with the hide and tried to sleep. In this attempt he was unsuccessful for the first few hours, for he kept seeing mind pictures of Sam catching up to Meadow and of all that would naturally follow; but then, finally, the very horrors that plagued his waking mind helped to put him to sleep, for their maddening repetitions had exhausted him mentally and emotionally. He then fell into a deep, dreamless sleep—which, in a sense, was a temporary escape from the caboose into some otherworld where thoughts and facts were not important—nor did he come fully awake until the sun rose and his captors began to move about the camp.

Smiling and happy, all his good humor returned, Byron brought breakfast to Don. It was bacon and flapjacks hot from the fire. Don ate every last lick of the generous amount offered to him.

Sam had not yet returned. In spite of this, Byron, Harry, and Bull broke camp and started the wagon on its way. They knew that Sam would eventually follow them to the rendezvous at Shallow Creek once he had finished his job.

Since the time that Sam had been put on Meadow's trail, Roman would gladly have taken any opportunity for escape that might have presented itself—at least from the time that he had realized that there was a real danger of Sam finding Meadow. At first this possibility had seemed remote to him, but not anymore. Sam was an evil man and a very determined one. Now Don wished with all his heart that he could somehow get out of the caboose, grab one of the horses, and ride after Sam with the hope of getting to him before he got to Meadow. But no opportunity came.

When they got to Shallow Creek the other party was already there. Don heard Byron announce, "Well, Ruizo got here ahead of us. I kind of figured he would." But although Don pressed his face into the window bars it was some time before the wagon turned to an angle that enabled him to see Ruizo and his men.

When he did see them he was startled by the effulgent splendor of the dozen horsemen who displayed themselves against the backdrop of an unusually tall growth of cactus plants. Just beyond these prickly spires trickled a muddy little stream that threatened to evaporate at any second. Some of the men stood beside their mounts, some straddled their fancy saddles, indicating, with both types of postures, that they had just arrived. It seemed to Don that this was remarkable timing, considering the long distance the wagon had come—unless these Southwestern men had sent out a rider to scout for the wagon's arrival; but that seemed unlikely, for Don had not been aware of any such contact or communication. The wagon pulled to a stop.

In all his life Don had never seen a group of riders so gloriously attired nor horses so lavishly accoutered. He had to admit to himself that even a scarlet-coated patrol of North-West Mounted Policemen riding through a green forest in Canada was not quite this spectacular. There were silver mounted saddles with huge pommels and tapadera-covered stirrups ornamenting the backs of pintos, blacks, whites, and odd looking yellow horses with cream colored manes and tails. The riders themselves, dark skinned and rugged looking, were so gaily bedecked with stunning bright shirts and silver-spotted gunbelts that they seemed to strut without moving. The brims of their hats were wide almost to the point of ridiculousness. A few of them sported heavy cartridge belts slung over their shoulders and crossed over their chests. Rifles in scabbards protruded from under every stirrup fender. It seemed likely to Don that these men were Mexicans, but what Mexicans!—the president's special bodyguard?

Don wondered which one was the leader, Ruizo. This question was quickly answered for him as Byron climbed down from the wagon and walked toward one of the smallest of the men. This thin gentleman, looking a bit worried—possibly because he feared that the weight of his two revolvers and oversized hat might sink him down into the sand—came forward from the rest of the group to meet Byron.

"Hallo, Triage," greeted the Mexican, revealing Byron's surname.

"Hello, Senor Ruizo!" returned Byron heartily.

Ruizo's face remained sour. "Chut up with the senors, yes? You theenk I cannot understood Eengleesh. Eef you wan' to call me sometheeng beside my name, call me meester."

Byron laughed shortly, probably because he couldn't think of anything suitable to say, then reached into his shirt pocket for his makings.

"We weel have to hurry," stated the grumpy sounding little Mexican. "Our fran' eez gatting mad. He say eet take too long. I just gat word from heem…. I see you got the cage. Eez the bird eenside?"

"He sure is," said Byron. "Take a look."

The two men came toward the door of the caboose. Don was tired of standing hunched over so he sat down in the straw. Ruizo, short as he was, managed to look in through the rear window, possibly by standing on a convenient stone. Don stared back at him. After a few seconds Ruizo ordered, "Gat op!" Don leisurely got to his feet and stood stoop shouldered under the low ceiling. Ruizo studied him for a moment, then said, "I gass he weel do."

"Nothing wrong with him," said Byron, "and if you're satisfied we might as well close the deal right now."

"Ho, no," snorted Ruizo. "First I got to know eef he's real."

"Well, I can show you his bloody uniform. What more do you want?" Byron's great good humor seemed suddenly to be wearing thin again at this apparently critical point of the enterprise.

Don became aware that Ruizo's men were now at both side windows, elbowing one another about as they all tried to get a look at the prisoner. At first they had been silent, then they began to laugh and to talk in Spanish.

"Hokay," said Ruizo, "you gat the uneeform, an' while you are gatting eet, I weel ask your bird a few quastions."

"Go right ahead," said Byron. He lit his cigarette and left the other man's side.

Don wished he could put questions to Ruizo instead of the other way around, but he knew that he might learn at least a little by paying attention to what kind of questions the Mexican asked him.

With his huge-brimmed hat pushed well back on his head, Ruizo's sour face was squeezed in between two bars now. "Wal, my fran,' what eez your name?"

"Why should I tell you?"

"I know of some very good reasons. I know my boys would like to have a leetle fon…. They would like to hang you downside up on a cactus an' teekle you with their knifes to see eef they can make you laugh…. Bot I weel not lat them eef you are good boy…. I do not really care what's your name, bot tal me thees—are you really from Canada, an' are you really from North-Wes' Mounted Police?"

Don hesitated only momentarily before he answered, "Yes, I'm a member of the North-West Mounted Police in Canada."

"What eez your rank?"

"Sergeant."

"That eez good eenoff. What chaep are you een?"

"Chaep? Shape? You mean, am I sick or healthy?"

"Yeah, sure…bot I mean, can you fight a man right now, weeth your bare hands?—een a fair fight? Or have you been hurt on thees treep? Or are you seek from all thees travel?"

"I'm not sick, I'm not crippled, and I'm in fine shape to fight with anyone if I have to…. Whom do you want me to fight?" But it didn't work.

"Ah, that I weel not tal you, bot eet's hokay—you weel fin' out soon eenoff." He turned around and plodded away out of Don's sight. The peeping Toms at the side windows also left.

A little later Don could see, through a side window, that Ruizo and one of his men, plus Byron, Harry, and Bull, were squatting together in a little circle in the shade of a growth of cactus plants. *The big meeting*, thought Roman. *If only they were a little closer so that I could make out their words.*

Byron turned to Harry and said something. The stocky henchman at once got up and came over toward the wagon. Don supposed he was coming to take him out of the caboose to turn him over to Ruizo, but Harry did not immediately arrive at the door. Half a minute passed, along with some creaking of the stationary wagon, before the round face, with its blue and purple bruise on the forehead, showed at the rear window. Harry worked a bulky package through between the bars. "Here's your duds," he said. "Put 'em on."

It was a pleasant surprise. Don eagerly picked up the cloth-wrapped parcel and untied the lace leather that held it together. He ripped off the outer cloth, unveiling the beautiful sight of scarlet serge, navy jodhpurs with their yellow stripes, and the brown leather gun rig. However, Don could tell by the lack of weight that the flap-covered holster was empty. Harry had left the window, but now he came back. Through the bars he passed Don's high, brown

Strathcona boots complete with their spurs. Next came the stiff-brimmed brown hat. Once more Harry left, and this time when he returned he opened the door. He stood there with his gun in one hand and a large tin basin of water in the other. A leather kit was under his elbow. He set the basin on the floor of the caboose, then the kit. "Git rid a' the beard an' use the same water to take a bath. I'll git y' some soap an' a towel. An' Byron will come later an' give you a haircut…. Yore gonna be a yoomin bean agin." He bolted the door and left, but was back shortly with a bar of soap which he pitched in through the bars and a towel which he hung over the sill.

The leather kit held shaving/grooming equipment including a scissors, a hair clipper and a small mirror. Roman found it a great pleasure to clip off the long hair of his beard and then shave. The razor was sharp and he did a neat job with only a couple of tiny nicks. He thoroughly washed his face, ears, and neck; then he took a bath as best he could with the little water he had. But the greatest pleasure of all was pulling on his underwear, pants, socks, and boots. For many days he had been like a naked animal. The pants and boots brought a feeling of new confidence in his ability to cope with the situation he was in, and a very true sense of protection for his body. He restrained himself from putting on the top parts of his uniform, partly because of the heat and also because it was better to get his haircut first. While he was waiting for this he went to the side window to see how Byron and the Mexicans were getting along.

The meeting beside the cactus plants was still in progress. Just then Ruizo handed Byron a leather pouch. The latter opened it and emptied the contents on a bandanna he had laid on the ground—gold coins, no doubt in payment for goods delivered. There seemed to be quite a lot of coins, and this pleased Don; for, if he must be sold, he at least didn't want to be sold cheaply.

The meeting broke up and then Byron and Harry came into the caboose. Harry held a gun on Don while Byron gave him a haircut. He did a fairly good job of it too, mainly because he used only a scissors and comb and didn't attempt anything short or fancy. When he was finished he let Don check it out in the small mirror. The hair had been left full around the ears and was simply whacked off straight at the back so that it was about collar length. Byron hadn't said much while he cut, giving Don the feeling that he had still not been forgiven for having let Meadow out of the caboose. Before Byron left he ordered Don to put on the rest of the uniform.

Don assumed that he now belonged to the Mexicans and wondered what they would do with him. The surprise came when he found that he was not going to be immediately transferred into Ruizo's keeping. The Mexicans all mounted in preparation to ride away and Byron and his men also took to saddle and wagon without any further ado. It would have been a complete mystery to Roman had not Ruizo turned in his saddle and yelled to Byron: "Remamber! Eef you don' gat heem there safe, an' eef you don' put heem to work right, you don' gat the other half. Thees theeng has got to work out right. They all got to like what they see."

"Don't worry!" returned Byron. He didn't wait for Ruizo to say any more, but urged his team into motion and headed the wagon in a southwesterly direction.

12

After a while Don removed his red coat and the shirt because of the heat, and Byron, becoming aware of this, approved, saying something about not wanting to get the monkey suit all sweaty. So these items of clothing, along with the hat and empty gunbelt, were again wrapped up in cloth and put into their hiding place somewhere under the caboose. Don was annoyed at himself for feeling such relief at being stripped to the waist and even more annoyed that he wanted to take off his pants and boots as well. At first the clothes had felt wonderful, but before long they had seemed unnatural and restricting. After having been naked for so long he knew it would take a little time to get used to wearing clothing again.

Don steadied himself against the swaying by holding onto the side window bars. Ruizo's last sentence seemed somehow to have opened his mind. *"They all got to like what they see,"* the little Mexican had said. Don wasn't completely sure, but he would have been willing to make a bet that the "all" referred to the Indians gathered at the sun-dance-war-council that Meadow had told him about. But why would Ruizo want him there? And what would Ruizo have to do with an Indian war council? Immediately Don thought of the possibility that the Mexicans might be gunrunners who hoped to supply the Indians with weapons. By no means would it be the first time that guns had been bootlegged across the Rio Grande; on one occasion some had been smuggled from Mexico all the way to Canada. The gun angle seemed to make sense, thought Don, but he couldn't understand where he himself fit into the picture. And he admitted that even the gun-selling idea was only conjecture — that he really had no solid facts to go on.

As the wagon rattled on, and as he stood stooped at the window watching the slow-passing arid landscape with its sparse sprinkling of parched desert grass and an occasional patch of cactus plants of one kind or another here and there, his thoughts began to return agonizingly to Meadow and to what her fate might be at the moment. She could well be dead by now for there was no good reason why Sam should not have found her. This was a terrible thought to Don, but he grasped at a weak consolation in the likelihood that by now it had to have gone one way or the other. Either she was gone from this world and no longer suffering, or else she had gotten safely to her own band under Chief Strong-Hand.

Don continued to gaze out over this great expanse of southwestern desert. The sun was high now; the time must be close to noon. Heat waves shimmered in the distance, animatedly distorting a long jagged ridge of amazingly red rock. Some of the tallest peaks of this outcropping stood considerably higher than the rest, so that the whole thing could be thought of as a great sprawling castle with ruggedly constructed towers and spires. The deep-blue sky was cloudless from Don's point of vision, contrasting handsomely with the various shades of yellows, duns, and dull reds of the desert in general. In spite of his uncomfortable hunched-over posture at the window and the thoughts that troubled him, Don could not help but enjoy the strange beauty of this increasingly barren land he found himself in. He was grateful that Harry was riding on the other side, so that this particular view was not contaminated by the sight of him. Just then something rather evil looking did appear however.

It was the biggest lizard Don had ever seen—a good two feet from blunt snout to blunt tail tip, and decorated all over with a beady pattern of yellow and black. It was only about twenty feet away from the wagon but increasing that distance as it scuttled from the shelter of a small rock to a somewhat larger one. *Ugly*, thought Don, *but probably harmless—still, you couldn't say for sure.* Then he remembered a Canadian called John Cody who had lived part of his life in the U.S. Southwest. He had told Don, among other things, about large lizards called Gila monsters, and that these had the rare feature of having poisonous fangs—quite unusual in a lizard. In spite of the heat, a shiver worked its way through Don's frame. He supposed there was probably a whole assortment of ugly and dangerous little critters slithering around there on the hot sand. He would have to keep that in mind when and if he managed to escape.

At least an hour more of travel went by. Don rested on the floor of the caboose part of this time, but he spent proportionately more time hunched over looking out through one or another of the three windows than he had so far on this nightmarish journey. The reason for this was that he knew he was close to the end of it. He wanted to have at least a basic concept of the land layout near the place where he would be unloaded; for sooner or later he would have to make his bid for freedom.

Very gradually the ground began to slope downward in the direction they were going. Soon it was plain to Don that the wagon was progressing into a shallow valley — Yellow Valley, this would be, if he was right in his hunch that he was being taken to the Indian war council.

Then a group of Indians on horseback — a half dozen — appeared and the wagon pulled to a stop. Don's shirt, red coat, hat, and empty gunbelt were handed to him again and he was told, by Harry, to put it on while Byron, from up on the high seat, told him to hurry and to "look sharp." While Don was once more donning the remainder of his uniform, Byron was conversing with one of the Indians; but nothing very revealing was said. The wagon started moving again, in the same direction, and the six mounted Indians fell in, three to each side but to the rear.

There was more grass now, and of a healthier green. In the distance was something that was either trees or an extra-tall stand of cactus plants. When Don looked in the direction the wagon was heading, as best he could through a side window, he saw a bluish haze darkening the sky. Smoke, and quite a bit of it. That would have to be coming from a large camp with many cooking fires.

The trail leveled off and led the wagon on for another mile or so. Don heard sounds — human and animal, the sounds of a camp. He realized then that he was looking out through the wrong window, but before he could go to the other side, the wagon turned abruptly and sharply, and the great Indian sun-dance-war-council camp swung into place before his eyes.

He was much impressed by the size of it. There were hundreds of grass wickiups and teepees surrounding a huge squarish looking tent. This great central structure, no doubt the place of meetings and ceremonies, had walls of paint-decorated hides. Although Don was no expert on Indians this far south, he guessed that the grass huts were temporary Apache dwellings, while the teepees and the big sundance tent had likely been brought in from somewhat farther north.

Geronimo was certainly trying to bite off a big chunk, thought Don, to bring a representation of all the southwestern tribes together like this, as well as some from farther north, to try to talk them into war. It was frightening; and the farther the wagon progressed, now moving toward the camp at an angle, the more unbelievably huge the place looked. The sound of voices—mostly children's laughing, crying, playing voices—could be heard now.

Soon the wagon was moving along between two rows of grass huts. On the shade side of most of these were squaws and cute, dirty-faced little children, and here and there older children played in groups. They, along with the adults, quickly dropped what they were doing and showed much interest in the wagon as soon as they became aware of it. Don was impressed with the dark beauty of some of the squaws and girls. The wagon progressed a good quarter of a mile into the camp before Don saw the first brave other than the ones who were riding with the wagon.

The rig came to a stop. As always, the cessation of the creaking and groaning of the old caboose was a relief to Don's ears.

The Indians began to cluster around more and more. Obviously they were quite excited; the crazy thought came to Don that maybe the entire general populace of the camp had been expecting the wagon with him inside.

Sergeant Roman studied the men and thought he could make out which ones were Apaches because of their unbraided shoulder-length hair held in place by wide, colorful cloth brow bands, as well as by their equally colorful cloth breech-clouts and the almost knee-high moccasins they wore, and the long, slender lances that many of them carried. Some of these were tipped with cavalry sabers which, no doubt, had been taken as spoil after bloody battle. A few of the Apaches wore leather shirts, but there was also a generous sprinkling of white man's clothing—brightly colored shirts, wide-brimmed hats, and bits and pieces of cavalry uniforms. Intermingling to some extent with this display of Apache color were the beaded buckskin and bright feathers of warriors from farther north. Every black flashing eye was turned on the caboose; there was veiled interest and anticipation written on every masculine, stoic, bronze face.

Some of the braves with lances were striding toward the rear of the wagon, so Don moved from the side window to the window in the door and saw that these armed warriors were forming a double line from the door of the caboose to an entrance into the large ceremonial tent. The others pressed against their backs but did not push through onto the narrow path that had been cleared.

Byron was there now, opening the caboose door. "All right, Sergeant, you can come out," he said. "Your journey has come to an end."

Don's heart did a short palpitation as he stepped down beside Byron into that sea of savages. He had heard about the cruelty of the Apaches—cruelty equaled nowhere among all the Indians of North America, unless possibly by the Iroquois. What did these Indians want with him? He straightened his shoulders so that the brass buttons down the front of his scarlet tunic stood out like a challenge to the equally colorful apparel of the red men. He adjusted the wide, stiff brim of his hat to his favorite rakish angle as he moved ahead of Byron down the human corridor.

A few steps later he was in the dim interior of the gigantic ceremonial tent. Byron and three Apache braves escorted Don toward the center of the tent where several more Indians squatted on furs in a semi-circle. These were mature looking men, very dignified in their sitting postures and facial expressions, although their dress was even more garish than that of the warriors outside. Chieftains, no doubt, thought Don. He counted them quickly and found that there were sixteen. Don realized that these could be the most important and powerful of all the leaders gathered here for this war council. Don counted five with the loose hair and other markings of the Apache. The remaining eleven displayed braids and feathers. Three of these wore full-fledged war bonnets.

Byron brought Don close before the Indian chiefs and then addressed one of them in particular. "Geronimo, here is the man I said I would bring to you."

One of the Apache chiefs solemnly rose to his feet and stared unwaveringly at Don. Don stared back with equal interest, for he knew that he was looking at none other than the infamous Geronimo—the "Red Devil."

On his head Geronimo wore a close-fitting leather cap decorated with two short steer horns—perhaps only the tips—and a yellow feather in between them. His buckskin shirt, leggings, and moccasins were fringed and beaded. The shirt was held close to his waist by a well stocked cartridge belt through which was thrust a long-barreled Colt Navy revolver. His face, wide and squarish, had enough wrinkles to indicate that he was well past middle age, but the lines of his lean body, now that he was on his feet and ramrod straight, were that of a younger man.

His wide, almost lipless mouth opened slowly. "What is your name?" he asked in easy-to-understand English with only a slight accent.

"Don Roman."

"Where are you from?"

"From Canada."

"Why do you wear that red coat?"

"It's part of my uniform. I'm a member of the North-West Mounted Police."

Geronimo was silent for a few seconds, then, with his face still in total poker-mode, said, "That is good." For several more seconds he studied Don from hat to boots. Then he took a step backward. "Sit with us," he invited.

Don was startled. It seemed incredible that he had just been asked to sit as an equal with the most powerful Indian chiefs of the Southwest. He was careful not to show his surprise and at once squatted down Indian fashion, facing the semi-circle of impassive bronze faces.

Geronimo had re-squatted himself at the same time, and now he spoke to Byron. "You go now, and make your camp in the camp of my people."

"I am pleased to do so," said Byron, and at once started for the exit together with the three lance-carrying braves who had escorted them in. These, however, went only so far as the exit where they remained standing within the tent after Byron had left.

Fifteen pairs of dark eyes were fastened unswervingly on Roman as Geronimo introduced his fellow chieftains. Most of the names were new to Don. There was, for instance, Gray-Horse of the Comanches. He was a bony, gaunt man with strangely glowing eyes—perhaps caused by an excess of moisture due to the windy, sandy climate. The four Apache chiefs beside Geronimo were: Tudeevia, Victorio, Mangus Colorado, and Cochise. Cochise was the only one of these that Don had heard about in Canada. He was probably the most powerful Apache leader of all. A rather handsome man was Cochise, with a strong but sensitive face and penetrating eyes.

Geronimo said, "Do you know why you have been brought here, Don Roman?"

"No, I do not," replied Don, trying to keep his language as formal sounding as that of Geronimo, "but I would very much like to know."

"I will tell you now," said Geronimo. "This is a great war council— not a sun dance. It is the greatest war council there has ever been. We have come together to decide if we should make a great war against all white man and drive him from the land of our fathers...or if we should not. If we do, then it will not be a work half done, for we will drive out the white man from the great waters of the rising sun to the great waters of the setting sun, and from the land of the snows to the land of the devils. All white man will flee over the waters and will not come back. But the Mexicans, the devils, we will kill even when they try to flee—all of them!" Honest fury had sprung into his eyes and voice on the last sentence, but he quickly regained his composure. A moment of silence passed.

Don, quite on impulse, asked, "If the Mexicans are your enemies, why do you buy guns from them?"

Geronimo remained silent for several seconds and Don was satisfied that he had hit a nail on the head. Then the chief looked at him intently and said, "If the devils want to sell us the guns to use for shoot them, why should we not buy?...But that is not for you. The devils are in the South, you are in the North. Your people will be sent from the land and many will be killed in brave battle....... I am ashamed of my own people," he hung his head as he said this, "for they are afraid of your people." He looked up again, squarely at Don, and continued, "They have heard many stories of the men in redcoats who do great wonders in battle that no other can do. Stories have come to us about the redcoats from the North—how they ride into battle on great black horses and leave behind them a trail of blood like a river; how they fight both Indian and white man, whoever does evil; how they always win their battles; how they can kill any man with only their hands and their eyes; how their red coats keep them safe from bullets and arrows so that they cannot be killed; how ten of them fought a band of thirty and killed them all. My people say that the men in red coats from the North are not men at all, but people from the north stars who have come down to make justice in the world. My people have heard stories and are afraid. They will fight in the South, but are afraid to go north.... But now we have you here with us...and we will find out if you are what the stories say you are. My people and all the tribes gathered here will see for themselves what you are."

As the incredible situation began to penetrate into Don's consciousness he felt the numbness of shocked nerves creeping over his entire body. An actual wave of dizziness assailed him momentarily. He recovered quickly without showing it, concentrated for a few seconds on willing strength into his vocal cords, and said quietly, "What kind of test are you going to give me?"

"Many tests," answered Geronimo. "Many tests before the eyes of all the tribes. We will find out if you are from the stars, or if you are only a white man like the rest. If you can show that the stories we heard are true, then my people will not make this great war against all white man — for it would be foolish to fight against people who are not people, but who are from the stars. But if we find that you are only a man as we are, and that the stories are lies, then we will begin the great war.... And in five summers there will be nothing left of the white man in all this land — only a little dried blood and a bad dream at night."

* * *

The jagged outer rim of Yellow Valley was dark against a glaring brightness in the eastern sky. Clouds just above the horizon, blushing pink before the partly visible eye of a peeping-Tom sun, contrasted sharply with the long, gray shadows that the rugged rimrocks cast over half the length of the valley.

A dog barked at one end of the great Indian camp, was answered from a long distance by another dog at the other end. A fractious stallion, tied by himself to keep him from bothering the other horses, contributed a long, almost chanticleer-like whinny. Then from the center of the camp the age-cracked voice of a medicine man began to chant a song of prayer. In a little while there were more voices, some talking, some chanting, and before long the whole war-council city was awake.

Don Roman crawled out of his warm blankets inside of his private teepee and wondered, fearfully, what this day would bring. The Indians had been treating him well since he had been turned over to them yesterday. After having sat with the chiefs in the big tent, he had been fed and then shown around the camp with all the ceremonious courtesy befitting a guest of great honor. From the awe-filled, respectful looks he had received as he had passed among men, women, and children of the camp, as well as from what he had been told directly by the chiefs, he soon began to realize that he was indeed being honored in sincerity. He was supposed to be a man dropped down from the stars—one of the mighty red-coated warriors from the North, a super being of action who could do things no mere mortal could do. Likely many of the Indians had doubts, but apparently they weren't taking any chances on not showing him respect in case the wild tales turned out to be more than a storyteller's dream. Not that they would kowtow to him in humble submission even if they were convinced that the stories were fact; but the Indian philosophy required giving credit where credit was due. A mighty man must be treated with concordant honor; if he was an enemy he received, if and when overcome, torture, death, or both—with respect and honor.

But how were the Indians of this war council going to go about finding out if the story about the redcoats was true or false? This was the question that bothered Don now as he reached for his shirt and tunic and began to dress. How would they test him?

The whole thing was ridiculous. And Geronimo had overblown grandiose ideas of what the Indians could accomplish even if he could unite the whole continent of red men. In such a case there would be great bloodshed, but Don could not see the white man's purpose of controlling the land being thwarted. There were too many whites and their technology was superior; and there was all of Europe to back them up with more white immigrants and more weaponry, along with more plows to change forever the face of the new world. Secondly, Geronimo would never convince all the natives of North America to join his cause. Too many of them, particularly those farther north and east, had already seen the face of the future; and although they did not like what they saw, they knew that the hooves of history were thundering over the land like some supernatural herd of giant bison, that, unlike the natural ones, could not be turned aside or decimated.

Nevertheless, all this did not insure that there would be no great war. It simply meant that the war would be limited to the Southwest; and, if Geronimo had his way, this could easily turn out to be the bloodiest Indian uprising in history. Thousands might die, both white and red.

And he, Sergeant Don Roman, was going to be tested to see if he was an ordinary man or something superior. He was to be tested to settle the matter; and the decision to go ahead with the great war might well be made as a result of the revelation that Don was just a man, nothing more. He knew he was in for an ordeal—an extremely hard ordeal of some kind, or rather of many kinds, for Geronimo had said he would be given many tests. With stomach-tingling impact, he wondered what would be left of his quite human flesh and blood by the time his tormentors were satisfied that he was indeed only human.

The thought of attempting an escape before the ordeal began had been with him almost continuously since he had found out what the purpose of his long journey was. He might get away with it too, for the Indians didn't seem to be all that worried about such an attempt. Possibly they didn't care if he did, for his running away would prove satisfactorily that the redcoats were not what the campfire storytellers had said they were.

And that was why Don had not yet tried to escape. With his scarlet tunic now on, he sat motionless in silent thought for some time, then hit his thigh hard with his fist in a gesture of desperation. If only so much didn't hang on it, he thought. At the very least, the whole Southwest would soon be drenched in blood; and it seemed quite possible, even probable, that whether or not this terrible thing happened depended on what these war-council Indians decided about himself, for he represented the one force they feared: the North-West Mounted Police—the red-coated lawmen of Canada about whom imaginative tale-tellers had obviously exaggerated to the point of ridiculousness. But the Indians could accept the possibility of there being at least some truth to these stories which were carried from camp to camp by those who passed them on; for they believed many other things no less fantastic. And perhaps they had good reason to believe some of it, for they often watched their tribal medicine men do impossible things that nobody, neither red nor white, had yet been able to explain.

So Sergeant Don Roman knew that he was a very real and important matter in the minds of the members of this war council. What they decided about him could well make the difference between peace and war. Should he make an attempt at escape or simply go ahead with the testing? If he escaped or tried to escape, the war would almost certainly go ahead. But if he stayed and failed the tests—and it seemed almost certain that he would fail—they would still go ahead with war. Either way the great Indian uprising appeared to be inevitable; the thing was, however, that one way might let him live, while the other way, that of allowing himself to be tested, was almost certainly the short route to a painful death.

He continued to think about the matter as he began to eat from the basket of food that a young brave had just pushed into the teepee. The brave had not said a word and was gone in a second. Don was sure there had been a look of fear on his face.

Roman chewed on a chunk of blackish dried meat and was too absorbed in his anxious thoughts to know what it tasted like, which was probably just as well. He ate it all, then started on the next course which could have been a vegetable of some kind, or maybe a root. There was yet something else that looked like a cross between a loaf of bread and a flapjack; it had a good enough taste (that of corn) to bring Don's mind around to the fact that he was eating—and not only eating, but stuffing himself. He wiped his mouth with his hand and took a drink from the leather water pouch hanging on one side of the teepee's interior.

Now standing in the very center of the teepee, the only place where he could stand straight, he stretched his muscles. He was still thinking, but a look of determination was now firming on his face. He stood quite still for a moment, then picked up his empty gun rig and buckled it on over his tunic. He thought, *I just can't be totally sure that I can't convince them that the redcoats are not to be messed with. And if I don't try I'll never know. And if all those people, Indians and whites, are killed...and I think that maybe somehow I could have prevented it....*

He picked up his hat, at the same time muttering to himself in a voice just loud enough so that it could possibly have been heard immediately outside of the teepee. "So if I can't live with myself, what's the use of living?"

He put on his hat at a rakish angle and stepped out into the early morning sunshine.

13

On that same day Jim Longfeather, alias Dave Lindner, had been riding since before sunrise, his trusty deputy beside him.

Three days earlier they had come across the prison wagon. After seeing the apparently insane prisoner and checking the papers of the men in charge, Jim and the deputy had carried on homeward after a rather fruitless mission.

The army had called him from his regular sheriff's duties at Garner Flats to investigate reports of large Indian movements to the southwest. Jim was still surprised about that, although he knew how the superintendent's mind had worked, in general, in selecting him. Fort Cummings did not have, at that time, any Indian scouts in their employ. He knew that Jim was an Indian, that he was large and intimidating, and that he didn't have a hell of a lot to do at the moment in his jurisdiction, having taken care of all that in his first week of carrying the sheriff's badge. The superintendent had reasoned that if any contact was made with these rumored prowling bands, an Indian might have a better chance of finding out what was going on. He didn't know that Jim's grip on the Apache language was next to nonexistent. Since Jim didn't want anyone to know from how far north he had come, he had lied about what native language was his. By this time he had picked up just enough Apache to get away with posing as a civilized one if he was lucky. It helped that he had made up a story (slightly similar to his true background in Canada) about being an orphaned Apache brought up by a pioneer family in the Oklahoma Territories. This story also accounted for his southwest lingo which he had practiced day and night while working on a cattle ranch in Montana—his first job after crossing the border into the USA.

The mission the army had sent him on had been more or less fruitless, although in a couple of places he had found a lot of shoeless horse tracks; but they had lost these on hard ground and in one case in a stream. He could have pursued the matter further, but he had been given a time limit for reporting back. That suited him fine, for he didn't really think the Indians were up to anything, and riding around on this stovetop wasn't his cup of English tea. Also he didn't really want to talk to any Apaches who would immediately identify him as something other than one of them. And if that happened his deputy might catch on that he'd been lying about his past.

However, Jim and Deputy Cliff Fullbright were no longer heading back toward home.

* * *

After having left the men with their mental patient, Jim had an uneasy feeling about that bunch. He would think about it every now and then, and before long he put his finger on at least part of what was bothering him. It was the looks on the men's faces—not the leader, but the others. It wasn't anything very definite, and yet he had caught glimpses of…uneasiness, maybe even fear, and sometimes sly looks of satisfaction. Satisfaction about what? It took hours and miles of riding before he thought that just maybe they had unwittingly presented these fleeting looks because of feeling satisfied that they were pulling the wool over a sheriff's eyes. But it was all so tenuous that Jim-Dave and Cliff had ridden almost a half day before Jim pulled his dapple-gray to a stop and shocked his poor deputy out of a year's growth—which the young man could have used to advantage, not being very big and looking like a midget when close to Jim. They were turning around, Jim told him, and going back after the wagon.

However, by this time they were only three miles or so from the stage-line station where they had changed horses on their way through the first time. This line, *The Kelton Comfort Stagecoach Line and Horse Rental Company, Kelton Bros. Proprietors*, was the line farthest to the south, with this particular station also being the southernmost entity of that company or anything that resembled it. So they returned to it and got back their own horses. Although Jim had gotten along well with the gray, he was happy to be astride his big bay stallion once more. The deputy also rode his own bay again. Both of these rich brown, black maned, black tailed animals were now well rested and faced the desert ahead of them with prancing strides and a mixture of courage, ignorance, and confidence. They assumed that their riders would continue to provide them with watering places and even a little oats now and then. This was true because the sheriff and deputy each carried a little sack of the grain behind the cantles of their saddles.

Jim and Cliff left the station well before nightfall, heading back the way they had come. They made camp near a foot-wide muddy stream beside an overhanging rock that, by the look of campfire remains, many travelers had slept under from time to time.

The next day they managed to pick up the trail of the wagon and followed this to the *Little Sandy*, a river that hardly deserved that designation and that, Jim decided, would in Canada have been called a creek. What they found there was interesting though. There was every indication that the wagon had upset and been dragged on its side for some distance down the riverbank. There were plenty of skid marks in the sandy soil. The wagon had been put back on its wheels, however, for the tracks continued on the other side of the stream.

With some difficulty, sometimes losing the tracks on hard ground before finding them again, the sheriff and deputy pressed on. But they did not catch up that day and again made camp for the night.

The third day was a repeat of the second. They were again often slowed in their progress because of losing the trail for long stretches. This was the depth of Apache country, but they saw no Indians nor smoke sign. However, they did come across another stretch of sandy trail through which a large party of unshod Indian ponies and moccasined feet had passed, and there were travois ruts as well. Jim paid little attention to this find other than to jot it down in his memory as something to tell the superintendent at Fort Cummings if they ever got back there.

All of Jim's energy was being focused on catching up to the wagon, and with each hour that passed he somehow felt it increasingly important that he do so. He kept thinking that if the men were not legitimate nut-haulers, then likely their naked prisoner was not a legitimate nut. What was he then? At the same time Jim was plagued by doubts. If the crazy-man nurses *were* legit, then he was guilty of a great waste of time and energy.

Fortunately his deputy went along with everything he said and did, for never had a deputy admired a sheriff more than young Cliff Fullbright admired "Dave Lindner." The admiration was mutual, for in just a very short time they had been through hell and high water together.

Now they were in their fourth day and still had not caught up to the wagon, but the tracks were fresh. Jim didn't push too hard. He was sure these strange haulers of human cargo would make camp soon, at least briefly, perhaps at some water hole they knew of, and this might give Jim and Cliff a chance to study them a bit before closing in. It could help, at that point, to have some inkling of what these men were up to. Particularly Jim was hoping to find, by observing them from a distance, some indication of how dangerous they might be when approached and further questioned. But so far they had not sighted the wagon.

The day was still early enough to be pleasant. The two men rode along in a comfortable silence for a long time. They both kept alert and never went far without scanning the horizon in all directions, including to the rear; sometimes it was one man looking to the left, sometimes the other looking to the right, etc., but seldom both at the same time in the same direction, almost as though they had practiced the whole thing as a drill. Actually, they weren't even thinking about what they were doing; it had become a habit. Fullbright was thinking about what it would be like to be married to the new waitress at the *Yellow Bird Cafe* and to be in bed with her on their wedding night; and Longfeather-Lindner was thinking about how in the Sam Hill he had ever gotten into being a sheriff in a southwestern cow town.

* * *

He had made it across the US border without incident. His original intention had been to head far south before looking for work, but an opportunity had come up for a job on a fair-sized ranch in Montana. He had liked the man who had hired him and had gotten along well with the other hired hands. He gave them a phony story about where he was from, but no one seemed to care one way or the other. The job, however, had been a temporary one; he replaced a man who was recovering from a broken leg.

Several of the cowhands had come up from the Oklahoma Territory and they talked in a fascinating way. Not only did they have an accent, but their way of expressing themselves also showed clearly that they had gotten out of school before they had gotten out of short pants. Jim at once threw his heart and soul into learning to talk as they did. They noticed the change and complimented him on being "a damn site easier t' un'erstan' now than you was jest a couple a' weeks ago. We think you got some big-tit school marm hid away somewheres, givin' y' grammerical lessons."

By the time the broken-leg man recovered, and Jim was ready to move on, he had a pretty good handle on his new way of palaverin.' He could have stayed longer, for the ranch owner, the foreman, and the hands all liked him, and they knew that in a pinch he could do the work of two or three men; but he felt he was still far too close to Canada.

* * *

So he carried on southward and eventually arrived in the Arizona Territories at a town supported by the military but run by eastern big shots. These paid big bucks to top brass at Fort Cummings who, for this consideration, allowed them to go on operating. Their operations involved gambling, prostitution, and selling whiskey to the Indians. The town was hell, and only about half of its citizens wanted anything other. When the corrupt sheriff counted his gains and decided to leave while he was ahead, the men in control tried to wangle in another or their own so business could go on as usual.

And they would easily have managed that if it hadn't been for a young cowboy by the name of Cliff Fullbright whose dad had just died. Jim learned later that Cliff, this small, rather good looking man, had cared for his failing dad for a number of years while running their near-worthless ranch. He had also been spending about half of their meager income on forty-five caliber shells for his old revolver. Not a day had gone by, for years, without his putting in some practice with it. And always he had done so in anticipation of one day becoming the sheriff of Garner Flats and cleaning out the rats' nest that the town had become. His dad passed on about the same time that the rotten sheriff had pulled stakes; and young Cliff saw this as his opportunity to attempt what he had always dreamed about.

At great risk to his life, he had campaigned for the office of sheriff, appealing boldly to that half of the population who took their families to church on Sunday and secretly complained about the moral muck in which they were forced to live. The town bosses put up a slimy candidate and backed him; and Cliff Fullbright's life, in spite of all his practiced shooting ability, hung by a precarious thread. Yet he didn't back down but, rather, continued to campaign mightily, arousing the population into a greater realization of the need for change. They became more dissatisfied, but could not really believe that this twenty-year-old dirt-poor rancher, who sometimes played his guitar and sang hymns of love and peace in church, could clean up their town.

And then one day, in the middle of all this, big Jim Longfeather rode his towering bay stallion down the street and pulled to a stop in front of the *Paradise Hotel* where the slimy candidate and young Fullbright were taking turns making speeches.

It had taken Jim about a half hour of listening to the speakers and the comments from the crowd to get the gist of the overall situation, including that the kid was not about to be sold a life insurance policy.

Before the bay stallion had finished eating his oats in the livery stable, Jim, calling himself Dave Lindner, had officially entered himself as a third candidate in the sheriff race. But he let it be known that if he won, he would take office only on the condition that Cliff Fullbright would be accepted as the deputy. Then Fullbright, after a meeting with his new rival, decided to withdraw from the race and give his support to Jim. This did the trick and turned the tide solidly in favor of this duo that actually offered hope to the good citizens that their town could be redeemed.

And it was. For Jim, as Dave Lindner, won the election and he and Cliff joined forces and lived a story that would be told to that generation's great grandchildren. Covering each others' backs, they went into action—a big Indian who could toss people around like small sacks of potatoes and a white kid who could shoot the balls off a flea while said flea was hopping from dog to dog.

The prestige and money of the town bosses had no effect on them. They arrested and jailed whomever they chose, ransacked their offices without warrants, piled up evidence, and got away with it. This drew in the corrupt army officials and they were also arrested. There was now a new superintendent at the Fort.

During the heat of the fray, "Dave" and Cliff lost track of the attempts on their lives and almost lost track of the dead bodies they provided the undertaker who was so busy he had to give up gambling. By the time a couple of stage loads of law officials of various stripes arrived from a bit farther northeast, the dust had settled, the evidence was piled in neat stacks in the sheriff's office, and it was time for the judge's gavel to bang out justice like an echo to the recent gunfire.

But Dave and Cliff had not done it all themselves. As they had shown themselves to be willing to fight to the death, more and more of the townspeople had joined in with them, packing guns and on occasion using them.

Even the pastor had gotten into a shootout. In self defense he had shot and wounded Charlie Orson, the hard-case who had hoped to wear the sheriff's badge.

Jim smiled in memory of that. He had seen it happen. The slime-bucket, shot in the arm and weaponless, had begged for mercy. It had been both hilarious and beautiful to Jim to see Pastor Wilfred Looch actually blow smoke off the barrel of his Colt, holster it, and say, "Of course, neighbor. And right now we need to patch up your arm so that, hopefully, you'll be fit to come to church on Sunday."

Even more funny and beautiful was the fact that the man *did* go to church about three Sundays later, willingly, his right arm in a sling and his left handcuffed to the deputy. That was the Sunday the good people of Garner Flats celebrated the winning back of their town from the human devils who had corrupted it.

* * *

The sun was getting hotter now. Cliff, looking at Dave for a moment, said, "What you grinning about, big man?"

Dave, embarrassed that his face had been so readable, said, "Nothin' much…. Aw, well, I may's well tell you. I was jest thinkin' 'bout how Pastor Wilfred plugged Charlie Orson an' then give him an invite t' church."

Cliff chuckled. "Yeh, thet was sure 'nuff one a the funniest damn things any man ever seen or heard."

Sheriff Dave was still looking at Cliff as that young man turned his face to the front and then let his jaw drop. Dave at once jerked his face in that direction—and saw a lone figure running, a good quarter of a mile away, almost at right angles to their own path but slightly toward them.

Both men unconsciously pulled their horses to a stop.

Dave squinted his eyes against the heat waves that somewhat distorted the figure. He said, "Looks like a woman, don't it?"

Cliff's eyes were younger and better. "Looks like a woman, you say?! Can't you see?! It's a woman all right! An' she's as naked as my face!"

"I do believe you're right," said Dave. "Yeah, I kin see her better now. She ain't even wearin' a garter belt."

"You ain't belchin' bull turds!" said Cliff, who, even though he sometimes sang in church, often used colorful language. "Where the hell did she come from?"

"Could be just a mirage," said Dave jokingly, "or, more'n likely, she skittered out from behind that stand a' rock."

"Yeah, that's where she come from all right. She's no mirage." He was encouraging himself and no doubt hoping to have a closer look at her. "She looks like an Indian. I ain't never seen a naked Indian woman before."

Dave said, "You ever see *any* naked woman before?" He was immediately sorry for saying that, for he appreciated the kid's moral upbringing and clean living—except for his bad language—and didn't want to make him feel that there was anything wrong with him.

Cliff started to reply. "Oh, I seen a little bit of—" He didn't finish because at that moment a rider came trotting his horse out from behind the rocky outcropping. But he at once spurred him into a gallop. He was apparently in pursuit of the woman and had now decided to quickly close the gap between him and her. He did not look to be an Indian.

"What the hell you make of that?" said Cliff.

"I dunno," said Dave, "but we're gonna find out. Be ready for trouble." With that he boot-signaled the stallion into a fast start.

Cliff got his own horse excited into a gallop and soon the two bays were kicking up sand side by side as they followed a course intended to converge upon that of the woman.

Dave now noticed two things about the pursuer. He was one of the prison-wagon men, and, because he was so intent on catching the woman, had not yet become aware of the fact that the sheriff and deputy were racing toward him. The sound of his own horse's galloping hooves were blocking out the sound of the other two horses to some extent.

In a few seconds the pursuing rider had caught up to the running woman and at once she went down, hit by the man or possibly bumped by the horse—Dave couldn't tell. The man cranked his horse around savagely, almost upsetting the poor beast, and took a spectacular dive out of his saddle, connecting bodily with the naked woman just as she was attempting to rise. They went down flat and began to wrestle, at the same time hitting at one another, although the woman was doing more clawing than hitting.

Dave and Cliff pulled their horses into a skid, and before they had stopped sliding were already swinging out of their saddles. And Cliff already had a gun in his right hand.

Three quick strides brought Dave close to the fighters. He turned the stride into a kick that caught the man squarely on the side of his head and knocked him off the woman. He rolled over once, got up on one knee, and in the same movement drew his gun. Before he could get it leveled at Dave, the sound of another gun, that of Cliff, shattered the morning air; and the gunman on his knee had his arm whipped back by the force of the bullet striking it. Amazingly, he still kept a grip on his gun.

Cliff yelled, "Drop it or your dead!"

The man decided to obey, slowly loosening his fingers on the weapon and letting it fall to the sand. Blood dripped from his sleeve. The man's face was bloody as well, from a number of scratches that the woman had given him. And he looked frightened.

The woman had gotten into a squatting position. Dave was going to say something comforting to her, then changed his mind and instead drew his gun and pointed it at the bloodied man. Dave said,

"Cliff, I got this here cuss covered now. You talk to the lady. Comfort her and ask her what all this is about."

"Me?" said Cliff.

Dave managed not to smile. "Yeah, *you*, depity. To start with, offer her some water. She's prob'ly needin' a drink right bad."

Dave stepped over to the kneeling man and kicked at the gun; it went skittering over the sand to a safer distance. "When you go fer the canteen," Dave told Cliff, "bring along some a' that cotton rope."

"All right," said Cliff. He was already on his way toward the horses.

"You don't need t' tie me up," said the prisoner. "Look, I'm bleedin' purty bad."

"Yeah, you are," said Dave.

"You sheriffs are right guys," said the kneeling prisoner. "You can sure 'nuff reckon it's appreciated. I need to get a bandage on this bleedin' arm."

Dave said nothing but backed off a couple of steps and positioned himself so that he could see not only his prisoner but also the woman and Cliff. The woman had gotten to her feet now, and remained as apparently calm as though she was having a rather ordinary day. She was truly beautiful, not only because all her physical femininity was revealed, but because of her fine-boned, graceful look from head to foot. Her nudity was bound to have serious shock effect on any man living in that long-skirted, high-collared culture, yet her face remained the highlight. Dave thought it was the most perfect face he had ever seen—high cheekboned, full lipped, and with those lovely dark eyes. He had an overwhelming desire to get closer to those eyes, for at this slight distance he was sure he was not able to appreciate their full beauty; he needed to be about two feet in front of her. She *was* looking at him though. Cliff was now returning from the horses, a canteen in one hand and a little bundle of thin cotton rope in the other.

The woman turned to face toward Cliff. She stood with her arms at her sides, not at all trying to cover herself. The thought flashed through Dave's mind that someday in the near future he would have fun teasing Cliff about how his blushing had made the morning desert look like a sunset. But he was not sure his own face was not contributing.

"Ma'am," said Cliff, "would you like a drink a' water?"

"Thank you, yes, I would," said the Indian woman.

Poor Cliff did not even appear to notice that the lady spoke in perfect English with a sophisticated accent; nor did he hold out the canteen to her, but just stood there motionless; and it occurred to Dave that the lucky rat was doing exactly what he himself wanted to be doing; he was looking into those lovely dark eyes at close range.

But then Cliff came-to long enough to say, "Ma'am...would you like to wear my shirt?"

"That's very kind of you, to offer that. But how about if you let me have a drink of water while you're removing your shirt?"

"Oh...yes, ma'am," said Cliff and held the canteen out to her in a sudden jerk. She took it and drank, and Cliff fumblingly began to unbutton his shirt, which was a well cut but plain-colored brown one, while at the same time letting his eyes move up and down over the woman's delightful body that would soon be covered at his own suggestion.

"You gonna let me bleed t' death?" said the kneeling man. The wound appeared to be on his forearm, for he was squeezing that with his other hand.

"Maybe," said Dave. "Depends."

"'Pends on what?"

"On whether or not you tell me what you an' your buddies is doin' with that wagon and who the man in the wagon really is and what the hell you're doin' with him. An' fer starters you kin tell me what your name is."

After a moment of hesitation, the man replied, "Bill."

"Bullshit!" said Dave, at the same time twisting more directly toward him and kicking him in the jaw. He fell on his side. "What's your name?!" yelled Dave.

"Sam Corely!" answered the man quickly. "Don't kick me no more!"

"All right, Sam. Now I want you t' tell me all about the wagon an' the prisoner. An' be quick about it, or I'll make you look like leftover hamburger meat thrown out to the dogs."

With Dave towering over him like some giant angel of death and destruction, Sam replied, "All right, all right. Jest don't kick me no more. An' git my arm wrapped to stop the bleedin.'"

Dave took a threatening half-step toward him. "You don't start talkin' right quick an' you won't even know yo're bleedin.'"

"All right, all right!.... We got hired by a Mexican name a' Ruizo to go up to Canada and fetch him a red-coated police officer—y'know, one a' them North-West Mounted policemen."

This sounded ridiculous, but Dave asked, "What fer?"

"Wal, it seems the injuns around here has heard these funny rumors about the red-coats—that they ain't quite yoomin, thet each of 'em is like ten men, or maybe a hunert."

There was a brief silence, so Dave said, "Okay, so what?"

"Wal, Geronimo is plannin' on a big uprisin,' or more like a war thet's supposed t' be bigger'n anything ever come before. But he don't want his followers t' be skeered a' these redcoats, 'cause they might not fight if'n they thinks the redcoats ain't yoomin."

"All right, that's enough horse crap!" said Dave. "You start tellin' the truth right now or I'll kick your head off!"

The woman's voice came from fairly close behind Dave. "I think he's telling the truth."

Dave turned enough so he could see her but still keep Sam in his peripheral vision. She was wearing Cliff's brown shirt now, all buttoned up, and it came close to fitting her, but the tails reached almost to her knees. She moved to within four feet of him before coming to a stop, and now Dave's sudden and powerful dream of wanting to see her eyes close-up was fulfilled. He was not disappointed. Those big dark eyes threatened to turn his knees to water; but he regained his presence of mind and said, "Why do you say that?"

"This man—" she poked a hand toward Sam and quickly withdrew it as one might point at a venomous snake that was too close for comfort, "—and his friends ambushed and killed a small party I was with. They kept me alive to abuse me, then put me into the wagon with their prisoner, but he helped me to escape. He really is a member of the North-West Mounted Police in Canada."

Cliff, who was also nearby, his naked upper body as white as milk, exclaimed, "No shit!" Then he began to excuse himself profusely. "I'm sorry ma'am! I'm *so* sorry! That weren't no way to speak in front of a woman! I'm really so damned sor.... Damn!—I said a bad word agin!—and agin! I better jest shet up."

"I accept your apology," said the woman, smiling in spite of her bruises and the terrible experiences she had just come through. "And believe me, I've heard a lot worse." She turned back to Dave and continued, "If the plan is for the police officer to be tested at the war council—and that *must* be the plan—then his life is in great danger. His name is Don Roman—Sergeant Don Roman."

"Don Roman," repeated Dave.

"You know him?" asked Meadow, apparently noticing something in his facial expression and the sound of his voice. "How could you?"

"Oh, no, ma'am," said Dave, feeling like a fool. "Reckon I heard a name somethin' like that sometime." A mental image of the naked, bearded man in the prison caboose flashed back into his mind. The man had pretended to be crazy as a loon, and with that beard...but yes, the eyes, the voice. Now he could make the connection. Then came the question: *Did he recognize me?* That was hard to say; he certainly hadn't shown any sign of it.

Dave then turned his face directly toward the kneeling, cowering Sam. "What does this...Mexican who hired you get out of the deal?" He realized then that he had not been using the lingo when he said that, and thought that this lapse had probably been brought on by hearing the woman's perfect English. He hoped that Cliff hadn't taken notice.

Sam answered the question. "Ruizo's plannin' t' sell lot's a guns to the injuns if the uprisin' happens. He'll bring 'em in from Mexico. The injuns'll pay fer 'em through all the lootin' they'll do once the fracas starts."

Dave let all this soak in for a moment; then the woman said, "Sheriff, my name is Meadow, and I'm a daughter-in-law to Chief Geronimo. My husband and I came back to the Indian way of life only recently. It's true that there's a great war council in session right now. But I know that at present most or all of the other great chiefs are not in favor of Geronimo's plans for war."

"Ma'am," said Dave, "I'm right pleased to meet you, an' I see that yo're a lady. I'm Sheriff Dave Lindner from Garner Flats, near Fort Cummings, an' this here is my good depity, Cliff Fullbright. If it weren't fer his quick and acc'rit shootin, we'd likely none of us be standin' here."

"I'm bleedin' t' death!" whined Sam. "Ain't nobody got a heart?"

"Go git the bandages," said Dave to Cliff. They always carried some basic medical supplies in their saddlebags, for in the clean-up of Garner Flats there had been plenty enough droning bullets to suggest the wisdom of such a precaution.

Then Meadow said something that almost leveled Dave in the sand. This bleeding man was one of the bunch who had tormented the woman and no doubt she assumed, rightly, that he had been sent after her to kill her. Meadow said, "I've had some training and experience in applying bandages. Let me take care of this. He's bleeding badly and really does need attention."

14

After some discussion it was decided that Cliff would start out for Fort Cummings at once, taking Sam with him. Dave would take Meadow and try to find her band, led by Chief Strong-Hand, before that group got all the way to the war council in Yellow Valley.

The message that Cliff would deliver to the new superintendent at the fort was to be carefully worded so that it did not provoke the army into a confrontational panic. Fortunately, Dave's playing the part of an uneducated sheriff had not prevented him from keeping a notebook and pencil in his saddlebags, so he composed the several pages of his message with clarity and yet with a good sprinkling of spelling mistakes and Southwest lingo:

Dear Superintendent Adams:

As you suspectid, we did discover signs of large bodies of Indians on the move and have learnt what that is all about. Lukly we come upon a friendly and peaceful Indian who knows all about it and informd us. There is a large council in seshion right now at which many of the Indians are pursuading Geronimo and others not to start an uprising. The council is being held in Yellow Valley. Inclosd is a page showing land marks which your scouts will be familyure with and anyhow I reckon they know where Yellow Valley is. Now if you trust me at al and I know you do then you will take hede to what I say next. It is very important that you DO NOT come here at this time with a large group of cavilry in a confrontayshonil manner. That would trigger a great uprising. Come only with a small group and a white flag, and with gifts for the Indian chiefs—clothing and flour and other itims of peace. Come and talk peace with Geronimo and the others. I repeet, most of the other chiefs do not want ferther fighting. They will respond to a show of good wil at this time. So please do hede what I say and hopefuly al wil go well. Let the white flag

*be seen at al times threwout the whole trip with your small group of men,
for you may be observd at any point. And let a peace ful wise negosheator
be in charge of the group.*

    Sincerely,
    Sheriff Dave Lindner

Dave did not feel nearly as confident about the matter of most of
the chiefs not wanting war as he indicated in the letter; but he
believed that to give any other impression would be disastrous. He
only hoped the superintendent would take his advice, and that
Meadow was right about many of the chiefs wanting peace.

Knowing that the desert sun would peel the hide off the shirtless
deputy, Dave gave up his denim jacket which had been a comfort to
him during the cool nights. Meadow kept Cliff's shirt to cover her
beautiful body, and Dave supposed that if Cliff ever got it back he
would never wash it.

Because Cliff had no stomach for riding double with Sam, and
Sam had lost too much blood to be walking, it was decided to let him
keep his horse; and Meadow would ride double with Dave as they
started out toward Yellow Valley. For this latter to work, however,
Dave's saddlebags, bedroll, and oats bag had to be fixed in an
awkward position in front of the saddle instead of behind it, thus
allowing Dave to sit behind the saddle and Meadow in it.

The group split up then and headed in their opposite directions.
Cliff had his lariat looped around Sam's waist and was holding the
other end, just in case the wounded man tried to outride his captor.

Dave had his arms loosely around Meadow, simply because he
was holding the reins of his horse; and he thought, jokingly, that it
might also prevent him from falling if he passed out from the sheer
delight of Meadow's proximity.

After Cliff and Sam were out of sight behind a rocky outcropping,
and Dave's big stallion had settled into his smooth walking stride,
Meadow spoke up. "I've suffered much during the last three days.
I'm hoping and praying that you wont take advantage of me because
of your manly feelings toward me."

This shocked Dave a little, but he realized at once that from her
point of view there was reason for her concern. After all, she didn't
know him. He said, "Ma'am, I want you t' be at ease, an' put such a

worrisome thought right outa your mind. I reckon I done some bad things in my life, but forcin' women ain't one of 'em, an' never will be.... But whilst we're on the subject, let's git this here all straight.... I want you t' know that you're the most beautiful an' brave woman I've ever seen, bar none. An if'n I tried t' tell you that you didn't git me all stirred up, I'd be one hell of a liar. But the bottom card here is that I don't hurt women, beautiful nor otherwise. Nor do I try t' seduce widows who have jest lost their husbands and been badly used by the likes of them that done so t' you.... As a sheriff and as a man, my goal is to pertect you an' git you back to your friends where you'll be safe." It was a fairly long and pious sounding speech, and Dave felt a bit foolish.

But Meadow said, "Thank you very much. You're a good man...just like Sergeant Roman. He also treated me like a lady, even though we were...well, you know, we were both naked in the wagon.... It's good to know that there are some men like you and Sergeant Roman." After a pause she added, "Bill was like that too— my husband.... He was always so good to me."

After a few seconds had passed, Dave realized that Meadow was crying, but obviously trying hard to keep it silent. Dave felt that his own heart would break. He concentrated on keeping his voice steady as he said, "You don't have t' hold it in. Go ahead an' cry. You need t' let it out."

And she did, sobbing in his arms as the big stallion strode on through the bright morning. In about a minute she quietened and Dave let her use his neck bandanna to dry her eyes. After that they rode on in near silence for about an hour, with only a brief exchange now and then in regard to landmarks and the progress of their journey.

And then they heard gunshots.

This was immediately followed by the equally harsh sounds of men yelling. The mixed cacophony continued.

All this was straight ahead but could not be seen because it was coming from down in an arroyo that Dave had been hoping would not be too hard to cross. He had brought his horse to a stop at the first shot, and now he hopped off its rump but told Meadow to stay in the saddle. "I'm gonna sneak up fer a look," he said. "If I should get shot, King should be able to outrun any horse they got down there. An' you make sure you git him to stretch out fer all he's got." He turned away and Meadow had to hold the stallion back from following him.

"Be careful," she said.

He gave her a quick smile over his shoulder and carried on, now drawing his revolver.

The shooting continued. It was obviously no small thing. Moving forward in a crouch, Dave came within view of the action, but at this point got down on his chest and snaked along still farther until he had worked his way to the very edge of the arroyo rim where he got between a rock and some tumbleweed.

Below him was bedlam. The arroyo was much wider than he had expected. It was filled with dust and squealing, bucking horses and with yelling men wielding firearms, and with the continuing thunder of gunfire. It took Dave a moment to sort it out; but he soon realized that the riders in the center of the melee were caught in a crossfire from two groups of well armed Indians on foot. It seemed fairly obvious that the ones in the middle had ridden into an ambush while crossing the arroyo. There were plenty of rocky hiding places for the attackers. Their horses, along with women and children, were probably hidden elsewhere.

In spite of the dust and the fast action, Dave quickly made out that the party under attack had a particular look, namely that of Mexicans. However, they did not appear to be a scruffy bunch of outlaws who had slithered across the border to raid small Indian camps. These men, along with their horses, were the fanciest group of riders Dave had ever seen. Their pants were sequined and their saddles were silver mounted. If they were outlaws they were successful ones. Although he couldn't be sure, Dave supposed these were the crew that Sam had told them about — the Mexicans who had hired Sam and the others to kidnap an officer of the North-West Mounted Police, namely Sergeant Roman, and bring him to the big war council as proof that the redcoats were only human.

If anything was totally clear about these men it was that their chance of survival was that of a toad's fart in a tornado. The Indians' crossfire was cutting them down so rapidly that already there were more empty silver saddles than those still covered by velvet pants. There was no good escape route available, for toward one end of the arroyo the two groups of Indians were fairly close together and numerous enough to prevent anyone from getting through; at the other end was a rugged mess of boulders in shale, creating an obstacle course that could not be gotten around quickly.

In spite of the dust and the fast movement, Dave thought he counted a dozen Mexicans, dead and alive. There were at least twice as many Indians—Apaches.

As the clamorous gunfire continued, the count quickly changed to a dozen Mexicans dead and none alive, with a few Indians dead and/or wounded. Even after none of the Mexicans were moving, the Apaches kept firing at their sprawling scattered bodies. But then they eased off and a tall broadshouldered Indian with a polka-dotted bandanna around his head and a belt of silver medallions around his waist, stepped forward and began to speak in his native tongue which Dave could not understand.

Dave carefully retreated out of the Apaches' line of vision, then hurried back to Meadow where she still sat on the bay. Coming to a stop at her side, Dave said, quietly. "There's a party of Indians down there—about two dozen of 'em—an' they jest polished off a dozen Mexicans. Ambushed 'em, I guess. I think the Mexicans might be the group that hired the wagon bunch to kidnap Sergeant Roman. They're all dead."

Meadow looked excited. "The Indians—are they Apaches? Could you see what the leader looks like?"

"Yes, ma'am. They was Apaches all right, and the leader is a tall man with a polka-dot headband and a lotta silver bangles around his waist on a chain."

"That's Strong-Hand! This is my band. This is the band I was trying to reach when I escaped from the wagon!"

"I reckon that's good," said Dave. "I jest hope they simmer down enough to let a sheriff live. They's pretty het up right about now."

"Don't worry," she said. "Strong-Hand is a gentle and good man. And, anyhow, you're with me. Nothing bad will happen to you."

"All the same, ma'am, we gotta make sure things look right—like you're in control. The mood they're in right now, wal, I reckon if'n they thought you was my captive they'd shoot me afore I had a chanct t' blow my nose."

"All right," she said, "I'll ride and you walk. And, by the way, how about if you quit calling me may-am and call me Meadow instead."

"Fine, Meadow Instead. Now let's start toward the arroyo, slowly."

"I'll show myself first. They might think you're a Mexican."

"You don't look enough like an Indian," said Dave. "Here, tie my bandanna around your head." He quickly removed it from his neck.

She took it and in a moment had fixed it across her forehead and knotted it at the back of her head. He walked beside the horse as they started toward the edge of the arroyo. She said, "Are you a full blooded Indian or part white?"

"Full blooded," said Dave.

"You're not an Apache."

"No, ma'am—I mean, Meadow.... I hope t' tell you more about that sometime. Right now how's about we think about the business at hand. Some a' your friends is likely to pop up over the edge of that arroyo any second, an' I'm tryin' to git ready to meet my Maker."

They were both silent after this as they moved on and soon arrived at the decline's edge. They were there for some time, looking down at the scene below, Meadow still on the horse, before any of the Indians saw them. For the most part they were busy looting the Mexicans. No doubt it was the biggest haul they had ever made—silver saddles, fancy clothes, beautiful gun rigs, and money. A few of them were tending their own wounded which appeared to number only four. Two braves were dead.

"Oh!" exclaimed Meadow, suddenly.

"What is it?" asked Dave, quietly.

"One of the braves that was killed is Strong-Hand's son, Jumping-Horse."

It seemed that Strong-Hand had just discovered this himself. He knelt beside the body of his son for a moment, then rose, and, after a few seconds of standing straight and tall, spun about and walked in among the dead horses and dead Mexicans. He came to a stop beside one fancy corpse—a rather small one—and kicked a moccasined foot at his head, connecting solidly with the unfeeling block of flesh and bone. Then Strong-Hand pulled aside his breechclout and peed on the body.

Dave said, just above a whisper, "I know you say he's a good and gentle man, but I suggest we git outa sight fer a bit till he simmers down some."

"Too late," said Meadow. "We've just been seen."

Several braves, then more and more, began looking and pointing up at them. Dave raised his hands to show that they were empty of weapons, and Meadow waved at them. Strong-Hand had seen them too now, and silence fell over the arroyo. Then Meadow called out something in Apache, and in a moment Strong-Hand called back.

"He recognizes me," she informed Dave. He wants me to dismount and come down. You are to stay up here with your hands raised…. Don't worry. Once I'm down there I'll explain everything and then you'll be okay." She dismounted. "Can I drop the reins of your horse, or do you need to hold him."

"Drop them."

She did so and started down the incline. In places this was so steep that she had to use hands as well as feet. It was the shortest way down, but Dave's scanning eyes quickly found a place where he could bring his horse down, if that would be allowed. He continued to stand there with his hands raised to his shoulders. The stallion whinnied nervously, smelling blood.

Meadow arrived at the bottom and approached Strong-Hand. Dave could not hear their voices but they talked for half a minute. Then Meadow turned, looked up, waved, and called out, "You can come down now, but leave your horse."

This suited Dave fine. The stallion was trained not to stray when his reins were hanging to the ground, and going on foot would allow a quicker descent. Dave looked forward to finding out definitely that these Apaches were not about to scalp him. So far it was looking good. He made the descent quickly and stood beside Meadow, facing Strong-Hand.

Dave then had a conversation with Strong-Hand—who apparently couldn't speak a word of English—by having Meadow interpret for both. Dave was assured that he was in no danger, and was thanked for having saved Meadow's life. Not everything that passed between Strong-Hand and Meadow was translated for Dave, but he was satisfied with what he did learn:

Strong-Hand's band had come across the bodies of the party that Meadow had been with when Sam and the other wagon-men had attacked. The band took the bodies with them and carried on, heading toward the war council. One of their point-riders spotted the Mexicans. Assuming that these had killed Meadow's husband and the others, Strong-Hand had planned and executed the ambush which was totally successful except for one thing: The Mexicans were innocent of that particular crime; although in an indirect way they were probably just as responsible for the murders and the rape of Meadow as were Sam and his bunch, having hired them for no good purpose and so brought them on the scene. Dave tried to explain this to Strong-Hand, emphasizing that in any case getting rid of the Mexicans had worked out for the best. He wasn't sure it all got through. Strong-Hand seemed happy with the day's work but very unhappy about the death of his son.

Dave then suggested that they start out for the war council in Yellow Valley, hoping to ride in there with Strong-Hand's band for protection. It seemed the only way he might have a hope of rescuing Roman. But this didn't work out. Strong-Hand wasn't about to go anywhere until he had organized a big ceremony in honor of his dead son. The women, children, and horses had been left about a mile to the north, and Strong-Hand lost no time in sending a brave there with word of what had happened and to let the women know that they were to begin preparing for the ceremony. Then the brave and some of the older boys were to return here with the horses so that the warriors and their loot, and the bodies of the two dead braves, could be transported back to that camp in an honorable way.

Strong-Hand seemed a bit upset about Meadow's insistence on herself and Dave starting out at once toward the war-council meeting, but he allowed it. No doubt it helped that she was daughter-in-law to the mighty Geronimo. He even went so far as to give Meadow a horse complete with saddle. Most of the Apaches rode bareback, but a few, including Strong-Hand, had snaffled onto some pretty nice stock saddles, probably during raids decades ago. Strong-Hand gave his own saddle to Meadow, but it was not a sacrifice, for he replaced it with one of the showiest of the Mexicans' silver mounted outfits.

And so it wasn't long before Dave and Meadow were once more on their way, with Meadow now mounted on a slim white gelding that seemed like a desert horse-ghost. He drifted along as quietly and smoothly as one, paying no attention to the snortings, sniffings, and nickerings of the big stallion—who was apparently quite disappointed that Meadow had not been given a mare.

Meadow also had been given moccasins—off the feet of one of the boys who returned with the band's horses—and some strings of beads for her neck and waist. But she still wore Cliff's brown shirt, which Dave thought looked pretty much as good as any of the doeskin shirts the other squaws had been wearing and was probably cooler. The beads and moccasins had been given to Meadow because Strong-Hand would not have a member of his band—and particularly the daughter-in-law of Geronimo—go to the war council, and to Geronimo, looking poor.

Meadow was confident that she knew the landmarks of the area well enough to lead them to Yellow Valley, and Dave had no choice but to trust that she did and could.

As the two rode along in silence, Dave began to wonder about the crazy mission they were on. In the first place, how did one rescue a lone police officer from a zillion Indians? Secondly, if that attempt was somehow successful, surely the sergeant would recognize him. Would Don Roman know that Jim Longfeather was a fugitive who had murdered a bounty hunter? There was a good chance that the sergeant had already been kidnapped before all that had come out. But if Jim somehow rescued Roman now, letting him go back to Canada, he would then learn the truth—and it would be known that Jim was in the Southwest and had taken on talking like an uneducated cowpoke. He would have to give up being Sheriff Dave Lindner, give himself a new name and get moving, probably to some big eastern city. One good thing, if this happened, was that Cliff was very capable of taking over the sheriff's office. He had proven his capability as a lawman time and again.

A sadness descended on Jim-Dave. This happened whenever he thought about the mess he had gotten himself into. He hated being a fugitive. And he felt this even more strongly since meeting Meadow. Here was the woman of his dreams—a beautiful full-blooded Indian who was also educated and refined. She was brave, caring and gentle. She could fight like a wildcat—he had seen that—and then she could gently and caringly bandage the wound of the enemy who had just been trying to kill her.

Meadow was also a grieving widow, but in time that wound might heal...and if he waited long enough.... But he was a fugitive from justice. How could he burden her with that? He couldn't; and so he was sad as he rode along so close to the most wonderful creature in the universe.

He longed to get to Yellow Valley and whatever danger awaited there, because that would take his mind off his predicament. How far did they still have to go? He wondered if they would get there before sunset.

15

No one bothered Sergeant Don Roman as he walked about the great Indian war-council camp that morning in his brilliant red tunic with the sun flashing off its brass buttons and off his high boots that had not lost their glowing polish, having been packed away. He was being given complete freedom, or so it seemed. But everyone took a definite interested notice of him. The looks directed at him held mixtures of fear, respect, admiration, and wonder.

He was hoping to run into Geronimo or some of the other English speaking chiefs so that he could tell them that he was in a hurry to get the show started (if he was going to go through with this, he might as well start displaying bravado right now), but he had made a big circle and was almost back to his teepee before he had a chance to do anything along this line. A broad shouldered Apache, all decked out in beaded ceremonial trappings and face paint, approached Don and in halting English informed him to the effect that his presence was desired in the big tent where the great chiefs were awaiting his arrival.

When Don got there and stepped inside, he saw that not only the great chiefs were there squatting in a semi-circle in the center of the place as they had been yesterday—with the exception of Geronimo who was absent—but there were many other Indians present as well. These others were busily at work preparing the place. Don couldn't at once catch on to details of what most of them were doing, but at the moment two of them were opening a large hole in the hide roof. He supposed that they had somehow climbed up from the outside. He noticed that the hole was positioned toward the south side, toward the sun, and extended as well down into the south-side wall.

While he was still looking up, Don was approached from one side by Geronimo. "Great red-coated-warrior-from-the-North," he addressed, "we are making ready for your first test. I want you here to see what will happen and will tell you if you do not know."

"Tell me," said Don, "I do not know."

"The first test is not mine but from Chief Standing-Smoke, one hunderd mile to north. He say that all man who would be call warrior should do sun dance. For many Indian braves this is first test to be called man. You must be test this way too—your first test."

Don knew what the sun dance was, for it was practiced yearly by the Blackfoot nation of the Canadian Northwest. It was a harsh initiation into manhood that every young male of those tribes had to undergo if he wished to be counted among the full-fledged braves of his band. Now Don watched the high sun dance pole being raised in the center of the lodge. As it came completely vertical it dropped into its hole; then dirt was packed around it to render it solid. To someone who didn't know its purpose, the high pole might have looked innocent enough; but Don knew exactly what it was for. He became aware that a batch of grasshoppers had just hatched out in his stomach.

He turned more directly toward Geronimo. "I know what a sun dance is. Where I come from we don't do it because it's much too easy. It's good for baby boys, maybe, but too easy for a grown man. We don't bother with it."

Geronimo's wide mouth attempted a smile, but because the corners of his thin lips had been so well trained to curve downward, all he could manage was a straight line. "You must do sun dance. It is only first test."

"Well, then we might as well get it over with, but it's a waste of time," said Don. "When do we start?"

"At noon," said Geronimo, and he looked up toward the high ceiling. Don did likewise. The roof now had a ten-foot wide opening in it so that the top of the sun dance pole was silhouetted against the pale blue of the morning sky. "At noon," repeated Geronimo, "when the sun shine down on you." He turned away and strode toward the other chiefs.

Don left the lodge and went back to his teepee. It was cooler inside, but he tied open the door-hole flap so he could catch some breeze and also so that he could see the progress of the sun. It seemed perverse in its insistence on continuously moving higher into the sky. He waited.

The desire to attempt an escape came back strongly, but there was something yet stronger inside of him that kept him from giving in to this natural urge. About an hour before noon a meal was brought to him. He still had a steady stomach and was able to eat it all.

Then, just before the sun reached its highest point, a group of elaborately dressed warriors came to summon him to his first challenge—the sun dance.

He was escorted into the lodge which was now filled with Indians squatting all about, facing toward the high pole in the center. These were the privileged ones who rated a ringside seat; but the common masses had not been forgotten, for the bottom six feet of hides had been removed from the framework of the lodge so that the crowd standing all about the huge tent would also be able to watch the first testing of the mighty redcoat from the land of the snows.

Around the pole in the middle of the tent was a fairly large open space where no one sat except three aged braves with tom-toms, and just beside them squatted an equally old fourth person whom Don took to be a medicine man or shaman. His outstanding feature was his nose which was like the beak of a large bird of prey. It hooked out smooth and shiny, contrasting sharply with the rest of his face which was crisscrossed with a billion wrinkles. His eyes were two small black marks that stared straight ahead intently, never moving and seldom blinking. He wore a headdress of feathers, painted sticks, and other eye-catching things not easily identified. The rest of him, except for a breechcloth, was covered only with various hues of paint— which did not particularly beautify his withered old frame. At his side was a rectangular piece of cloth on which was laid out his medicine paraphernalia. The noon sun brightly illuminated a large central part of the tent—and heated it.

Geronimo and the other big chiefs sat on hides at the very edge of the open space, with a bit of elbow room being kept free around them to show respect. Don was brought before them.

Geronimo looked up from his squatting position. "Are you ready for first test?"

"I'm ready."

"You know what you must do in sun dance?"

"Yeah."

Now Geronimo, still squatting, made a considerably long speech in his native tongue. He spoke in a loud voice, and as his talk continued it seemed to Don that the atmosphere of the tent became more somber and intense than it had been before. Then Geronimo was finished and the whole place remained hushed. Now the Apache chieftain spoke to Don again. "We will start now. Take off red coat. Make chest naked."

Don removed his hat, gun rig, coat, and shirt, dropping it all on the ground as he did so. Stripped to the waist now, he stood tall and straight, waiting for the next order. He knew what it would be.

"Go to medicine man," said Geronimo. "Kneel at him."

So Don knelt before the old shaman. *Here it comes,* he thought, and braced himself as he saw the wrinkled, hook-nosed man reach for a long-bladed knife.

Don had thought that it might be a good idea to try to keep a smile on his face all through the ordeal, but when he actually saw the long ceremonial knife coming toward him he wisely decided not to attempt the near impossible. If he should start out smiling and then be forced to grimace in pain a little later, this would be worse than if he hadn't smiled at all. So he settled for a poker face and braced himself.

The medicine man ran the knife into Don's left pectoral and made a vertical cut. Blood flowed freely over the sergeant's abdomen and onto his pants, but he was not aware of this or of anything else beside the waves of intense pain that spread out in angry circles through the flesh surrounding the open gash. Then the pain was less sharp as the waves seemed to go into ebb tide and Don began to feel other things again, like the warm blood soaking the underwear between his legs. But in a moment everything was crowded out of his mind once more as the medicine man made the second cut. This one was parallel to the first and about an inch away from it. Now the witchdoctor worked the tip of the blade under the flesh so that the two cuts were connected. He thrust one finger through this passage and with his other hand reached for a piece of lace leather. He pulled one end of it through the hole, then tied it securely. Next, he picked up his knife again and coolly went to work on Don's right pectoral muscle, rendering the same set of parallel gashes with a connecting tunnel underneath. Into this he tied the other end of the slim strip of leather. With both ends of it now tied into the flesh of Don's chest, the middle part hung down a little lower than his waist.

The medicine man got to his feet. Don knew that he was expected to do likewise. He wasn't at all sure he could do so steadily, so he waited a few seconds to collect inner strength. Then, from somewhere surprisingly close, he heard Byron's cheerful voice saying:

"See, Geronimo—see how the sweat pours from him…as it would from any young brave. He's only an ordinary man."

Don had been starting to feel quite sorry for himself during the work on his chest, but now the words of Byron served to switch both of his adrenal glands to high speed and they pumped a great surge of enraged energy to every part of his body including his vocal cords. These latter would have given out nothing more than a half-hearted croak a moment before, but now they vibrated strong and clear in a loud laugh that was almost happy sounding. "I always sweat when I'm having a good time," said Don as he faced Byron who turned out to be sitting not far from where the honored chieftains sat.

Don had his adrenal energy well under control. He said no more but stood up with perfect steadiness and faced the medicine man who now fastened a much longer strip of leather to that tied into Don's chest muscles. The far end of this long cord was already fastened to the top of the high pole.

The medicine man stepped out of the way. Don knew what was expected of him next. The moment the three old braves began to beat their tom-toms, he must fling himself backward and then begin to dance around the pole, leaning back and jerking his weight against the leather thong in an attempt to break free. To pass this test and so become a brave, it was always required that the young Indian continued to dance until the flesh of his chest gave out so that he was free of the leather. How soon this happened depended a great deal on how much effort was put into it, but also on how deep the cuts had been made and on the strength of the flesh. Sometimes it took hours. Don knew that in some cases when it took very long, the leather strip was removed from the top of the pole and tied to a horse instead. Someone would ride the horse, dragging the would-be brave behind in an effort to cut through the flesh and bring the thing to an end. Don couldn't help but wonder if he would need this and hoped not.

The three tom-toms simultaneously began their rhythmic black sound. Don gritted his teeth and threw himself backward.

As the leather thong jerked taut, his chest seemed to be struck by white-hot fire. He could feel his muscles lift from his rib cage, threatening to tear loose in many places. He almost blacked out, but in spite of this no sound escaped his lips. His subconscious mind, having been told over and over by his surface mind that there must be no cries of pain, was now doing its part by keeping his voice disengaged even though he was in a half faint. And he did not straighten up to relieve the pressure of the pull; that, he knew, would have been as bad as screaming. But he hung back on the thong without putting his full weight into it for a few seconds while his mind cleared; then he began to circle the pole, jerking against the leathers tied into his chest as he did so. Each time he made an effort to tear loose the pain was ghastly. And yet he had to keep trying. This was the sun dance.

Don prayed that the flesh of his chest would tear.

He had no way of calculating the passage of time—not even by that blazing sky-furnace called the sun, for as he moved in a circle about the pole, the sun also seemed to move in a circle. After some time he was no longer sure about what was stationary and what was not, or, for that matter, which was up and which was down. It didn't help that his head was often hanging over to the back. But he did know that he had to keep on jerking against the leather line, for the more he tormented himself the sooner his suffering would be over. It is wonderful that not once did he think about the fact that after the sun dance was over there would be other torments ready and waiting for him. Some merciful mechanism kept his mind from remembering that this was only the first test.

He kept his eyes closed a good deal of the time, but when they were open they took in a dizzying, kaleidoscopic, moving panorama that was like something out of a nightmare. As he continued to circle, and at those times when he let his head hang back, he saw upside down dark faces and feathers; and the glaring sun; and more faces, surrounded by many copies of the sun; and the brightest sun again; and Byron's upside down face with a red sun at his chin; and three upside down tom-tom beaters working furiously at creating that ugly rhythmic sound within a furnace of the ever increasing number of sun-copies; and the white sun again, this time split in two by the top of the pole; and the upside down, wrinkled, hawk-nosed face of the medicine man, his toothless mouth now open as though he was sucking in all the ugly energy of the place to give him new magical strength. No, it wasn't that. The open mouth was where that horrible wailing sound was coming from, sometimes almost drowning out the drums.

The muscular flesh of Don's chest held fast. He realized with sudden clarity that he would soon pass into unconsciousness; or worse, he would simply not be able to continue his dance around the pole. He would sag forward and lean against the pole so that the terrible pull would be taken from his chest. Maybe Indians could sun dance for hours; he could not. Or had hours passed since his torment had begun? He didn't think so. Well, maybe he had done his best. If he failed and the Indians went to war it wouldn't really be his fault. He had done his best—yes, he had. God didn't expect him to do the impossible. He slowed in his circling movement and straightened up somewhat to ease the awful tension of the thong.

Once more Don heard Byron's happy voice above the drumbeat: "He's givin' in now…. See, he's givin' up."

Again an extra large shot of adrenaline spurted into Don's blood stream. But instead of falling back, he continued to move forward, further releasing the pressure of the leather. Dead ahead of him he could see a long smiling face under a cowboy hat, staring at him through a pile of glowing red suns—Byron's face. And to Don it had suddenly become a target. He moved past the pole toward this target until he could go no farther because of the thong, which was now pulling at him over his shoulder and tightening up and beginning to pull him over backward. But he lashed out with his leg, and the toe of his boot caught Byron squarely under the chin, knocking him over backward into the lap of the Indian who sat behind him.

Don backed up enough to catch his balance so that the pressure was released from his chest. But he knew by the way that his surroundings were undulating and spinning that he would not be able to remain standing for more than a few seconds. Gritting his teeth, he flung himself backward all the way to the place where he had been before he went after Byron. The leather snapped tight and he felt and heard the flesh of his right breast rip. The left side gave somewhat too, but still held enough to keep him dangling, twisted sideways now. He straightened up a little, fell back hard, and the next moment was rolling free in blood and dust close beside the three old men with the tom-toms. They stopped beating and the whole place was intensely quiet.

Don was still conscious. He wanted to get up but knew that this was impossible so he didn't try. He lay there motionless in the strange dead silence of the crowded lodge and waited patiently for a little strength to come back to him.

Geronimo was looking at him squarely; then Don became aware that the expression on the old chief's face held more than a little of respect and wonder. Don glanced briefly at some of the other faces, and read much the same there. Then he willed strength into his limbs and rose to one knee.

"You have done well," said Geronimo. "You have suffered bravely in the sun dance just as have many Indian warriors…. But you are the first to kill your enemy at the same time."

Don glanced about and quickly saw Byron lying motionless on his side, his head back too far.

Sergeant Roman got to his feet. He knew he had passed this test, but it needed a finishing touch. He was a grim sight as he stood there with his legs wide apart, black locks of hair hanging over his ears, his chest an ugly mess of blood and torn muscle.

He tipped back his head and laughed a mighty full throated laugh that almost shook the hides on the lodge roof and, in a sense, *did* shake up the Indians who squatted underneath.

Again there was silence; then, after a long moment, Geronimo began to speak in his native tongue and this was followed by one of the other chiefs who had something to say. Geronimo spoke again, then a few others took their turns. Some of the braves got up and left the lodge. All this while Don remained standing motionless.

Finally Geronimo looked straight at him and said in English, "You have done good here, warrior…. Go to your teepee and rest."

Rest? Don could hardly believe his ears. He was very grateful but did his best not to show it. He walked forward past the chieftains, making his way among the other squatting Indians along a path that seemed to have been cleared for him.

Behind him now, Geronimo's voice came again. "To get to your teepee you must go through between brave warriors who will try to kill you. You must try to run fast."

So this was the catch. Don came to a stop and looked up ahead. Outside the lodge were two long parallel rows of braves—the rows leading away from the ceremonial tent. Every man of them had a weapon of one kind or another in either hand. Don understood that he was expected to run along between the two rows—which were only about four feet apart—and try to get through to the other end without being clubbed or knifed to death. He took note that the parallel rows of warriors began about twenty feet away from the tent, and he began to wonder if he might be able to slip away to the side; however, he also saw that there was a lance-armed guard standing one to either side to discourage him from attempting such a detour.

As Sergeant Roman continued to stand there, he was so tired he doubted he could lift his feet. Every added second of motionlessness did two things: It allowed a bit more strength to return to his muscles, and it made him look cowardly. He knew he could not hesitate much longer without losing face. In the meantime he made an inward effort to prepare himself to run for his life through this gauntlet of warriors; but the situation had all the earmarks of a run toward death.

16

What good would it do to try? It almost seemed to Don that this taunting question was being whispered in his ear, but he knew that it came from somewhere in his own mind—perhaps from a cowardly part. Yet it seemed like straight-out suicide to rush forward into that corridor made up of savage warriors who had been given instructions to do their best to kill him before he got to the other end. There were at least twenty men in each of the two rows. Most of them held a long-bladed knife in one hand and a heavy club in the other. A few had stone-headed weapons, some blunt, some sharp. What chance did he have of getting past even the first pair of braves? And if he got by those through some strange fluke of fortune, what hope did he have of getting past the next, and the next, sets of beating, slashing arms? Geronimo had made it clear that this was no ordinary running of the gauntlet where a severe beating was the worst that could happen. These men had been given instructions to kill him.

But if he refused to run they would kill him anyway. He was reasonably sure of that. Either way it was death, and the council would go ahead with plans for the great war. In the face of this second test, Roman's sun dance victory of a moment ago had turned to ashes. This rankled the policeman even though the cold fear of death had come upon him, for he had much enjoyed those fleeting seconds of painful triumph when the expressions on the faces of the Indians had given him hope that he could pull this thing off after all—that one man with a wild, fantastic legend behind the uniform he wore could single-handedly hold off the greatest Indian uprising ever conceived. It had been a good feeling and he hated to give it up.

The Indians—chieftains, general public, and the gauntlet—waited quietly as Roman continued to stand where he was.

Don looked around, then back at the gauntlet. Each face he happened to look at directly held a mixture of curiosity, anticipation, maybe even fear...and in some distinctly a cruel hope to see him suffer, or maybe a hope to see him beg for mercy. *Blast them!* Thought Roman. *I won't lie down for them! I'll run their bloody gauntlet! And I'll get through to the other end!*

Coming to life with a suddenness that startled everyone, Roman charged to the right, not at the gauntlet as they expected, but at one of the lance-armed sentries who stood by himself a few feet away from the two rows of men. Roman was upon him in a half-second, striking against him with his shoulder and all his weight, at the same time getting a solid grip on the lance. The brave hit the ground on his backside as Roman wrenched the spear out of his hands. Holding it in both hands, Don spun to face the gauntlet and immediately ran at the men with all the speed he could muster. As he ran he quickly changed his grip on the spear, now holding it in front of him like a quarter-staff or the handle of a push cart, so that the ends stuck out on either side of him.

The element of surprise played its part; the warriors in the gauntlet had little time to make up their minds about how to deal with this new situation. Don raised the lance to shoulder height as he lunged in between the first two men in the row. The long knife of the one on the right grazed his side at the same instant that both ends of the spear made solid contact. The warrior on Don's right was struck on the head, the one to the left received the force of the shaft on his shoulder. Both men went down with Don and the spear on top of them, pinning them to the ground.

The Indians next in line had been thrown backward, stumbling into the ones behind them so that many were off balance to some extent. The blade of the long knife that had grazed Don's side was caught in the dirt and the handle was slipping out of the stunned Indian's hand. In a second Don had the knife in his own hand and in another second he had plunged the blade between the ribs of its owner. The other man caught under the spear fought his way upward and this levering action of the spear's shaft forced Don backward off the man he had just killed. He was in a squatting position as the other Indian threw off the spear completely and lunged down on him with an upraised knife blade just as long as the bloody one that Roman held in his hand. Don straightened out his knees and his knife arm at the same time, saw and felt the jolt as his weapon struck muscle, glanced past bone, and came to a cushioned stop deep in the man's chest. Roman drew back on the knife, and what had been his attacker fell to the ground spurting blood, with his own unused knife still in a raised position above his head. As he squirmed about in his death agony, Don took the weapon from him. Now, holding a long blade in each hand, Don took a slow, deliberate step toward the other Indians in the lineup. They were disorganized, and as this bloody monster with a knife in each hand came slowly toward them, a fear of the supernatural fell over them. They had expected him to run the gauntlet with great speed; instead, he had already killed two of them before hardly getting started.

Now he was approaching them slowly and deliberately. He walked straight except for his head which was thrust forward somewhat. His eyes were bloodshot. His face was as expressionless as that of a dead man. Each hand held a knife at hip level with the long blades pointing down. He moved toward them relentlessly, without a trace of hesitation.

The first pair of Indians next in line fell back a bit, stepping on the toes of the ones behind them. Both lines, already out of shape, now became even more broken up. Then, as the monster from the northern stars came ever nearer, the Indians in both lines moved well back to either side so that the passage between the two scraggly rows was a good ten feet wide in most places. These warriors could have been rallied back into action by a few shouted commands from the chieftains, but the chieftains sat watching in silence; they would not interfere with this contest to see whose medicine was the greater — that of the warriors or that of this legendary being from the north. Silence hung over the scene as heavily as the heat of the day.

As Don slowly walked in between the two rows of braves, he suddenly felt very weak and thought he might fall. From the time he had attacked the sentry and had taken the spear from him, he had felt no pain in his chest and no physical discomfort of any kind. His mind had been completely taken up by the action. Not so now. He had to force every step, and his legs seemed to weigh at least a hundred pounds apiece.

He was well in between the two lines of men now. They stood quietly, their weapons lowered. But then Roman heard a barely audible sound behind him—a moccasin in the sand, along with a nervous breath. Don turned part way and jabbed his knife out blindly behind him in a quick, straight stab that used up the last of his fighting strength. Out of the corner of his eye he could see his victim shudder and begin to buckle; but he was still on his feet as Roman, with very mechanical looking motions, withdrew his knife and continued to walk, unwittingly giving the impression that he did not consider that anything worth thinking about had happened just then. Behind him he heard his victim drop heavily to the ground, then claw about in the sandy soil in his death throes.

The grotesque walk continued. Roman's steps were so stiff and unnatural looking that they did much to add to the grizzly effect he was creating in the minds of his watchers. They did not know that a quick breeze could have blown him over at this point, nor that as he walked he was saying to himself: *Now my right foot. Now my left. Now my right foot. Now my left.*

He got to the end of the two lines of men and continued on, not looking back, not moving any part of his upper body, but going on at the same speed, like a stone statue with stiffly moving legs. *Now my right foot. Now my left.* Only when he had made it about halfway to his teepee did he begin to hear the sound of low-talking voices among the large groups of those standing in and around the ceremonial tent.

At the flap door of his teepee he got down on his hands and knees to crawl inside but almost didn't make it. The world began to spin around his head. His chest dropped down so low that a few loose ends of it came close to dragging in the dirt. He hauled himself forward once more and managed to get far enough into the teepee so that by curling up he could draw his feet all the way inside. The door flap fell shut. And so did every sensory doorway that had connected his mind to the world around him.

* * *

When he woke up he was on his back. In the dimness of the teepee his blurred vision could make out a dark shape hovering above him. He blinked a few times, commanded his eyes to focus. It was a

185

woman bending over him—a fairly big one, in buckskin and with her hair in braids that dangled forward onto his own chest. Roman decided at once that her face was beautiful and knew the main reason for this was the gentleness it held.

He next noticed that his chest was bandaged. There was a strong, not unpleasant smell in the teepee. He guessed that the woman had treated his wounds with some kind of medicinal plants and had probably bandaged these healing ingredients in place. There was no pain in his chest, nor anywhere else for that matter, but he expected that would change when he tried to move. So he did try a little of that, moving his arms and legs a bit. The pain was minimal, but he felt so stiff and weak that he doubted he could rise to his feet. For the time being there was no point in trying.

The woman put a water bag to his lips and held it for him while he drank. He hadn't realized how dehydrated he was until he felt that cool liquid soaking into his throat. "Thanks," he said when he had finished. She did not reply except with a smile. He doubted that she understood a word of English.

Roman's mind was clear and he wondered why this kindness was being allowed him. Could it be that his testing was over and that he was now being treated as an honored hero? He didn't really think so. The two tests he had successfully come through would hardly be enough to satisfy Geronimo and the others. Still, it was a happy possibility.

He wondered how long he had been sleeping. It was a question that he didn't attempt to answer even with a wild guess. The kind woman was still looking down at him, smiling slightly; but then her expression changed to one of annoyance and apprehension as voices sounded just outside the teepee. The words were in an Indian tongue but Don could tell by their intonation that they were words of command and possibly constituted a threat of some kind. The woman moved away from Don, lifted the flap and poked her head out. When she spoke there was little respect in the sound of her voice. She closed the flap and came back to Don.

The voices outside grew sharper and more demanding. Don pushed himself up into a sitting position. The movement came easier than he had expected and he was about to progress up to his knees when the flap opened and an Apache brave entered. Another one followed close behind. They stood silently for a moment, leaning forward a bit because of the slanting teepee walls, looking down at Don and the woman. One of the braves was the one who had summoned Don to the first of the testing. The two took turns speaking to the woman now, but in a somewhat quieter manner. The firmness was there however, in their voices and faces. It was plain to Don that they were ordering her to leave. And she was ordering *them* to leave. Just outside the teepee were more voices.

Don got to his feet. The two braves stood aside as he moved toward the door flap. He knew that they had come for him and that the kind squaw was trying to protect him; so the sooner he left the better it would be for her.

He stooped through the exit. Outside, Roman found himself facing Geronimo and four of the other big chiefs. From the earlier introductions he remembered one of them as Cochise. The next thing that Don noticed was that the sun was low in the west. If this was still the same day then he had, at the least, slept several hours.

Geronimo was standing there very straight with his arms folded in classic cigar-store Indian fashion, but with his steer-horn cap making him look more like a Viking than an Indian. He spoke. "Are you ready for your next test?"

"I'm ready," said Roman.

"You must come with us." Geronimo turned and walked away. The other chiefs and Don followed. While he walked, Don did a seemingly insane thing. He removed the bandage from his chest and threw it to the ground. The chiefs who saw this showed no reaction, but Don knew that the effect was not lost on them.

The wounds on his chest were lightly crusted. Any little exertion was sure to break them open again. The bandages would have helped considerably, but Don could not imagine a super-being from the stars wrapped up in bandages, and he was pretty sure the Indians couldn't either. Blood, yes; bandages, no.

Don was aware that much strength had returned to him. He felt rotten, but, considering the ordeal he had come through, he was doing well. As they continued toward the center of the camp where the ceremonial tent was, the stiffness began to ease in the joints of his legs. He would have liked to work his arms a little in order to loosen them up as well, but this would not have helped to make the desirable impression. He wondered what his next ordeal would be.

Geronimo surprised Don by leading him past the ceremonial tent rather than into it. On the other side of it the same great mob of Indians who had watched Roman do the sun dance and run the gauntlet were now waiting eagerly for the next act. They were squatting and standing around a fairly large open space in the center of which was a bonfire and a six-foot-high stake. This pole was not for the purpose of sun dancing. Don was reasonably sure, without anyone telling him, that he would be tied to this post and that he would be tortured. But what the torture would actually consist of he didn't know and didn't at all try to imagine. He tried instead to keep his mind blank.

They were about to tie him to the stake when abruptly there seemed to be some disagreement among the chiefs. Don tried to look uninterested in everything while a discussion went on. All sixteen of the big chiefs had their say. Don couldn't understand any of the words, but some of the sign language being used had a bit of meaning for him. That didn't matter though, because when the little impromptu meeting was over, Geronimo turned to Roman and told him plainly what it was all about.

"Chief Victorio say you have already prove to us that you are no coward," began Geronimo, "so there is no use for the test at torture pole. Most other chiefs say same. I say same. We take you to next test. Come." He turned and led the way again with Cochise walking beside him. Roman, surrounded by the other chiefs, followed. And the great crowd followed behind them.

So he had been spared one brand of agony. Don couldn't help feeling relieved even though he was fairly sure that something even more horrible awaited him somewhere just ahead. Now that he wouldn't be tortured at the stake he could allow himself to contemplate what they might have done to him. He supposed they would have further tormented and mutilated him with steel, stone, and fire.

The long procession led by the chiefs and Roman finally reached the edge of the camp. The chieftains came to a halt. To one side grazed a large number of horses, some hobbled, some completely free. They were enjoying what was possibly, by the look of it, the best grass in all of this southwestern desert.

Immediately in front of the chiefs was a large pile of sandy dirt beside a hole in the ground — a pit, its opening about ten feet square; and when Roman was brought up close to the edge of it he saw that it was at least twelve feet deep. Some of the sandy walls were already showing signs of cave-in, but basically the pit was intact. Those were not the only observations Don made as he looked down into that dim excavation. He needed every bit of his will power to keep from stepping back away from the edge.

Geronimo said, "They are not very big, but they are death."

"I know what one of them is," said Don, "— a rattler. But what are the other two? We don't have anything like that in the North."

Geronimo seemed pleased. "You know what rattler is — that is good. I will tell you what are other two." He pointed down into the pit and Don's eyes followed the line of his finger. Geronimo said, "That is a scorpion. He is call the black scorpion and death is in his tail." He then pointed at the remaining member of the ugly little trio. It was a heavy looking lizard, about two feet long, and Don remembered that he had seen one just like it through the window of the caboose. He had wondered then if it was dangerous; now Geronimo set him totally straight on that. "Like rattler, the death is in his fangs. White man call him *Gila monster*." He turned his back on the pit and faced Don squarely. "You must go down into the pit and try to kill them...without any weapon. They will fight you — hard, for they are afraid and have no place to hide. They maybe attack you all three at same time. If you come alive from this hole in ground you are more than just a man."

An Apache brave wearing the top half of a cavalry uniform over his breechcloth came forward and drove a short stake into the ground near the edge of the pit. He tied one end of a rope to it and dropped the other end over the side. In the meantime the spectators — men, women, and children — continued to crowd in on all sides, closer and closer. There was some apprehension on the part of the chiefs that someone other than Roman might end up in the pit, so they hastily set up a circle of husky braves to hold the crowd back a safe distance.

"Climb down the rope," ordered Geronimo.

Don hesitated only a second before he moved toward the rope. But then he stopped and once more looked down at what awaited him below.

Roman shivered in the heat. It would have been hard to decide which of the three critters was the ugliest. The black scorpion, over six inches long, with four many-jointed legs on each side and two crab-like pincers in the front, sat perfectly still with its tail arched over its back. Don could make out the deadly little barb at the end of the tail. About a yard away from the scorpion, the two-foot-long Gila monster looked up at Don with nervous blinking eyes. Its hide seemed to be an intricate pattern of black and yellow beads. It kept moving its head from side to side with a quick limber motion. *The death is in his fangs*, Geronimo had said. The rattlesnake was coiled. It too was alert. It was a big one; Don estimated its length at six feet, which he knew was just about as big as rattlers come. Both its head and rattle were up, the head bobbing a little, the rattle giving out its heart chilling warning every few seconds.

Don's mind was working hard, casting about desperately for a means of dealing with this triple threat. At the same time he was wondering if he could even force himself to climb down there among those nervous, frightened, deadly creatures as his tormentors required of him. But Roman had already come through two tests as a super-being in the eyes of the red men and he didn't want things to start changing now. He continued to study the three critters closely.

"Climb down the rope," ordered Geronimo for a second time.

Of the three critters, Don realized, the rattler was the only one he knew anything about—knew roughly what kind of action to expect from him. Therefore the other two were possibly more dangerous to him.

"Are you afraid?" asked Geronimo. Silence had come over the crowd again so that the rattling sound from the pit was plainly audible.

"No," answered Don. This was, of course, an outright lie.

"Climb down the rope."

"I don't need the rope," said Don. He took a step forward and jumped into the pit.

But he jumped carefully, aiming one boot at the head of the Gila monster and the other at the tail of the scorpion. And he leaned backward as he fell, for he didn't want to fall forward in the direction of the snake, which was coiled farther toward the other side. He felt the squish under each boot as he hit bottom. His legs buckled under the stunning jolt of the twelve-foot drop. The rattler uncoiled and sprang at him in a movement too quick for the eye to follow. Don fell back against the wall of the pit. Stumbling about, he got his feet under him more solidly and managed to keep from falling to the pit's dirt floor. He stood twisted toward the wall for a moment but then turned back quickly to face the danger. His first glance showed him that the scorpion was not dead, but badly mangled on one side. The Gila monster, however, was a mashed potato. Don had missed the head but had connected with the back area squarely. He noticed these things during the seconds of time that passed while his eyes swept around looking for the rattler. Where was the bloody snake? He quickly looked down at his feet and at the same time felt a whipping around his legs. The snake was there, all six feet of him, now coiling and uncoiling. Don jumped back, bumping against the wall, and found that one end of the snake was fastened to the toe of his left boot. The fangs were sunk into the hard leather, and possibly through it, but hadn't reached his toes. Don quickly stepped on the snake with his other foot, making sure that he connected right behind the head, and squashed that part to a complete pulp. He wiggled the ugly creature around a little with his feet so that the fangs came loose from the toe of his boot. Then he stepped on the head. Leaving the snake twitching around rather violently for a dead thing, Don went over to the injured scorpion and put it out of its misery by carefully crushing it under his heel. He took another glance at the smashed lizard and at the rattler which was still bouncing around but more slowly now. Then Don took hold of the rope and began to climb out of the pit.

He saw the sixteen chieftains and a few privileged braves looking down at him and at the mess he had made of their mighty scourges of the desert. The increasingly familiar expression of awe and wonder was strong on the faces of all of them. Don knew he had won another powerful victory—or almost won it, for there was still a chance that he might spoil everything by losing his hold on the rope and falling back to the floor of the pit. That would certainly obliterate the effect he had created thus far. Ordinarily the climb would have been child's play, but at present he had little strength left in his limbs. He knew now that the time of rest and sleep had not been enough to bring back his full muscle tonicity or anything near it. And blood was once more oozing out of this chest wounds. His legs felt numb from the shock of the twelve-foot drop but there was enough strength left in them so that they could do their part in the climb by walking up the side of the pit while his arms pulled the weight of his body hand over hand up the rope. It was his arms and chest muscles that threatened to give out. By the time his head reached the top of the pit he was soaking in sweat. The pain in his chest was intense now. He hung back motionless with his arms stretched out straight in order to rest the biceps. He dared not stay that way for more than a few seconds for fear his muscles would stiffen. The chieftains stood looking down at him like a lifeless circle of grim statues. Don began to contract his biceps with all the will and strength left in him, and found himself moving upward very slowly. His shoulders were above the top of the pit now. The stake that the rope was tied to was only about a foot away from him. He chanced taking his left hand off the rope, lost only a few inches as a result; then, with a quick and heroic effort, he managed to get the crook of his elbow around the stake. He knew he had made it. He let go of the rope altogether now and, after resting for a moment, changed from biceps to triceps as he pushed down on the ground and so brought himself up out of the pit entirely. He would have liked to crawl a few feet away from the edge before attempting to get to his feet, but knew this wouldn't look good. He stood up.

Geronimo was right there in front of him, looking him squarely in the eye. He spoke the same words he had used immediately after the sun dance. "You have done good here, warrior." He was silent for a few seconds, then said, "Your next test will be to fight our most strong young warrior. He is one of braves in this camp who have no fear of you. He have no fear of anything. He have kill many men. You will fight him till him or you will die. If you are what stories say you are, you will kill him quick. You are tired and bloody. He is not tired, not hurt. But you will kill him very quick if you are what stories say you are. He is a mighty warrior. His name is Face-over-Fire…. You must fight him now, and one of you will die."

Later Don could not understand, at least not completely, why he had replied to Geronimo as he did: "One man is too easy for me to fight. Bring me Face-over-Fire and two others of your best fighters and I'll fight all three of them at the same time."

Geronimo took a few seconds to digest this and said, "I will talk to other chiefs." He immediately began to do so in Apache or whatever it was, and each of the others formally took his turn to answer; but because the replies were short the whole thing did not take more than a minute or two. Geronimo turned back to Roman. "You will fight three men—the best and most fearless braves we find in camp."

Don hoped desperately that the searching process would take a good long time so that he'd have a chance to recoup some of his strength. He was led back to the torture stake and the bonfire where the crowd once more gathered around; but they were made to leave a large area open for the action of the fight.

Don's hopes for a rest were then dashed, for things moved forward quickly, and Don found himself facing three of the biggest, toughest, and meanest looking men he had ever laid eyes on.

The tallest of them stood between the other two. He wore only a headband, a breechcloth, and knee-high moccasins. His revealed muscles were not impressive in bulk but they were well defined, much like those of Roman, only the brave's were more stringy and hard looking. Most of his face was grotesquely disfigured with burn scars; so Don knew this was Face-over-Fire, the man who feared nothing—not even a super being from the northern stars.

His two comrades looked about as fearless, and their unscarred faces were able to show more maliciousness. Their eyes seemed to glow with the evil hope that they would soon see pain inflicted. These men too, like Face-over-Fire, were stripped down for battle. All three had unbraided shoulder-length hair held in place by brow bands in the Apache tradition, and the outer two had war paint on their faces. Don wondered if war paint was painful to Face-over-Fire, or if he realized that his scares were considerably more intimidating than paint. All three held stone-headed war clubs in their hands.

Another brave came into the large cleared circle and handed the same kind of weapon to Don, then left. The club had a good stout handle about a foot and a half long with a smooth rock fitted into the split end of it and held there securely by many bands of shrunken rawhide. Don wielded it experimentally to get the feel of it. He watched Fire-Face closely and saw the brave's eyes narrow slightly.

What was the man feeling? Did he truly have no fear?—or was it all bluff?

Don himself was very much afraid, and he had good reason to be. In fact, he felt strongly that this time he had come to the end of his rope. He was exhausted and bleeding, sick. He had come through three grueling tests of wit, might, and endurance that had left him with the strength of a child. Why had he said that he wanted to fight three men instead of one? Although he couldn't quite understand what had prompted him to ask for that, he knew that the most obvious part of his motivation had been to carry on with the impression he needed to create—that he was more than human and that the redcoats in numbers would be impossible to defeat. It had been a sort of crazy, all-or-nothing decision. Logically he was no match for Face-over-Fire alone, so why not throw in two more and hope for a miracle? Anyhow, it was too late to backtrack now. His goose was cooked and well done. He had bluffed his way through the men in the gauntlet, but he knew he would not bluff these; for they had been hand picked for their fearlessness.

Geronimo had seated himself, but now he stood up from among the squatting chiefs near one side of the open space. The encircling crowd of onlookers—some squatting, some standing—all looked toward the great chief. Most of their faces carried the stoical near-expressionless looks that their culture had bred into them; yet there was a somewhat morbid expectancy and impatience escaping from many eyes.

"Begin to fight now," said Geronimo.

17

The three Apaches moved toward Don. Face-over-Fire came in a straight line; the other two spread to the sides in a flanking movement. Don stood still waiting for them, and he had no plan for defense. He was already so beaten physically from all he had been through that it required considerable concentration just to stay on his feet. In a moment the three Apaches had formed a triangle with Roman in the center of it. Then they closed in, not fast but not slowly either, brandishing their war clubs.

Suddenly Geronimo yelled something in a loud voice. At first Don supposed it was a command for the warriors to speed their attack, but when the three quickly returned to their places and stood in a line as they had before they began their advance, he realized that it was just the opposite. The chief had called them off.

Working their way through the great crowd of Indians were four braves with two people in tow. Don blinked his bloodshot eyes. One of the two was Meadow. The other was the big sheriff who looked so much like Jim Longfeather and who had stopped Byron and his men on the trail to inspect the contents of the caboose. Meadow seemed to be fine and was no longer naked. She was unfettered, but the sheriff appeared to have his hands tied behind his back.

The man and woman were brought before the chiefs. Geronimo was the only one of those standing rather than squatting. He looked coldly at the sheriff for a moment but spoke to his daughter-in-law first. Don could not understand what he said to Meadow, nor what the beautiful woman replied, but both seemed calm and under control.

Don was very happy at the moment, partly because his massacre had been temporarily interrupted, but also because Meadow was alive and apparently well. He had not had time to think about her lately; however, now that she stood there it all came back to him and his relief at seeing her alive was so great it startled him. It took him a moment to figure out that she was wearing a man's shirt, brown in color, with tails long enough to cover her thighs; and she had colorful beads at her waist and neck. The shirt almost fit her shoulders, so it could not be an extra one the sheriff had pulled from his saddlebags; it had to have belonged to the little deputy who was apparently not with this party.

Don could not get over how much the sheriff looked like Jim Longfeather. Could there be two men with the same face, the same towering height, and the same wide-shouldered muscular frame? His holster was empty, but they had let him keep the sheriff's star pinned to his shirt.

These observations about the sheriff were not what mainly occupied Don's mind. He was wondering if this appearance of the lawman could somehow benefit the overall situation and, particularly, the situation of his own imminent doom. Then he knew there was a way that might help, but it would be putting the sheriff's life in grave danger. That was unfortunate, yet Don felt it had to be done—not just for himself but for the good of all.

"Geronimo!" addressed Roman.

The chief turned to face him. "What do you want?"

"I'm very happy to see that you've captured a lawman of the United States of America," began Roman. "See the star on his chest? As you know, the star means that he stands for the law in all this land except for the far North, just as my red coat, that I usually wear, stands for the law in the far North. Your people tremble at the sight of my red coat because of the stories they've heard about the might of the red-coated warriors of the North. They do well to tremble, for the stories are true—as I have already begun to show you by my mighty deeds. But listen well to what I have to say to you now. I say that there is strong medicine here in the South that you do not know of. You have fought the long-swords, the riders in blue, and sometimes you have won. But should your great uprising go forth, all the lawmen who wear the golden metal sign on their shirts would be gathered together and come against you. Then you would find that the men of the golden star—and there are thousands of them—are just as powerful as I am. Their medicine is just as strong. The men of the golden star can do even more wonders than can the men of the red coat."

He paused a moment to study the faces of all the chieftains, for he thought that a few of them besides Geronimo could probably understand some English. Then he looked at the sheriff. It was plain that the giant had taken in every word with interest and perception. Don felt fairly sure that Meadow would have told him about the war council situation. The only thing he would probably not be clear on was that Don was being tested as a sample of the white-man's strength in the North.

Don turned his eyes back to Geronimo. "You have been testing me to find out if the men of the red coat are as mighty as in the stories you have been told. You want me now to fight with these three Apache warriors. I will be happy to do so...but I wish to prove to you now that the strength of the golden-star men, here in the South, is just as mighty as that of the redcoats in the far North....... Bring three more or your mightiest braves into the circle, and bring this lawman of your own south country here to my side. And the two of us together will fight your six brave warriors...and we will beat them.... What is your answer to what I say, Geronimo?"

Geronimo stood there without motion and with his normal poker face unchanged. The sheriff, however, now looked a bit surprised; yet Don felt confident, strangely enough and for no distinct reason, that the big man would be willing to go along with the proposal.

Geronimo then replied that he would speak to the other chiefs about the matter, which he did, and the new bill was quickly passed. The spectator crowd had followed this discussion by their leaders and an almost imperceptible, yet definite, ripple of interest passed over them as they grasped the new shot of excitement that had been injected into the day's entertainment.

The sheriff's bonds were cut and he was handed a war club. He left his hat with Meadow who was still standing there looking frightened; then he moved into the human clearing.

As the big sheriff walked toward Roman, he ran a large hand through his straight black hair, as though to make sure it would be well out of his eyes. "Howdy," he said to Don. "You know how t' git into all kinds a' fun, don't you?"

"Yeah," said Don, "but it wasn't exactly my idea."

They stood facing each other now. Don, who was no dwarf at just a touch over six feet and used to looking down at people rather than up, felt suddenly miniaturized. In the same way, the war club in the sheriff's hand looked small. He was also studying Roman. He said, "I've always wanted t' meet a jenwine member of the North-West Mounted Police. But I'm a mite disappointed. I heard that they kept themselves groomed slick as a wet pumpkin."

When Don thought of how he must look to the sheriff—blood crusted chest, wildly unkempt hair, a beard stubble of at least twenty-four hours, black and blue marks, dirt and sweat, sick-eyed, haggard—he let himself laugh a little, even though the exertion threatened to tip him over. "Do I look worse or better than when you saw me in the caboose?"

"A hell of a lot worse."

Geronimo spoke to Don and the sheriff from the edge of the clearing where he now stood beside Meadow. "We must find three more of our best fighters. You rest while we find them." He stepped closer to the other chieftains.

"I reckon you look like you could *use* a rest," said the sheriff to Don. "Here, let's park our butts on the ground."

"Yeah," said Roman as he sat down at once. The sandy soil was hot, but this was better than standing. The sheriff also sat down. Don continued in a low voice that was not likely to carry to the nearest Indians, although they probably couldn't understand English anyhow. "I hope it takes them longer to find these extra fighters than it did to find the first three.... Apart from my big mouth, how did you get into this mess, Sheriff, and how come you were with Meadow?"

"When me an' Depity Fullbright stopped the wagon we was pretty well taken in by them bastards. A' 'course you did your level best t' help 'em. I know you did it to pertect us, an' I'll admit if you hadn't made out t' be crazier'n a shit-rollin' bug high on whiskey, Fullbright an' me prob'ly would've ended up gittin' our asses shot off. Wal, we fell fer it, but after we rode off I began t' have me some doubts."

Dave Lindner carried on, in colorful language, telling his story of how he and the deputy had changed horses at the stage station and turned back to follow the wagon. He told about how they had come across Meadow fleeing from Sam and had rescued her, giving deputy Fullbright the greatest part of the glory, praising his remarkable shooting ability. Lindner carried on about how Sam, after a bit of persuasion, had spilled everything, and how Meadow had verified that the prisoner in the wagon was indeed a member of the North-West Mounted.

Don put in, "She's a wonderful woman."

"Yeah," agreed Dave, and for some reason looked sad about that. "I reckon she likes you a lot. Truth is she said she did. Reckon you treated her like the lady she is."

"Yeah, she's a lady."

After a further moment of looking sad, Dave continued, "Wal, we put Sam on his horse, after Meadow had bandaged his arm, an' I give Cliff a written message to deliver to Inspector Adams at the fort."

"That sounds like your first bad move," said Don. "What we don't need right now is the cavalry riding in here. I can see that from your point of view it seemed like the right thing to do, but I wish you hadn't. If anything could set off a war right now, the cavalry coming here would be it."

"Wal, I thought a' that too, an' made it as plain as I could in the letter that this here is a very touchy business. If they got the brains of a runt flea they'll walk easy. An' the new inspector, Adams, is smarter an' more peaceable than most. I recommended he send out a small group carryin' a white flag, and t' come with a mind t' talk peace."

"Think he'll do that?"

"Don't know. Hope so. I know one thing though—they won't git here in time to save our necks."

"They wouldn't be able to even if they got here right now."

"Damn true.... After that I took Meadow on my horse an' we started out to come over here. She had been wantin' to rejoin her band under Chief Strong-Hand, but she hadn't been able t' find 'em. Then we comes across 'em just as they're finishin' off a bunch a' fancy Mexicans."

"Ruizo's bunch. That's the outfit that hired Byron to kidnap me and bring me out here."

"That's what we figured. Wal, Strong-Hand's band massacred the lot of 'em. He thought they was the ones that had killed off the small group that Meadow was in. I tried to explain the way it really was, but also told him that his mistake didn't make much difference. Meadow and me both wanted t' git here to the war council as quick as possible, t' try t' git you outa the silly mess you're in, but Strong-Hand didn't seem t' give an owl's hoot about that. Really I think he didn't much like the idee of bringin' a sheriff to what was supposed t' be a secret war-council meetin.' Can't say as I blame him. He's agin the war hisself, an' bringin' a lawman along to the meetin' would be goin' a step too many fer his own good. Besides, he was heartbroken about his son just havin' been killed in the fight with the Mexicans and didn't figure on goin' nowhere till they had finished with a big ceremonial dance in his honor right there on the battleground. But he give Meadow a horse and we started out right away t' git here. It was as much her doin' as mine. She was dead set on tryin' t' save your hide. I had some hope in the fact that she's the daughter-in-law of Geronimo, but I also knew that she and her husband had been more or less kicked outa this camp, 'cause a' Geronimo's son's strong talk agin the war. Anyhow, we come. I jest rode right up to the sentries an' Meadow talked to 'em. They tied my hands and brought us in.... I don't have any idee how t' git you outa this mess you're in, an' that you now got me in too, but 'cordin' to that little speech you made, it seems you haven't been doin' too bad in savin' the country from Indian war. But all I kin say is if these red men think you look anything like a mighty hee-ro from the moon, or whatever the hell you're supposed t' be, then they must be pretty easy satisfied. The way you look right now...I think a five year old boy could whip you."

"Probably could," admitted Don, "but this rest has helped some."

"I been doin' a whole lot a' chin flappin,'" said the sheriff as he once more stroked back his hair. It was an almost feminine gesture and looked ridiculous performed by this buffalo bull of a man. "But I figured it was only right I should entertain you—you bein' a visitor from Canada an' both of us not havin' long t' live."

"Don't talk like that," said Roman. "We have to win this fight. I've come through three hard tests already and won out in every one of them. This could be the last one. If we can win this fight outnumbered three to one...well, it might be the finishing touch on what I've done by myself so far."

Sheriff Lindner looked at the ground, apparently thinking humbly about what Don had just said. All around a quiet hubbub of conversation from the natives continued. But then came louder voices—an altercation of some kind, it seemed—but this quickly faded back into the general drone. Don wondered if those louder voices had involved disagreements about the choosing of the extra three fighters. Lindner looked up again. "Wal, I kin handle them three standin' there by myself without raisin' a sweat," said the giant, and, crazy as it sounded, Don believed him. The sheriff continued, "But I don't know about three more besides them. I beat ten white men once, in a saloon brawl, but they was drunk. But six bloody Apaches trained to kill from the time they was old enough to stand up and piss...I dunno. But I'll give 'em somethin' to remember anyhow.... Yeah, I expect I'll kill most of 'em."

"Now, look here," said Don, "I dragged you into this mostly because I knew there was no chance of me handling three of them by myself and I could see by looking at you that you're the kind of creature from the stars that I'm supposed to be. But let's not discard me altogether, eh? I may not look it, but there's still some fight left in me. And, anyhow, I wouldn't want to spoil the reputation I've built up for myself."

"I see what you mean," said the sheriff. "It wouldn't be good if I got lucky an' finished off all six of 'em with one sweep of my tommyhawk an' left you standin' there lookin' like a schoolgirl. All right, I'll let you have a share in the fightin.'"

The sad look came back to the sheriff's ruggedly handsome face. After a long moment, he looked squarely at Don and said, "Let's stop fer a bit with all the brave talk t' git us primed up t' fight. We kin start in on that agin right quick. But jest fer now let's admit we got as much chance of gittin' outa this alive as a mosquito has of pokin' a elaphint." He turned silent for a bit.

It seemed to Don that the big man had more to say, so he didn't reply.

In a moment, the sheriff continued, "I got somethin' on my mind—been thinkin' about it a lot lately, an I reckon I don't wanna keep it to myself or go on livin' the way I been...whether I live or die here today. I jest ain't cut out fer it.... An you're the right man fer me to tell this to."

"Go ahead," said Don.

The sheriff looked at him a moment longer, then asked, "Don't you really know who I am?"

It took Don a few seconds to get his thoughts together after that, but then he said, "When I first saw you at the wagon I thought you looked exactly like Jim Longfeather, but then I thought, how could *that* be?—so I gave up the idea. I guess I was right though."

"Yeah, you was right."

"But you don't talk like Jim. You talk like you grew up in the middle of longhorns and coyotes and never got close to a book."

Jim smiled. "You said, 'you talk like you grew up.' That's poor grammar. You should have said, 'You talk *as though* you....'"

"Thanks for the lesson," said Don. "Now tell me this in good English. What the hell are you running away from?"

"Don't you know?"

"No, I don't."

"Well, what I've been running away from is the gist of what I want to tell you about. I'll try doing it in good English, but forgive me if I slip back into range lingo here and there. I reckon it ain't that easy t' switch back.... So...I guess you must have been kidnapped before word got out about what I done—I mean, what I did."

"I guess so. What did you do?"

"I heard that Chuck Scote had gone after the dead-or-alive reward money being offered for bringing in my blood brother, John Pinetree. I expected Scote to try a cold-blooded ambush, and I knew I had to warn Pinetree. That's all I wanted to do—just warn him. But when I found him, the shooting had already started. I got involved. It came to a shoot-out between Scote and myself...and I won."

Don thought about this. "Not exactly a cold-blooded murder then."

"No, but a murder all the same," said Longfeather. "Scote was within the law in what he was doing. I interfered and ended up killing him. There was another man helping Pinetree at the time, and he knew what I had done. I'll never say who that other man was, but when he began getting a loose tongue about the matter, I saw the gallows looming and headed south.... But I can't live like this. Being a sheriff suits me fine, but being a fugitive doesn't. If we should somehow get out of this alive, I want to go back to Canada and give myself up. If we're both alive, you can bring me in.... So...from this moment on, I'm your prisoner."

"Jim...I would gladly let you go."

"Well, you shouldn't. It's your duty to bring me in. I greatly respect the law. And you should too. After all, you're a member of the North-West Mounted Police!" Jim was raising his voice a bit and Don now did the same.

"You're a good man who got into a tight corner! It's not right that your life should be wasted!"

"I'm a murderer and a fugitive and I'm sick an' tired a' lyin' t' people an' makin' out I'm somebody I ain't!"

By now the surrounding crowd was taking notice of what had become a quarrel of sorts between the man from the northern stars and the sheriff.

"All right, all right!" said Don. "If we get outa this alive, I'll take you back to Canada and stuff you into a jail cell. Only promise me you'll quit talking like a bowlegged, foulmouthed bronc rider!"

"Fine!—only give me a little fartin' time t' git over it!"

"Fine!"

At this point the chiefs returned with the extra three warriors. This second trio was as tough looking as the first. Stripped down for action and with more war paint than the first three, they looked seasoned, confident, and vicious. Don supposed that they, like the first three, had been picked for this fray not only because of their strength and fighting prowess but also because they were fearless—or at least they lived by a code that did not allow them to show fear.

The six chosen braves now stood together on one side of the circular clearing, but Roman and Longfeather continued to sit on the ground near the torture stake and the low-burning fire. They had quickly agreed that by refusing to stand up till the very last moment, they would give an impression of being entirely unconcerned about this trivial matter of fighting six Apaches.

But then Geronimo gave the order. "Start to fight now."

Don and Jim got to their feet slowly, seemingly without care; but actually both were very alert, watching for a sudden rush from their enemies.

It came.

Face-over-Fire yelled a screeching battle cry, which was taken up with great gusto by the other five, as all of them together ran in converging lines toward Roman and Longfeather. Those two split up and ran in opposite directions—strictly on impulse, without any planned strategy other than to run fast and live a few seconds longer. It worked out even better than that, because just for a moment it left the Apaches in a neat bundle that made a target too big for Don to miss when he suddenly decided it might be a good idea to throw his war club at them. Aiming toward the center of the mass, he wound up with the stone-headed club for as hard a throw as he could muster. At the last moment before release the weapon slipped in his hand and went higher than he had intended. There was an ugly cracking sound as its stone end connected with a head and one of the heftiest of the warriors dropped like a sack of mud.

Of the five left, four came after Don. The remaining one—truly a brave man—headed a lonely path toward the towering bulk of the sheriff.

Don ran. The sight of those four painted Apaches coming at him with uplifted war clubs was enough to momentarily drive everything out of his mind except the desire for escape and survival. But his legs were stiff and tired and he didn't go far. All four got to him at the same time. Hard stone ground past his ear, crushed into his left shoulder; he went down and felt one set of heavy moccasins on his back. The Apache inside of them stumbled over Don and fell on his face. Don's left arm was completely paralyzed but he was only vaguely aware of this. He scrambled to his haunches and sprang at the downed Indian, landing on him. But that man turned over more quickly than a flopping fish, upsetting Don and gaining the upper position.

As they struggled, and as the other three warriors who were after Don moved in to try to get at him, Don caught sight of something grotesque coming toward them from farther away. At first glance he didn't know what it was, but then he grasped that it was the sheriff holding an Apache above his head. The next moment that same Apache came hurtling toward the men bent over Don. It was a good strike. Of the three braves who were on their feet and hit by this human weapon, two were knocked flatly to the ground while the third stumbled back awkwardly but managed to keep his feet under him. The fourth one was still on top of Don, for the flying Apache had passed over both of them.

Now Don struggled with all his strength to get out from under his opponent. He needn't have worried. The sheriff was there in a few steps and, with a boot the size of a corral corner post, kicked the

Apache off of Don. If the Indian had received the blow on his head it would likely have killed him, but instead it was his shoulder that took the damage. As he rolled to the ground, Don realized that the man had become more of an even match for him, for now each of them had only one good arm. The Indian's limb was dangling, completely broken close to the shoulder. Don saw something else. The Indian that the sheriff had used for a discus was lying there completely motionless with his skull split open. Without really taking time to think about it, Don understood that this man had been dead before the sheriff had picked him up to throw him. It was the sheriff's war club that had caved in the skull of that brave warrior who had dared to face the giant alone.

The giant, having picked up two war clubs—one of them Don's—so that he brandished one in either hand, moved past Don and closed with the three braves who had been hit by the dead Indian but were now all on their feet. They had not lost hold of their war clubs, nor of their courage; they moved in on the giant without a moment's hesitation.

Don got one foot under him and made a dive for the brave with the broken arm, just as that person was beginning to do the same for him. They collided and Don pinned the brave down for a second; then, because the brave was strong and put more than enough effort into dislodging Don, they began to roll over and over with one broken arm and one paralyzed one flailing about uselessly from out of the human bundle.

The sheriff met his three opponents with magnificent confidence—perhaps too much. He struck at the center one but the warrior sidestepped the blow with an ease that indicated he had practiced that evasive move many times. Because the sheriff hit empty air, he was off balance now. The brave to his right made quick use of the opportunity by swinging a war club into his side to further throw him in the direction he was already stumbling. The sheriff staggered against the man on his left, knocking him off balance also. That Indian managed to stay on his feet however, and the sheriff went down alone—onto his knees. He still held a club in each hand. The three braves came in for the kill.

Don and his immediate antagonist continued to roll—toward the bonfire. This had been prepared earlier to be used for some method of torture at the stake before it had been decided to bypass that step; and now the flames had shrunk to embers and hot ashes. Every spectator watching this part of the action just then couldn't help but wonder whose naked back would first be pressed into the dimly glowing embers—Don's or the brave's. Only a short, rapidly decreasing space separated the fighters from the fire as they continued to roll, man over man, toward it.

The kneeling sheriff had crossed both his war clubs above his head so they became a shield, and, as his opponents began to swing down on him, he straightened his great legs and stood up. The down-coming clubs did not have time to gather full momentum, but two of them struck the crossed clubs and the arms that held them with enough force to stun the sheriff and to break up his improvised shield, yet he made it back up into a standing posture. One of his clubs fell to the ground. He managed to hang on to the other one by the very tip of its wooden handle. He started to run forward between two of the Indians before they could raise their clubs again, but one of them grabbed a hold of him and hung on.

Don and his opponent rolled onto the still smoldering bonfire and the brave's bare back ground down onto the live embers. In spite of his training and fearlessness, he let out a nerve-jangling scream. The roll continued, but Don's back came down on the other side of the fire. His good arm, however, had been badly seared along with the Indian's back. Don felt the brave go limp on top of him.

The sheriff made another lunge forward and the warrior who had grabbed him was left standing there with the biggest part of a tattered shirt in his hands. The sheriff ran, zigzagged around a bit—because he thought the three were after him—and came to a stop close to where Roman was throwing the limp Indian off his chest. That brave had passed out completely from the pain and frightful shock to his nervous system. But the three remaining Indians were not chasing the sheriff. They had stayed where they were in order to catch their breath for a few seconds and to get a better hold on themselves before they made their next move.

One had dropped his war club; he picked it up. The three glanced at one another, and the tallest one, Face-over-Fire, grunted a few words of instruction or encouragement, or maybe he was cursing.

Then the three of them advanced, slowly this time and with a great air of determination.

Don was on his feet now and stepping to the side of the sheriff. In the open space, more or less between them and the three advancing braves, sprawled the unconscious Indian that Don had just thrown off himself, the dead one whose skull the sheriff had cracked with his war club, and the one that Don had knocked down at the very start of the fight by throwing his club.

The three remaining braves, with the disfigured Face-over-Fire in the center and somewhat to the fore, advanced steadfastly.

Don was sick with fatigue. His whole body cried out to just let go and drop. His nervous system was ready to snap. He realized that he had no weapon in his hand, saw a club lying not too far away, but didn't have the strength to run and scoop it up.

The sheriff's voice, low and calm, said, "Let's retreat slowly."

They did so, walking backward side by side.

The sheriff spoke again. "I see you ain't got no hammer. Here, take this one." He handed his war club to Don.

"Better keep it," said Don. "You can do more with it than I can."

"No, take it," insisted the sheriff. "I'm gonna git me a bigger club."

Don took the stone-headed weapon from him then and continued to walk backward. But the sheriff turned to one side and grabbed a hold of the six-foot-high torture stake. Roman realized the importance of keeping his eyes on the advancing braves, but he could not help but look at the sheriff just then. Shirtless now, except for a shred of sleeve that hung from one wrist, the sheriff flexed unbelievably huge muscles against the post. It didn't break, but the force against it was causing it to lean. The sheriff pushed it the other way, then quickly began to wiggle it. At the same time he constantly kept his eyes on the braves. They had momentarily stopped in their tracks, but then Fire-Face said a few words to the others, and Don was sure it was an order for the three to renew their advance—only now it would not be slow.

As Don saw their legs bend slightly at the knees and their powerful leg muscles bunch up in preparation for a united forward spring at the sheriff, Don already knew what he had to do. He threw both hands above his head, one brandishing the war club, and yelled at the top of his voice:

"YAH YAH, YAH-YAH-YAH-YAH...YAH!"

It worked better than he had hoped. The Apaches suddenly considered Don to be more of an immediate threat than the sheriff and so changed the direction of their charge. All three of them came rushing toward Roman. He turned to run, tripped over his own feet and fell. As he got to his knees, expecting his skull to be bashed in momentarily, he heard the most terrible, nerve-rasping sound that had come to his ears in a lifetime. He realized at once that it was coming from the sheriff. The giant was using Don's idea of distracting the braves from their course of action by making threatening vocal noises. But what noise! He had pulled the post out of the ground and was getting a better grip on it. While he did this, his vocal cords issued a sound that would have done credit to any eight-hundred-pound bull-gorilla in the darkest of Africa. It was that kind of a sound: a great quavering scream, ear-stunning, nerve shocking, frightening—and apparently totally unrehearsed.

The three Indians came to a stop between Don and the sheriff. They stared unbelievingly at the monster who had made this sound—a battle cry that no Apache in his most fervent hour of heated slaughter could ever hope to duplicate—and they saw the now eight-foot-long torture stake being raised above the monster's head. But then the sheriff seemed to change his plan and brought the pole down to waist level and held it in front of him in the manner of a quarter-staff, but an oversized one. The three Indians were muttering to one another, probably exchanging ideas of how to best deal with the situation.

Continuing to wield his mammoth club at waist level, with both biceps flexed out strikingly and his chest muscles looking like two big slabs of metal, Jim moved toward the three Apaches. These had lost the stern determination that had marked their advance of a moment ago. They jockeyed about, shifting their positions as though to confuse the sheriff, but they were certainly also doing it in order to try to stay out of his reach a little longer.

Don, still on his feet but almost completely done in, got behind the sheriff's back where he looked and felt for all the world like a boy hiding behind his father in the face of danger. For the moment he had forgotten entirely about the super-being impression he had been trying so hard to make on the Indians. The sheriff threw the post up in the air and caught it again, causing all three of the Indians to step back in unison. Now the sheriff was once more gripping the pole in the manner of a club—one that few men could have wielded, for its business end extended a good six feet upward from where he gripped it.

Don stood limply and watched as the sheriff suddenly charged forward swinging the long, heavy post. Flailing it back and forth, wielding it like an average man would wield a stick, he bore down on the three braves. These, still grouped fairly close together, should have scattered; but their code of battle did not permit them to run outright in such a fight to the death.

The sheriff came in close and swung the post in a wide, high arc toward all three of the warriors, as though he intended to knock off the heads of all of them at once. The Indian first in line broke away to one side. It was the reasonable thing to do, but he should have ducked at the same time. The swinging post rattled against his skull, dropped him in his tracks, and carried on with the same sweep to glance more lightly off the head of Face-over-Fire. That man staggered but held his balance. The swing of the post had now lost its drive and for a moment its end swept the ground. The third Apache tried to get in close and found the sheriff's boot in his crotch. He sagged back against Fire-Face who was just beginning to get straightened out. Both Indians fell and Fire-Face struck his head on his own war club. The other one was halfway back up when the sheriff lowered the post onto his head in a way that stretched him out on the ground with a look of finality.

This was not the case with Fire-Face who was still conscious—or at least he was getting back to his feet, and he was even picking up his war club at the same time. But his eyes had a far away look in them. The sheriff was about to bat him, but then changed his mind and stepped back, and continued to retreat until he got alongside of Don. Fire-Face followed, walking fairly straight but with a groggy look showing through his facial scars.

Between heavy breathing, the sheriff spoke to Don in a low voice. "Takin' life pretty easy, ain't you?—lettin' me do all the work."

"You didn't seem to need any help just now," said Don, "and, anyhow, I wouldn't dare come within twenty feet when you're swingin' that fly swatter."

Fire-Face continued toward them, although he occasionally stepped backward instead of forward. He looked like a drunk person determined not to be deterred by such a handicap. There was fresh blood on the stone part of his club—likely his own from falling on it.

The sheriff hefted the torture stake as though trying to guess its weight. "This here thing's a mite heavy. Next time I'll bring me a fence post." Then, in a voice just above a whisper, he muttered, "Now, listen—you take care a' this last one. He's about ready to keel over, so you should be able to handle him. You haven't been livin' up to your reputation lately, and that's bad. But this here's your chance t' git back into the act."

Don was already picking up a war club. He went forward to meet Fire-Face.

They came within a few feet of each other and both swung their stone-headed weapons at the same time. The two war clubs struck together. Both men almost lost their balance—Don because he was near dead on his feet, and Fire-Face because he was so groggy from having fallen on his head. For a few seconds, however, they continued to fence with their war clubs as though they were swords. The blows of both were pathetically ineffective. Fire-Face's eyes were becoming more glassy by the second, and Don was about ready to just give up and collapse. Then he found that he didn't have the strength to lift his club anymore. Fire-Face didn't have any trouble in this regard, but he did seem to be having difficulty in seeing his opponent. Quite possibly he saw a double image of the bloody-chested white man and didn't know which one he should strike at. And he had a hard time to keep his balance.

Both men fell forward into each other's arms and then dropped to the ground like a couple of hasty lovers. Don happened to be in the upper position, and he thought vaguely that this probably meant he was the winner.

But Fire-Face had other ideas. He let go of his club and his hand made awkward but quick groping movements between his own back and the ground. In a moment that hand flashed into sight holding a short-bladed knife. At the same time his other hand pushed Don's shoulders up and back.

The knife came up and Don felt the blade stab into his chest.

But suddenly there was no pressure at all behind the knife. Fire-Face's arms both went limp and fell to the ground. Don, now holding himself up above the other on the strength of his right arm, realized with great relief that Fire-Face had blanked out completely. Then Don looked at his own chest and saw that the knife, which had penetrated an inch or more into his pectoral muscle, was still dangling there, it's point probably lodged in a rib bone. The area felt numb, as though pain, overworked, had given up. A slow flow of blood ran down the blade and handle. Then the knife fell loose and lay on Fire-Face's chest.

Don saw that the cuts and torn muscle he had sustained during the sun dance now had been reopened on one breast and was bleeding along with the shallow stab wound from Fire-Face's knife, the tip of the blade having entered a bit to one side of that former wound. The realization of how cut up he was had an interesting psychological effect on Don's overtaxed nervous system. He was suddenly fed up with being mutilated, and very angry. He remembered that this warrior under him was his mortal foe, fully dedicated to killing him. Don grabbed up the knife from where it lay on Fire-Face's chest and held the tip of the blade close over the unconscious man's heart.

He was all set to drive it down, but then there was a conflict of emotions inside of him and he hesitated. Still holding the knife poised, he looked up and all around. In the strange silence of the place his eyes swept slowly over the motionless forms of the other five warriors who lay within the cleared circle, and on to big Jim Longfeather who had dropped the post and stood there completely still like a monolithic statue of King Tut. Don looked back across the circle of awkwardly sprawling defeated warriors, then at the silent onlookers. And his eyes came to a stop on one face—the beautiful face of Meadow.

She was as silent and motionless as the rest, but in her eyes he thought he could see an intense longing—of some kind. Roman's gaze moved on a little farther to where the chiefs squatted, and settled on the expressionless face of Geronimo. No, it was not quite expressionless. Something was there in his eyes—something even more intense than what he had seen in Meadow's face, yet entirely different.

The complete silence continued as Don looked back down at Fire-Face's relaxed ugly countenance, at his slowly rising and falling chest, at his right hand that twitched a little, and at his own hand that held a sharp instrument of death in readiness to plunge it downward.

That hand, with the blood-covered knife, looked strange to Don. Quite suddenly it looked very strange. Was he, Don Roman, actually thinking of murdering a defeated, helpless, unconscious man in cold blood?

He threw the knife away to one side. Then he slowly got to his feet. He walked over to the sixteen squatting chieftains and stood before them. "Geronimo," he addressed, for he was facing that chief in particular, "I'm ready for my next test."

The strange, intense look was still on Geronimo's face, if anything stronger now than it had been before. He slowly got to his feet, then stood silently glaring at Don for a moment before he said, "There will be no more test."

They stood facing each other in silence for a few further seconds. Then Geronimo asked, "Why you not kill him?" When Don didn't know what to reply at once, the old chief asked another question? "Are you a Christian?"

"Yes," said Don.

Geronimo's eyes seemed to burn into him, as if seeking to discern the depths of his soul. After a long moment he turned slowly toward the other chieftains and toward four braves who had come up to him and were awaiting his instructions. Don, intent on Geronimo, hadn't noticed them making their way through the crowd. The four of them surrounded two prisoners whose hands were tied behind their backs. They were Harry and Bull.

Geronimo spoke a few words of instruction in his own language and the two men were brought a bit deeper into the circle, forced to lie down on their backs. Small stakes were driven into the ground all around them and they were secured to these with strips of rawhide.

Now Geronimo spoke to Don again. "The squaw of my son have told me how these devils kill my son…and the others, and how they take her with them to hurt her. One other has been taken away to face white man's justice, and their leader you have kill when you kick him and break his neck in sun dance…. Now my people will kill these two." Again that strange, burning look in his eyes. "My people want to torture them to death very slow...but I say no. They will be kill quick."

Again Geronimo was silent for a while, looking sternly at Roman. Finally Geronimo said, "There will be no great war. You have show that you are a mighty warrior from the North. And big man with star have show that he is a great warrior for white man's law here in South.... But that is not why I say no war.... We have seen that you are mighty warriors, but we have also seen that you are only men as we are. We are not afraid to fight you."

He stopped for a moment but continued to look Don squarely in the eye, and when he spoke again it was obvious that he was forcing himself to say words that were hard for him to get out. "I say no war because...because my people, and other great tribes, do not want war. They are tired of blood.... I see that they all come to my war council not because they want war...but they come because they want to say that there shall be no war.... Before you were given test I have say to you that they would fight if they did not fear the great red-coated warriors of the North, but we have had much talk, an' now I see what I did not want to see—that my brothers no longer want to fight." He stopped speaking for a few seconds and looked at the ground in front of him in a gesture of honesty and submission to the truth that he had learned about his people, and perhaps to supply a dramatic pause to set up his next statement. Lifting his eyes to Don's face again, Geronimo said, "They no longer want to fight white man......and they no longer want me for their leader." Again there was a lengthy pause, and no one denied what he had said. Geronimo carried on, "I will go. I will go back to Fort Sill, for there is no other place for me now.... And maybe that is good." He did not explain why he thought it might be good, but continued, "When I go, I will go alone to show that I come a free man.... And you, redcoat warrior, can go back to North and tell people there that there will be no great war. I will give you twenty-five good braves to ride with you three suns into the north. Then they will come back and you will go alone from there."

Now that Don knew that the fate of a large part of the continent had after all not depended on the testing of himself, he was surprised to find that his biggest inner reaction was a feeling of relief. Even though it was all over now, it somehow felt good to know that if he had been a complete failure the war would still not have gone forward.

And Geronimo, sometimes known as *the Red Devil*, one of the greatest of the Apache warrior-chiefs, was no longer wanted by his people whom he had led to victory in many a bloody battle. There was a sadness about it—to think of the old proud chieftain having no place left to go except back to imprisonment or, at best, a confined life on a well-guarded reservation at Fort Sill. And yet, strangely enough, Geronimo did look entirely unhappy. Don felt convinced that there was a sense of relief showing in the old man's stern face. It almost seemed that Fort Sill was beckoning to him. Don hoped that somehow the old fighter would find peace.

* * *

Sergeant Don Roman, freshly shaved, the bandages on his chest and arm completely hidden under his red tunic, his gunbelt strapped around his waist, and the stiff-brimmed hat angled to shade his eyes from the early morning sun, was beginning to once more look and feel like himself. The sorest, stiffest part of his body was the shoulder that had received a war-club blow from the rear, but even that was coming along. At least his arm was not paralyzed anymore. Meadow had done the bandaging of his chest and also of his other arm on which the skin had been burned considerably during his roll through the fire. A full week had gone by since the end of Don's ordeal.

He stood beside a sleek, black war-horse that had a standard white man's riding bridle on its head and a cavalry saddle on its back, very much like the kind used by the North-West Mounted. All of this was a personal gift to Roman from Geronimo, and included the blankets and supply of food behind the cantle of the saddle, the leather water bag that hung from the pommel, and the handsome Springfield rifle secure in a handmade buckskin scabbard under one stirrup fender.

A little to one side stood twenty-five more horses with some of their riders standing beside them and some already mounted. They were the braves that Geronimo had promised would escort Don for the first three days of his long journey home. The party was all but ready to start out.

Don had already done his official farewell to Geronimo this morning. For the first time since their meeting, the old chieftain had not been wearing his usual horned cap, but had replaced it with a plain brown brow band. No doubt there was symbolism involved in this change of headgear, for Geronimo was going through some great life shake-up that Don understood only partly.

Jim Longfeather, alias Dave Lindner, came toward Sergeant Roman leading his bay stallion. He also had received a gift from Geronimo and was wearing it. It was a soft leather shirt, beautifully beaded—the biggest one that could be found in the whole camp.

He no longer wore his badge. Immediately after the fight, the sheriff had left camp, riding to intercept the group of cavalry that had been on its way to investigate the war-council meeting. Jim had convinced them that it was best for all concerned that they turn around and head back where they came from, and not to stir up trouble where there no longer was any trouble. Of course there was bound to be further investigation of the whole matter, but at least now the army would not aggravate the situation just when things were going well.

Jim had written two letters and sent them along with the army riders, one to the superintendent at the fort and the other to Deputy Fullbright. And with that one he sent along his badge and instructions that the letter be read to the town elders. Both letters stated that Dave Lindner had been called away from the area on urgent personal business. The one to Cliff and the town elders highly recommended that Deputy Fullbright be upgraded to sheriff and suggested that a particular man who had done well during the town clean-up become the deputy if he was available. Jim, as Dave, also assured them that in due time he would contact them and let them know more about why he had suddenly been called away.

Jim came to a stop beside Don, glanced back over his shoulder toward where Meadow was saying good-bye to some acquaintances, then said quietly. "I've gotta know something."

"Oh, yeah? What's that?"

Jim spoke even more softly, apparently not wanting Meadow to hear. "She's coming along with us because of you, isn't she?"

"No.... What do you mean by that?"

For just a moment Jim lapsed back into his cowpoke lingo. "I mean it ain't likely she's willin' t' gallivant all the way up t' Canada jest t' see a bloody moose eatin' frozen quack grass."

Don tried to rub in the lingo slip-up by attempting some of his own. "Wal, I reckon I ain't talked her into it."

"You sure?"

"Shore as there's balls on a...on a bullfrog."

"Oh, shut up. I'm serious. And anyhow, even if you didn't talk her into it, she must be doing it because she's—" He glanced toward Meadow again. "—because she's sweet on you."

Don was silent for a moment, wondering if he should clue-in Jim on his suspicions, went ahead with it. "Has it occurred to you that she might be wanting to come with us not because of me but because of you?"

This seemed to genuinely surprise the big man. "Nonsense!" He dropped his voice lower and leaned forward. "I'm a wanted man with a noose looming over my head, so I've made sure I didn't do anything to encourage her to like me."

"Just because you didn't encourage it doesn't mean she's not attracted to you.... But if you're serious about having your neck stretched, you really should tell her about it."

"No, I don't want her to know. Make sure you don't tell her...But I still think it's you she's got her heart set on. She said you treated her like a lady when you were together in the wagon...both stark naked."

"Well, don't make it sound like we planned that. You know, I've got a beautiful, hot-blooded, blonde woman waiting for me in Canada—waiting for me to marry her.... At least I hope she's still waiting."

Jim said, "Well then, you ought to tell Meadow that." After apparently thinking about it for a moment, he added, "Ah, maybe she's not interested in either of us. After all, her husband just died a few days ago."

Don's next words were spoken as though he was a ventriloquist, with very little lip movement. "She's coming."

Jim then tried to give the impression that they were in the middle of a different subject. "Well, Geronimo has been treatin' us right smart—I mean, treating us real good."

"Yeah," said Don as Meadow, smiling, leading her white gelding, walked up to them. Geronimo had wanted to give her a beautiful doeskin outfit of long skirt and thigh-length shirt. She accepted the shirt but got his permission to trade in the skirt for a man's breechcloth and leggings which would allow her to straddle her horse with less difficulty. The shirt was held to her slender waist by a belt decorated with a variety of shiny metal ornaments, and some of these same kind of baubles were in her braids. On her feet were new moccasins, replete with fancy leather tassels. She was all Indian, and all lovely. For a moment Don tried to visualize her in a white woman's dress and with a white woman's hairstyle, and was fairly successful in conjuring up this transformation. But he was not as successful in deciding which way he liked her best.

"Well," said Meadow, "I guess it's really time now to mount up and leave. I hope that neither of you thinks it's wrong of me to be anxious to leave here…. I mean…they are my own people. But I know I don't belong here, and, after all, it is a good thing to look forward to the future." She spoke to both men in front of her, looking from one to the other, but the beautiful smile that followed was directed at Jim.

The three climbed into their saddles, and the braves who had not yet mounted did so, and the party got under way. It was an exceptionally colorful party with its assorted hues of horses, brilliant brow bands on the Apache riders, the beaded-buckskin-attired Longfeather, the lovely Indian woman on her snow-white horse, and the scarlet-coated member of the North-West Mounted Police.

They made their way out of the big camp and rode north. They rode willingly—Don toward what he hoped would be his long-awaited wedding to Rita; Meadow toward what she hoped would be an exciting new life in Canada; and Jim toward easing his conscience by confessing his crime and therefore possibly facing a hangman's noose.

PART THREE:
AN OUTLAW'S LAST STAND

18

By the time winter closed in, the northbound travelers had gotten as far as North Dakota. Although the area had won statehood seven years previous, many still referred to it as the Dakota Territories. It was great farming country. Even before the white man had reached it, the basic native population had been cultivating some of the level landscape. Don, Jim, and Meadow arrived in a little town called *Windy Valley*.

The Apache Indian escort had taken them about seventy-five miles from the war council camp in Yellow Valley, and from there the trio had gone on alone. In time they had acquired a packhorse, and, as the days grew cooler and the nights distinctly cold, warmer clothing and better camping gear. Don had packed away his uniform and replaced it, from hat to boots, with the normal wear of a working westerner. He had even bought a used cartridge belt and open-topped holster along with an old Colt Navy. He was afraid that the police rig, as well as the issue hat and boots—even without the red coat—might start people wondering if he was a deserter from the U.S. Cavalry. And wearing the whole red-coated outfit would only have drawn attention and a lot of questions. It was better to just blend into the scenery.

Meadow had also changed her attire, first to boys' clothing for comfort on the trail—namely denim pants and work shirt, along with boy-sized western boots and a wide-brimmed hat.

Of the three, Jim was the only one whose style of clothing hadn't changed, but it was his money that covered the expenses of all of them. It was fortunate that he had made it a habit to carry his savings around with him in one of his saddlebags.

Upon arrival in Windy Valley, and with the decision to winter there, Meadow's appearance changed again, for she bought materials at the general store and cut and sewed them into delightful creations that made her look like the townswomen except that she was more beautiful. Her sewing skills had been acquired along with her good English through her upbringing in her affluent eastern home. Fortunately nothing had ever been able to change the bronze of her skin, nor the high-cheekboned stunning beauty of her face.

At the first opportunity, long before getting to North Dakota, Sergeant Roman had sent a telegram to police headquarters in Regina, explaining briefly what had happened to him. But there had not been a direct connection to Regina. Don wasn't clear on whether there was no direct line or whether it had been temporarily down, for the Western Union man had been feeling overly cheerful and carefree due to booze; but he had assured Don that the message would get through, partly by horse and rider. This was strange, since the Pony Express hadn't been in operation for thirty-five years, and stranger still since there had never been such a service in this area. Don had not elected to trust himself to this tenuous communications set-up by waiting there for a return telegram. Instead, he had included in his message that a reply was to be sent to the nearest telegraph station on the Canadian side, at *Qu'Appelle*. He made no mention that he had a willing fugitive in tow, nor did he say that he was traveling in the company of a beautiful Indian woman. Now he hoped that if and when they finally made it into Canada and to Qu'Appelle, a message would be there waiting for them, from police headquarters and also from Rita. The one from the force would say, hopefully, that they would be so happy to have him back, and the one from Rita would say how glad she was that he was safe, and that she was looking forward to their wedding. He encouraged himself that he could expect such messages and felt quite hopeful about it. He knew that Rita would wait a long time to hear from him...and yet, when he considered her tremendous sexual need....

Meadow was the first of the three to get a job in Windy Valley— as a waitress at the *Paris Café*, which was part of the *Empire Rooming House*. All three had rooms at this establishment.

The town of Windy Valley, situated at the side of a wide creek or small river that flowed through a hollow in the ground hardly deep enough to be called a valley, was, in many ways, a normal looking pioneer town of the Northwest. However, there were more farmers around than ranchers, and few of either type packed a gun. This pleased Don, and both he and Jim soon learned to walk the streets unarmed. The sheriff, Adam Williams, carried a gun however, and he seemed to have the place under reasonable control in spite of an occasional drunken brawl at the *Big Wheel Saloon.*

Don was next to find employment. The owner of the livery stable, old Carl Peterson, passed on due to age-related health problems, and his son, Wilfred, took over. But Wilf Peterson was more interested in gambling than in running a feed barn, and gave the job of managing it to Don.

Then the schoolmarm quit teaching because of her booze problems and left to get help from her family and friends in Chicago. Meadow applied for the job, and, in spite of a few parents who didn't want their children taught by an Indian, got the position. In about two days all the children were in love with her, particularly the older boys who suddenly wanted to go to school.

One evening Sheriff Williams was a little late in getting to the Big Wheel Saloon to stop a brawl, and before it was over the bouncer, "Lank" Fitzgerald, had been injured badly enough to have to give up his job. Jim applied and got the position almost before he was finished asking for it. There weren't any brawls after that. The potential troublemakers would take one look at him and comment to one another that he looked like a nice man so why should they give him a bad time.

Wilf Peterson, when he wasn't gambling at the Big Wheel or checking up on Don at the feed barn, was spending a lot of time courting Meadow—seemingly without the slightest success. Wilf was a rather good looking sport who kept himself perfectly groomed, which included the wearing of expensive suits, riding britches, fancy neck scarves and so on. He owned several matched driving teams, plus a wagon, a couple of buggies with springs, a two-horse cutter-type sleigh, and a larger sleigh that was used to haul freight. He hired someone for that. Wilf had a charm about him and women seemed to like him in spite of the fact that they never saw him working. Men put up with him and didn't take him seriously. Jim Longfeather, in particular, didn't like him very much.

Don found it amusing to see how Jim was obviously annoyed by Wilf's interest in Meadow, although the big Indian would have jumped into a well before admitting to that. After all, he was going to Canada to get hanged, so how could it matter if another man got friendly with Meadow. The problem became more pointed however, one sunny noon just before Christmas, when Meadow caught Jim alone crossing the snow-covered main street and hurried to his side.

* * *

"Hello," said Meadow, smiling. "Slow down a bit. I want to talk to you about something."

Jim was pleased and worried at the same time. He smiled back and took shorter steps. "Good, we can talk while we eat. That's where you're going isn't it?"

"Yeah...but...I don't want to talk in there. This has to be a very private conversation."

"Okay, so let's head for the sidewalk and then toward the harness repair. Don't see anyone around." He had the urge to add, *The street's as bare as a newborn baby's ass*, but restrained himself, partly because he was talking to a lady, and partly because he had been making good progress in getting over the crude cowpoke lingo and didn't want to regress. So instead he said, "What're you planning to do—rob the bank?"

"No, it's more serious than that," said Meadow as they arrived at the snow-loaded plank sidewalk. Jim got onto it ahead of her and reached for her hand, giving her a gentle lift as she stepped up beside him. She was as beautiful as always, even though bundled up in her long winter coat. But the weather was mild for this time of the year and she was hatless. Her solid black hair, no longer in braids, had been curling-iron bent into a fluffy, becoming face-frame.

They began to crunch along the snowy sidewalk. Jim felt good just to be walking with her, alone. He couldn't remember ever doing that in all the time they had been together. He said, "So, what's on your mind, pard?"

"Pard—I like that. You and me and Don really are partners, aren't we? We've learned to trust one another and take care of one another, almost like we're a family."

"Very true...and you sound like you're about to ask me to do something."

She laughed and it was music. She spoke English without the slightest trace of Indian accent, but it seemed to Jim that her laughter sounded native somehow, and he hoped that would never change. The tail end of her tinkling laugh transformed seamlessly into words. "You're right. But I don't think you'll mind—at least I hope not.... Still, I'm being very daring to ask this."

"What you're being is mysterious." He turned up the collar of his heavy jacket so it met with the brim of his hat. "My ears are getting cold. You sure we couldn't discuss this over a bowl of soup?"

"It won't take long." But she hesitated a bit before she went on. "You know how Wilf keeps trying to start something with me.... And you know that I'm not even slightly interested in him."

"Can't rightly...can't really say that I know that last part."

"Well, I've told you before, and I've refused him a million times already, but he just doesn't give up."

"I've seen the two of you walking down the street together, more than once."

"Sure. What am I supposed to do? He sees me walking and he's at my side. I've been so cold toward him it's a wonder we both haven't frozen to death. He just won't take no for an answer, whether subtly implied or spoken outright in his face. It's tiring."

"So you want me to kill him. Sorry, I'm not for hire."

"No, what I'm going to ask of you might be harder to do than that, although I hope not."

"Try me."

"All right, here's the problem. Since I've been going to church regularly, Wilf has gotten the idea, and rightly so, that my Christian faith means a lot to me—as it does to most of the people in this town and surrounding countryside."

"Yeah," said Jim, "except for the boozers and gamblers that collect at the Big Wheel, this is the most religious town I've ever set foot in. And I like it. I know I haven't been going to church, but I'm not without faith. I was brought up in a Christian home just as you were."

"Then you won't mind going to church on Christmas eve for the big program—the Christmas concert."

"No, I don't mind. I was planning to go."

"All right, here's my problem. Wilf is sure to ask me to go to the concert. I don't think he cares anything about Christmas concerts, but he'll want to impress me with his spirituality, and, anyhow, he'll want to be with me. If I was a gambler like he is, I'd bet...I'd bet pretty heavily that he's not going to overlook what to him will seem like a golden opportunity. He'll think that I won't be able to refuse to go to church with him. After all, if I refuse he might lose all interest in church and go to hell."

They were walking past the town laundry, closed for the winter. Most households did their own washing, but there were always bachelor cowboys and farmers needing the service in summertime when they got dirtier but had better things to do than wash underwear.

Jim said, "So...is there something to that? I mean, do you think maybe you should go to the Christmas show with him to help him along the right path?"

"It's not a show," said Meadow. "It's a program of worshipping God as the Christ child.... And no, I don't think I should. It doesn't work that way. He knows about the concert. If he's genuinely interested, there's nothing to stop him from going by himself. And if I went with him I'd be misleading him. Later on, when he'd eventually have to admit that I'm not interested in him, he could feel cheated and this could work against him. You know, he could think, if that's the way Christian women behave, leading men on and then disappointing them, then I don't want anything to do with it."

"I see what you mean," said Jim. "You know, I didn't realize quite how religious you are. How did that go over when you were trying to live like a regular Apache?"

"Not so great, but Bill was a Christian too. I guess I should have told you about this before, but I still don't like to talk about Bill.... You see, in our own way we were trying to be missionaries to our people, but I don't know how successful we were. It was difficult."

"You don't have to talk about it."

"Thanks. But I should point out that I'm not all that religious. I don't mind skipping church, and I like going to the dances—or I *would* like that if it wasn't for Wilf swooping down on me like a bloody hawk the moment I show up.... Religion seems to have a lot to do with customs. I'm basically just interested in the heart of it.... Well, I guess by now you know what I want from you."

They had arrived in front of the harness repair shop and also the end of the block. Jim brought them to a stop. The shop was open but there weren't any customers at this time and Henry would be in the rear part making a harness or catching up on repair work. Jim said, "Well, I could guess, but I'd rather hear you come out with it."

"I suppose that would appeal to a man's vanity."

"I suppose."

"All right then, here it comes," said Meadow, kinking her head back severely to look up into his towering face. "I would like you to take me to the Christmas concert, and I'd like you to agree to that right now so that the next time I see Wilf, and he asks me to go with him, I can say I'm already spoken for."

Jim felt this definitely called for a few seconds of suspenseful, dramatic silence, before answering, but he softened the effect by smiling down at her. The feelings inside of him, however, were somewhat different than what his face showed. She was too close and looking up into his face too much. He wanted to grab her into his arms and kiss her—long and hard. No, long and tenderly. And by saying yes to her request he would be setting himself up for more of this exquisite torture. It was bad enough, damn it, just to see her every day, without her being this close, looking up at him with those intoxicating brown eyes. But what could he do? He couldn't refuse her request.

He said, "Of course I'll take you. As a member of our little family, how could I turn you down?"

Her face showed that she was not entirely pleased with his response. She said, "Will it be such a sacrifice then? Will you find it so unpleasant to spend an evening with me?"

He was stabbed to the heart. Of all the things in life he did not want to do—such as orphaning a child by boiling its mother in oil—very near the top of the list was his overwhelming desire to never, never, never in any way hurt this dark-eyed beauty whom he would gladly have died for. And he had just hurt her.

He said, "Oh, no! Spending an evening with you, unpleasant?! That's the funniest thing I've ever heard. You're every man's wildest dream. Don't you know how beautiful and wonderful you are? I'm very pleased that you want me to do this." He knew he had gone way overboard, but, what the hell, it was all true and even though nothing could come of it, he had at least told her this one time how he felt about her.

It had the desired effect, erasing the hurt from her eyes and replacing that with a genuine look of pleasure. But she was clever enough to temper that look by saying, "Then I'll be looking forward very much to Christmas eve and going to the concert with my big brother—my big, big brother…who is also one of the most amazing men I've ever met."

Jim couldn't help wishing she had left out the brother part, realizing at the same time that it was better that way. After all, he didn't want her to fall in love with him, for that would only hurt her in the end. He was a man without a future.

Well, not quite. Right now his future was going to a Christmas-eve church service with the most wonderful woman in the world.

* * *

The church was on the outskirts of town and a barn had been built along with it for those from the surrounding countryside who came in wagons in summer and sleighs in winter. Older folk from town also were driven to church, but most townspeople walked, even in wintertime unless the weather was too bad.

The current extreme warm spell held for Christmas eve. There was a light cloud cover through which a soft-focus near-full moon could be seen, and not even a touch of a breeze.

Jim and Meadow walked toward the church, by themselves at first; but soon a number of couples and families, including themselves, had coalesced into a small group. There was lighthearted chatter and the incredibly happy sound of children laughing. With Meadow on his arm, Jim had an indescribable feeling of suddenly having been transferred to a paradise world that he was unfamiliar with but liked very much.

As the small group arrived on the churchyard, some sleighs were pulling up at the barn and horses were being unhitched. At this point Don rode up on his black gelding. He saw Jim and Meadow and waved to them; they waved back.

Jim said, "Do you think we should wait for him and sit together?" and was immediately sorry he had said that.

"No, he's a big boy," said Meadow. "Let's go in."

The happy feeling Jim had experienced on the way to church did not forsake him as they entered the building. It was not a fancy place, basically, having been put together by local carpenters with the help of the community, but not with a lot of financial resources. There were no stained glass windows and everything was roughly finished and practical. For this special night, however, the interior had been decorated. The main feature of this was a Christmas tree ornamented with shiny baubles and ribbons, and there was a red cloth bow on each window. Even as the couples and families settled into the pews and the happy conversation was replaced by a worshipful silence, the mood somehow remained festive.

Not everyone there was part of a couple or a family. One of these exceptions was Wilf Peterson, looking sharp in a gray suit with a narrow stripe. Not all the men wore suits; a few of them, particularly the younger ones, displayed their most colorful shirts and sweaters. Jim caught sight of Don, sitting between some teen-agers and a woman who was well into her nineties; and he looked to be in season in his newest shirt, a bright green one.

Jim would have liked to be wearing a suit and tie, but he had none, and the stores didn't have anything to fit him. There were at least two women in town who could have made him a suit, but they would have needed more time. So he came in his best pants and somewhat worn yellow shirt, and looked pretty much in line with everyone else in this none-too-affluent community. It was not a place where people looked down their noses at a patched elbow.

Pastor Conrad Fleck, although dressed in his usual dark suit, at least had a festive smile on his face; and he had an anticipating look about him, as though he had something good to tell everyone—as though maybe he had just received a letter from heaven informing him that winters would never be cold again. He was a fairly young man, thin and energetic. But he was old enough to have a pregnant wife and three children.

The news that he was smiling about was, of course, the good news about the Christ child; and, after some prayers and Christmas hymns, the pastor spelled out the main details of the story in a short sermon. It had been a long time since Jim had heard this story, but it made him happy and he agreed with all of it.

At one point the thought flashed into his mind that he had killed a man by the name of Chuck Scote—not as he had killed a number of others, but that particular one in an unlawful way. He had often asked God to forgive him for this, but he still felt confused—not about God's willingness to forgive, but because of the circumstances of that shootout. As always, he came to the conclusion that he never should have become a blood brother to John Pinetree. But he had. Now, which was the greater guilt?—killing Scote to protect his blood brother, or running out on his blood brother after the killing?

This Christ child of long ago had come into the world to help people; the Christian faith, which Jim accepted, taught that. Somehow that help would come, but maybe not before he returned to Canada and admitted his crime to the authorities.

As the program of carol singing got underway, many of the songs being performed delightfully by children, Jim was able to forget about the negative details of his situation and feel only the hope and faith that this wonderful evening was bringing to him. Whenever the congregation was asked to sing along, Meadow, close at his side, would join in wholeheartedly, obviously familiar with the words. Probably she had been practicing them. But Jim could only remember them vaguely from his childhood. This didn't bother him, for he felt that his singing was about as good as that of a raven with a bad cold, and he didn't want to spoil the good singing of the others.

The wonderful evening moved swiftly toward its final parts, the highlight of which was a nativity scene with real people and even a real baby. The baby had enough sense to not cry and just about everything came off without a hitch except that one of the shepherd boys tripped over his blanket-robe and fell. But he got back up quickly and didn't seem to be hurt. Joseph was played by a farm boy called David, and Mary by Sarah, the daughter of the owner of the Empire Rooming House, a sweet teen-aged girl who had become a good friend of Meadow.

How religious this community was could be assessed not only by the names of their children but also by the fact that no Santa Claus showed up at this celebration. The general consensus of the church people here was that the jelly-bellied old gift-giver was a usurper trying to take the real meaning out of Christmas. The children couldn't miss him because they had never made his acquaintance.

This, however, did not prevent gifts from being given. A lot of them were passed out along with homemade candies and baked goodies.

While this distribution was going on, Jim took notice of Don leaving the church. "Don's takin' off," he said to Meadow. "Why would he be in such a hurry to leave? We haven't even had a chance to talk to him."

"I dunno," she said. "I hope he enjoyed the concert."

"Well, *I* sure am enjoying it," said Jim. If there were any angels hovering around the church on that special night, they may have been amused at how this big man, who had been through fist-fights, shootouts, and had for some time practiced talking like a mule skinner, was now so deeply moved by this simple little celebration of the birth of the Prince of Peace.

When it was officially over, people didn't rush out the door. They moved slowly toward it, visiting at the same time and wishing one another a Merry Christmas as they got into their coats. Jim and Meadow did the same.

When they eventually got out of the building they saw that the sky was clear of the thin veil of cloud and now the almost-full moon was totally free and lighting up the snow-covered countryside on one side and the town on the other. The temperature seemed even milder than earlier and the smoke from the chimneys and stovepipes curled straight upward in the quiet air.

Some of the people were on their way to the barn to ready their horses for the drive home, but no one had begun hitching them up at this point. Nevertheless, there came the distinct sound of horses' feet crunching through the snow in a lively trot, sleigh runners creaking, and harness bells jingling. It was just a matter of turning one's eyes to the road to see the handsome matched team pulling an open cutter type of sleigh, coming toward the church.

"Oh, well," said Meadow, "we all arrive late at one time or another."

"That's Wilf's outfit," said Jim, "but he was in church."

"Yeah, he's standing right over there," said Meadow in a low voice, "looking at me."

Jim said, "Someone must have rented his team and cutter. He rents them out whenever he can."

"Yeah, and look who rented it."

"Don. What's he doing with that outfit?"

The cutter was not heading for the barn but straight toward where Jim and Meadow stood among others in front of the church. The horses were one of the prettiest matched teams for miles around, chestnuts with flaxen manes and tails, perfectly groomed and accoutered in shiny black harnesses ornamented with nickel spots. The spreader reins between the horses' heads had lengths of red, white, and blue rings made of horn, and the top of each fancy bridle was decorated with a plume of red-dyed horsehair. Jim knew the outfit well, having previously admired it from close range. And tonight sleigh bells had been added.

They jingled merrily and then settled into the occasional clink as Don pulled the team to a stop. Jim and Meadow stepped over to him where he sat smiling in the bright red cutter that looked like something out of a toy store.

Meadow said, "What're you up to?"

Smiling but not saying anything, Don got out of the cutter, stood before them, and then handed the reins to Jim. "Jim and Meadow, this is my Christmas present to you, my best friends. No, I'm not giving you this team and cutter, but I rented it for you to use tonight."

Meadow looked amused. "That's pretty nice. You're going to drive us home in style."

"I'm not gonna drive you anywhere," said Don, "and you're not going back to your dingy rooms—not yet."

Jim said, "So what're we doing?"

"Well, I'm going to walk home to my dingy room, and after I hang up my stocking, I'm going to bed."

"Won't do you any good to hang up your stocking," said Meadow. "Santa doesn't come to this part of the world."

"Oh, yeah, I forgot," said Don. "If he tried he'd be shot down like a duck."

"So you're going to walk, and Jim and I get to ride in this fancy rig?"

"That's right," said Don, "but you're not going home right away."

"Tell us more," said Meadow.

Don turned from Meadow to the big man. "Jim, you are going to take this lady for a ride in the moonlight. You're going to take the old-bridge trail because no one else will be going that way. The bridge isn't safe so don't cross it. But go right up to the bridge. It must be very beautiful there tonight."

Jim was puzzled. "Why're you doing this?"

"I told you," said Don. "It's my Christmas present to the two of you." He looked directly at Jim. "If you refuse it, you'll be insulting me—me, your best buddy. You wouldn't want to do that, would you?"

Jim looked at Meadow. "Ah...how do you feel about this?"

Meadow was smiling radiantly. "I think it's wonderful!" She turned to Don and said, "What a great idea you had!" Then she threw her arms around him. Don at once enclosed her in his own arms and held her for enough seconds to annoy Jim. At the same time Don was looking at Jim, and, although his mouth was shut, the police officer in disguise seemed to be saying, *See, if you go for the sleigh ride you might get some of this—if you're not too much of a fool to accept it.*

There was, of course, no way for Jim to refuse this gift, even though it meant treading on dangerous ground in his effort to not let Meadow get emotionally involved with him. So, as she and Don finally got out of their friendly hug, Jim said, "Well, buddy, I certainly do thank you for this thoughtful and original gift. Of course, Meadow and I are both delighted."

"Yes, thank you so much!" said Meadow.

"You're both very welcome," said Don. "The horses and sleigh are yours till sunrise." He smiled, then turned away and started walking home, but after a few steps someone who had overheard some of his conversation with Jim and Meadow offered him a ride home and he accepted.

As Jim helped Meadow into the open cutter, he wondered why Don was being so foolish. Why was he determined to bring him and Meadow together when he knew that Jim was going to give himself up to be brought to trial? Did Don think he was doing something good by stirring them up for nothing? Well, the damage was done now. Somehow, Jim told himself, he had to get through this ride in the moonlight while causing as little pain as possible to Meadow, and to himself.

There was a big cushion on the cutter seat, reaching from side to side, and blankets over that. And there were plenty of blankets to cover up with as well. Jim sat on the right side, as was the custom for the driver of any rig, and Meadow at once leaned into him and began to tuck the blankets cozily over their laps.

"Oh!" she exclaimed. "There's a foot-warmer stone in here. He thought of everything."

Jim moved his feet a bit and found the warmth radiating from a loaf-sized stone on the floor under the blankets. It was a common practice, in colder weather, to let such a stone absorb heat in a fireplace or oven and then transfer it to the sleigh where it would radiate heat for at least a couple of hours. They didn't really need it on a night as warm as this one, but obviously Don had gone all out to make their Christmas sleigh ride as warm and romantic as possible—the bastard. He repented at once for having called his best friend that, even though it was only in his mind and he hadn't felt malicious about it. Still, it wasn't any kind of thought to have on a Christmas eve toward a friend who must somehow think he was doing a good thing. As Jim got the horses into motion, he saw Wilf Peterson standing there poker faced, not all that far away, watching his team and outfit pulling away with Meadow in it. It occurred to Jim that Don certainly had not told Wilf why he was renting the outfit.

The horses crunched their way at a slow trot along the old-bridge trail, the bells on their harness tinkling like music from a fairy orchestra. The town and the church fell away behind them, and they were alone in a magical world of snow and moonlight. Jim brought the horses to a walk; the fairy orchestra did a piece in slower tempo.

"I've never seen the snow sparkle quite like this before," said Meadow. "It's as though God spread out barrelfuls of diamonds on the snow—just for us."

"That's very poetic," said Jim, trying to sound pleased instead of desperate. He could tell that this whole thing was not about to get easier. And now Meadow got her arm under his and pulled herself even closer.

The winding trail led through a grove of bare trees, so that for a while little bars of moonlight-shadow flickered over them as the moon bounced along through the black silhouettes of the naked aspens.

The old bridge was only about a half-mile from town, so they quickly arrived. The trail dipped downward briefly toward the creek, then leveled off before reaching the bridge. Jim brought the team to a stop.

There were a few trees along either side of the frozen, snow carpeted creek, but more willow shrubs, and these were hung with globs of snow. The old bridge, only about twenty feet long, was mostly snow covered, but here and there parts of it were exposed, mainly parts of the railings which showed up black in contrast.

"It's so beautiful here," said Meadow. "Don was right."

"Yeah.... Would you like to walk out onto the bridge?"

"Is it safe? No one's supposed to use it."

"That's horses and sleighs. Some of the wood's rotted and might not support much weight. But it'll hold people. C'mon, let's go." He had the idea that anything was less dangerous than going on sitting so close to her.

He held her arm as she was stepping down out of the cutter and found no opportunity to let go of it as they walked the few steps toward the bridge, for she quickly slid her arm under his. He was familiar enough with Wilf's well trained team to know that they would stand unattended with no thought of leaving. The gambler had Aubrey Smithers train all his horses, and Smithers was good at it.

Jim and Meadow walked only a yard or so onto the bridge, and were cautious even at that. With his gloved hands Jim swept snow off a short area of the plank that made up the top of the railing. "Care to sit, ma'am."

"Thank you, sir," said Meadow, playing along with his polite game. The railing was low enough so that she could get up on it with only a little hoist with her arms. Jim didn't need to hoist himself and sat down leaving a good foot of space between them. "Oh, come on," chided Meadow with a half-tinkle of laugh mixed in with her words. "When a man and woman are sitting on a bridge in the moonlight, they don't sit that far apart."

"Oh, I guess you're right," he said and moved a few inches closer. She quickly closed the remaining gap, and so once more he felt the pleasant pressure of her form leaning into him. So it didn't matter — sleigh or bridge, he was forced to undergo this exciting torture.

They sat there like that for a few seconds, silent, motionless, and then Meadow said, "Jim, what's wrong?"

"Wrong? What do you mean?"

"You know what I mean…Why're you so cold toward me? Is it because I've recently been widowed and you think it's wrong to show an interest in me this soon?"

"Well…ah…I guess…yeah, I guess that kind of bothers me."

"You're lying. If that's what it was you wouldn't have hesitated before you answered…. No, it's something else…and I wish you'd tell me what it is."

"Go on. What makes you think that."

"Because—because you're a contradiction."

"A contradiction? I guess you'll need to explain that," said Jim, not really wanting an answer.

"All right," said Meadow, "I'll give it to you straight…. Whenever I make a move in your direction you give me the cold shoulder. And the rest of the time you look at me with hungry eyes."

There was a long silence.

Then Meadow said, "Am I right or wrong?"

Jim hesitated only slightly before he said, "You're right."

"So? What's the problem?"

Jim knew what he had to do. He had to tell her the truth. There was no other way. He turned more toward her and picked up one of her gloved hands in his own. "Meadow…I'm…I'm a fugitive from the law. I can't let you be involved with me because of that. I killed a man in Canada and now I'm going back to give myself up. I'll probably be hanged, or, at the best, I'll get a long prison term…. If it wasn't for that, well…well, there's no use talking about it."

She sat very still, and after a while she spoke, but her voice had grown quiet and there was a slight tremble to it. "Tell me what happened…in Canada."

He told her. It took about five minutes; he didn't leave out anything.

When he was done she sat looking at the snowy bridge for a while before she said, "You didn't murder him in cold blood. If you hadn't shot him he would have shot you."

"True, but according to the law I shouldn't have been interfering with what he was doing. Like I told you, there was a legal bounty on Pinetree's head, and Scote was simply out to get it."

"This Pinetree, your blood brother—he didn't really have a grip on things, did he? I mean, like you said, he thought he was going to be hanged for killing a government cow to keep his band from starving. That wasn't true, but he really believed it. One can't blame him for trying to defend his own life…when he killed that police officer who came after him."

"I know, but I had no right to interfere with the law. I'm a murderer, Meadow. We can't get away from that." He felt tears stinging his eyes and for a moment thought he might make a complete fool of himself. But he kept quiet so his voice wouldn't betray his overwhelming feelings of frustration.

They were still holding hands, but now she put her other hand on his shoulder. "You're a very brave and wonderful man…. But I think you're making a mistake to go back to Canada and give yourself up. Would Don try to stop you if you turned back?"

"No," said Jim and was glad to find that his voice was steady. "Sergeant Don Roman would like to kick my ass all the way back to the Arizona Territories—or to anywhere other than Canada. He shouldn't feel that way. After all, he represents the law. He should bring me in even if I didn't want to go." Then he added, "I'm sorry about that bad language. It was a slip-up."

Meadow ignored the apology and, after a moment, said, "Jim, why do you think Don is willing to go against his duty and recommend that you not go back to Canada?"

"I don't know. It's kind of hard to figure. He's always been a good, upright police officer."

"If you don't know, then I'll tell you," she said. "Don knows that there are some things even more important than upholding the law. He loves you. He admires you as the good man you are. He can't stand the thought of you throwing your life away when that would serve no good purpose. And he's right. You shouldn't go back."

He said nothing, so after a few seconds she added, "What's so terrible about being a fugitive anyhow—especially since they don't know where you are and will probably never come looking for you."

"I don't know," he said. "At first, when I ran off, I sort of got a kick out of it—you know, there was something…romantic and adventurous about it. But then, after some time…well, I think it was because I couldn't tell anyone about it. I had to keep it all to myself, no matter where I went…. It was amazing how much better I felt after I told Don about it."

"And now you've told me."

"I'm sorry, I was sort of forced into it."

"Don't be sorry for telling me…. But if you leave me and go get yourself hanged, then, just before they do that, when you're standing there on the gallows platform, take a moment to be very sorry—sorry for plunging me into a lifelong torment."

In that moment Jim's mind opened up. Here was a woman with whom he was in love, and who was in love with him, and who had just a few weeks previously come through more suffering than some people have in a lifetime, and here he was about to cast her into another hell. Which was more important?—himself being brought to justice, or Meadow being saved from another great hurt? The answer was clear to him.

He put a gloved hand to her cheek and saw that her eyes were brimming with tears. He said, "I'm so sorry…. Please forgive me for being so stupid and unfeeling. I was wrong. I won't give myself up. We won't go back to Canada."

She exploded into sobs of relief, put her head against Jim's shoulder; but then she got it under control and looked up at him again, now with rivulets of tears on her cheeks glistening in the moonlight. "So what does this mean…for us?"

Jim said, "For me it means I don't have to hold back any longer from telling you how much I love you."

"I love you too, and want to be with you always." Her face came closer to his as she said this; then he realized that this was mainly because his own face was moving down toward hers. Her lips were cool against his own for a fraction of a second, then they warmed as her body heat came to the surface.

They held each other and kissed for a long time. Some of the kisses were short and some were long, but they were all like dynamite exploding and heaving huge rocks in all directions. The rocks were cares and problems that had weighed heavily and now were suddenly meaningless.

Jim took a break for air, then said, "Do you love me enough to marry me?"

"Yes," she said. "I'm so glad you asked that now. It would have killed me to have to wait for you to get around to it."

"Let's get married right away."

"How about on New Year's day? Can we wait that long?"

"A whole week?" said Jim. "All right, but not a day longer."

Meadow laughed happily and snuggled up close to him with her head against his shoulder.

19

It was early summer. The bright, green-leafed poplar trees showed up strikingly against the darker green of the pines. The floor of the forest was covered with a thick carpet of grass, shrubs, and decaying pinecones. Here and there small pink roses hung on thorny branches. Above it all a hawk circled leisurely in a blue-tinted crystal-glass sky. The forest was stabbed by rays of sunlight and filled with the twittering of a million songbirds.

Through this scene of woodland splendor rode the hunted outlaw, John Pinetree. At his side was his beautiful squaw, Flying Blackbird, on her brown and white pinto gelding. And close behind rode two young braves, each leading a loaded packhorse.

These men had only recently become the trusted companions of Pinetree. He had wanted someone to ride with him, to fight with him, to stick with him in any situation that might arise. When Jim Longfeather had shirked his responsibility as a blood brother, Pinetree had begun to shop around in his mind for other possible volunteers. Sleeping Wolf had also refused to cast in his lot with the outlaw, but he, at least, had suggested to Pinetree that he get in touch with two very brave young men, Redleaf, and Born-on-the-Hill, both of whom lived on the One-Arrow Reserve. These men were ready for action anytime, anywhere. Wolf had promised that he would contact them to see if they were willing to take to the woods and a life of outright rebellion against the authority of the white man—for this was what it amounted to now. These two were young, rebellious, and hungry for excitement. They were willing. And so they now rode with Pinetree.

The four were on their way to the One Arrow Reserve, for Blackbird had been yearning to see her child again, and Pinetree himself wished to be reassured that the little fellow had remained healthy and safe in the care of his grandmother.

For many days the outlaws rode southwest. At night they camped; in the daytime they traveled. Since the bounty-hunter incident slightly over a year ago, Pinetree had moved much farther north. Now the journey to the reserve was so long that the travelers found it necessary to do a bit of hunting along the way.

Then one day, nearing the end of their journey, they made camp about twenty miles northeast of Duck Lake. The three male Indians stayed in camp and the woman alone went on to the reserve. John Pinetree dared not go farther at this time; but Blackbird was to come back and let the others know if there were any redcoats patrolling the vicinity. If there were not, then Pinetree would ride in and get to see his son again.

On the morning following the day Blackbird left for the reserve, the three men mounted their horses and rode out of camp. Pinetree expected Blackbird to return in about two days, and during that time he and his men would try to find and bring down a deer. This hunt brought them within the borders of the reserve but still far from the permanent village-camp where Pinetree and Blackbird had left their child.

The air was cool and pleasant at this hour, but the cloudless sky forecasted a hot afternoon. The three riders cantered their horses side by side over the level landscape. Weed flowers bloomed in blazing patches of color. Here and there stood a grove of bright green poplar trees. Pinetree didn't have much hope of finding a deer or an elk in this immediate area, but he knew of a creek where game regularly came to drink, and so the riders headed in that direction.

Redleaf, who rode on the left side of the trio, suddenly pulled the reins of his horse so violently that the animal skidded to a stop and reared up on his hind legs. Pinetree and Born-on-the-Hill, surprised by this unexpected action, also brought their horses to a stop.

"Look!" said Redleaf. He pointed with his buckskin-fringed arm.

The hawk-eyes of Pinetree did a quick sweep of the open landscape toward which his friend pointed. Not a half-mile distant and magnificent in the morning sun, rode a patrol of red-coated members of the North-West Mounted Police. There appeared to be about two dozen riders.

For three seconds Pinetree sat in his saddle as still as a bronze statue before he said, "Quickly! Ride to those trees." He pointed. "They may not have seen us if they are all looking straight ahead."

He wheeled his horse about and the other two followed; they charged toward and into the nearest growth of poplars. Dismounting, they led their horses deeper into the grove.

"Check your guns," ordered Pinetree. He drew his revolver and made sure that all six chambers were loaded, then checked his rifle.

Now they could hear many horses' hooves drumming the prairie. The sound grew rapidly louder.

"The redcoats have seen us ride in here," realized Pinetree out loud.

In a moment they could see, indistinctly through the foliage, a splendid array of mounted policemen in their red coats and wide-brimmed brown hats. They were bringing their horses to a stop near the bush. The animals—mostly blacks and bays—excited by the quick dash they had just accomplished, were now prancing about in place. Pinetree reaffirmed his calculation that there were about twenty to twenty-five mounted police officers. The three outlaws crouched low. Then they heard the leader of the patrol speak.

"All of you go around to the other side. I'll take this side by myself."

As soon as this strange command had been given, the Indians heard the patrol obediently ride around to the other side of the grove. The man who had spoken was now alone.

Pinetree told his men, "You wait here." He got to his feet and started to walk.

"Where are you going?" whispered Redleaf.

"To kill their leader," returned Pinetree.

Revolver in hand, he started toward the edge of the grove where he knew the redcoat was on guard; but the foliage prevented a sighting at this point. As Pinetree cautiously worked his way among trees and underbrush, it suddenly came clear to him why the leader had made the apparently foolish move of separating himself from his men. Very likely he had thought that the three Indians would go straight through the bush and escape from the other side, in which case all of his men might be required there. But he himself had stayed on this side just in case he was wrong and the Indians backtracked.

Even under these circumstances the man was certainly doing a brave thing, decided Pinetree.

A moment later Pinetree was close enough to the edge of the grove to put him face to face with the redcoat. Pinetree recognized him at once; he was the little man with the large black mustache who headed up the Duck Lake police detachment. The lawman, standing beside his horse now, also had his revolver drawn. For a splinter of a second the two faced each other without moving. The small redcoat began to raise his gun.

Pinetree fired from the hip. The redcoat stood as though paralyzed, except that his gun hand lowered. With the gun slipping from his fingers, he fell forward on his face. But he was not dead. "Drop your gun and give yourself up," said the downed leader. He was forcing his head back to look up at the man who had shot him. The redcoat's forehead was wrinkled with pain and his voice was strained—and full of angry venom. "Give yourself up, Pinetree, you bastard. It's your only chance."

The Indian's finger toyed with his trigger. He had heard white men call other white men *bastards*, but had never learned what it meant, so he was not insulted. He wanted to take the policeman's gunbelt, but he knew that in order to do so in safety he would have to shoot him once more. But the little man looked so weak and pathetic. Strangely, Pinetree hesitated. Then he lowered his revolver, turned, and ran back among the trees. He stopped, still undecided. He peered back through the foliage and at that moment the rest of the patrol, or at least a large percentage of it, came thundering around the grove. They had, of course, heard the shot.

Pinetree quickly slunk back deeper into the grove where his companions were. The Indians could hear the sound of horses trampling about and the creaking of saddle leather, along with words about how best they could help their wounded leader. A tenor voice spoke up more clearly than the rest.

"Well, the command now devolves on you, Sergeant Saben."

"Yes," said the sergeant, and began to say something more but was cut off by the voice of the wounded leader: "I'm not dead yet, so I'm still in charge of this bloody outfit!"

"With all due respect, sir," said Sergeant Saben, "to be in charge you'd have to be on your feet. However, I'll respect your wishes and stay in contact with you as much as possible."

There was more cussing from the leader, then a few moans of pain.

The sergeant said, "Cartney, you and Melrose carry Commissioner Bancroft up to the top of that low rise. Take him behind the willow bushes and tend to his wound. The rest of you follow me on foot. We're going in after them!"

Bancroft's voice came again, more shaky now, but full of angry energy. "Yeah, you go in there and kill the sons of bitches!"

They wasted no time. "Charge!" yelled Sergeant Saben as he led his men in among the trees.

"They come," said Pinetree. "Start shooting."

His two companions were armed with rifles. Pinetree used his revolver. They crouched behind the slender poplar trees and fired rapidly at the approaching redcoats.

The heavy six-gun bucked and roared in the hand of Pinetree. He saw a redcoat twist back, grab his wounded arm, and retreat hurriedly.

Bullets buzzed through the air like angry bees. Pinetree noticed a redcoat lower himself to one knee and take careful aim. The Indian outlaw fired quickly. The police officer did a backward flop but managed to get to his hands and knees; he crawled away. The other two Indians were rapidly firing their rifles. Groans of pain sounded here and there from the enemy.

Then Pinetree realized that the redcoats had abruptly begun to retreat—in great haste. He would have continued to fire after them, but his gun was empty. His two companions released a few more shots at the running policemen.

"We may have killed some," observed Pinetree, "or maybe only wounded them, but we have put fear in their hearts and wings on their feet."

"And what will we do now?" asked Born-on-the-Hill.

"I do not know," admitted Pinetree. He wished that they could make a run for it, but felt that this was just what the redcoats wanted them to do. Out in the open they would have no chance whatever.

Pinetree slowly and cautiously moved toward the edge of the grove once more. He peered through between leafy branches.

Frowning, he turned away and, crossing through the bulk of the grove, had a look at the other side. He returned to his companions near the center.

"They have made a circle around us," he announced. "We cannot flee.... We must stay here."

"They are waiting for more redcoats to come," suggested Redleaf. "Then they will try again."

Pinetree agreed.

Redleaf then said that while Pinetree had been checking out the redcoats, Born-on-the-Hill had discovered that his horse had been shot dead and that he was now trying to find the other two. In a moment Born-on-the-Hill came back and reported that those two had likely fled the bush.

Morning gave place to afternoon. The Indians were fortunate in that they had brought food and a little water with them when they had started on their hunt; now they ate and drank sparingly.

Pinetree decided to build a barricade. The Indians gathered fallen trees for this purpose. None of these were large, for the *quaking aspen*—or *poplar*, as they're known in the area—seldom grows more than five inches in diameter; and some of them regularly die and fall from winds. When the crude bulwark was finished they dug a shallow hole behind it. They had no spade so they did this job with hunting knives, hands, and sometimes rifle butts. They arranged their guns and ammunition in handy positions. They waited.

Sometime later Pinetree detected the sound of hoofbeats by placing his ear against the ground. He saw that the patrol still had them surrounded, and not much later all three of the fugitives distinctly heard hoofbeats in the distance. Soon they saw the second patrol arrive—about thirty more men. There were two riders among them who did not wear red, and Pinetree supposed that they were either scouts or volunteers from Duck Lake. He wondered if any of the people he knew in Duck Lake would be willing to help the police. He guessed that they would. The riders dismounted and a little later he saw them check their weapons.

Pinetree went back to the barricade. "They will come soon," he told the others. "Be ready."

His companions accepted the news grimly. Tall, slender Redleaf wiped sweat from his face with a red bandanna. He was stripped down to leggings and breechcloth. Pinetree and Born-on-the-Hill also removed their buckskin shirts now.

They heard the sound of many leather-booted feet approaching. Through the foliage they caught glimpses of the red-coated white warriors drawing near on foot. Pinetree lowered himself behind the barricade and crouched tensely beside his brave companions. The heavy six-gun lay in his right hand, loaded with death. A moment later a number of the enemy arrived near enough to the grove to bring them more clearly into sight. They were only a few feet from the edge of the bush.

Pinetree fired over the barricade at the nearest redcoat, and missed. The police officers returned a volley of lead. Flying wood splinters and dirt struck the face of Pinetree. A bullet burned his ear. He ducked low behind the barricade, then straightened up quickly and fired three shots as rapidly as he could thumb and trigger them. He saw Mr. Garnue, the postmaster of Duck Lake, on his knees and clawing at his stomach. Again Pinetree wondered how many volunteers from Duck Lake were risking their lives to help the police in this effort to kill him.

The air vibrated with the rumble of exploding gunpowder. Blue smoke clouded the poplar grove.

Pinetree aimed his revolver through a crevice in the barricade, and when he saw a flash of red move by he pulled the trigger. The police officer leaped wildly into the air and came down on his back. He kicked around a bit before lying motionless.

Pinetree crouched low and looked to the side at his companions. Redleaf was firing boldly over the barricade. Born-on-the-Hill was hurriedly reloading his rifle. A long smear of red ornamented his cheek where a bullet had made a furrow. Pinetree fired one more shot, this time over top of the barricade, and then his revolver was empty. He reloaded it while the other two used their rifles to blast shot after shot at the redcoats.

Pinetree cocked his six-gun and straightened up. A ricocheting bullet whined past his ear; he heard it thud into a tree somewhere behind him.

Some of the redcoats were now in among the trees, but they were no longer advancing. Instead they did their best to find cover behind trees and shrubs. One officer flitted from behind a tree and ran a short distance in an attempt to gain a place of safer refuge. He was stopped by a rifle bullet that knocked him to the ground.

Pinetree fired twice at the redcoat he suspected was the leader of this frustrated attack. The second shot caught the man's hip, bringing him down on one knee. A moment later he had dragged himself out of sight behind weeds and underbrush, but he was still within the grove.

Pinetree squeezed his trigger again and another officer grunted and tumbled.

Then a loud command sounded above the violent rhythm of the gunshots. "Retreat!"

The leader of the outlaws breathed a sigh of relief. He continued to shoot quickly and carefully at his red-coated enemies as they hurriedly, while still firing, backed out of the poplar thicket. It had likely been the wounded man, the leader, who had ordered the retreat from where he lay hidden in the grass, thought Pinetree. He did not see anyone come to his aid and supposed they did not know the man was wounded.

Soon Pinetree stood erect behind the barricade, confident that every officer still on his feet had left the bush; but then he caught sight of the one he thought was their new leader, Sergeant Saben—the one he had wounded in the hip. The man was clearly visible to him through an opening in the foliage. Pinetree had always respected the redcoats for their bravery, so he was sure the other officers would have taken their leader with him had they known he was still alive. He certainly was showing signs of life now. He raised himself up to a half-standing position by holding on to a tree. And at the same time he lifted his revolver to fire another shot at the outlaws.

Pinetree deftly raised his own six-gun and pulled the trigger. The roar of the discharge seemed extra loud now that the other guns were silent. Through the smoke that drifted up from his own revolver, the Indian saw the police officer crumple like a falling blanket.

The other redcoats continued to retreat hurriedly and did not stop until they were a good distance away. Pinetree moved closer to the edge of the trees, staying on the alert now for other possible wounded enemies who might pop up suddenly and shoot. When he got close enough to the edge he saw that the retreating men had come to a halt on the slow-sloping hill that overlooked the grove of poplar trees. This was the hill—although it was hardly high enough to be called that—where earlier some of the men had taken the first wounded leader, Bancroft, and concealed him behind willow bushes. The highest point of this rise of ground was less than a quarter of a mile away from the outlaw ensconcement. Pinetree also noticed at once that a good number of police officers—those who had not participated in this last attack—still held the grove surrounded. He went back to the barricade.

"There are still many redcoats left," he said to his friends. "Some are surrounding us and some are on the higher ground, where they are licking their wounds. There are many of them and they all want us dead. We cannot run now, so we will wait—wait for a chance to run. And if no chance to run comes, we will fight together to the very last and die together bravely like the true warriors we have already proven ourselves to be."

Suddenly a bullet whined through the treetops, then another and another in quick succession. Next came the corresponding sounds of gunshots in the distance.

Pinetree released a loud laugh. "They are shooting at us from the hill," said he. "They have found it is better not to come close."

* * *

The tables had been removed from the mess hall in the police barracks at Regina and the large room had been decorated with red, white, and blue garlands. There was laughter and merriment. Ladies in lovely gowns glided about gracefully with their uniformed partners to the lilting rhythm of a two-step.

A contingent of policemen had been selected to sail to England and there ride in the Diamond Jubilee procession of Queen Victoria. The present celebration was a send off.

Everyone appeared to be happy. The room was filled with light from many wall-hung oil lamps and with music from red-coated musicians on a bandstand.

Colonel Schmermer, the Commissioner, guided his attractive partner onto the crowded floor and they began to dance. She was not his wife and she was not any woman he had ever touched before. She had a lovely smile.

He said, "And how are you tonight, my dear?"

"Enjoying the celebration," she said, turning up the delightful wick of her smile a little higher.

Schmermer unglued his eyes from her face and as he looked over her shoulder he saw a door swing open. He recognized the man who stepped inside as Sergeant Coleson, the officer in charge of the town station. He was in his work-uniform jodhpurs, booted and spurred, and his face wore an urgent expression.

Commissioner Schmermer quit dancing and said to his partner, "Please excuse me for a moment."

"Certainly."

"Something seems to have come up and probably needs my attention. I hope to get back to you."

He walked her to a chair before striding over to Coleson who was already coming toward him. Schmermer said, "Well, Sergeant, what is it?"

"Telegram, sir." Coleson handed the message to the colonel.

Schmermer read it quickly. Immediately he walked over to the orchestra and stopped the music.

"Ladies and gentlemen," he began loudly so he could be heard above the cheerful hubbub. He waited briefly for the room to grow quiet and when it did he continued. "Ladies and gentlemen, there is Indian trouble in the North. Commissioner Bancroft, whom many of you know, has been wounded and there has been some loss of life. I do not yet have the details on who have given their lives in the line of duty…. This looks like an Indian uprising. The Mounted Police have something else to do besides dancing. As soon as it can be arranged, for those ladies who were brought here by members of the force, conveyances will be at the door to take you to your homes. Good evening, and may God be with us."

And so the celebration came abruptly to an end. A well equipped party, Under the command of Assistant Commissioner Rintley, took the early morning train. They went north toward the town of Duck Lake. One boxcar was filled with their riding horses and another with tack.

And on a flatcar, chained to the platform, was a field gun.

* * *

The wife of Pinetree cradled her infant son in her arms and wished fervently that she could take him with her when the time came for her to leave. She sat alone, save for the presence of her child, in the teepee of Pinetree's mother, Laughing-Buffalo-Calf.

The flap door opened then and Buffalo-Calf entered. She was out of breath and crying, but managed to announce, "They have caught him! He and the other two are trapped in a little bush near where you said you made camp.... The redcoats are going to shoot them with a big thunder stick!"

Clutching the child to her breasts, Blackbird rose to her feet. For a moment she was silent; then she said fiercely, "Who told you this?"

"None other than Strong-Man, the son of Chief One-Arrow," sobbed the elderly Buffalo-Calf. "It is true. He came here to tell me."

The younger woman sank back to her blankets on the ground. Then she laid the child in his own little nest of blankets, and once more rose to her feet. She started toward the exit.

"Where are you going?" asked Buffalo-Child. Then, realizing the answer in advance, she continued quickly. "Do not go. They will kill you too!"

"I have to go."

Soon she had saddled and mounted her pinto gelding. She lashed him once with the loose end of her reins. The horse sprang forward like an attacking snake. She held the reins loosely on his neck and he streaked across the level grass-carpeted prairie, his hooves drumming out a tom-tom rhythm of fear.

Blackbird knew of no way to help her lover. Only one thing was clear in her anxiety stricken mind. She wanted to be near him.

20

They came around a bend in the trail and caught sight of the road station only about a quarter of a mile away. There wasn't much to it— a two-story log house, a medium-sized log barn, corrals, a stack of hay, and a wagon parked near the barn. Even at this distance everything had the look of needing repair. And the concept of paint had likely never come into the mind of the builder. All the wood was a weather-beaten gray with shadings of brown. But the surrounding grass was in its early-summer green glory, along with the numerous thickets of emerald-green poplar trees. The sky was a near-cloudless brilliant blue.

Don felt good about being back in Canada and only a little more than a day's ride from Duck Lake, but he still was not wearing his uniform. After having the *Windy Valley Laundry* clean it for him, he had once more packed it away, but he knew he'd be wearing it again soon—when he'd be welcomed back by some of the brass of the force, and, even more wonderfully, when he'd be reunited with Rita.

Casting a shadow over all this were his worries about Jim and Meadow who were still with him, only now in a single-seated buggy with a fair-sized box area behind the seat in which the trio's belongings and travel supplies were packed. The rig was pulled by a team of chestnuts with flaxen manes and tails—the same beautiful horses that had taken Jim and Meadow on their life-changing Christmas eve ride. The horses were, incredibly, a wedding present to Jim and Meadow from Wilf Peterson, which proved, beyond a doubt, that there was still some goodness left in the heart of mankind; for Wilf's pain at not being able to win Meadow would be something he would live with for the rest of his life. But by making such a generous gesture of love-under-any-circumstances, Wilf proved, according to Don's philosophical reasoning, that he would survive the disappointment and, hopefully, go on to better things than gambling at the Big Wheel Saloon.

Jim and Meadow had not given up their riding horses, however. Jim's bay stallion and Meadow' white gelding led well, and so, with their halter shanks tied to the rear of the buggy box, were making this leg of the journey with no weights on their backs. The saddles were in the box along with all the other things. Only Don continued to keep butt to leather on his handsome black gelding that was a gift from Geronimo.

When Jim and Meadow had announced their intention to be married, along with Jim's decision to not give himself up to Canadian authorities for the murder of Chuck Scote, Don had been immensely relieved. The marriage ceremony had been beautiful, and the happy couple had rented a small house on the outskirts of the town of Windy Valley. The rest of the winter had gone by peacefully, and, for Don, slowly. While Jim and Meadow were romping about—as Don imagined—in their cozy bed of marriage bliss, he himself was sleeping alone on the pins and needles of doubt. Was Rita still waiting for him?

Apparently she was, for there had been some communication by way of travelers to and from Canada who happened to pass through Windy Valley; there had been three envelopes, two going and one coming. Not that these had made it all the way in the hands of a single wayfarer, for no one traveled that far in wintertime nor even in spring while the thaw made roads near impassable. But in wintertime some traveled shorter distances, and these had connected with others, and, somehow, the messages had gotten through.

The first envelope from Don had contained two letters—one to his bosses, explaining in greater detail what had happened to him and saying that he hoped to get as far as the *Southland Station* by a particular date, and one to Rita. The envelope had made it to police headquarters in Regina and from there the enclosed letter to Rita had been delivered to her in Duck Lake. In the same way one had come back from her, carried in an official looking envelope along with a letter from the North-West Mounted.

Rita indicated that she was very happy to hear that Don was safe and could hardly wait for him to get back. But she said nothing about their interrupted plans for a wedding.

Commissioner Bancroft wrote that the force was awaiting Don's return, and informed him that he would be required to appear before an investigative committee to officially relate what had happened to take him away from his regular duties for so long—even though Don had already described that in considerable detail in his letter to headquarters.

There had been another item in the letter from Bancroft—an item that had worried Don a lot, and still did. The Commissioner informed Don that the adoptive parents of Jim Longfeather, who was being sought by the North-West Mounted, had arrived from the east and were staying at Duck Lake in the hope of once more seeing their runaway son. Bancroft wondered if Don, before or after being kidnapped, had come across any information on Longfeather that might indicate where he had run off to. Don had toyed with the idea of not sharing this information with Jim, but had quickly decided that he had no right to withhold it.

Jim was too soft-hearted to ignore the information. It hadn't taken him long to decide that he would return to Canada, to Duck Lake, with the hope of meeting his parents secretly. He would explain to them what had happened, so that, perhaps, they would understand somewhat better why he had done what he did. Then he and Meadow would return to the United States, probably to stay there for the rest of their lives.

Meadow tried to talk Jim out of going to Canada. Don probably tried even harder. It was no use. Eventually all three worked together to come up with the best plan to enable Jim to successfully pull off this dangerous adventure.

Jim and Meadow took on the identities of Mr. and Mrs. Parenteau, Howard and Elly, a cultured Metis couple who hoped to start up a general store somewhere in the Northwest Territories. They traveled in a nice spring-supported buggy pulled by an expensive looking team. Mrs. Parenteau was dressed conservatively and tastefully, and Mr. Parenteau sported a narrow brimmed hat, a fine suit, and a gold-looking watch chain. And he had a beard—a removable one that someone had found at the back of the Big Wheel Saloon and had sold to him for the outrageous sum of five dollars. But it was a realistic looking one of black, human-looking hair streaked with gray, and had a lining that when moistened held the thing precariously to the face. It had probably been left behind by some of the traveling thespians who occasionally made their way through smaller towns. Jim slapped this thing on only when there was a possibility of meeting up with someone, and at such a time, if he was in the buggy, he would slouch down low in the seat to disguise his great size; and when he was out of the buggy he would walk stooped over and leaning on an ivory-headed cane that had cost him considerably more than the beard. Standing and walking in a stooped posture didn't really make him look any smaller; it simply made him look like a big cripple. But the three agreed that this did contribute considerably to his disguise.

When they got closer to the roadhouse they could read its homemade, poorly hand-lettered sign: *SOUTHLAND STATION— Food and Lodging—Prop. Sylvester Ellrose.*

Jim, putting on his beard, sounded a little muffled as he commented on the sign. "Sylvester Ellrose. With a name like that running the place I guess we can expect to be eating caviar for dinner."

"And drinking tea out of delicate teacups," added Meadow.

Don knew better, for he had been through the place on journeys from Regina to Duck Lake and back, but he didn't say anything.

Jim's and Meadow's hopes of finding even a smidgen of genteelness at this roadhouse were shattered when they pulled up between the barn and the house, and a large and roundly built manure-splattered man holding a pitchfork came out of the barn and introduced himself as Sylvester Ellrose. He did this by saying, "Hallo, I'm Sylvester Ellrose. You can dump your horses in the barn or in the corral, as you please. I gotta git back to pitchin' shit…. Will you be wantin' dinner?"

The three were silent for a whole two seconds before Meadow responded, "Well, if it's not too much bother for your cook…."

Sylvester further verified their fears. "*I'm* the cook, an' no, it ain't too much bother."

"I'd be happy to help you out by preparing our meal," said Meadow, "if you'll let me use your kitchen." She was still in the buggy, but Jim was climbing down, trying to look crippled, and Don had dismounted.

Sylvester used a callused hand to wipe a bit of soggy manure off a prong of his pitchfork. "No," he said, flicking the manure to the ground, "I ain't got a kitchen, an' I do the cookin' around here…. An'

I'll feed your horses too—you don't need to bother yourselves with that either. It's a quarter of a buck per day per horse, an' if yous decide to stay fer the night, it's fifty cents fer a bed—seems you'll be needin' two—an' a quarter per person fer each meal. An' you gotta pay in advance."

Jim was already unfastening one of the harness traces, looking as though his back was giving him a lot of trouble.

Sylvester continued, "I'm meaning that you pay me now, afore yous unhitch."

"I'll get it," said Don. He dropped the reins of his horse and turned to his saddlebags. Sylvester quickly stepped up, and when Don handed him the money he noticed that the man's teeth were either half rotten or badly stained with tobacco juice—maybe both.

* * *

Dinner, the noon meal, was pretty much as unpleasant as expected, or worse. They sat around a square wooden table with two other travelers who had arrived just in time to test their molars on the meat. It seemed to be that of a bull that had died of old age and then had been left where he fell until he had petrified. Even the big scraggly brown dog that kept putting his snout on the edge of the table had a hard time coping with it when Sylvester finally threw him a chunk. The dishes the food was served on looked as though they had been spit on for washing and held up to the dog's wagging tail for drying.

As Sylvester had said, there was no kitchen. The ground floor had only one room, quite large and cluttered with things that should have been in the barn or in a shed—things like a set of harness under repair, a manure shovel, and a horse-drawn-type of grass mower, also obviously under repair since about half of it was missing. But there was also a cookstove.

In one corner a narrow stairway without a railing led up into sleeping quarters, the possible horrors of which were at this time still a mystery to all of the newly arrived travelers except Don.

When the meal was about half over, Sylvester, who was eating together with his guests, suddenly sat up straighter and quit chewing. "Oh, I damn near forgot," he said. "A redcoat came through here just the other day. Said he was comin' from Duck Lake and headin' fer Regina. An' he left a letter fer you folks."

"For us?" said Don.

"Fer you, I guess," said Sylvester, looking at Don. "Yeah, it was fer Sergeant Don Korman...or whatever the hell you said your name was."

"Roman," said Don, "Sergeant Don Roman."

"Yeah, it was fer you, sure as shit."

Jim spoke up in his best stilted, formal sounding English. "My dear sir, I would greatly appreciate it if you would control your urge to use disagreeable language when in the presence of this lady."

From under hair as rumpled as the room around him, Sylvester glared at Jim for a moment, apparently not quite comprehending, but then he said, "Oh, yeah. Sorry. Shit, I keep forgetting. Don't see many women around here. I'll go git the letter." He got his bulk up on his feet and waddled toward the stove.

One of the other two travelers, a bony man of about fifty, looked angry. Now that Sylvester's back was turned, he began to shake his head sadly for the benefit of the others as though to let them know that he also disapproved of their host's crude language. His sidekick (for the two had arrived together), was a younger man and his reaction to the conversation was one of smiling amusement.

Sylvester opened the warming cabinet over the cook stove, and, from behind some dirty dishes stored there along with a variety of small junk, pulled out an envelope. He brought it back to the table and more or less threw it at Don. Sylvester sat down, chased flies off his plate, and got back to eating.

Don was on his feet. "If you'll all excuse me, please, I think I'd better see what this is." He was surging with excitement as he walked toward the door, at the same time carefully tearing off the end of the envelope.

He opened the screen door and glanced back at the table before stepping outside. He knew that Jim and Meadow would be wanting very much to know what the letter was about. Sylvester said, "Why's he gotta go outside t' read it? There's enough light in here."

Don didn't let himself pull the letter out of the envelope until he was comfortably seated on a chopping block that had been sawed out of a large log. A small pile of firewood gave off a pleasant smell of drying sap under the noon sun. It was a beautiful day and one that might become even more beautiful if the envelope contained a letter from Rita. He knew it hadn't been addressed by her, but, rather, by Colonel Shmermer who had been stationed at the Regina headquarters at the time of Don's kidnapping. That name was up in the left-hand corner of the envelope, but there was a good chance that Rita had again managed to put a letter of her own in with this one from the brass.

And she had. Don hardly glanced at the other letter, the one from Schmermer, laying it aside on the woodpile and hurriedly unfolding the one from Rita. Her very feminine and amazingly curly handwriting, read:

Dear Don,

I am so lonesome for you. I do not know which will get to you first, this letter or me. You see, once I found out that you would be coming on the Regina trail and would be stopping at the Southland Station, I decided to try to meet you there! Everyone thinks I am crazy to do that, but who cares? It means that I could get to see you a day or two sooner. Of course you could be off on the time you hoped to get there, but what is the difference? If you are late I will wait there, and if you are already past that point, I will meet you somewhere on the trail, wherever that might happen to be. I love you very much and look forward to a warm hello!

Don's heart was beating ridiculously fast for a man who had calmly faced death a number of times. This was more exciting. The *warm hello* sounded real good, but, again, she said nothing about their wedding plans. That worried him a little.

I expect to arrive at the Southland Station roadhouse on June the fourth.

June the fourth? What was the date today? He didn't know. Don was tempted to go running back into the house like a silly kid, shouting out his desire to learn what day of the month this was; but he controlled himself and finished reading the letter. There wasn't much more, but it was all good stuff. She surrounded her signature with one circle of o's and one of x's, meaning hugs and kisses, and another circle made up of o's and x's cleverly combined so that one upward angled branch of each x appeared to pass through the center of each o. Only Rita would think of doing something like that. Her powerful sexuality frightened Don a little, yet he was confident that when the time came he could handle her.

He refolded her letter, tucked it safely into a shirt pocket, and reached for the one from Colonel Schmermer, expecting it to be nothing more than further formalities. He was surprised enough at its contents so that he momentarily forgot about wondering when Rita would arrive.

Dear Sergeant Roman:

Thank you for your missive informing us of the progress of your journey back to our native land. It had been decided that a small contingent of riders would come out to meet you at the Southland Station, but, unfortunately, something has come up that has necessitated a change in those plans.

As you no doubt will recall, when you left, the Indian outlaw, John Pinetree, was still at large and wanted for the murder of Sergeant Walker. On May the twenty-sixth, only three days ago at the time of this writing, Pinetree and two cohorts were discovered on the One Arrow Reserve. They were at once surrounded but refused to surrender. There has been considerable loss of life. Commissioner Bancroft has been wounded but is presently in fair condition and still at the site. All available members of the force within the Duck Lake area and a contingent from Regina have been called to help. That is why no welcoming committee will be available to meet you. For that I am sorry.

Although I am not ordering you to help in this situation, you are certainly welcome to come to the One Arrow Reserve and join in with the others if you are so inclined. The site is only about a mile south of where the Twin Creeks meet, and I know you are familiar with that area.

You must understand that this is not simply a matter of three Indians making trouble. A negative outcome, involving a few more deaths in our ranks, could possibly encourage other natives to rebel and come to the aid of this long-time troublemaker, thus possibly initiating a serious uprising.

In any case, I heartily welcome you home, and look forward to hearing from you personally regarding your amazing adventures south of the border.

Sincerely,
Colonel James Schmermer

Don headed back toward the house. He came to a stop, wondering if he should share this latest information with Jim, who still considered himself to have some kind of ridiculous blood-brother relationship with Pinetree. There was no telling what he'd do when he found out the outlaw was surrounded and facing death. But Don realized he couldn't very well keep this to himself. For one thing, he felt duty bound to follow Schmermer's suggestion (it was almost a thinly-veiled order) that he head out to the scene of action to help in any way he could.

When he got back into the house the others were still all sitting around the table. Don said, "What day of the month is this?"

"The third," said Sylvester unhesitatingly and threw another piece of meat at his dog who risked mouth injury by catching it in midair.

"And tomorrow's the fourth," said Don, smiling as though he had just learned to count.

"No shit," said Sylvester.

* * *

There were four small bedrooms upstairs and they weren't quite as bad as Meadow and Jim had feared. The bedding looked and smelled reasonably clean, and each room had a couple of chairs plus a small handmade dresser holding a large tin basin, a pitcher of water, towels, and soap. The five guests were shown three of the rooms and Meadow, being the only woman, was given first choice. Since they were all the same it was no big thing. The two men who had arrived together decided to use the same room to save money, leaving Don the only one who didn't need to share his room with anyone. Sylvester explained that he himself was presently using the fourth

room, but that if more travelers arrived he would give it up and sleep in the barn hayloft.

The horror of the evening meal was past and darkness had come before the trio got around to cleaning themselves up from their dusty hours of travel that day. Don's room was next to that of Jim and Meadow and the walls were not thick enough to keep out sound. He could hear every word they said and the splashing of water as they probably bathed together stark naked with the tin basin between them. It was enough to drive a single man crazy to think of it—to imagine what Meadow looked like. This was easy because he had seen her naked; but he could only guess at how exciting she must look smiling up at Jim, knowing she was turning him on and liking it.

Don was naked too, and bathing with a washcloth dipped in the basin. They had talked Sylvester into heating up enough water on the cook stove to bathe everyone, but it had cost them an extra four bits.

With Meadow occasionally whispering something on the other side of the wall, and then moaning with pleasure, Don's libido kept building. Normally he would certainly have released the pressure with a few strokes, but because he had some kind of half baked idea of wanting to be his horniest self when he met with Rita the next day—to not be outdone by her—he determined to suffer through it.

* * *

They spent most of the next morning arguing about the John Pinetree situation. It was two against one—Don and Meadow against Jim. Jim wanted to go and try to talk Pinetree into giving himself up; Don and Meadow were reasonably sure that if he embarked on this impossible endeavor, he himself would be arrested and Meadow would likely spend the rest of her life as either a widow or a "prison widow." It was this thought that kept Jim from what would otherwise have been a quick decision to go and try to help Pinetree somehow.

Another concern was that if Rita showed up today as her letter had stated, she must not see Jim, for even with his phony beard she would likely recognize him. Don was certain he could trust her not to tell anyone, but did not want to saddle her with this information that would make her an accomplice to Longfeather's dodging of the law. Jim totally agreed with this and decided that he would ride out alone

to a nearby stand of trees from which he could keep an eye on the road station from concealment. He promised to wait there until he got an all-clear signal, and also that he would not start out for the One Arrow Reserve without telling Meadow and Don. At this point he still had not made up his mind.

So Jim saddled his stallion and rode off. Sylvester Ellrose was told that he had gone out for a day's ride to enjoy the countryside and possibly to do some hunting, and that the whole party would likely stay at the station for another night.

Then Don, all clean and shaved and uniformed, waited nervously for Rita to arrive. Somehow he could hardly believe that she would — not for any sensible reason, but simply because it seemed too good to be true. Meadow kept herself in her room, ostensibly to read some outdated newspapers she had found, but, more likely, thought Don, to worry and pray that Jim would not go to help Pinetree.

* * *

Rita showed up at sunset. Don was looking out of his upstairs window toward the west, not thinking about Rita just then — for no one ever arrives at the moment one is looking for them — when a movement on the trail to the north caught his eye. He whipped his face in that direction and saw, about a quarter of a mile distant, the approaching buggy. It had a top and this dimmed his view of the occupants, but he could make out that there were two — the driver and the smaller figure of a woman. He was sure that it was Rita, partly because a narrow ray of the setting red sun managed to squeeze through the tiny peekaboo window in the leatherette side of the buggy's covering and reflect off a bit of her blonde hair, and partly because he just knew.

His heart pounding, Don turned away from the window and looked at his image in the cracked mirror that hung above the water basin. He was uniformed but still bareheaded, clean, shaved, and with his hair neatly combed — had been like that most of the day. Now he put on his stiff-brimmed hat at just the right angle and hurried quietly out of his room and down the stairway, hoping that no one would see him and follow him outside, for he wanted this reunion to be as private as possible. But before he had made it all the way down the stairs the stupid dog began barking and Sylvester's voice, floating from out of a dark corner of the still unlit main room, said, "Shit, someone's coming." He was probably upset, Don realized, because another guest would mean that he'd have to sleep in the barn.

As Don worked his way through the dim room, sidestepping things, he told Sylvester, "It's someone I'm expecting. I'll take care of meeting them and welcoming them, if you don't mind."

"Go ahead," said Sylvester, "an' you can help 'em unhitch an' feed their bloody horses too if you want, just make sure they know ahead a' time what it's gonna cost 'em. You got that part straight?"

"Yeah," said Don, then realized he wasn't really clear on all the costs. But he kept going and said, "I'll take care of it, and would you please light a lamp?"

As Don stepped through the doorway into the rose-tinted sunset evening, he could hear Sylvester behind him grumbling something about the high cost of kerosene.

When he got around the corner of the house, Don saw that the approaching buggy was only about fifty yards away now. He wondered if he should walk forward to meet Rita, but decided to stay where he was, assuming an at-ease military posture—feet somewhat separated and hands behind his back. He had always thought that it was a posture that showed off the uniform to full effect.

The buggy approached slowly and almost silently, a black silhouette against the sunset. Suddenly, from another direction, came jogging footsteps and the rustle of skirts. Meadow came running up to him from in the direction of the barn. Her white horse was tied to the corral there. He had thought that she was in her room, but obviously she had been with Jim in his little bush hideout overlooking the yard. The low sun revealed rose-tinted tears on her cheeks. He realized that she was not aware of the approaching buggy.

"Meadow," he said, "why are you crying?"

"He says he's going. He's gonna start out in the morning…and I can't talk him out of it…. Oh, Don, I'm so afraid that he's gonna be killed if he goes out there!"

She stepped in close, put her arms around Don, her head on his shoulder, and sobbed.

What could he do? He put his arms around her and tried to think of some comforting words.

* * *

Rita had no trouble recognizing Don. The low sun had been full in his face until he had turned toward that woman who had suddenly come running into his arms. A dark pain came into Rita's heart. It was almost as though that glorious sun behind her had suddenly dropped the last few miles behind the horizon, casting darkness over everything. Yet she could still see Don and the woman embracing.

The man beside her was obviously quite aware of her thoughts and feelings even though not even a gasp or a moan had escaped her. "Take it easy, Rita," he said. "There can be a hundred satisfactory explanations for this." He looked to be in his forties and had a dashing look about him, mainly because his handsome face was decorated with a narrow mustache. He wore a clean felt hat with its brim just a shade narrower than most, and his shirt and pants looked a cut above average.

Rita responded, "But only one likely one.... Well, what could I expect when we've been separated for so long."

"All right, it's good for you to be prepared for the worst," said the handsome man, "but at the same time don't jump to conclusions."

Don and the woman were out of their hug now, but still standing close together.

Rita leaned back more into the buggy seat and looked down at her feet. She said, "I feel like jumping into a river, but I don't think there's any nearby."

* * *

Meadow said, "Oh, Don, I'm so sorry! I didn't see the buggy coming! But I'll explain to your fiancée why I was hugging you. I'm sure she'll understand."

"Yeah, she will...but I'd rather explain it to her myself."

"All right.... Well, then, I'm out of here. I'm going up to my room and you can call me down when...whenever you think it's the right time. I'm certainly looking forward to meeting your girl." With that she left and hurried toward the front of the house, quickly disappearing around a corner.

The buggy came closer and now Don could see both Rita and the man reasonably well, although the sun was just barely peeking through red clouds behind them. Rita was even more beautiful than he remembered her, and the man…he was too damned good looking to suit Don. And Rita didn't look happy—as though maybe she had some unpleasant news for him.

The driver pulled the horses to a stop, and before Don had taken two steps toward the buggy, the handsome man proved that he was quite athletic by hopping down off the rig faster than a frog could have done it and holding out his arms for Rita, to help her down. She accepted that help without a blink, and, as her slender, shapely body was easily hoisted to the ground by Mr. Biceps, a thrill surged through Don in spite of his misgivings. She was wearing a dark blue dress, snug at the waist and low cut at the front, but with a silky scarf mostly covering the otherwise exposed top curves of her breasts. "Thank you, Darcy," she said to the mustached man. Then, still unsmiling, she came toward Don who was also moving toward her. As he raised his arms to enclose her in that long dreamed of hug, she came to a sharp stop and held out a hand as though to ward him off.

"One moment, Handsome!" she said, and the sound of that golden voice thrilled Don deeply even though there was an edge of hardness to it. "You're still warm from that woman you were hugging. While you're cooling, you can tell me who she is and what's going on."

"Of course," said Don. "And I'm very sorry that she…that she had a need for a hug just when you were arriving. She was emotionally upset and didn't see or hear you."

"Well, I guess I can't blame her for being emotionally upset when your old flame comes along."

In that terrible moment Don knew that he had no choice but to tell Rita everything. There was no other way. "Rita, I need to talk to you alone."

She gave the handsome man a glance. "Oh, you don't have to worry about Darcy. I don't have any secrets from him."

When Don had recovered from this slap on the head, he said, "Well, *I* do!…I'm sure that Darcy, being the gentleman he obviously is, will not object to you and I stepping around the corner of the house for just a moment, so I can tell you what I need to tell you!"

Darcy said, "Certainly, that's just fine. In fact, I'll drive over to the barn and you can both stay right where you are to continue your discussion."

Don and Rita stood stiffly until Darcy had driven the rig reasonably out of earshot. Then Don said, "All right, here's what you need to know. The woman you saw me hugging is the wife of Jim Longfeather. As you probably know, he's wanted by the Police. I came across Jim in the Arizona Territories. That's where I also met the woman you saw—Meadow, and we've become good friends. Jim and Meadow are married and very much in love. Jim is here too, hiding in a little bush only about a quarter of a mile away. He's found out that his old buddy, John Pinetree, is up to his neck in trouble on the One Arrow Reserve and plans to go and try to help him. Meadow is scared spitless that he'll go and get himself either shot or arrested. That's why she came crying into my arms. She had just been talking to him and he told her that he plans to start out for the reserve tomorrow morning."

For a few seconds Rita just stood there staring up at him. Then she removed the silky scarf, revealing the top bulges of her breasts, and said, "Well, then, what do *I* have to do to get that hug treatment?"

"For a starter you can tell me a little about *Dandy Darcy* and what your relationship is with him."

Rita seemed surprised. "You're jealous of Darcy?" She seemed to think about the matter for a moment, then continued, "Yeah, I guess he is kind of good looking, and he's a sharp dresser, but he can't compare with your looks and your uniform…. And he's not the one I'm in love with. Darcy is my new pastor."

"So what's he doing driving you around instead of tending to his flock?"

Rita smiled for the first time since she had seen Don hugging Meadow. "Well, I got this wild idea…. I thought maybe we could get married right away, you know, since it's been put off for so long. I brought a wedding dress and the pastor to tie the knot. I figured we could probably find a couple or so travelers to be witnesses. Darcy thought it was real funny but was willing to go along with it. So, what do you think? We could get married tonight and sleep together."

Don was smiling now too; in fact, he was close to laughing. But he held that back and instead stepped close to Rita and took her into his arms. "Rita, you're the most wonderful woman in the world." He kissed her with a lengthy kiss, and she not only put her heart into it but her tongue as well. When Don was about ready to explode, he drew back from her and tried to speak in a controlled, level voice, one worthy of a police officer in uniform. "I really appreciate you being willing to marry me tonight, and I can't tell you how much I want to do that, but...."

"But what? If I need to strip naked right now to help you to make up your mind, I'll do it." She put a hand to the top button of her dress, just below where the exposed parts of her breasts met in an inverted V.

He was sure she would do it if he gave her the slightest approval, and he was tempted to let her, even though he thought Sylvester and his dog were probably watching from a dark window. He still had not lit a lamp.

"I'd say *yes* to all that your suggesting...only the timing isn't right." He stepped to her side and took her arm. "Let's walk a bit farther away from the house. I want to make sure no one hears us."

The sun was behind the horizon and the western sky had dimmed into a dull glow like a partly ashy ember when Don brought them to a stop near a patch of willow bushes. A few frogs were croaking contentedly in the little slough behind the bushes. Don carried on his explanation of why the wedding-right-now was not a good idea. "I've already told you about this awful problem I have with Jim Longfeather. He's on the brink of putting himself in a position where he'll get killed."

"But you're a police officer yourself. Shouldn't you be bringing him in?"

"Of course I should be—at least according to the letter of the law.... But he's a good man. The death of Scote took place under very mitigating circumstances...and...Jim saved my life and has become my best friend. Then there's Meadow. Her life will be ruined if she loses Jim.... I could never turn him in."

"I see what you're saying. I agree."

"Do you realize what I've just done to you? I've made you a co-conspirator abetting a fugitive in staying out of the hands of the law."

"You know, that's kind of exciting…and okay since it's really for a good cause. Just last Sunday Pastor Darcy was preaching that it's the spirit of the law that counts much more than the letter of the law."

"Well, let's leave him in the dark about this particular case."

"Of course."

Don said, "I don't want our wedding to be spoiled—not to mention our wedding night—because of this heavy thing hanging on my heart."

"Oh, well," said Rita, "we've waited this long, I guess we can wait a little longer."

"I'm so glad you understand."

"So, if I can't sleep with you tonight, I hope there still are some rooms available in this luxurious mansion."

"We'll work out something," said Don. "Likely some of the men will be bedding down in the barn loft."

An excited look came into her eyes. "I know we're not getting married tonight…but just think, if we had, we could have slept together up in the hayloft if we wanted to…. I've always had this daydream of doing you in a hayloft."

Don wondered how they would survive this night. He was about ready to mess up the inside of his clean uniform; but that didn't stop him from grabbing up Rita and kissing her until their mouths were slippery.

* * *

In some ways the night passed by better than Don had hoped, in other ways worse. There were several reasons for this. First of all, he had not wanted Rita to sleep in Sylvester's room, even with him in the hayloft and the sheets changed. The room smelled of tobacco, dog dander, and sweat. Rita and Meadow were hitting it off wonderfully, and, being women, took it upon themselves to solve the bedding problem: Meadow and Rita would sleep together in Meadow's and Jim's room, and Jim, Don, and Pastor Darcy would sleep in Don's room, two in bed and one on blankets on the floor. The good part of all this was that Don, in the company of two other men, could get his mind off sex more than if he had been sleeping alone; the bad part was the recurring thought that if he hadn't been so stupid he could be married by now and sleeping with Rita.

Don was not seriously tempted with the thought of having sex with Rita before marriage, and he knew that she wasn't either. In the clear-cut culture they lived in, and with the strict Christian upbringing that both of them had experienced, it seemed there were only two kinds of people in a sexual sense: the loose-living ones who had no sexual morals, and those who lived by the commands of God, abstaining from fornication and adultery. So if you were trying to be a good person and you wanted to have sex, you got married.

Jim had come back from his hideout shortly after sunset, at Don's prearranged signal: an up and down movement of a barn-lantern. Don, Rita, and Meadow met him at the barn, and Don let him know that Rita was now one of the inner circle. Jim took it well, apparently realizing that Rita could be trusted — or, maybe, not caring because he felt he would probably be riding to his death the next day anyhow.

Jim insisted on sleeping on the floor, which made sense because his size would have left little room in the bed for anyone else. This meant that Don had to sleep with a pastor, a new experience for him.

The pastor had not been told that Jim and Meadow were married, so he thought it only proper that the women share one room and the men another. He also had said a very nice prayer for everyone in the building just before they all went up to their rooms.

The pastor turned out to be a dangerous bed partner. At first he did nothing more violent than snore; but sometime during the night he began to bounce about and fling his arms and legs around, while at the same time yelling, "Down! — down, you evil beast!"

Don flung himself to one side to avoid being hit and almost fell out of bed. The pastor quickly settled down, apparently without having awakened; but Jim had been roused. From his blankets on the floor, he said, "What's going on?"

Don answered quietly. "It's okay now, but for a moment there the pastor turned into Saint George fighting the dragon. I think he won."

"Well, tie him down and gag him if you have to," grumbled Jim. "I'd like to get a little sleep."

Yeah, thought Don, *you want to get your sleep so you can be fresh and alert tomorrow when you go out to get killed.* Don was not looking forward to the next day.

21

In the morning things were better than Don had hoped. Jim, after sleeping on the matter of John Pinetree, apparently had developed second thoughts about going to his aid. The critical factor seemed to have been the same as on Christmas eve, when Meadow's welfare had won out over his sense of sacrificial duty and a deep-seated need to be law abiding.

Although Don was relieved that Jim was holding back from racing off to the One Arrow Reserve, the bad side of the situation was that he himself now had a somewhat similar problem. Don felt a great need to get out there and do his duty as a police officer and help bring the killing to a stop as quickly as possible. But Rita, having just received him back into her arms after his long disappearance, was not at all willing that he should again ride away over the horizon where he could get his head blown off as likely as not.

Added to the uncomfortable brew was the fact that Jim and Don had two very different slants on Pinetree. To Jim he was a misguided person and a blood brother who had once saved his life and whom he had promised to stand by in times of trouble; but Don saw Pinetree as a troublemaker who had killed a police officer in the past and was now killing more of them.

Rita could not talk Don out of going. He saddled up his black, packed some food into a bedroll and tied that behind the cantle. It was a western roping saddle rather than the cavalry-type used by many members of the North-West Mounted, and he supposed he would soon have to get used to one of those again.

He had already kissed Rita good-bye, and she was now in the house being consoled by Meadow. As he filled his canteen at the well near the barn, Jim came walking up to him. Coming to a stop, he set one booted foot up on the edge of the plank water-trough, but said nothing. He was wearing his beard and the whole respectable merchant outfit, and today looked particularly uncomfortable in it.

Don's horse, having already had his fill of water, had wandered over to the corral where some hay was stacked. Don closed the well lid and put the cork into his canteen. "I guess I better go get 'im," said Don, referring to his horse, "before Sylvester sees him taking a couple of bites of slough hay and charges me an extra two bits."

"No...leave him," said Jim. "What I have to say won't take long."

"Sure...all right."

"I've decided not to go out there myself, for Meadow's sake.... But, you know, it's not easy to see you goin' out there to do your duty in regard to Pinetree. You're my best friend now, but my friendship with Pinetree goes back much farther.......... All I'm asking is this: If you see any opportunity at all to get the police to negotiate with him, to try to get him to surrender, please do anything you can to make that happen."

Don thought about it for a moment before he answered. "I promise to do that."

"Thank you," said Jim. After studying the ivory top of his cane for a moment, he said, "But we both know there's very little chance he'll give himself up.... So I have one more thing to ask of you.... Please try to not be the one who kills him. I'd have a hard time living with that."

Don said, "I respect your feelings in this matter. When I'm out there, I *will* do my duty—I guess you know that. However, I also will do what you've asked. I will *try* not to be the one who does it."

"That's all I ask," said Jim.

They shook hands, Don turned to go retrieve his horse, and Jim limped toward the house, stooped over and leaning on his cane. Watching him for a moment, Don felt deeply sorry for the man.

He was about to mount when Rita came out of the house, ran past Jim and hurried toward Don, her golden hair competing with her breasts in a bounce contest.

She ran into his arms and he held her close. She surprised him then by saying, "I didn't come to have another go at trying to talk you out of this. In a funny way I even want you to go. After all, part of the reason I love you so much is because you're the kind of man you are—you know, the brave hero type. So, how can I justify trying to stop you from going out and doing your work as a police officer? So, go out there and do what needs to be done. Then come back, marry me, and do what needs to be done."

He kissed her long and hard. He felt that kiss on his lips for at least an hour after he was on the trail heading for One Arrow's.

* * *

Jim waited for about an hour, from the time Don had left, before he saddled up his bay stallion and packed a few things into saddlebags and fixed that and a bedroll behind the cantle. He had already changed into riding clothes—brown, hard-twill pants and a dark green shirt that he hoped would blend in well with outdoor surroundings if he needed to play chameleon. He had removed his false beard but had it hanging nearby on a stall partition.

Meadow was there with him in the barn, looking sad but brave. "I don't understand," she said. "If you knew you were going, why'd you lie to Don and tell him you weren't?"

"I wanted him out of my hair," said Jim, picking up the beard as though that was the hair he was referring to. "Riding over there side by side with him would have been an impossible situation—with him basically out to stop Pinetree at any cost, and me out to try to somehow save his life. I need to ride alone so I can think."

"I know now that I can't stop you, but just tell me this: How much hope do you yourself have of coming out of this alive and free?"

He put a hand gently on her shoulder. "A lot," he said. "I fully intend to not get caught and to come back here to you. We'll then carry on with our plan of secretly visiting my parents, after which we'll head back to the States."

"But how do you hope to help Pinetree without letting yourself be seen. That's impossible with all those policemen around there. Some of them are bound to recognize you, even with the beard. You are gonna wear the beard, aren't you?"

"Yeah, when I'm near anyone…. Look, the truth is I don't yet know what I'm going to do, if anything. But at least I want to go there and look the place over, even if only from a distance, just on the chance that some kind of opportunity might come up. If there's no opportunity…well, I won't do anything stupid."

"All right," said Meadow, "thanks for telling me that. Please be careful. I love you so much! I don't want to lose you."

He took her in his arms and kissed her gently. Then he stepped back and looked down into her dark eyes. "I should be back in a few days. In any case, you and Rita stay here and take care of each other until Don and I return or you hear from us with further instructions. If Pastor Darcy has to get back to his congregation, let him go, but he seems to be willing to stay till this is over."

"Oh, he said he'd stay and he will, so we have a man to protect us."

"And who will protect everyone from you and Rita?"

In spite of the heavy situation, they both laughed a little. Jim put on his beard and led his horse out of the barn with Meadow clinging to his arm.

Jim asked, "You want another kiss with the beard on?"

"How about a tight hug instead?"

So they went for that. Then Jim turned away and swung into his saddle. The stallion was not one to prance around, but stood quietly waiting for the lift of the reins and the click of Jim's tongue.

The beautiful face of Meadow smiling up at him was almost more than Jim could bear, for he thought there was about a fifty-fifty chance that he would not see her again until they met in heaven. He pretended that he didn't see the tears in her eyes.

He said, "See you soon, sweetheart."

"Yeah," she said, keeping up the smile.

He turned the stallion away and rode off at a walk, not looking back until he was clear of the yard area; then he did and she was still standing where he had left her. She waved and he returned that.

He lifted his reins and touched heels to the big bay and cantered off along the trail, determined not to look back again.

* * *

From the time Jim left the road station, it took Meadow and Rita about an hour to get ready. They loaded food and water, and oats for the horses from Sylvester's stock (a whole dollar's worth), and then saw about getting themselves ready before hitching up the horses.

When Rita found that Meadow was going to wear pants and boots, she thought that was wonderful and wanted to do the same, only she hadn't brought any. Fortunately Meadow had an extra pair of trousers which Rita at once pulled on. They were a bit loose on her but she decided to wear them anyhow. Meadow still had her moccasins, which she let Rita wear, and Rita was as delighted with these as she was with the pants. Meadow had made five shirts for herself (as well as the ones she had made for Jim) while wintering in Windy Valley, so they had little feminine touches to them—a bit of embroidery here and there, and fancy pockets, and larger buttons than she put on Jim's shirts. A couple of them even had lace around the collar and cuffs. Rita chose a plainer one however—a red one—apparently fascinated with the idea of dressing considerably more in male fashion than she was used to. The shirt, though, did nothing to make her look more masculine, for—just as Meadow was wider in the hips than Rita was, Rita was fuller up front, so the shirt stretched across her breasts, threatening the buttons and preventing several of the tops ones from being closed.

Meadow would have worn her hat, but, since Rita didn't have any, she didn't wear hers either. She threw it into the buggy just in case the temperature climbed a lot.

Next came the weaponry. Jim had taken their rifle and his gun rig, and Don had taken his uniform belt and gun but had left his other more regular open-holstered rig complete with its long-barreled Colt Navy. Beside this, Meadow had her own personal gunbelt and six-shooter—which she hadn't strapped on after arriving in Windy Valley where she had made a noble effort at once more being a lady. She buckled it on now.

Rita was as excited as a little boy when she tried on Don's gunbelt. It was far too big on her so they improvised by putting the holster on his wide pants belt which fit him around the waist, but on Rita allowed the gun to ride low on her hip in the style of a professional gunslinger.

They hitched Jim's chestnut team to the open-topped buggy and said good-bye to the pastor, asking for his prayers which he at once began and carried on with for so long that they began to think he was using this as a tactic to delay them. He did not approve of their plans but couldn't really do anything to stop them, and since they had left him with his own buggy and team, he was not being inconvenienced.

However, he let them know that he intended to wait for them at the roadhouse.

And so the two women, armed and determined to follow their men to hell and back if necessary, climbed into the buggy. Meadow, sitting on the right side and holding the reins, tongue-clicked the chestnuts into motion. The women waved good-bye to Pastor Darcy who returned the wave from where he still stood with his hat off after praying.

The flaxen-maned chestnuts, refreshed after almost two days of rest, looked perky as they trotted the buggy off the yard and along a trail.

Meadow asked Rita, "You sure you know the way to the One Arrow Reserve?"

"No problem," said Rita as she adjusted her gunbelt to accommodate her sitting position. "This is the only trail that leads in the right direction, and we'll likely come across the occasional traveler or roadside rancher who can give us further directions. We should get there before dark."

"I thought it was at least a day's travel from here to Duck Lake."

"It is," said Rita, "but the One Arrow Reserve is east of Duck Lake and Don said that this trail is a shortcut that leads through the badlands."

"Badlands?"

"Yeah, I guess there's a bit of rough country with the trail winding through some steep ravines and stuff, so that it's usually tackled only on horseback. But I expect we'll get the buggy through all right."

Meadow appeared to be letting this digest. Then she encouraged herself by saying, "Well, if we end up walking through your version of badlands, at least we won't have to worry about poisonous snakes, way up north here, as we would if we were back where *I* come from."

"Right, no poisonous snakes," said Rita. "But then there *are* the wolves."

"Oh, you mean coyotes," said Meadow. "They're nothing to worry about. They're scared of people."

"I don't mean coyotes," said Rita, seeming to enjoy this conversation and stroking the butt of the six shooter in her holster. "We have lots of those too, but I'm talking about timber wolves. Some of them are as big as Shetland ponies and their paws can measure six inches across. They've been known to bring down a full-grown horse. Of course, most of them are a bit farther north, in the forests, but occasionally some of them wander along riverbanks or creek banks and so they *could* wind up in the badlands…along with grizzly bears and stuff…. But it's unlikely."

"Well, thanks for setting me at ease," said Meadow.

Rita said, "I hate to change the subject, but I've been wanting to ask you……. Is having sex really as good as…as…people seem to think it is?"

Meadow turned her face, with a smile forming on it, slowly toward Rita. Meadow said, "I think for me it's even better than what people think…. And for you—for you it'll be like tons of dynamite exploding."

"I think you're right," said Rita, and they both laughed.

* * *

Later, some gave the pastor the benefit of the doubt, assuming that he had not lied when he had told Meadow and Rita that he would stay at the road station. He could simply have changed his mind. In any case, after the women left, only about half an hour passed before he had his team hitched to his top-buggy and was on his way, following the same trail that everyone else had taken—the one that led toward the One Arrow Reserve.

It had occurred to him at some point that if there was so much action going on there, it was quite possible that there would be further violence, death and dying, and mourning. The comforting words of a pastor could well be needed. He didn't much like the idea of bullets whistling around his ears; but, he told himself, he was ready to die, having long ago made his peace with God. And getting killed by a stray bullet would be a small price to pay if he could first lead even one dying man into accepting forgiveness for his sins through the suffering, death, and resurrection of Jesus.

Like those who had left on this journey before him, the pastor felt that he was moving in the right direction.

22

Jim, no longer wearing the beard, had been pushing the big stallion, hoping to gain on Don but not enough to catch up to him. When crossing the badlands, however, and while still up on a high bank on the near side, Jim saw his red-coated friend a hundred feet below, riding through a dried out creek. Quickly turning his horse aside behind some scraggly foliage, he dismounted and rubbed the stallion's nose to try to keep him from letting out a whinny of greeting to Don's horse. But the only reason the stallion didn't make any sound was probably because they were upwind and higher than the other horse. Likely neither one had seen or smelled the other.

Jim waited where he was for about a half-hour before he started down a rocky path that only antelopes and sure-footed horses could navigate.

Once across the badlands, he slowed the pace of his progress, making sure he didn't catch up to Don.

* * *

Two hours after leaving the badlands behind, Don drew in sight of the standoff. He could see a lot of people on a low hill, many of them members of the force. These were lower down on the almost-level slope; the people in plainclothes were at the highest level, several dozen of them. Don assumed they were a mixture of curiosity seekers and Indians concerned about one of their own.

It was not hard to see that the grove of trees closest to the low hill was the one in which the outlaws had taken refuge, for that one was surrounded by police officers on foot, but with a lot of space between themselves and the bush. This indicated strongly that the situation had not yet been resolved.

* * *

Meadow and Rita arrived at the first ravine. They found two sizes of hoof prints and assumed that these had been made by Don's and Jim's mounts. But they could find no way to drive their buggy down the steep incline.

They gave their team some oats and had a bit of food themselves — bread and sausage they had bought from Sylvester. Tired of sitting, they ate while standing beside the rear of the buggy. They could hear water flowing somewhere but the creek bed below them looked totally dry.

Meadow said, "What we hear sounds like a creek, so it must be in a larger arroyo that this one leads into."

"Arroyo?"

"Oh, yeah, you call them all ravines here. Jim told me about that."

"What're we gonna do?" worried Rita.

"We have some options," said Meadow. "We can unhitch the horses and ride from here on. Or we can go back. Or we can try to find a way around this rough terrain."

"It seems to lead as far as the eye can see in either direction," said Rita.

"I know, so that third option wasn't a very good one. That leaves two—ride or go back. Have you ever ridden a horse."

"Sure. Is there anyone who hasn't?"

"Plenty," said Meadow, "at least in the city where I grew up. I only learned to ride after I returned to my own people, the Apaches."

"What an exciting life you've lived!" said Rita. "Here, you want another sausage?"

As it turned out the woman didn't have to ride the buggy horses, nor did they turn back. Another option arrived in the form of that man of God, Pastor Darcy. He must have been making somewhat better time than the women, for they were barely finished eating when he pulled up.

"Pastor! What are you doing here?" said Rita.

He brought his buggy to a stop near where they were standing and wrapped his reins around a little post for that purpose that stuck up out of the dashboard at the front of the buggy. "Well, everyone was heading in this direction, apparently to be useful, and I got the idea that I might be able to be useful too." He climbed down out of the buggy with the springy ease of a teen-ager, then looked out over the ravine. "And I suppose this is where we sprout wings and fly, like angels, at least if we're going to keep going in that direction."

Rita said, laughingly, "Only a pastor would think of that way of getting over this badland area."

It turned out, though, that the pastor had some practical ideas as well. He informed the women that before becoming a minister of the Gospel, he had worked on a road gang in the east. He explained — while eating the last sausage — that in some cases the roads under construction wound through uneven terrain so the workers and their engineer bosses had to find ways of moving wheeled, horse-drawn road-building equipment in ways that prevented these from tipping and rolling. Basically it was a matter of tying sturdy restraining ropes or chains to the vehicles in such a way that men, and/or horses, when positioned properly, would apply enough pull to the ropes to keep the vehicles from upsetting. It was not always easy to find good positions, and, also, whoever was in charge of the restraining rope had to pay it out carefully, never letting it go slack, but also not holding back the moving vehicle from making progress. So, when it was horsepower applying restraining pressure to the rope, it took an expert horseman to keep such teams, sometimes made up of four or six animals, under careful control.

After hearing about all this and the dangers and difficulties involved, Meadow said. "You're not really planning to do this here with our buggies, are you? It sounds like a recipe for disaster."

"Not really," said the pastor. "After I had helped with a fair amount of that kind of work, I was put in charge of it. If you don't mind my saying so, I got to be so good at it that I was sometimes called out to other job sites where they were having a particular problem along that line. I always got them through it."

* * *

Pinetree yawned and stretched his long arms above his head. In spite of the hopeless situation he had managed to get in a little nap. The three Indians were taking turns standing guard, but there had been no further attack—only some ineffective long-range shooting from the low hill.

He walked slowly among the poplar trees. When he came near the edge of the grove he squatted down and through the leaves that hid him watched the activity of his enemy.

He observed that another large party of redcoats had arrived and were gathered on one side of the hill. Higher up were a lot of people not in uniform. Onlookers.

"They are making a celebration out of it," said Pinetree to himself.

Birds sang gaily in the branches above his head. A gentle breeze played through the leaves.

* * *

When Don arrived at the hillside camp of the North-West Mounted, he was warmly greeted by the man in charge, Assistant Commissioner Rintley, who had been a sergeant when Don had last seen him a couple of years ago. And further words of welcome came from many others as well. He knew all the members from Duck Lake and some of those from Regina. For a while there were a lot of handshakes, but that had to be cut short for the time being because of the situation.

Before he got involved with anything, however, Don was taken into the medic tent to report to Commissioner Bancroft who had been wounded early on in the fighting. He was horizontal now, but otherwise looked as angry and unpleasant as the last time Don had seen him.

Don had arrived just in time for a strategy meeting. It was held in a second large canvas tent that had been pitched for that purpose; and Don could see by the many bedrolls stacked in one corner that it also served as a bunkhouse. Several folding tables had been set up to make a larger one, and the brass, including sergeants, sat around this. Don was offered a chair across the corner of the table from Assistant Commissioner Rintley, apparently an honor of sorts, acknowledging Roman's hazardous experiences in the United States and his safe return.

He quickly learned that all three of the outlaws, in the bush, were believed to still be alive and as dangerous as ever. The immediate concern and problem was that Sergeant Saben—briefly Acting Commissioner Saben—had been shot, thought to be dead, but then had been seen crawling out of the thicket and there collapsing. Although he had crawled no farther, a viewing through field glasses had revealed a slight movement of one hand, so there was a good chance that he was still alive. The problem was how to get him out of there without further loss of life. Any such attempt would obviously be extremely dangerous since he was lying only of few feet away from the grove of poplars in which the renegades were hidden.

One of the few civilians at the meeting was a medical doctor by the name of Drummond. He looked to be about forty and was dressed in a respectable dark suit in spite of the warm day; but this was no more contrary to the weather than the red surge that the policemen were wearing. Don, like many of the others, had grown used to this over the years and now hardly gave it a thought, even though he had not been wearing the uniform for a long time. Dr. Drummond said, "I think a wagon, with the end-gate removed, would be better than a buggy—easier to lift Sergeant Saben into it."

A sergeant who's name Don didn't know replied, "But a buggy is lighter and could be pulled faster."

"It can also tip over more easily," said Dr. Drummond. "The driver is going to have to make one hell of a fast turn to get away from there…. In any case, I volunteer to drive the team—my own horses. They're fast."

For a few seconds the room was silent. No one had expected such a quick offering. Then Rintley said, "Well, in that case, doctor, you shall have your choice of vehicle. You realize, of course, that you may not come out of this alive, so I must ask if you have any requests—anything to be carried out in the event of your demise."

Dr. Drummond was fishing an envelope from out of an inner pocket of his suit coat. He passed it to the Assistant Commissioner. "It's all in here—not much, though. I don't have any family here, but my next of kin is in Winnipeg. Don't bother reading it now. We don't have time. What we need now is one or two volunteers, armed men, preferably police officers, to pick up Sergeant Saben and put him into the wagon—likely while under fire."

Five seconds of dead silence passed. Then Don discovered that he had lost his mind, for he heard himself saying, "There's no need for two officers to risk their lives. One strong, agile man is enough to spring down off the wagon, hoist Sergeant Saben into it, and jump back up into the wagon. Two men could get in each other's way. We only need the driver and one officer...and I volunteer to be that officer."

Again there was silence. Then Rintley said, "Are you sure you want to do this, Sergeant? I mean you've just returned. You haven't even had time to be reunited with your friends."

"Sir," said Don, "for every second we go on talking, life is draining out of Sergeant Saben. Let's do this as quickly as possible. If Dr. Drummond is ready, and I know he is, then I'd like to get started on this rescue as soon as his team can be hitched to a wagon."

"Very well," said Assistant Commissioner Rintley. "Sergeant Neufeld, grab up a constable and see to the horses and wagon—on the double!"

Sergeant Neufeld was on his feet. "Yes, sir!" He left the table and hurried out of the tent.

Poor Rita, thought Don. *I'm always slipping away from her.*

* * *

The second ravine was deeper and steeper than the first, but by the time they started crossing it, Pastor Darcy was totally into the operation and it almost seemed to him that no time had elapsed from when he had quit working on the road gangs to the present. Using his own team as the anchor, connected to the rear of Meadow's buggy by the long lariat she had provided from out of equipment stored in the buggy-box, he carefully controlled their movement so that the rope remained taut. Meadow risked life and limb by driving her team that was pulling the buggy, sitting on the high side of the sloping rig. And Rita added her own slight weight by standing on the boarding step on the high side, gripping the backrest.

Darcy knew that he himself was in greater danger than the women. This was because in controlling the anchor-team he had to walk in front of them, hanging on to their bridles, at the same time looking over his shoulder to the front to keep the rope and buggy in sight. If the horses he was controlling quit trusting him and panicked, he could easily end up under their hooves. The women knew that if things got out of control they were to jump clear of the buggy immediately.

A good pastor's voice can be soothing, to people and also to animals. His horses continued to trust him, downhill and up on the other side.

When it was over everyone collapsed into a much needed rest. Pastor Darcy noticed that his hands were shaking and tried to hide this from the women. *Why did I do it?* he thought. *Is it that important for these women to get to the men they love?* Sometimes he doubted his calling as a pastor. He was too reckless, it seemed. Yet he knew that a deep inner guidance always carried him through so that things turned out right. *Obviously,* he told himself, *God is with me.*

Yet he tended to get himself into trouble. Right now his top-buggy was on the other side of the ravines where someone could come along and steal it. He would have to tie his team behind Meadow's buggy. As for himself, he'd be riding in the box, fighting for space with all the stuff Meadow had in there. And he'd have to listen to the delightful voices of two beautiful women, mile after mile. That could work on a man.

As so often before, he wondered why the good Lord had not yet given him a wife.

* * *

Jim Longfeather, keeping to cover of bush, arrived near the scene of the standoff. He tied the stallion to a tree and pulled binoculars out of a saddlebag.

Crouching between two clumps of wild shrubbery, Jim put the field glasses to his eyes. There was activity in the police camp. Horses were being hitched to a buckboard type of wagon. A police officer and a man in a dark suit were walking together toward it.

Then Jim noticed the gun off to one side of the camp—a great menacing field gun on wheels; its barrel looked to be at least five or six feet long. It was chilling. Would they actually use that? Had they used it already? Not likely, for there was no shell damage visible in the police-surrounded grove where Pinetree and his men obviously were ensconced. The surrounding policemen, however, were a long distance away from the grove, no doubt not wanting to make easy targets of themselves. But close beside the grove lay a police officer, either dead or wounded.

Back on the side of the hill, the two men he had noticed a moment ago—a police officer and the man in the dark suit—were now climbing into the wagon, but only the suited man mounted the seat at its front. The officer settled himself down on the floor of the box. He looked like…. Jim turned the central knob on the glasses and brought him in closer. It was Don all right.

"What're they up to?" Jim mumbled to himself. He panned the glasses over to the thicket and held steady on the redcoat lying there. He now had him in close enough so he could see, although vaguely, flies buzzing around the corpse's nose. The corpse's nose crinkled and then the face rolled to one side a bit as though trying to avoid the flies.

So that was what Don and the man in the suit were up to! Out loud but quietly, Jim said, "Damn it, Roman! Do you always have to be the hero?"

* * *

Pinetree, peering through foliage at the police camp on the low hillside, noticed a strange looking object off to one side. At first he thought it was a funny new kind of cart, for it had two large wagon wheels, and some redcoats, on foot, were pulling and pushing it. But then, as its angle changed, and Pinetree saw the sun reflect dully on a long, metal barrel, he realized that he was looking at a field gun. The redcoats moved it only a few yards into a position that suited them better for some reason and then maneuvered it around so that it was aimed at the grove of trees, and quite directly, it seemed, at Pinetree himself.

He grimly considered this new threat. He could not think of anything much to do about it. He watched a furry caterpillar crawl over the toe of his moccasin and disappear into the grass. When he next looked back to the hill his mouth opened slightly and his muscles became rigid.

On one side of the elevation, not far from the host of onlookers, stood a paint horse. Its head was erect and it was impatiently prancing about. Its rider was Blackbird.

Pinetree worked his way through the trees back to the barricade.

"What are they doing now?" inquired Born-on-the-Hill.

"They have brought a very big *gun*—" Pinetree said the word *gun* in English, "—with which to smash us to pieces. Come and see."

He led his partners to the edge of the grove. The redcoat who had been the leader still lay near the trees where he apparently had managed to crawl after Pinetree had shot him. He appeared to be dead now. The Indians looked up at the hill. They saw a couple of redcoats behind the field gun and assumed that they were loading it.

Suddenly Pinetree and the other two became aware of a buckboard drawn by a team of hard-galloping horses, dashing down the hill, heading straight for the grove.

"What is this?" said Redleaf in a startled voice. He cocked his rifle.

"I do not know," said Pinetree, and he drew his revolver.

The buckboard bore down on them with awe-inspiring speed. There were two men in it. The driver, sitting at the front, was hatless and wore a dark suit. He was slapping his reins down on the rumps of the team of horses to get more speed out of them. A moment later Pinetree recognized him as Dr. Drummond, a white medicine man who had been practicing his healing magic in Duck Lake before Pinetree became a fugitive. He did not recognize the redcoat who seemed to be just behind the seat rather than in it.

Pinetree instructed his men to move back, along with himself, a little farther into the bush, but not so far that they could not see the approaching wagon. The three Indians crouched in the undergrowth, their weapons in a ready position.

Dr. Drummond lashed his galloping horses furiously, now using the ends of the reins. The rig bounced over the rough ground and rapidly approached the Indians.

Then, in a flash, Pinetree realized what the men in the buckboard were trying to do. "They are trying to rescue their fallen leader," he said. "Maybe they have seen him move and so know that he is not dead."

"The men in the wagon are brave," commented Redleaf approvingly.

Pinetree agreed. Here was a very daring and noble rescue attempt—a deed worthy of great honor.

"When I say, *shoot*, kill both of them," he said.

The driver of the buckboard swung the rig around in a sharp arc that threatened to upset it, but it stayed on its wheels. With the horses now facing away from the grove, he reined them in so that the wagon was still fairly close to the limp form of the man they intended to rescue. The redcoat jumped down out of the rear of the rig with his revolver in hand. It was then that Pinetree recognized him as Sergeant Don Roman, the police officer who had arrested him for butchering a government cow—which arrest had started all this.

Sergeant Roman bent over to pick up the wounded man.

"Shoot!" said Pinetree.

Two rifles and one revolver thundered out a volley of lead. But there were too many trees in the way, making the targets difficult. The ricocheting, whining bullets tore splinters from the wheels of the buckboard; the horses reared and whinnied. Although the heavily foliaged trees interfered much with the Indians' shooting, it was yet nothing short of a miracle that Roman was not hit by the flying lead as he lifted his wounded superior into the rear of the buckboard. Roman still held his unfired gun in his hand as he did so.

Pinetree jumped to his feet. "Stop shooting!" he ordered his men. "I am going to kill this redcoat myself." He ran out into the open.

Sergeant Roman, having loaded the victim, was about to hop into the rig himself when he apparently saw the outlaw out of the corner of his eye. Instead of climbing up, he spun around quickly.

Pinetree fired—too quickly and his bullet missed.

Roman fired. A scorching pain seared the skull of Pinetree. A wave of dizziness rolled over him. The ground tilted up and hit him in the face.

Pinetree lay on his stomach in the grass. He could feel hot blood spreading over his head. He saw the back of Sergeant Roman as he turned and started climbing into the open-ended rear of the buckboard. Pinetree still clutched the revolver in his hand, and now, using the last of his strength, he raised the gun as best he could and fired another shot at the redcoat. The bullet kicked the sergeant's dangling leg forward as it knocked off about half of his boot's hard leather heel.

The six-gun slipped from Pinetree's numb fingers.

Roman, already partway up into the wagon, made it all the way and got a grip on the side of the box. The driver shouted and whipped his horses. They sprang into a gallop. The buckboard clattered back up the hill, rifle bullets now screaming in its wake.

Redleaf and Born-on-the-Hill hurried to where Pinetree had fallen and quickly dragged him behind some high brush. This manhandling roused him a bit from his near-unconscious state and he immediately tried to stand up, but he staggered and fell to one knee. "Take me back into the bush," he said as the two were already lifting him to his feet, one on each side of him. He put his arms over their shoulders and with this support was able to walk. But it took them quite a while to get back to the barricade. Once there, Pinetree relaxed into a sitting position in the pit, and Redleaf began to doctor his head wound.

The bullet had not entered but had left a long, deep tear, not only through scalp, but also scraping the skull. Redleaf knew it was a serious wound, but he could do nothing more than fashion a crude bandage from his own bandanna, and this brought the bleeding somewhat under control.

The Indians waited tensely, expecting the field gun to begin shelling them at any moment, but this did not happen.

Strength returned to Pinetree so quickly that Redleaf and Born-on-the-Hill could hardly believe their eyes. By evening the wounded man was walking about, flexing his muscles, and saying how he would like to kill every one of the redcoats who were out there on the hill. He seemed to have made a miraculous recovery, but his two companions could not help but notice a feverish look in his eyes—a delirious, wild look.

Night came, slowly spreading its dark cloak over the hill and the bluff as though to conceal the shameful doings of that location.

Pinetree woke up during the night and arose. Born-on-the Hill woke up too when he heard his leader moving about. Redleaf was already awake for he had been standing guard.

Pinetree spoke, but in a strange, tight-voiced way that did not sound at all right to his two companions who knew him well.

"I have been betrayed!" charged the feverish voice of the outlaw. "I have been betrayed by the white men, by my friends in Duck Lake, and by my own blood brother...who would not stand by my side.... My blood brother! Just as the others, he also wishes me dead!.......... If he stood before me now, I would kill him!"

23

Jim slept through most of the night, which was what he had intended to do. When he got out of his blankets, the pre-dawn light had not yet begun to lighten the eastern horizon. Only the owl and the nighthawk, with their sensitive night eyes, could see Longfeather as he strapped on his gunbelt with the Colt on his right hip and the long-bladed hunting knife on his left. He did not put on his hat but instead folded his neck bandanna and tied it around his head to ensure that his hair would not get in his eyes.

After peeing and then making up for it by taking a drink from his canteen, Jim checked on his horse. He had tethered the stallion to a foot-long metal ground stake that he always carried with him. He had left the bay a ways back and in the open where there was plenty of grass and where, if Jim was not able to get back, the animal would be easily seen, in daylight, by the people on the hill. This way the horse would not be left to eventually die for lack of water if he could not break free. Jim had also unsaddled him and hung all the tack in a tree, out of reach of most leather-nibbling animals.

After eating one of the sandwiches Meadow had sent with him, and taking another drink of water and another pee, this time just to make sure his bladder didn't give him discomfort during the challenges that lay ahead, Jim started out through the dark toward Pinetree's grove of poplars. He knew it had remained surrounded by policemen all night, but this did not stop him from moving forward. He was determined to talk to his old buddy face to face.

Jim was grateful, in a way, that, after yesterday's daring rescue of the wounded officer, no further effort had been made by the police to bring the standoff to an end. Yet one part of him—maybe a cowardly part—couldn't help but wish that some action had been taken to end it all. Then he would have had no reason to stay here and risk his own life. But he knew that this day, after daybreak, the North-West Mounted would not hold back from making further moves. They might even use the field gun. One way or another, it would likely all be over before another sunset.

One thing bothered Jim greatly. He had seen Don shoot at Pinetree and wound him. He did not in any way hold this against Roman; after all, what else could he have done? It had been him or Pinetree. Also, Jim appreciated that Don had been doing something distinctly good in carrying out that daring rescue. What bothered Jim was that he did not know how badly Pinetree was hurt or even if he was still alive. He very much wanted to help the man, if there was anything that could be done; but, on the other hand, if he was dead, then Jim was risking his own life in vain.

But he moved on. With his eyes well opened to the night, he could vaguely see the top of the grove's dense foliage against the slightly lighter shade of dark that was the overcast sky. When he was about a hundred yards from the grove, he lowered himself to the ground and began to crawl on his belly.

Silently as, but much slower than, a snake he wriggled forward—and proved to himself that he was indeed an Indian, for he passed through the circle of policemen who held the grove surrounded without even a bad moment. The lawmen were spaced at intervals of only about forty feet, and the two between which Jim found his way had not been sleeping. As the civilized Indian crawled in among the first trees of the grove, he felt quite pleased with himself. He worked his way a little farther in among the weeds and brush, then lay still with his eyes closed, resting and trying to think of the best way of making contact with his blood brother without getting shot by mistake. The only thing he could do, he decided, was to call the man's name and then wait for an answer before he proceeded any farther.

He rested a minute or so longer, then got to his knees. "Pinetree!" he called softly, saying the name in Cree. "Pinetree—I am your friend, Longfeather." He was almost certain that the police officers nearest to him could hear his words, but they would likely not understand what he was saying, and he also said his own name, Longfeather, in Cree. They would think it was one of the three fugitives talking. He continued, "Where are you?…. I come alone." He waited quietly for an answer. When none came he called again. Still no answer.

Jim got to his feet and began to walk forward, deeper into the grove, but with each step he became more tense inside; it was almost as though a red flag of danger was being waved in his face. He asked himself why he should feel this way. Maybe it was the silence, he thought—the utter silence when there should be a friendly answer.

He crouched down beside a tree and waited there, still hoping to hear some response from the people he had come to help. He began to consider the possibility of having Pinetree and his two companions attempt to sneak out through the circle of law officers just as he himself had come in; but he realized at once that it was too late for that, for the gray light of dawn was already seeping into the bush and he could vaguely see the vegetation around him. By the time he found his blood brother and talked things over with him there would be too much daylight to allow any hope of sneaking through among the circling lawmen. Too bad. He was confident that Pinetree could have made it, but didn't know about the other two. One thing he was sure of though: Pinetree would never forsake his friends by sneaking away from them in the dark simply because he thought he could make it alone.

Then Longfeather smiled suddenly as the idea finally came home to him that there was no one except himself in this bush. That was why there had been no answer to his call. The smile left his face almost immediately however, for the horrible irony of such a situation was apparent. If the three Indians had made their escape in the dark, then he had uselessly taken their place. And now there was too much daylight for him to have any hope of being able to sneak back out.

He got to his feet and moved forward with mixed contradictory feelings flopping around inside of him. He really didn't want to find Pinetree, for he hoped the man had escaped; but a small, stupid part of him hoped that the Indian outlaw and his friends were still in the bush—so he himself could have a worthwhile reason for being here.

There was a rustling sound to his right. When he turned to see what it was, all he could make out was a large, dark shape hurtling toward him. He had no time to duck. The thing made a solid impact against him, knocking him down. Jim could tell now that it was a large man, and, a moment later, that it was Pinetree.

Pinning Jim to the ground with his bodily weight and one arm, Pinetree raised his right hand high above his head. Jim's eye caught the dull paleness of a knife blade. Automatic reflex brought up his hand in defense as the knife started into its vicious downward arc. The wrists of the two men came together with a solid smack. Jim's arm gave twelve inches, but then, like a good strong spring, smoothly brought the downward motion to a stop. Pinetree could have drawn his arm back for another quick stabbing attempt, but instead he preferred to simply increase the pressure against Longfeather's resistance, apparently having forgotten just how big and strong his blood brother was. The blade did not go down any farther.

Jim's right arm was pinned to the ground by the left hand of Pinetree, but neither of the two men were fully aware of this sideline effort. Their attention was welded to a small intense area between them where two crossed forearms quivered and a sharp wedge of steel trembled. The faces of both fighters were contorted with the strain and the passion of each that drove them to this terrible exertion. In the fevered brain of Pinetree, the passion was the desire to kill; in Longfeather, it was the desire to live.

The mind is a strange thing. Even during those moments of extreme effort, Longfeather found that he was thinking clearly about another time when he had crossed wrists with Pinetree. Vividly he remembered how they had pressed together the cuts on their forearms so that the flowing scarlet intermingled; and, while tom-toms beat out the sound of a human heart many times amplified, he and Pinetree had become blood brothers.

And now, suddenly, Jim Longfeather knew for certain that it had been wrong—but not because the ceremony had finally brought him face to face with death in this final moment. It had been wrong because Jim Longfeather and John Pinetree were two persons who could not truly be blood brothers. Although pure Cree blood thundered through the arteries of both, and although they had fought side by side, and although Pinetree had saved Jim's life, yet in truth they were as far apart as north is from south and east from west. Peace and war can never be brothers.

The thought that only one of them would likely come out of this immediate violent contact alive weakened Jim. It was obvious that his opponent was determined to kill him, but Jim could not see himself killing Pinetree. The result of this realization was that the knife blade once more began sinking toward Jim's chest.

Pinetree was stripped to the waist. In the dim light of dawn the hard, sinewy muscles of his chest and arms stood out flexed and motionless like stone sculpture. His face, looking down, was all hatred and fury. A blood-soaked bandanna was knotted crookedly around his head. The knife tip became a point of pressure as it began, ever so slightly, to press into Jim's shirt.

Now that the knife was lower, it enabled Pinetree to put more weight on it, so Jim knew that he had no hope of saving his life by further resisting the pressure. He had to make a different move, if he could—a quick bodily twist, maybe. If it worked he might salvage his life; if it failed he would die a few seconds sooner than he would if he didn't try. It was an easy choice to make.

Quick and hard, he twisted his body to the left. The blade was plunged downward with all of Pinetree's weight on it, cutting through shirt and flesh but glancing off the new angle of rib bones. There was little pain—Jim's mind did not have room for it at the moment. Pinetree, following along with the downward thrust of his knife, was somewhat off balance. Jim wrenched his right arm free from Pinetree's grip and with the same movement clubbed his fist against the side of the man's head. Then he quickly turned his attention back to the weapon. He made a grab for the wrist of the knife hand, cutting his fingers on the blade but succeeding in getting his hold. Pinetree was pummeling him with his other hand now, but because he was off balance the blows were not crushing. Jim was able to hold on to the knife hand, and at the same time he made another twisting motion with his hips which further upset the upper Indian. Then Jim grabbed the knee that had been digging into his side and flipped it upward; at the same time he pulled down on the knife hand. Pinetree hit the dirt shoulder first and rolled over onto his back; but Longfeather only saw the first part of this, for he also was rolling— away from the other man.

They both gained their feet at the same time and stood facing each other, panting hard and letting strength seep back into their tortured muscles.

Jim was aware of pain and moisture on the side of his chest, but only in a vague way. He faced Pinetree over the six-foot distance that separated them and tried to make sense out of what had happened.

When he got some of his breath back, he said in Cree, "Is this my friend, Pinetree?"

"This is your blood brother," returned Pinetree, "—your blood brother whom you have betrayed! Your blood brother by whose side you would not stand in his time of need, although you promised to stand by him to the death. This is your blood brother who is going to cut your heart out and spill all your blood here upon this ground...for you have betrayed the great trust that I placed in you." While he spoke, his own blood, from the wound in his head, began to trickle down out of the dirty bandage. He eyes were red and unnaturally bright. He said his next sentence in a harsh sounding half-whisper: "I know you have come here to kill me...but I will kill you instead." He still held the knife in his hand. He took a cautious step toward Jim.

Jim said, "Wait! Before you once more try to kill me, let me speak. The wound in your head has made you sick. It is foolishness to say that I came here to kill you. I came to help you." But Jim could see that his words were having no good effect on the other; Pinetree was tensing his muscles in preparation to spring forward. Jim continued: "I do not know what has happened to you, but there is one thing you will understand. I must defend my life. I do not have the strength left to fight another hand to hand battle with you, so I warn you not to come any closer." His hand moved slowly to the holster on his hip. When it got there it found empty leather.

Pinetree smiled an evil smile. "You still have your knife on the other side. You will have to use that."

Jim knew that his revolver had to be somewhere on the ground within a few feet, or inches, of where he stood, for no doubt it had slipped out of its holster during the struggle. But he didn't dare take his eyes off Pinetree, much less bend down. So instead he reached, with his right hand, for the knife that hung on his left hip. The movement was not fast and not slow, its speed carefully calculated so that it wouldn't trigger the angry Indian into action. This was successful in that Pinetree seemed to take for granted that Jim must draw his knife before the fight could carry on.

But now Pinetree began to cautiously close the short distance still remaining between them. He held his knife with the blade pointing downward; Jim held his with the blade thrusting upward from his hand.

The grove was fairly bright now, and Jim suddenly noticed Pinetree's two companions standing in the background, calmly watching proceedings. They were not likely to interfere, knowing that this was Pinetree's fight.

Pinetree sprang within striking range and lashed out with his knife. Jim stepped back and at the same time his own blade swept forward to meet the other weapon, and, with skill and luck combined, literally cut the knife out of the hand of Pinetree with one clean stroke. It fell to the ground; Pinetree pulled back his gashed hand and took a retreating step. Jim at once let his own knife fall from his hand, formed a fist, and crashed it into his opponent's jaw. Pinetree staggered backward. Jim, following close, tried to bring his left fist into action but found that he couldn't lift that arm. Twice more he struck hard with his right. Solid as they were, they were not enough to upset Pinetree, who seemed to be held up by some super-normal inner strength; but then he did sag back against the slim trunk of a poplar tree. The tree bent under his weight, then straightened again and Pinetree used this spring, with the addition of his own effort, to catapult himself forward at his adversary. Jim could not react quickly enough and found himself being thrust backward by the force of the other's charge and weight. Jim's feet tangled in brush. He went down on his back with Pinetree once more on top of him. Close beside Jim's head was a tree trunk; he had missed hitting it by inches.

Pinetree's big hands fastened on Jim's throat and tightened, then slipped somewhat because blood from the gash in one of them was making the throat slick. But he retained his grip and applied more pressure. Jim clawed and kicked like a wildcat. His mind reeled from lack of circulation and oxygen. Still applying pressure on the throat, Pinetree suddenly gave a quick lift and then rammed Jim's head sideways and down against the tree trunk.

That was the end of the fight.

* * *

Jim became aware of three things at the same time. His head was sore, his one side hurt from shoulder to hip, and he was tied upright—actually in a standing position—to a tree. After this it took at least a minute before he even began to remember where he was or what had happened. His eyes cringed away from the bright sunlight, taking refuge once more behind uncomfortable eyelids. A passing fly decided to stop for a rest on his upper lip. He snorted it away but it came back. He began to struggle desperately with his bonds for it seemed very important to get rid of the fly.

A loud laugh from Pinetree made Longfeather lift his head and open his eyes wide. More consciousness forced its way into his foggy mind.

Pinetree was done laughing, but now he walked up close and stood before Jim. "I am glad that you are awake at last, blood brother. The thunder-*gun* on the hill will soon begin to speak. I was afraid that you might sleep all through it...and so never know that you had been brave enough to stay by the side of your blood brother to the very end....... We are going to die together, Jim Longfeather, as blood brothers should." He turned and walked away, shafts of early morning sunlight flicking over his naked bronze shoulders. His right hand had a dirty rag tied around it—a perfect match to the one around his head.

He did not walk far. About twenty-five feet away from Jim he stepped down into a shallow trench in which his two companions already squatted. The trench had a low log barricade in front of it. All this was in clear view of Jim because there were no trees in the area between him and the crude redoubt.

Jim was fully conscious now, and understood the present situation well enough. The way the three outlaws hunkered down in the trench told him plainly that they really did expect the field gun to start shelling the bluff at any moment. Not that the trench or barricade would do them much good, and they probably knew that, but still it could prolong their lives by minutes if they were lucky. As for himself, thought Jim, the first two or three explosive shells would likely bring his time on earth to an end, for he was standing there as upright and exposed as the trees around him—and the trees around him would soon be a tangled mass of splintered vegetation. Yelling for help would do no good; the policemen around the grove would by now have moved out of harm's way as well as out of earshot. Besides, Pinetree would never stand for anyone disgracing his standoff by yelling for mercy. He would end such an effort quickly with a bullet.

Jim studied his bonds. He was tied to the tree with several strips of leather—probably cut from a shirt—and behind his back, on the other side of the tree trunk, his hands were lashed together so tightly that he could not feel his fingers.

Pinetree spoke to Longfeather again. "We will not have to wait very long. The redcoats have already shouted one warning from the hill, saying that we must come out to surrender or they will use the big gun. There may not be another warning. We will soon all be smashed to pieces, but at least we will all die together bravely…. You and I, Jim Longfeather, will die together bravely as blood brothers should…. Are you not happy that you have decided to honor your vow?"

After a few seconds of effort, Jim found his voice somewhere at the bottom of a parched throat. "Do you wish to leave this life with a taunt on your lips and evil in your heart? And did I not come here freely of my own accord? You are doing me a great injustice, John Pinetree. It is foolishness to say that I came here to kill you, when I have always been your friend."

For a few seconds Pinetree looked at Jim, a sober expression on his face. Then he said, "Everyone is against me now……. I know you did not come here to die with me. If you did not come to kill me, then why did you come?"

"I came to try to help you," said Jim. "But it is true that I did not come here to die with you…. There is a way for you and your two friends to save your lives. It is not a certain way, but it is your only hope. If you do not try it, then you are sure to die here."

Pinetree replied, "I know what you want us to do. You want us to give ourselves up to the redcoats. I will not do that…. How much money were they going to pay you for making me surrender?"

Exasperated, Longfeather lost control of himself and broke into English. "What you're saying doesn't make sense!"

Pinetree smiled, nodding his head in satisfaction as though Jim's switch to English proved which side he was on.

Jim realized his mistake and went back to Cree. "If I had been sent here by the redcoats they would not use the big gun until I came back out. So why are you hiding in the hole?"

At least a part of Pinetree's fevered brain was functioning clearly enough to come up with a rather reasonable theory. "I think the white men know that you killed Scote. But they have promised to give you your life if you can make me surrender. If you do not succeed in bringing me out to them, they will be happy to kill us both." As Pinetree finished this last sentence he got up out of the trench and walked toward Longfeather.

Jim wondered what was coming now. He said, "What you say is not true. I came here to try to save your life. I know that if you and your two companions do not give yourselves up then there is no hope for you. But if you surrender now, there is always the chance of an escape later on.... Think carefully, Pinetree. Do not give up your only chance for life."

Pinetree was bending over now, picking a handful of grass. He straightened up. "Open you mouth," he ordered. When Longfeather, startled, did not obey at once, the outlaw drew his knife. Longfeather opened his mouth and Pinetree shoved the grass into it. He then unrolled part of the bloody rag from his wounded hand, cut off that part, and used it to finish gagging his captive. He left Jim coughing through his nose and returned to the pit. "I wish to die without having to listen to the cawing of a stupid crow." He hunkered back down into the trench beside his fellow warriors. Before completely dismissing from his mind the topic that had been under discussion, Pinetree made a final statement expressing his own way of thinking on the matter. There was certainly no doubt about his having the last word.

"You have been speaking like a white man," he said. "A white man will surrender and be led like the white man's cow to be butchered. No, he will even make himself lower than a cow, for he will get down on his knees and beg for mercy from his enemy. A true Cree will never do such things. He will fight his enemies until his last breath is gone and his heart no longer beats."

There was silence after this—for about fifteen seconds, and then came the sound of a man's voice calling from the distance, probably through a bullhorn. "John Pinetree! This is your last warning! We are going to shell the thicket! Come out now and give yourself up! This is your last chance! We are going to begin shooting with the field gun! Come out now and give yourself up! This is your last warning!"

This same information was repeated in Cree by an interpreter who could shout even louder than the first voice.

Then followed the most terrible silence that the four in the little bush had ever experienced. None of them could have said how long that silence lasted. It could have been one minute, or five, or ten, or fifteen; for time had changed somehow and could not be calculated.

During part of this time Jim wrestled with his bonds, but because his energy was so drained the effort could be nothing but futile. Utter exhaustion rather than despair finally caused him to cease struggling against the strong leather strips that cut into his body and numb arms. He had made no progress; if anything, the leather had tightened.

He hung limply now, waiting for the fearful cataclysm that he could hardly accept as reality and yet knew would happen.

The first shell exploded directly to the front of Longfeather. It was a bright flash of fire with smoke—a deafening blast that pitched uprooted trees in every direction. The trees didn't get to Longfeather, but he was hit hard by flying dirt. Before long the second shell exploded close to where the first one had fallen. This time a tree landed near the barricade. The next shell fell closer, but Jim was aware only of its first brightness which quickly turned into an even greater brightness inside his head. He had been hit on the forehead by a small piece of flying wood. It was a glancing blow, yet enough to render him unconscious for several seconds.

He came-to, partly, and in a semi-conscious state looked at the smoking tangle in front of him and wondered what it was all about. By the time the next shell hit a good distance to his right, he had his wits back to some extent but was still far from clear about the whole situation. He knew only that someone was trying to kill him and some other people, and that one of these others was Pinetree. Anything beyond this was too complicated.

The next shell dropped closer than any of them had, but Longfeather was left untouched except for a bit of dirt. When the ringing in his ears quietened down a little he heard a moan of pain from the barricade. He saw that one of Pinetree's men was halfway up out of the trench, squirming about. After a moment the young brave lay quietly.

Jim felt blood running down his forehead. He saw Pinetree get up out of the pit. The outlaw took a few steps toward Longfeather and then another shell exploded nearby. The blast of it knocked Pinetree headlong; but he got back to his feet shakily and once more started toward Jim. There was a smear of blood on Pinetree's chest now. Through dust, smoke, and a groggy mind, Jim watched the outlaw approaching, now running, toward him. There was a knife in his hand.

In a moment he was behind Jim's tree and Jim heard the blade slitting leather and bark—felt his body come partially free. Next the gag was cut away and he spit out the grass. Then his mind began to fade again, and though he was aware of someone doing something behind the tree, he didn't know what and didn't care. A second later he was falling over on his face just as another shell went off to the front. He heard something whiz by over top of him, crash against the tree where he had just been standing, and then fall on him. The thing seemed like a many-legged monster and was pressing him into the ground. Somehow this new abuse of his body served to bring his floundering mind up to a slightly higher level of awareness.

For the first time he realized that Pinetree had freed him. But now there was a great branchy, leafy tree on top of Jim. He began to struggle, made some progress. Then, when he managed to twist around enough so that he could look up, he saw that it was Pinetree who was doing most of the lifting. With his muscles flexed into hard bulges that were shiny with sweat and blood, he slowly lifted the green tree. It was a larger than average poplar. As Jim struggled to crawl out from under the easing branches, he realized it was these that had saved him when the whole thing landed on him. The green branches had served as a springy cushion between the ground and the weight of the trunk. And Pinetree had not been hit by the tree because he had been standing behind the upright trunk that Jim had been tied to.

One of the branches was hooked on Jim's clothing. He did a painful twist, got clear of it, and then another shell went off. Pinetree fell, the tree he had been struggling with fell, and Longfeather was pinned to the ground again, more solidly than before. When the dust had settled a little, the first thing that Jim noticed was that one of the other Indians was lying bloody and motionless not far from the barricade. He must have been on his way to give a hand to Pinetree, thought Jim. He did not look as though he would move again. The other brave who had been hit earlier was still lying partway up out of the trench as he had fallen.

And where was Pinetree? Was he down too? Jim tried to twist his head around to see, but there were too many leaves hanging in his face.

Then he heard a grunt and at the same time the pressure against his back eased considerably. Clawing wildly in the dirt with his one usable hand, and applying all of the little strength he had left, Longfeather dug himself out from under the tangle of branches while Pinetree continued to hold up one end of the tree—a superhuman feat for someone as badly injured as he was. When Jim was clear of the tree it dropped, and so did John Pinetree. But he was back on his feet in a few seconds. It was a different case with Longfeather. He tried to get up, but his strength was gone. Loss of blood from the knife wound on the side of his chest had been the main drain on his system, and having been knocked unconscious twice within the hour had done the rest. Now as he lay there, his head began to swim more and more until he lost contact with things in the sense that he didn't quite know what was happening—even though his eyes were open and he could see, hear, and experience other physical sensations.

He felt hands under his arms, felt and saw himself being lifted. Instinctively he began to once more use his own effort to try to get to his feet, and with this help Pinetree was able to get him into a standing position. Jim's mind came back a little just as Pinetree pulled the other's arm around his own shoulders. As they began to stumble along together, Jim realized with clarity that Pinetree was taking him toward the outer edge of the grove—in the direction from which the field-gun shots were being fired. But before the full hope of it could get to him, his mind fogged up again.

When next the ground trembled underneath them and poplar trees where shattered to pulp not far to the right of them, and the concussion cleared a few cobwebs off the top of his mind, Jim could see a brighter glow of sunlight through the foliage ahead. They were getting close to the edge of the grove.

Jim was awake enough to dread the next explosion. Maybe, he hoped, they could make it out of the bush before the gunners got another shell into that terrible weapon.

They stumbled on. The trees thinned out some. Then there was a big log in the way, and Pinetree more or less dragged Jim over it, but he managed to stay upright. A few more steps brought them out into the open. Just then another shell exploded among the trees behind their backs and the air blast knocked both of them down on their faces. As they struggled back to their feet, Jim looked up toward the hill.

There they were, still covering the hillside: red-coated policemen, buckskin-clad plainsmen, multi-colored townspeople and farmers. They were a good distance away, but almost immediately Jim's eyes picked out the field gun with the two gunners who stood behind it. And he saw one of these wave his arm and he heard a shout—a shout that turned into a ripple of voices and passed through the entire crowd of policemen and onlookers.

Jim knew they had been seen. The gunners would not fire again.

Pinetree let go of Jim who found that he could stand by himself although it took a considerable amount of concentration. The two men stood facing each other.

After a moment, Jim said, "This is the second time you have saved my life."

Pinetree, breathing hard, looked up at the array of red-coated policemen on the hill, then back at Jim. His face was relaxed and the feverish look was gone from his eyes. Finally he said, "My blood brother...you have *tried* to save my life." Then he turned and stumbled back into the bush.

"Wait!" called Jim. "Come back!" But Pinetree was out of sight and Jim could hear his retreating footsteps through the underbrush.

For a few seconds Longfeather stood where he was. A wave of dizziness came over him; he staggered, then recovered. He began to walk farther away from the bluff. He had to get to the police officers and tell them not to fire any more shells into the bush. Four scarlet riders were coming down the hill to meet him. That was good. But he wished he could get away to his horse. After he told them not to fire anymore he would try to get back to his horse and escape. Meadow needed him.

The riders got to him in a few seconds. When they saw how badly hurt he was, two of the four dismounted and, supporting Jim between them, slowly climbed back up the hill on foot. During parts of this trip Jim was conscious, but during most of it he was in a dense fog with his feet dragging. Yet he heard himself telling the policemen over and over that they must not fire any more shells at the grove. Or was he only thinking the words?

When they got up to where all the people were, the two police officers laid Jim down on some blankets in the shade of a long lean-to built of green poplar trees and leafy branches. Other wounded men were lying there. The shade was pleasant. He was glad they hadn't taken him into one of the two big canvas tents that stood nearby; they would be hot inside. His mental fog was lifting now and he could think more clearly.

A policeman in a handsome spear-tipped white helmet, and with an impressive display of stripes on his red tunic, came and stood looking down at Jim. He said, "I'm Assistant Commissioner Bob Rintley, in charge here. You're Jim Longfeather, aren't you?"

"Yeah."

"We've been looking for you for a long time, but that bush was the last place we'd have expected to find you. How'd you get in there?"

"Crawling on my belly—early this morning while it was still dark."

"Why?!"

"I thought I might be able to talk Pinetree into giving himself up."

A man in a white shirt came and, while saying that he was Dr. Drummond, began to cut Jim's bloody shirt to pieces with a scalpel.

Assistant Commissioner Rintley continued his talk with Jim. "It seems you weren't very successful in convincing Pinetree to surrender. Wasn't that him who came to the edge of the grove with you and then went back in?"

"He *brought* me to the edge of the grove," corrected Jim. "I couldn't have made it on my own."

"Well, if he didn't want to come out now, I guess he just isn't going to come out." The Assistant Commissioner began to turn away. "I'll get back to you later."

"Wait!" said Jim, straining against the arms of Dr. Drummond. "Don't fire any more shells into the grove! Give him a chance!"

"I guess he's had plenty of that," said Rintley. "I know he's your friend...but there are several good men dead because of him, and several crippled by gunshot wounds.... There aren't going to be any more." He turned and walked away.

Two minutes later another warning was shouted. There was no reply. As the field gun began to boom and the shells once more thundered into the grove below, Jim Longfeather slipped back into unconsciousness.

* * *

When Jim next regained complete consciousness he noticed at once that his head and chest were bandaged. He felt considerably better. Most of his pains were gone—so long as he didn't move—and his muscles were in a pleasant state of deep relaxation. He seemed to vaguely remember having been given a drink of water along with pills during some previous stage of semi-consciousness.

A male voice somewhere to his right said, "He's awake." He looked in that direction and saw four people standing there looking at him: Meadow, Don, Rita, and that pastor—what was his name?—oh, yeah, Darcy somebody.

Meadow, smiling, was now charging toward him. She knelt at his side. "Darling, how are you feeling?" The others were coming closer now too.

"I'm okay," he told Meadow as he enjoyed the nearness of her beautiful face and the love glistening in her dark eyes.

Don had moved around to his other side and now knelt there. Golden-haired Rita and the pastor stood near Jim's feet.

Jim asked Meadow, "How come you followed?"

"What a silly question," smiled Meadow, and kissed him lightly on the cheek.

"Yeah, I guess it was," admitted Jim.

Don said, "Dr. Drummond checked you over and said you didn't have any broken bones. But you've lost quite a bit of blood from the wound in your side so you'll have to take it easy for a while.... You'll be happy to learn that your adoptive parents have been notified about your surfacing and should arrive here later today."

302

"Good," said Jim, but he dreaded that meeting. He turned to Don. "Your rescue of the wounded officer seemed to be successful. Will he survive?"

"Drummond says he's got a fifty-fifty chance," said Don. "I sure hope he makes it....

When you've regained your strength a bit, you can tell us what happened there in the grove."

"What about Pinetree?" asked Jim. "What's been happening? — and what's happening now?"

"It's all over," said Don. "I'm sorry.... They've brought out the bodies already — all three of them."

Jim absorbed that silently. He found that he could raise his head, and as he looked more or less straight ahead past Rita and Pastor Darcy, he became aware of the wife and also the mother of Pinetree standing close together not so far away. He had no trouble recognizing them, particularly the younger woman. "What's going to happen to Blackbird?" he asked.

Don looked in that direction. "Nothing. There's no reason to put her under arrest. I'm glad she won't be alone. She has her mother and her child, and her band.... I'd like to go and say something to comfort her, but I'm afraid it wouldn't do any good. I guess she considers every policeman to be her enemy...especially after today.... Now *you* could probably talk to her and give her some comfort. Should I call her over?"

"Yeah," said Jim, "call her over here — but not just yet.... Have you talked to your superiors about me?"

"Yes, since the story about you is all over this camp."

"When I first came to I admitted who I am," said Jim. "Tell me, if you know — how did the police find out about Scote? Did Sleeping Wolf tell them?"

"No," said Don. "It was pure accident. Two trappers, Krake and Davis, saw the whole thing. They were across the creek from you — under cover of bush but only a short distance away — when you shot Scote. They had no idea of what was going on, but they hightailed it out of there — and the worst of it was that they kept their mouths shut about it until just lately."

"Well, you've got your man," said Jim, taking on a philosophical calmness. "Where are you going to take me?—to stand trial in Regina?"

"No one's taking you anywhere," said Don, smiling. "I'm pleased to be the one to be able to tell you about this."

"Tell me about what?" puzzled Jim.

Don said, "Scote was wanted on the west coast for murder. His real name is Donald Retman. There was a thousand-dollar reward on his head, dead or alive, just like the one on Pinetree." Don let out a little laugh. "You're not under arrest. The North-West Mounted was looking for you only to tell you that you're in the clear, and that you can collect the reward money."

Jim passed out again.

* * *